The Old Witches Home

by
Avian Swansong

Do you have a story to tell? What's your animal spirit? Share it with us. #hellobeesties

Copyright © 2024 by Avian Swansong

Wildebeest Publishing Co.

Wildebeest Publishing Company, LLC
6456 Collamer Road
Syracuse, NY 13057

All rights reserved, including the right to reproduce this book or portions thereof in any form. Unauthorized copying or distribution of the book is forbidden.

For more information about copyrights and usage, special discounts on bulk purchases, workshops, and engagements, please contact Wildebeest Publishing Company, LLC at (315) 220-0217, info@wildebeestpublishing.com, or online at www.wildebeestpublishing.com

Wildebeest Publishing Company, LLC paperback First Edition June 2024, United States of America

Cover Art and Illustrations by Courtney Hopkins
Author photo by Pedro Gutierrez

ISBN 978-1-958233-25-2 (paperback)

The publisher and artists can accept no legal responsibility for any consequences arising from the application of information, advice, or instructions given in this publication. The author, artists, and publisher have made all reasonable efforts to contact copyright holders for permission and apologize for any omissions or errors pertaining to credit for existing works. Corrections may be made to future versions. The opinions expressed in the book are those of the author and do not necessarily reflect the views of the publisher or the foreword author.

Acknowledgements

I owe a deep well of thanks to the many people who have helped me on the way to this debut novel. I knew I could write training manuals but fiction? That was a whole new kettle of fish. I didn't realize at the beginning how much I needed all of you, and I am so grateful you showed up for me when you did. It truly was magic!

Thanks so much to the teachers at the Syracuse YMCA Downtown Writers Center who guided me through my first tentative forays into the world of storytelling, especially Chris DelGuercio whose Writers Life courses provided a framework for the endeavor I had begun. Thanks also to Linda Lowen who got me thinking about the structure of a plot, commercial viability and loglines. Finally, thanks to Georgia Popoff and Kayla Blatchley for their support and encouragement.

The realization that no writer works alone led me to writers' groups where I could be in a community of like-minded souls. Many thanks to the Stamford Library Writers Circle, especially Chris Hauser, who invited me, and Terry Bradshaw who offered publishing guidance. I learned so much from hearing everyone's work, and having the opportunity to read with them at the Liberty Rock Bookstore in the Hobart Book Village, NY. Thanks also to the Winter Writers Group, whose members write such compelling pieces and who have offered valuable comments on pieces of the book.

Most importantly, thanks to my Sunday Night Authors Group – Kelley Donaghy, Rebecca Butterworth, Jim Wright, Chris Travis, Catherine Farrell, Victoria Larson and Karen Chamis. They have been steadfast critics and cheerleaders, always offering suggestions to make the work better and encouragement to keep going. Thanks, Chris DelGuercio, for introducing us in your class. Even though I have never met any of these friends face to face, I know them intimately, and they know me. Thank you!

Thanks much to my beta and early readers, who suffered through my learning curve: Judy Stachowski, Yarrow Angelweed, George Franklin, Diane Perazzo, Mary Morska, Shawn Usha, and Kathleen Hayek. Renee Prive and Marjorie Kellogg had the luck to read later versions – somehow there were still more revisions to be made! I thank everyone for their feedback!

Thanks to Reedsy Marketplace for providing access to a fabulous editor, Adrienne Kisner, and a brilliant illustrator, Courtney Young. Thanks to Lisa Tait and Sharon Reeves for helping me design an Old Witch House website. I also have to acknowledge Laura Thorne and Jess Neiding of Wildebeest Publishing who took a chance on me, and made it possible for me to get this book into your hands.

I am so fortunate to have people in my life who bring me joy, and keep me going even when I think I'm too old. To Ariana Krawitz, Judy Stachowski, Ted and Kathleen Hayek, Debbie Cole, GG and Toni Leslie Stankiewicz, I am so grateful that you are in my life. I will try to make you proud!

To Opus, who reminds me of the basics – food, play and sleep. Thanks.

For anyone I might have missed, know that you have my deepest gratitude for your support.

Finally, I would not have been able to envision the magical world of *The Old Witches Home* without SpiralHeart and the Reclaiming Community of Witches. To them, I say, Blessings! Another world is possible! What happens between the worlds changes all the worlds! So mote it be.

"We are all longing to go home to some place we have never been — a place half-remembered and half-envisioned we can only catch glimpses of from time to time. Community. Somewhere, there are people to whom we can speak with passion without having the words catch in our throats. Somewhere a circle of hands will open to receive us, eyes will light up as we enter, voices will celebrate with us whenever we come into our own power...Someplace where we can be free."

~Starhawk, <u>Dreaming the Dark</u>

TABLE OF CONTENTS

Acknowledgements iii
Prologue ix

1	Wednesday Morning 1
2	The First Inkling 12
3	Maya visits Angie 18
4	Council Meeting 27
5	Binding Ritual 42
6	Mnemosyne is Afflicted 48
7	Thursday Morning 61
8	Building the Bonfire 68
9	Maya Makes Lunch 77
10	Lunch with Huffstickler 86
11	Huffstickler's Plan 95
12	Twig 104
13	Gathering the Healers 115
14	Oscar at the Farm 121
15	Healing Ritual 128
16	Friday Morning 139
17	Hardware and Naps 151
18	The Sleeping Sickness 159

19	Dinner at Birdie's House	164
20	A Restless Midnight	183
21	Birdie and Tom	194
22	Saturday Morning	203
23	The Hydration Project	218
24	The Summer Solstice Ritual	224
25	A Week Later	254
26	Epilogue - Later	259

List of Chants 265
Avian Swansong Bio 271

PROLOGUE
LIGHTNING'S LAST DAYS

"No tears now! I just won't have it." I sat up too quickly, and the room started spinning around me. The faces of my friends, the founders of The Old Witches Home (Maya, Maple, Mnemosyne, and Birdie), came in and out of view.

"Oh, shush, Lightning," Maya said. "Silly man. We're allowed to cry if we want to. We love you. Also, I brought muffins."

Maya. Dear Maya, whose colorful Mexican skirt swirled around her shapely body, moved toward me. I had been able to keep the non-Hodgkin's lymphoma that the handsome doctor discovered a year ago secret for months. But four months ago, Maya, sensitive Maya, started noticing my weight loss.

"Oh, darling, I'm just trying to get back to my dancer's weight," I tried to tell her. "I wouldn't want to let any sweet young men pass me by. Not if I can help it."

She wrapped her arms around me and gave me a smile that showed she didn't believe a word.

So I had to tell them all.

Maple was my rock, taking me to chemo and doctor's appointments and keeping track of everything. I flirted incessantly with him behind the sexy oncologist's back, and Maple laughed, that big, round belly laugh, and flirted right back. I think he felt free with me, in a way he couldn't be free in the insomniac world, the world without magic.

With me, he could be himself.

And that's what it's all about, isn't it? Being ourselves? I leaned back, closed my eyes, and remembered this land as it was when we first looked at it when I inherited it ten years ago from that fabulous old lesbian—my great-aunt Estella.

She said the land had a soul like mine—wild and wooded, filled with sunlight and shadows. My friends and I saw a small hunter's cabin where the Heart is now, next to a deer trail skirting the pond and leading to the top of the mountain. We spied fairies peeking out from behind bushes filled with blackberries, catching rides on dandelion puffs floating in the breeze.

That's when we knew what we had to do.

Together, we built The Old Witches Home, a sanctuary for outcasts and pagans of all kinds. A place where we could just be us, crazy and wild and happy.

I raised my head and looked at the dark brown baked good Maya set on the tray before me. Morning-glory muffins were my favorite, and she had swirled the icing on top just how I liked it.

In the last few months, Maya had done everything she could for me. She was a gifted cook and an intuitive healer. She enlisted Diego, one of our few non-witch residents, a curandero from the Yucatán, to perform a limpia. He was accustomed to working with spirits like Oggun and Yemaya, Afro-Caribbean deities, sometimes fierce, always powerful. When he beat away the negative energies with a tight bundle of herbs, a mist of clear energy enveloped me. He rubbed an egg over all of me, circling my lymph nodes, under my neck, under my arms, over my abdomen, and around my torso. I shrieked when he reached my groin and suggested he should buy me dinner first, but he remained focused and continued chanting words I didn't understand. I dozed and felt better for a week after they finished.

They started round-the-clock visits after that. They moved me to one of the second-floor rooms in the Heart (the community building in the center of the village) to be close to the Healing Center, just in case.

In case of what I could never figure out, but they had insisted.

So many nights, I lay in bed, pretending I wasn't too weak to move. I heard the sounds of the witches doing rituals below, the rise and fall of their voices as they chanted and danced in a sacred circle. I fell into dreams. The air in the room filled with the scent of incense rising from below.

Now I smelled peppermint tea in the mug Maya held. She sat in a chair beside me.

"Oh, darling, that muffin looks divine. Maybe later. Thank you so much." I wanted to sit up, but my stomach was doing pirouettes and jetes the way Eric circled the stage during our shows.

Eric.

I would be with him soon, and we would dance together like we used to when we were both in Les Ballets Trockaderos, touring the globe and upending the staid world of classical dance. I closed my eyes and heard the music from *Giselle*. I could feel the long tulle skirt flowing around my legs as I spun and flew through the air, enchanting unsuspecting peasants. I could have flown forever, lighter than air, a wisp of smoke, twirling up into the heavens.

"Lightning, would you like some water?" Maya's clear voice brought me down to earth. Her own skirt swished as she rose from her chair. Her plump hands poured water into a glass with a rainbow-colored straw.

"Yes, please," I croaked and lifted my head.

"Here, let me help." Maple moved behind me and lifted my back, tucking another pillow under my head, raising me up. He was a bear of a man, a papa bear, soft and cuddly.

I looked around. They were all there, arrayed around the room like horses on a carousel, some up, some down. Birdie was scowling, talking low with Mnemosyne, who stood next to her, towering over her. Birdie's short gray hair was spiked from her morning swim. I used to see her in the dawn light, traveling back and forth, creating little eddies as her arms dipped forward and back. Birdie's strength had carried me when I got discouraged. She was the one who told me to fire that stupid lawyer who made fun of my graceful stature, who called me a fairy behind my back. I soaked up her pride. Even though she was not much over five feet, together we stood tall.

Mnemosyne's dark face exuded calm, as it always did. The light from the window behind her cast her in a halo as she patiently explained something important to Birdie. "An African princess," I used to call her. She would look me straight in the eye, at my level, as few could do, and say, "And?" I chuckled every time. Mnemosyne had the business sense none of the rest of us had, and I loved her for it.

She would take care of everything, I was sure.

"Lightning, can I read it to you? Make sure it's what you want?" Mnemosyne's low, sexy voice cut through the swirling fog of my mind. She had a clipboard in her hands. Her notary public kit, stamp, and circular seal sat on the wheeled table over the bed.

She read my last will and testament to me, the words gliding over one another and lulling me to a pleasant state of mind. I shook myself. I had to stay present. I wanted this to be done right.

I knew my friends would take care of and cherish this land I loved. The community we built would live on. The witches who had found refuge here, who had found their last cabin in the woods, who had found their final resting place, would be safe.

The Old Witches Home was my legacy.

I trusted that it would survive, even if I had to leave.

No one would be able to destroy our vision.

My mind was pulled to the creek near the home where I grew up in Kansas. I was once again near the edge, watching the water caress the rocks and boulders, creating pools for frogs and dragonflies, before slipping away down the stream. I jumped and splashed, free of the brothers who punched me in the arm and had no imagination. I skipped rocks and built stone cairns. I disappointed no one.

I woke again when the visiting nurse and that handsome doctor from town arrived to witness my signature. I rallied and wrote my legal name, large and with a flourish, Edward Vincent O'Neill! My pen faltered just a bit as I circled the O and added the apostrophe, but I recovered by the time I looped the "l" and "l" in the end.

The land was now safe.

Finally, I could rest.

That evening, Maple and Birdie helped me into a wheelchair, and we rode down the elevator to the ritual room below. Gently, they coaxed me onto a hospital bed in the center of the circle, decorated with sequined flowers and sparkle ribbons. Everyone was there, in their finest ritual robes, with witches' hats and starry magic wands. They twisted my hair into a knot at the top of my head and tucked my silver lightning bolt into it.

For the last time.

The ritual was a simple farewell. The harmonies of the Summerland Choir rose and fell and entranced me as I dropped
    further

                      and

      further

                      into

    the

                          other

world.

Eric stood there with open arms, flanked by the other dancers we had lost over the years.

My parents greeted me, smiling. Were they really happy to see me?

Great-Aunt Estella, my benefactor, my champion, walked forward, her brow furrowed, moving her mouth, but I couldn't hear.

What was she saying? *Tell them* . . . what? It seemed important. What was it?

I succumbed to warm serenity.

At peace.

Well . . . mostly.

1

Wednesday Morning

Birdie McAllister wanted to die at The Old Witches Home. Like Lightning, with all of her friends gathered around to mourn her passing and celebrate her life. She wanted to linger in the ether, hovering above her friends, who would be sad, crying, and talking about how amazing she had been. Really, she just didn't want to be alone.

"I'm sorry, I'm sorry!" She burst into the dining hall where her friends were at their regular table in the corner, near the window looking out into the meadow full of wildflowers and tall grasses, ready to be mowed in preparation for the Summer Solstice Festival that weekend, the most elaborate Festival of the year. The luscious Catskill Mountains and perfect summer temperatures would entice the townspeople of Winkton to their annual fund-raising event to buy and sell arts and crafts, feast and mingle, dance the Spiral Dance, and be charmed by the magic of The Old Witches Home.

She could already feel the excitement building.

"About time!" Maya said as she grabbed another cup from the sideboard and poured coffee for Birdie. "Are you trying to take Lightning's spot as the most time-challenged of us all? Have you adopted pagan time?"

"I'm sorry. I just lost track while I was swimming." Birdie wasn't usually late, but as she floated in the pond during her morning swim that morning, she had been drowning in memories. It was ten years since Lightning inherited the land and the five of them had dreamed this place. In ritual trance, Birdie, Maya, Maple, Mnemosyne, and Lightning imagined a retirement village – a welcoming community for pagans and witches of all kinds to live out their lives in nature, friendship, and magic. They had dreamed and re-dreamed their vision, tapping into the energy of the Goddess and using plain old hard work to make it real.

But now Lightning was dead, and their dreams had to change.

Maya's plump frame jiggled a little in her full peasant skirt as she walked back and forth. Birdie thought she looked much younger than 81 years old but knew better. They had known each other for over 50 years since they first became ReDreaming witches in the woods of Vermont, where Lightning had proposed The Old Witches Home one morning during a weekend retreat.

"I still miss Lightning," Maple said.

"It's only been six months," Birdie grunted in agreement. As she added cream to her plain porcelain cup, Birdie coveted the elaborate tree of life ceramic mug in Maple's hands, one of the last pieces his late wife, Juniper, had made. But she wouldn't dare borrow it, and his wife's inventory was long gone.

"Well, he's not here," Birdie said as she placed her towel on the chair and sat at the table with them. She hadn't had time to dry her short hair, and now it was dripping down her back and making her irritable. "We've got work to do. How is probate coming? Do we have title to the land yet?"

"No," Mnemosyne said. "And I don't understand why not. I realize it's only been six months, but I filed all the paperwork I thought we needed the day after Lightning died. The county clerk still hasn't found the deed transfer from Estella to Lightning, but that shouldn't have held things up this long. There has to be a record of it somewhere."

Birdie loved the sound of her friend's name, *ne-MA-sa-knee,* so gentle, such a contrast to the steely demeanor she had to adopt during her years as an insurance executive. Like many Old Witches Home residents, she adopted a magical name when she was initiated, and most people didn't even know her legal name. She was simply Mnemosyne, Greek goddess of dreams and memory, mother of the Muses, The Old Witches Home Administrator.

Birdie thought she should have been more creative when she named herself a devotee of the Goddess – "Birdie" worked, but it didn't inspire much.

"Have you talked with the guy who used to be his lawyer?" Maya asked.

Birdie scoffed. She was glad Lightning had taken her advice and fired that man. He was a greedy capitalist. She didn't trust insomniac lawyers, nackers who didn't dream. They didn't understand that the dream world was as real as the daytime one. The ReDreaming witches had been calling these folks insomniacs, nackers for short, for as long as she could remember. The name fit.

ReDreaming witches believed in Dion Fortune's definition, that magic was "the art of changing consciousness at will." Magic starts in the dream world, and if you can re-dream your dreams, you can make magic. Anyone can. All it takes is focused energy, a clear intention, and a circle of allies. The Old Witches Home was their magic - a better world.

"He hasn't responded yet. I'll try again today." Mnemosyne sighed. The tall, stately woman had circles under her eyes, which were difficult to see on her dark skin, but she looked more tired to Birdie than usual. She knew Mnemosyne was a night owl and wasn't crazy about morning get-togethers, but still, something felt off.

"Are you okay? How are you feeling?" Maya asked. "Would you like some peppermint tea? A cinnamon scone?"

"I'm fine. I just feel like I didn't sleep at all. I was working on the financial projections for the Festival, and I woke up with my head on the desk at about three in the morning. I went to bed after that, but I don't feel like I slept. I just kept having strange dreams that I don't remember. I'll sleep tonight, I'm sure."

"So where do we stand? Financially speaking?" Birdie asked, eager to return to the business at hand so she could go home and change. The wet swimsuit was making her butt cold.

"The bank is asking for a huge balloon payment for the mortgage on the Heart. Since no one seems to be able to find the deed transfer from Lightning's Aunt Estella to him, we can't show that he owned the land. So they can't transfer the land to us, and the bank claims there's no collateral for the loan. We also owe taxes at the end of June, and we still have to pay the bill for the second solar array," Mnemosyne said. "We really need sizable donations from the Festival this weekend. We don't have Lightning to fall back on anymore. And until probate is finished, we have no land."

"And we need to upgrade the septic when the new people move in," Maple reminded her and bit into a morning glory muffin. Birdie savored Maya's morning-glory muffins, made with whole wheat flour, carrots, apples, raisins, walnuts, orange juice, coconut and wheat germ. They reminded her of the little coffeehouse where she used to spend hours writing poetry in the San Francisco Mission District in the 70's.

"Yes," Mnemosyne agreed. "We're in a precarious position. The Collective has no assets if we don't own the land. All we have are debts and liabilities." She brought her coffee to her lips and sighed.

"We can't lose this place," Maple said. "I can't live with my kids. They'll make me crazy. And I don't have enough money to move somewhere else."

"Me either. I love my daughter, but her hands are full with her kids. She doesn't need me in her kitchen," Maya said, refilling everyone's cup and checking the cream container.

At least you have kids, Birdie thought. *If I weren't here, I would be in a nacker retirement home playing Mahjong with a bunch of old ladies who wear diapers under polyester pants.*

Birdie tried not to be resentful, but she felt no one understood what it was like to be old and completely alone. Her parents were dead, and she had no siblings. Her only family was a cousin she had stopped talking with years ago. She wasn't even sure she had his current address. The Old Witches Home had saved her from isolation even as it had used up every bit of her retirement fund. She looked out the window and saw a crow on the tree by the path. Hermes, her 9-year-old tuxedo cat, sat under the tree, looking up.

"We need to focus," Birdie said. "No one needs to know that we don't have title to the land yet. The nackers in town have been generous in the past; let's assume they will again. Right?"

"Right," said Maya. She sat down and folded her hands in front of her.

"So what do we need to do? Mnemosyne is figuring out the money. Do you need help with the feast, Maya?"

"No, I don't think so. I'm sure Angie and I can handle the food." Maya, the head cook, and Angie, her assistant, organized the magical dishes that were the festival's main attractions.

"Oscar and I will make sure the grounds, the bonfire, and the vendor area are good to go," Maple said, referring to his partner-in-crime, a retired general construction manager.

"Who's doing decorations?" Mnemosyne asked.

"Twig and Angie. I think they're doing a 'Bountiful Berries' theme with strawberries, blueberries, raspberries, and blackberries painted on all the banners and tablecloths," Maya said. "I'm not sure how much they've finished yet. I overheard them singing and laughing when they worked on it last week, but I didn't see any finished products."

"They don't have much time left," Maple looked concerned. "We'll be setting everything up on Friday and today's Wednesday. They better get moving."

"They will, Maple. Have faith. You know how young people are," chided Maya.

"Angie's in her 50's," Maple responded.

"Well, that's younger than us!" Maya laughed.

"Okay. I'm working in the Healing Center today, but I'll wrangle everyone for the ritual," Birdie said. "I think we'll be ready." Something made her uneasy, but she thought it was typical nerves before a big event.

The four of them stood for a group hug. Someone said, "May the Old Witches Home thrive and nurture us."

Someone else said, "May we live long and prosper."

They all chuckled.

"So mote it be," they said in unison.

After everyone hugged each other, not missing anyone, a process which took a full five minutes because you don't want to rush hugging people you love, Birdie picked up her towel and crossed the building to the south exit onto Joy Lane. As she reached the doorway, Hermes crossed before her and nearly tripped her. How did he get there? How did he always know where she was?

Mnemosyne passed Hermes as she entered her office, where the air conditioning was always set at 68 degrees, and her files were color-coded. She scanned the pile of envelopes on the corner of the desk where the mail carrier always placed them and opened the big one.

"Will Contest..." was all Mnemosyne saw before her legs felt weak. She held on to the edge of the desk for support and sidled over to her chair. This didn't make any sense. Who would contest Lightning's will, and why? And why was she feeling so woozy? Maybe all she needed was more water. But that could wait.

She set the papers neatly on the desk. She wasn't an expert at reading legalese. Still, his older brother, William Gordon O'Neill, claimed that Lightning was not of sound mind and lacked the "testamentary capacity" to bequeath the land to The Old Witches Home Collective, LLC.

His lawyer, Benjamin Huffstickler, had filed an objection with the court, claiming that the bequest had been procured by deceit, undue influence, or fraud. Fraud? This is what he wanted. She had been there at the end, had notarized the will herself, and the nurse and the doctor had witnessed it. Sure, it was right before he died, but he wasn't pressured. She and the others watched him sign it 'Edward Vincent O'Neill.'

So WASP-y, he had said with a sigh. He was thrilled to be leaving the land to the collective.

And coerced? She couldn't imagine anyone coercing Lightning into anything. He had four brothers – as a middle child, he had to fight for everything, from sitting next to the window in the station wagon to getting the last baked potato at dinner. She didn't know a witch strong enough to tell Lightning what to do, much less get him to sign over his land.

Dang! She was sure everything had been done correctly. But she wasn't a lawyer. Had she missed something? Everyone was so filled with grief when Lightning died. Had she messed it up somehow? Why did Lightning make her the executor anyway? Why didn't they get a real lawyer to advise them? These silly old witches don't trust anyone in the 'system,' but maybe this time they should have.

Now Lightning's eldest brother got a local lawyer, Benjamin Huffstickler, to send them this ridiculous letter stating that the will wasn't valid. He said he owned the land as Lightning's next of kin since Lightning was unmarried and childless, and their parents were deceased. And Huffstickler? Wasn't he the guy who was trying to make Winkton a weekend resort for rich people from the City? And didn't Lightning say they were related like he was a long-lost cousin or something?

Mnemosyne knew she would have to call Birdie and the Council. They would have to have a meeting about this. Hopefully, nothing will happen until after the Solstice Festival. They needed time to get donations from the townspeople. If rumors began circulating, people may not be inclined to donate as much as they had in years past.

She placed her feet firmly on the floor and began breathing deeply. She closed her eyes and imagined a large tree root growing from the base of her spine and reaching down to the rocks and dirt beneath the floor. This taproot dug until it found a crevice to crawl into and secure itself. Mnemosyne breathed the moist, warm air of the earth up through that taproot into her solar plexus to gain power and then into her heart to grow compassion.

She started to feel the earth energy in her neck, cleansing her throat chakra and empowering her voice and words. But as the energetic stream rose to the third eye in the middle of her forehead, she could sense the words in her throat getting jumbled and numbers taking their place. The flow to her forehead was tingly and sparkling and moved like a dotted line. Her head felt light, and she started seeing shapes and lines like they were on a genealogy chart.

Still, she pushed her will and her mind through the blockage. It felt like slogging through mud. When the energy burst out of the crown of her head into the branches of the trees around her and into the sky with the clouds and the birds, Mnemosyne knew she was ready.

She picked up the phone to call Birdie. Birdie was there at the beginning with Lightning, Maya, and Maple. Birdie will know what to do.

Still in her wet bathing suit, Birdie rushed down the hall to the DWI (Dealing with Insomniacs) Office, Mnemosyne's realm, aka Administration. Hermes trailed her. His tail was high, and he sauntered with confidence and purpose. Not the way she felt at all.

"What? How can he do that?" She held the letter from Huffstickler, feeling the urge to crumple it and throw it against the wall.

She felt inadequate and out of control compared to the orderliness and neatness of Mnemosyne's domain. The room resembled a normal office with a desk, lamp, computer, and chairs for guests, but subtle differences reminded visitors of Mnemosyne's magical power. A pentacle hung on the wall between the windows behind Mnemosyne's desk, almost blending into the background, emitting a slight amber glow around it. The sacred shredder behind her desk also had that glow, and Hagall, the rune for destruction, was painted on it. When Hermes entered behind Birdie, the red and green ceramic dragon on top of the bookcase to the left of the doorway appeared to growl at him. The scent of Nag Champa incense emanated from the wooden incense holder at the front of her desk, where a nameplate would have been at her old job.

"I don't understand," Birdie said again. "What happened? Why does Lightning's brother think he has a claim on our land? I thought Lightning left it to us."

"He did, or at least we thought he did," said Mnemosyne. "But you know he didn't have a will when we first formed the Collective. He didn't have one until he finally agreed to write it from his hospice bed. We all were there, and the doctor and nurse witnessed it. I notarized it. He made me his executor. The brother is saying he was coerced, and that's why he's challenging it."

"What does Huffstickler have to do with it?"

Mnemosyne continued. "Huffstickler is related to Lightning somehow, but he's also a local lawyer. He probably saw the obit in the Daily Star. The brother's name is William Gordon O'Neill, and he's still in Missouri. I notified him, like I was supposed to, that Lightning had died, but this is the first time we're hearing from him. I think Huffstickler probably contacted him and put him up to this. Huffstickler wants the land because he wants to develop it. I can't believe we have to fight him."

Birdie tried to remember everything Lightning had told them about his family, but he didn't talk about them much. He just talked about his great-aunt Estella, who left him the land. He loved Estella because she always came to his ballet performances, didn't care that he was gay, and encouraged his creativity. He loved visiting Estella and hearing her stories of the old days.

So who was his brother? She remembered one evening when they were all reminiscing, and Mnemosyne was bemoaning being an only child. Lightning remarked that he wished he didn't have brothers; they were 'the meanest meanies,' and he hadn't talked with any of them since his parents died. None of them had come to his funeral.

"Wasn't Huffstickler Lightning's aunt's executor when he inherited the land?" Birdie asked. "I vaguely remember Lightning talking about him and excruciating holidays at the aunt's home."

Mnemosyne's eyes were glazed over. Birdie wasn't sure where Mnemosyne had gone, but her question seemed to bring her back to the office.

"Yes, he was. But that's because he was the aunt's great-grandson, which makes Huffstickler Lightning's second cousin once removed. At least I think he's removed – maybe he's a third cousin or something. In any case, I don't have the details, but Lightning said something about Estella having a kid out of wedlock back in the day. Her kid was Huffstickler's grandmother. Estella never married but lived with a companion, Alice, for almost 60 years. She wanted to leave everything to Alice, but Alice died just a few months before Estella. Lightning was devastated by both of their deaths. He was pissed when he found out that Estella made Huffstickler her executor. He didn't like Huffstickler. He said Huffstickler took advantage of Estella when she was still grieving for Alice."

My goodness, this is complicated, thought Birdie. We need a chart or something.

Mnemosyne sat down quickly and swayed a little in the chair. She opened her mouth, shut it, shook her head, and opened it again. Hermes jumped on her lap and head-butted her.

She looked up. "Do you know where Lightning kept his important papers?"

"Probably under his mattress." Birdie chuckled. "You know he didn't trust anyone, not banks, lawyers, or even us all the time. Didn't he have a safe? What are you looking for?"

"The transfer of the deed from Estella to him. I thought he got it back from that old lawyer he fired. But I can't find it anywhere. We need it for probate. It wasn't in his little safe."

"I've got his ritual stuff in a couple of boxes in my shed. I'll look in there. We'll find it. Isn't there a copy in the sky or something?"

"The cloud, you mean. No, I can't find a record of the transfer online, either. There should be a file in the County system, but it doesn't seem to be there."

"Well, shit. We'll have to find the actual paper then. Meanwhile, what are we going to do about his brother?"

"We have to call a Council meeting," Mnemosyne said.

"I'll call Maple," Birdie said. "He's the anchor these days." She hesitated. "I'm not sure he's up to the challenge. Maybe I ought to facilitate the meeting."

"No, let him do it. It's his turn, and you should have faith in him."

"But this is so important. He always gives in to Dandelion and Dirty Swan. He's so afraid of being accused of being sexist or racist."

"I know," Mnemosyne sighed. "But I'm sure he'll be okay. I'll tell the others."

Reluctantly, Birdie agreed, even though she always felt better if she could do it herself. She went outside and sat on the steps of the entrance. She pulled her cell phone out of her pocket and called Maple.

2

THE FIRST INKLING

"I can handle it," Maple told her when she called. "We'll call a Council meeting and figure it out together." But she was skeptical.

When Birdie had left her cabin that morning for her daily swim, she felt danger was looming. Now she knew what the threat was, and even the warm summer air, filled with the scent of magnolia and lilacs and the sounds of the blue jays and sparrows, didn't reassure her.

She had always been an outcast, the strange one that didn't quite fit – not with her family, not with her job, not with her town. The Old Witches Home had been Lightning's idea, but she embraced it and energized the others. She was proud of what they had built – a sanctuary for misfits, a haven for weirdos, a safe place for pagans and witches of all kinds to age gracefully among their own kind. Would they lose their homes if they couldn't get the title to the land? She always believed the Goddess would take care of her and put food in her mouth, and so far, she always had. But what if she didn't?

On her way back to change her clothes after the morning meeting, Birdie passed homes under construction and some that had been there for a while. She saw a couple of small log cabins similar to her home, a tiny house with brightly colored flags flying from the roof, and a fully functioning yurt, which had always impressed Birdie with its simplicity and beauty. That's an example of stacking functions, she thought, a basic permaculture principle – everything has more than one purpose.

Birdie felt content in the community they had built.

Then, an overwhelming feeling of grief slowed her steps. Lightning is dead, she thought. Nothing I can do about that one.

The discordant snores from the sagging green tent on Whale Tooth's site called to Birdie.

His construction had been stalled due to lack of funds.

The dewy lawn chair outside, free from its usual burden, seemed to sigh in relief in the early morning sun. Whale Tooth cooked on a barbecue grill and slept on a cot – it was comfortable enough, he said – Birdie wouldn't have spent more than one night lying on that squeaky old thing. Sometimes, she could hear it as she passed in the evening and was surprised it didn't collapse under Whale Tooth's weight. Of Hawaiian heritage, Whale Tooth adopted his name as a symbol of power when he began to explore his native spiritual beliefs, an important step in his healing from addiction.

Birdie had no idea when Whale Tooth could start working on the house again. That nasty bank manager, Louella Cartwright, denied his bank loan shortly after the foundation had been poured, just when they started the framing. Without an influx of cash from somewhere, the tent might also be his winter home. That wouldn't do. They would have to find him a room in the Heart or help him out with a loan from the Collective. She was angry that the bank had rejected his application. But that was the way these insomniac capitalists worked, wasn't it? You had to have money to make money. Since Whale Tooth (aka Walter Tennyson) had no money, and the land was held up in probate, Louella didn't think investing in his home was a good risk. What will Louella think when she finds out the will is being contested?

Lending him money was better than him ending up on the street, though, wasn't it? Birdie was aware that Whale Tooth, a veteran and former addict, knew what it was like to sleep beneath bridges. This was probably his only chance for a safe harbor as he aged. Curse Louella! When she thought about Whale Tooth's life and what he was facing now, it was hard to believe the Goddess had their backs. Maybe magic only goes so far in this world.

Then she saw Oscar and Rabbit.

As she neared her cabin, she could hear Oscar and Rabbit arguing amiably as they weeded in their garden next door. Rabbit's tall frame appeared amid the vegetables, topped by her pink sun-kissed neck and the shaggy cut of her short silver-blond hair. Oscar's dark wavy hair, white t-shirt, and brown-skinned arms moved slowly down the rows on the other side of the garden.

"Oscar, leave the clover. It's holding the soil and providing nitrogen," Rabbit, who used to be known as Laura Washington, said.

Oscar Gonzales bobbed his head up and down. "I just want to make sure the squash has enough room to spread," he said in a very loud staccato.

"Shush, you're going to disturb the whole neighborhood."

"You shush. You're the one who started it. What a lovely worm." Birdie watched Oscar hold the squiggly thing up to the sun, holding his mouth open as if he were about to drop it in. He blinked, shook his head, and dropped the worm on the ground. It slithered away quickly.

A crow cawed in the tree next to the cabin. Birdie listened for a second. It didn't seem to be saying good morning to its friends. It seemed to be calling to her. Why, she couldn't tell.

"Owww!" Oscar squealed.

"Oh, my Goddess," Rabbit yelled. "Wait, don't move." Their heads disappeared into the vegetation.

Birdie heard scuffling and moaning. She rushed to their yard. Rabbit was leaning over Oscar sitting in the garden, eyes closed, moaning.

Birdie could see blood seeping through the cloth of the bandanna she was wrapping around his hand.

"What happened?" Birdie asked.

"I'm not sure. He was weeding this row, and I was on the other side. Then I heard him yell. When I got here, he was just sitting here, clucking like a chicken and holding his hand."

"Stay with him," Birdie said. "I'll get some bandages."

Birdie gingerly walked between the rows of lettuce on one side and kale on the other to get back to her cabin. The scent of rich dirt and healthy growing things followed her as she exited the garden through the open section in the six-foot deer fence. She looked back to see Rabbit sitting on the ground, holding Oscar against her chest, murmuring to him.

When Birdie returned, Oscar stared wide-eyed at a nasty gash in his left hand. Blood was oozing from where the trowel had torn a slice of his palm open.

She took a moment to ground herself by imagining a taproot from the base of her spine going deep into the earth. She thanked the Goddess for the energy rising from the planet's core that flowed through her hands and fed her healing ability. Her mind quieted as she held Oscar's hand, listening for anything his body could tell her about the injury. But all she heard was a low rumble and a sound like keys rapping on a typewriter.

"What happened, Oscar? You must have really hit your hand hard."

"I was – worms and bugs," he said, his head bouncing like a bobblehead, a strange guttural sound under his words. "The lettuce – Rabbit – ground, this thing." His eyes were unfocused, staring past Birdie.

"Don't worry," Birdie said as she held his hand, removed the bandanna, and cleaned the area. "You may have to let Rabbit do all the work for a few days while it heals."

Rabbit chuckled, but Birdie could see the concern on her face. Oscar was rocking back and forth.

His face paled. He looked like he was going to keel over. Birdie put a hand on his chest and looked into his eyes, "are you all right?" Rabbit scooched closer to him.

"Dizzy – pass out." He focused momentarily on Birdie and then closed his eyes, swaying.

Birdie looked down at the cloth she had been using and saw less blood than expected. She looked back at his hand. The bleeding had stopped. There certainly wasn't enough blood loss to cause dizziness.

She opened a bottle of water and gave it to Oscar. "Maybe you just need to drink something. Take this." Oscar took the bottle, started to lick it, then shook his head and poured the water into his mouth.

"Has he eaten this morning?" Birdie asked Rabbit.

"Not yet. We usually have breakfast after we finish weeding."

Birdie finished the bandaging and tried to give him a granola bar, but he looked past her. She was starting to get worried. It wasn't like Oscar to succumb to minor injuries. He usually just powered through. She took the water from him and set it beside her.

"Lay down." He began to fall to one side. His voice sounded strange. The undertone reminded Birdie of a cow mooing.

"Not here, Oscar. Let's go inside," Rabbit said. But Oscar had already folded his legs and put his head down on the dirt between his arms. It didn't look very comfortable. His eyes were closed, and he was muttering something, but she couldn't catch the words.

"It's probably just dehydration," she tried to reassure Rabbit. Birdie gazed at Oscar. She quickly ran through symptoms of strokes and heart attacks in her mind. No, those didn't make sense.

"Do we need to get him to the Healing Center?" Birdie said. "Can he walk?"

"Let's see," Rabbit said. Birdie tried to lift him on one side while Rabbit tried to lift him on the other, but Rabbit was almost a foot taller than Birdie, and Oscar was somewhere in between. He tilted to one side like he was in the middle of a ski slope. The three of them wobbled along and somehow got Oscar into the house. As soon as he was settled in his bed, Birdie hugged Rabbit and left to get changed and get back to the Healing Center.

This was the first inkling that something was really wrong at The Old Witches Home. It was just a cut, but there was something else, something she couldn't explain. As Birdie entered her home to change her clothes, a caw from the crow made her look up. Hermes scrambled up the tree and fell back down.

Birdie asked the Goddess what she should do. The Goddess had nothing to say.

3

MAYA VISITS ANGIE

Maybe the big Medical Encyclopedia in the Healing Center would have something to say about Oscar. His behavior was a bit odd, she had to admit. When she returned to the building, she saw Hermes hunting in the bushes outside. He was crouched, and his head was outstretched. She couldn't see any prey nearby, but there must have been something. She shuddered.

She thought about the letter Mnemosyne showed her. Those damn nackers! Well, they weren't any match for magic. She was sure about that.

She took a deep breath, asked the Goddess for patience, and opened the doors.

The Encyclopedia would have to wait. The warm sun on her walk had made her hungry. She needed a cookie.

The kitchen in the Heart of Old Witches Home was just down the hall from the Healing Center. Further around the building was the Dining Hall, where feasts and gatherings were often held. They had decided early on that no one should have to eat alone if they didn't want to. Residents volunteered for kitchen duties, supervised by Maya Craven, the head cook, or Angie, her assistant.

They cooked for festivals and for the residents who were ill, forgetful, indigent, incompetent, or depressed. Maya had kept several residents alive and healthy – Whale Tooth probably owed his robust nature to her. She believed in the magic of food and was just as sweet as the chocolate desserts for which she was famous.

When Birdie came in, Maya was sitting on a stool next to the kitchen counter. Her warm brown skin was tanned from afternoons lying out by the pond. Her dark hair braid lay gently on the back of a floral short-sleeved blouse. As she turned to Birdie, the ruffles on the open neck of the blouse revealed her ample bosom and the rest of the paper clips she needed to mark the recipes she wanted to revisit.

Birdie looked around, expecting to see Angie, but it appeared that Maya was alone. A spiral notebook filled with dog-eared and grease-stained pages was open in front of her. Birdie could see that Maya was anxious – chewing on a paper clip and rapidly flipping back and forth from one recipe to another.

"Got any cookies?" Birdie asked. She had a wicked sweet tooth and long ago decided there was no use trying to tame it. Every time she did it just made her cranky. Her favorite was the chocolate coconut cookies that Maya would make just for her.

"Here you go," Maya said distractedly as she pulled out a jar labeled "Keep Out – Poison!" from behind the coffee jars on the counter. She looked at Birdie. "What are you doing here? Shouldn't you be in the Healing Center today?"

"Yep. On my way there. Just wanted to fill you in on what's going on. Lightning's brother is contesting the will. He says Lightning was coerced as if we had put a spell on him or something and forced him to give the land to us. Can you imagine?" Birdie tried to laugh it off, but the need for chocolate gave her away.

"Holy Goddess," Maya said. "What are we going to do?"

"We'll have a Council meeting to figure it out, I guess. I called Maple." Birdie took another cookie out of the jar.

"Good. Maple will get everyone together," Maya said, returning to her notebook.

"Will he?" Birdie said. "Maybe I should do it."

"Birdie…" Maya said. "Give him a chance."

"Yeah, yeah. Oh, also – Oscar got hurt this morning when he was gardening. A nasty gash in his hand. He's home with Rabbit. He's acting kind of weird – he keeps making these clicky noises, and his head keeps bobbing up and down. When I tuned into him, holding his hand, all I heard was a low rumble. I thought maybe some food would ground him, but he wouldn't eat anything."

"If he's been making magic, protein is the best thing for him. I'm sure I have eggs, cheese, or something here if you want to take it to him." Maya walked over to the industrial-sized refrigerator set into the opposite wall.

"Thanks, but I'm sure Rabbit can handle it. She's been practicing as long as we have and knows what to do. It could be just blood loss from the cut, you know." Birdie generally preferred mundane explanations if they made sense. She was tempted to take a third cookie. Maya brushed her hand away.

"We better have a good festival. I'm not sure what we will do if we don't raise enough money to pay the balloon payment. Now we need money for lawyers, too."

"We'll get by. We always have. We're witches, remember?"

"Yeah, but witches can be burned at the stake. What if they believe these insomniac lawyers and give the land to his brother?"

"Have faith, Birdie. We've always gotten by before. We live in a universe of abundance, whether insomniacs can see that or not. They live in a world of scarcity. We'll be okay."

"I just don't know, Maya. I'm afraid I'll have to go to some state home where they don't have enough staff, and people are left to drool and wither away in their wheelchairs all alone."

"Birdie," Maya stopped and looked at her. "You're not alone. You're in community, remember? We do this together. We love each other; we're a family. You're so used to being independent and self-sufficient that you still haven't realized that there are others in the world who have your back. How many times do you have to be reminded? You're not alone."

"Right," Birdie said and looked down. She knew what Maya said was true but still had trouble believing it fully. She had always felt unloved. Her friends said they loved her, but she was sure they would leave her and go back to their biological families if they lost the land.

"Well, I can help with the cooking if you need it." Birdie tried to smile, but her lips twisted, and one side went up while the other side looked for the exit at the back of her head. The offer didn't fool Maya.

"Uh, thanks, but I'll manage," she said. "Angie had the whole feast figured out, who was bringing what, and what we needed to make. It's just that she put it on her computer in some sort of program with lots of boxes and numbers. I can't figure out how that thing works for the life of me. She isn't answering her phone, and I don't know what's happening with her. I have no idea what we need to buy or harvest – or what still needs to be done."

"She hasn't shown up? That's not like her, is it?"

"No, it isn't. She's usually so reliable. Not like a witch at all. It's weird!"

"Does she have a fever or anything?"

"I don't know. I'll go by her house in a little while to see what's going on." Maya poured hot water over a peppermint tea bag in a handmade ceramic cup with a crescent moon handle.

"I'm sure she's okay," Maya added. "Maybe she's astral traveling and hasn't come home yet." They laughed.

"Right, like when we used to take psychedelics. God, I miss those days," Birdie said.

"Me, too. But I am too old to stay up all night like we used to. Not that reality is all that great, but at least I can sleep through most of it." Maya winced as she remembered the hot nights in El Paso in her small bedroom over the garage. It was hard to sleep when her father visited her, and a quick trip on the astral plane was her only refuge.

"Well, let me know if I can help with the food. We have to have a good feast to convince the insomniacs to part with their money. We need that money, you know."

"I know. Don't worry. I've been doing this for years."

"Yeah, I know. I just don't want to see us come up short this year. I hate having to rely on the generosity of the town."

"Everything turns out the way it should. The Goddess will take care of it," Maya said.

"Yeah, right. Tell that to the nackers at the bank."

Birdie left Maya studying her notebook, a worried look on her face.

Maya was completely confused. In past years, she had kept track of what they were cooking and who was doing what with a series of index cards. She had an elaborate system of organizing the meals by ingredients, by type of dish, and by contributor. But this year, she succumbed to Angie's pleading to allow her to put the menu on a spreadsheet. Angie had sworn that they could still sort by ingredient or dish and that it would be faster and easier. The only problem was that Maya would look at the spreadsheet and somehow screw it up by tapping just one key.

Whenever Angie tried to teach Maya how to use the program, she would stand behind her, looking over Maya's shoulder and occasionally sighing.

"I know this is all new for you. You haven't had the benefit of being introduced to computers early in your life," Angie said in a sympathetic tone. Maya harrumphed and pointed out that Angie was only fifteen years younger than Maya, but Angie just smiled patiently.

Eventually, Maya gave in, and Angie took over the solstice feast planning and became the head cook for this occasion. Maya didn't like being relegated to assistant and said so loudly. Privately, she confessed to Birdie that she was enjoying the lack of responsibility and the ability to take it easy and simply support Angie rather than being in charge of the whole thing.

Until today, that is. She decided to go to Angie's house to ensure she was okay.

But when she arrived, the door was wide open. The deafening sound of Angie's voice singing "Defying Gravity" from *Wicked* almost knocked Maya down.

Wow, she's really good. But this wasn't like Angie, to completely ignore her commitments. No matter how much Maya wanted to enjoy the music, she had to find out what was going on.

Maya knocked on the door, but no one appeared. She knocked again, louder this time, but the only sounds were the song, strident, in tune, and full of joy. She decided the open door was an invitation and entered to find Angie standing in the living room, twirling around and jumping up with arms outstretched.

Maya looked around. She hadn't been to Angie's home for a couple of years since most of their time together was spent in the kitchen. Angie's small house was on the Fulfillment East Lane of the pentacle. Most of the younger people in their 60s lived there, as was fitting. They still had so much living to do. There was a fire circle at the end of the lane where they could drum and sing and dance into the wee hours of the night. Angie played her stump fiddle, Stumpie, with all its bells and whistles, literally – triangle, cymbals, wooden pipe, and tambourine. She loved goofing around with that thing and would make up chants and ditties right on the spot for any occasion.

To the side of the cabin sat Angie's little kitchen garden with herbs, peppers, and tomatoes guarded by her tiger kitten Kumquat. There was a wood stove against the outer wall in the living room and a kitchen that opened onto the main area. Colorful fabrics draped her windows, covered her couch and hung from the doorway into her bedroom. The last time Maya had been there, she felt like she was being carried in on a flag of freedom and justice, as though she were a baby in a carriage and could only see the sheets waving in the breeze above.

Angie's in a good mood today, Maya thought. Great! But Angie didn't stop singing when Maya tried to ask her about the day's activities. Angie was still in her nightgown, and when Maya suggested she might want to change her clothes, Angie simply threw up her arms and twirled in a pirouette. A bit of starlight peeked out from the faraway look in her eyes.

"Angie!" Maya yelled. "ANGIE!!" But Angie kept singing, dancing, and jumping. Maya went to the pile of clothes on the floor in the bedroom, grabbed a tee shirt, and stood behind Angie, guiding her into the bedroom. Once Angie was standing next to the bed, Maya climbed on the rumpled sheets and positioned the tee shirt on Angie's head. She tried to slide it down over her head and nightgown. The nightgown and the tee shirt got all tangled up with each other as Angie continued to sing. Maya got off the bed to pull the tee shirt down from the front, but Angie's arms waved in the air, moving the tee shirt up, making it impossible for Maya to pull it down.

Angie belted out the last verse, exhorting all who were listening to find her in the western sky, defying gravity, flying free. Maya thought the sentiment had never been so appropriate. No one was about to bring Angie down!

She finished the song. She hadn't missed a beat.

Maya gave up, plopping down on the floor beside the bed.

Angie plopped, too. Onto the bed and fast asleep. One arm was in, and the other out of the tee shirt, causing it to bunch up around her neck.

Maya sat on the floor, panting and pondering. The quiet was welcome after the raucous wailing but also quite eerie and unsettling. Angie had always been so steady – now she's singing and sleeping uncontrollably?

Was Angie ill? Drunk? Drugs? She never knew Angie to imbibe. She claimed she couldn't take the risk. Her Guillain-Barre syndrome made her more susceptible to the effects of drugs and alcohol, and she didn't like the feeling. Angie said she'd rather get high with ritual and music. The thought of Angie being stoned or drunk made Maya's stomach queasy.

Maya didn't know what to do next. Should she leave Angie like this? She could try to decipher the spreadsheet by herself. She needed to make out the shopping list. Eddie and Taylor planned to go to town that day to get their supplies, but they didn't have much time. Solstice was only three days away.

Or she could try to make out a list without the spreadsheet. Dang! Why had she allowed Angie to convince her that the computer was a better way to go? Paper and pen had always worked for them in the past, hadn't it?? Something about the way computers seemed to have a mind of their own always bothered Maya. They just didn't make sense to her. It was like they were speaking another language.

Maya rolled over onto her hands and knees. Her generous stomach hung down, and she couldn't resist the urge to pat the soft folds, every inch due to one joy or another. She reminded herself of her old Guatemalan abuela. She had loved the way her grandmother's embrace felt, like being held by a sturdy pillow. She always felt safe and loved in the lap of the woman who saved her from her father.

Enough daydreaming, Maya admonished herself. She grabbed the edge of the bed and hoisted herself up, hearing her left knee creak as she rose. Magic in those knees, she thought. Magic.

She bent over Angie, and Angie stirred, rolling onto her back and murmuring, *"When you're a jet, you're a jet all the way..."* Maya pulled the tee shirt off her and placed a blanket over Angie. What the heck is wrong with this woman?

Maya sat on the bed next to Angie and held her head in her lap. She closed her eyes and placed her palms on Angie's chest. Her breathing was steady. She then checked her forehead – cool and dry. All indicators from her energetic field suggested that she was fine and healthy, with all organs working the way they should. Maya sensed a lightness from her and thought she heard the strains of "Oh, What a Beautiful Morning" as she held her wrist. Very strange, but she didn't seem to be in imminent danger.

Might as well let her sleep. Maybe it's just a reaction to her medications. She'll probably be back with the living this afternoon. Maybe she just needs more sleep. Sleeping sickness, that's what this is. Silly sickness, more like. Maya decided to come back that afternoon to check on her again.

Maya worried on the walk back to the kitchen. What would she do without Angie?

It was a warm day but not the awful humidity that Maya hated. She preferred the cool summer days in the Northeast to the hot El Paso summers. There was always a breeze in The Old Witches Home Village, as though fairies were sitting in the trees fanning their little hearts out. The design that Maya, Maple, Birdie, and Lightning had created was perfect. Everything was close enough to be walkable. They could live out their last years among friends and magic. At least when everyone was awake and functioning.

4

COUNCIL MEETING

That afternoon, Maple was wide awake and functioning as well as he could. He hurried toward the ritual room where the council meeting would take place. He still wasn't comfortable running the community meetings, being what they called the anchor. He struggled with the process they used to build consensus, create space for everyone's voice, and ensure agreement on the final decision. It was a lot like herding cats, and he had always been a dog person.

The cats on The Old Witches Home Council were the representatives from the traditions the residents had brought with them. Maple, Maya and Birdie were ReDreaming witches, and the Collective was organized according to ReDreaming principles, which were collaborative and non-hierarchical. But there were also Druids, Norse pagans, British Traditional Witches, Dianic witches, and even a Mexican curandero, Diego, at The Old Witches Home. Everyone was welcome, and everyone had a voice. The Council simply attended to administrative matters and facilitated smooth running of the Home. They rotated leadership positions so no one tradition had a louder voice than anyone else.

Even though Maple had been a manager at a large hardware chain and had functioned quite well in the insomniac world, he had avoided being anchor for years. Now, the role had finally caught up with him, and this was his first big meeting. As a heterosexual cis white male, Maple understood intellectually how white supremacy, colonization, and racism had formed the culture they had all grown up in. Still, he always felt a bit uncomfortable when discussions got heated, feeling that somehow oppression was his fault, personally. He never wanted anyone to think he was exerting too much power or was trying to take over. So he stayed in the shadows, kept his mouth shut a lot of the time, and just enjoyed the camaraderie and energy swirling around him. If he possessed magical power, he wasn't sure how to tap into it. He just went with the flow.

I need someone to keep track of the stack, Maple reminded himself. He remembered when he first heard the term 'stack' when he was learning about the consensus process they used in ReDreaming. It was all so strange to him then, but over the years, he saw how it worked and came to appreciate the elegance of it. Efficient meetings required a facilitator confident enough to wrangle strong-minded witches who often had very different views of what needed to be done. They had to put aside their self-interests and prioritize the group's welfare. That's not how most people were trained in this individualistic culture.

He added to the to-do list in his brain that he needed someone to keep track of time. He reviewed the process for coming to decisions. First, get a proposal from someone, then discuss it, then ask for blocks – those people who can't live with the proposal at all – then stand-asides, and then consensus. I can do this, he thought. I've been in enough meetings; it's about time I led one. I can't expect Birdie to do everything.

Several people were already huddling when he walked into the large circular ritual room with the retractable glass roof and the assortment of folding chairs, overstuffed chairs, loungers, and large pillows. The ritual room was in the center of the Heart, enclosed by low stone walls that created an open space that could be used for meetings or rituals. He remembered the first time he had leaned against one of those walls during a ritual, the day they consecrated the building and dedicated The Old Witches Home to Chiron, the wounded healer of Greek mythology,

Kuan Yin, goddess of compassion, and Baba Yaga, the maligned Slavic crone, the archetype of the wicked witch. There were less than twenty people living at Old Witches Home then, and now there are almost a hundred.

At that time, Maple was still building the stone altars at each of the four directions. He grumbled as the assistants he hired from town laid each piece on the top of the structure. Finally, he burst out, "Be careful! The goddess spent thousands of years on that rock, goddammit." He noticed how the two kids looked at each other after he said it. They probably thought he was pretty strange. He didn't say it again.

Today, the warm summer sun shining on the shelves and bins lining the low walls revealed all kinds of ritual supplies, from candles and altar cloths to statuettes and crystals. As soon as Maple walked in, he felt the energy of the ten years of rituals and sacred workings that had taken place here. He breathed more easily and found a comfy chair to settle in. He looked around, imagining the many witches who had filled the space with their magic, and noticed the large wooden chair Lightning had called his throne. No one else filled that chair like he had. He missed Lightning.

As soon as he saw Birdie and Maya come in, with Mnemosyne not far behind, muttering to herself and carrying her laptop, Maple decided to start the meeting.

He asked for volunteers to ground, set the circle, and invoke the elements.

"Do we have to go through all that?" Charlie asked. Charlie and Bjorn, the newest council members, Heathens who worshipped Thor, the Norse god of thunder, were still adjusting to a non-hierarchical governance structure. They generally wanted to know who was in charge and preferred if it were one of them. Bjorn's red, white, and blue striped suspenders held his blue jeans over his ample belly. Maple felt a twinge of resentment as he saw Bjorn make himself comfortable on Lightning's throne. Charlie, taller but with the same protruding stomach, sat next to him in a back-facing folding chair with legs splayed and elbows on his knees.

As Nordic pagans, they prided themselves on their mead-making skills and hadn't skimped on consumption in their later years. They had joined the Old Witches Home community a couple of years ago when their local temple fell apart over disagreements regarding gay rights. Some Heathens supported changes in the laws – while others thought support of gays was against the religion and an affront to the fertility gods. Maple suspected that Bjorn and Charlie were among the latter, but they kept their opinions to themselves. Whale Tooth had told them about The Old Witches Home but for some reason, he didn't seem to spend much time with them these days.

"It's our process," Dandelion, the Black transgender woman from the Northern California ReDreaming community, said. "You know that. We want to ensure we're in a safe, sacred space when we do our work and everyone has a chance to be heard. We've been doing it this way for years; we're not changing it now."

Dandelion wore her politics on her ruffled sleeves. She had chosen not to have gender reassignment surgery. She simply wore women's clothes, which for her meant colorful t-shirts, pastel eyeshadow, frilly blouses and tight jeans. She said the surgery cost too much, and it hadn't been available when she started asserting her womanhood. It was safer back then if she could simply change clothes if needed. She remembers when they were called 'transsexuals,' as though it was all about who could get you off, and sex and gender were exactly the same thing. For rituals, she wore dresses she bought at thrift stores and often used black eyeliner and bright red lipstick. Many members of Dandelion's community had passed away due to AIDS or old age. When Northern California became too expensive, Dandelion took Lightning's advice and moved to The Old Witches Home.

"Yeah, yeah." Charlie gave up easily, but he didn't smile.

"So who's doing what?" Maple said.

Old Boreus, the slow-moving Druid, agreed to do the grounding. Boreus reminded Maple of an old oak tree in autumn; he was solid and wide with feet planted firmly on the ground with gray and orange hair. Of Scottish origin, he would occasionally drop into a deep brogue when he was tired. Victoria, the British Traditional Witchcraft representative, had invited him to join her at The Old Witches Home when Boreus ran into her at a Renaissance fair after his wife, Fern, died. He was adamant that he wasn't senile, but he definitely needed help remembering things. Some days, it felt like he was part of the furniture, silent and stable, always there when you needed him.

In a lilting voice, Amethyst offered to cast a rainbow circle to bring light and laughter into the meeting. She was a brown-skinned frail woman with turquoise nail polish, very attractive, and dressed in a lilac pantsuit, as though she had just arrived from a garden party. She wasn't sure if she was a witch, but she knew she couldn't afford most retirement communities. Amethyst tended to encourage everyone to love each other and imagine a white light around anything problematic. When she visited the first time, she proclaimed that "the energy was positive, and there were fairies in the woods." She always cast rainbow circles, even in the most tragic of situations. Maple didn't know where Amethyst heard about the Old Witches Home, she just appeared one day, and the Council admitted her, as if enchanted.

Dandelion said she would invoke the elements but only if she could do them all simultaneously instead of each separately. No sense in wasting time, she said.

"Anyone have a problem with that?" Maple asked, unsure if they needed consensus for this decision, but better safe than sorry.

"Not if it means we get out of here more quickly," Charlie said. Charlie used to sell cars for a living and always seemed to be racing from one place to another as if someone were chasing him.

"Okay, then, go."

Except for Amethyst forgetting where she started and trying to continue the circle a second time, the circle was cast fairly quickly and the group was in sacred space.

"We have only one agenda item for this special meeting," Maple said. "That's the letter that we received today. After Birdie explains it, we'll start a stack and take questions and comments. Hopefully, we can get a proposal to do something about this situation."

"Are we going to take a break for snacks sometime?" Dirty Swan asked. Dirty Swan, one of the at-large reps, a swarthy woman with wrinkles on her face for every day she was alive, was an anarchist and refused to be labeled or associated with any organized group. She generally disagreed with everyone and had no trouble letting them know. She always took care of herself. Maple suspected she moved to The Old Witches Home because she couldn't get along with people anywhere else. He liked her and knew he could count on her to shake things up when they got too boring.

"Also, I will probably need to pee soon," Amethyst said, and there were several nods in agreement.

"No worries, you can take a bio break whenever you want. I don't think we'll be here that long," Maple reassured them. Especially if we can get started soon, he thought.

"We got a letter from a lawyer representing Lightning's brother, William Gordon O'Neill. William's contesting the will, suggesting that Lightning was coerced to leave the land to us and that the will was written under 'undue influence,'" Birdie began. "If they can prove that Lightning wasn't in his right mind, then the land will go to the brother. We figure this lawyer, Huffstickler, will try to get the land from the brother."

"If that happens, I don't know what he'll do with all our houses. We think he's the one who's been sniffing around, wanting to make the place a resort for nacker weekenders."

"What happened? Why didn't you all take care of this when you first started the place?" Charlie said. He glared at Maple, who tried to ignore him. He always complained. He didn't understand they were all in it together.

"Okay," Maple said. "Who's keeping track of the stack?"

"I will," Dandelion said. "I see Charlie has his hand up. Go for it."

"So what are we going to do?" Charlie said. "I can't afford to move.

I used up all my savings just to build here. It's not my fault you all didn't take care of things the way you should have."

"Yeah," Bjorn added. "Maybe we shouldn't let so many new people in. The septic system can't handle it. It's already starting to smell. This place is getting crowded, and I didn't move here to be in another town filled with liberal lowlifes."

"Our mission is to be inclusive," Birdie responded. "If they agree to the Principles of Community and practice a pagan religion, we welcome them. You know that. And we'll use money from the Festival to upgrade the septic."

"Yeah, but we can't be too careful. And besides, they always need services – they're just freeloaders." Bjorn was on a roll. Maple had learned from Charlie one night after ritual when they were all drinking mead and watching the stars that Bjorn's family had been on welfare when he was growing up and that the kids at school had teased him mercilessly about it.

"What services?" Dandelion asked. "Water? Septic? Electric? You use those same services."

"Yeah, but I didn't need a loan when I came here, did I? If you can't afford to live here, you should go back where you came from."

"Oh, my Goddess, Bjorn. Everyone needs help sometimes, even you. And everyone has the right to a decent place to live. That's all we're trying to do." Dandelion was so exasperated that she huffed instead of breathing. She had completely lost control of the stack.

"We're victims of white supremacy culture," Dirty Swan said. "I knew it would come to this. Those nackers just don't want anyone to be happy unless they make money off it."

"Hold on. You're not on stack yet," Dandelion said, looking chagrined. At least she was trying to take control again, Maple thought gratefully.

"Okay. Stack," Dirty Swan said.

"Go ahead. Then it's Victoria, and after that, Mnemosyne." Now, they were getting the hang of it. Maple was sure she wouldn't let Bjorn derail them again.

"We're victims of white supremacy culture. The insomniacs want to get rid of us. They don't like the fact that we're inclusive and that we believe that everyone has a right to decent housing, no matter where they come from. I think we should secede from the state and create our own government," Dirty Swan said. "We can fight like they did at Standing Rock in 2015. We could pitch tents in front of Huffstickler's office and use his bathroom."

"Yeah, like the Indians. We could be our own sovereign nation," Bjorn said. "If they can do it, why can't we?"

"No one calls them Indians anymore," Dandelion said. "That's disrespectful. And they could do it because the land was stolen from them in the first place. It's not the same for us. Most of us are descended from the colonialists."

"I've always called them Indians, and I'm too old to change now," Bjorn grumbled. "Besides, I wasn't being insulting – I admire them. They fought the government!"

"Wait a second. What about the stack?" Maple said. "I think you said Victoria was next."

"I was going to suggest we do a binding spell," Victoria said. "But I like the idea of secession too." Victoria was strict about ceremony and protocol, as befitted a High Priestess of Avalon and a Gardnerian witch. Her waist-length raven black hair was falling over her shoulder in one long braid, almost touching the lacy black ankle-length skirt that was neatly arrayed about her on the folding chair.

"Yeah, we have our own power, our own water, our own food. What do we need the government for? They're just going to try to take our rights away," Bjorn said.

"Hold on! Stack! Mnemosyne is next." Maple once again wondered why he had volunteered for this job. This pack of rabble-rousers was a pain in the ass.

"I just wanted to explain the problem," Mnemosyne said. She seemed somewhat out of it. Maple figured she had a long night.

Mnemosyne told the group what she had told Birdie, hesitating more than once as if other thoughts were pushing their way into her brain, and she had to keep pushing them back out.

"I don't know," she continued. "I don't get it either – why did Huffstickler find Lightning's brother and get him to contest the will? Probably because he knows we're facing a balloon payment with the bank and don't have money for legal fees. We're vulnerable and broke. Great time to steal the land. 75 times 300." What did she say? She went on.

"Or maybe he's pissed off because Lightning always refused to sell to him. Lightning said Huffstickler thought Estella should have left the land to him. He managed her affairs after Alice died and had been there for her most of her life. But she gave it to Lightning. And he left it to us. I bet Huffstickler has been waiting for this moment for 10 years. 10, 20, 42 divided by 7." What the hell was she saying? Maple studied her, but no one else seemed to notice. They were all so riled about the will. She looked distracted.

"That man is evil," Maya said.

"We need to sue his ass," Dandelion said.

"We need to burn his ass," added Dirty Swan.

"Yeah, maybe we should get a lawyer and take him to court ourselves," Maya suggested. Maple watched Mnemosyne, who was caressing her computer.

"I don't trust lawyers," Charlie said.

"I don't trust Huffstickler or any insomniac," Birdie agreed. "Besides, we don't have the money for lawyers."

"Our legal system does not respect the common person," shouted Dirty Swan. "We need to dismantle the whole system!"

"It's an Antifa conspiracy," Bjorn yelled. He and Dirty Swan glowered at each other. Maya passed Bjorn the bowl of trail mix and handed Dirty Swan the basket of muffins. Soon, they were quiet.

"We need to defend ourselves. How about an AR-15?" Charlie said, snickering.

There was a loud chorus of no's. Guns were not allowed on Old Witches Home property and never had been. The Principles of Community were quite clear about this issue.

"Wait a second," said Maple. "We don't have to put up with this. We can fight back without guns. We're witches, aren't we?? What about some kind of magical activism? Dandelion?"

"Sure. This is just like People's Park. We can reclaim it!! Maybe some street theater? I still have my stilts."

Maple tried to picture Dandelion on stilts but only saw a waiting ambulance.

"Yes, let's fight back," Bjorn said. "We can use the power of Thor's hammer to rain thunder and lightning on him. We need to fight for justice. We can't let that miserable lawyer win!"

"For once, we agree," Dandelion said. "What should we do?"

"Maybe we should cancel the festival and concentrate on this," Boreus said.

"That might not be a bad idea. Without Angie, I'm not sure I can handle the festival feast alone," Maya said. "I'm too old for all of this."

"What's wrong with Angie?" Charlie asked. He seemed genuinely concerned.

Maple wondered too.

He heard Maya whisper to Charlie, "I'll tell you later."

"No. We have to have the Festival," Birdie said, steering the conversation back to Huffstickler. "We rely on the donations from the townspeople."

"We really need the money right now," Mnemosyne said. She seemed to be back in the room, but she was still holding onto her computer as if it were an infant. "Unless we can get a new loan – 78, 43, 62 – we will have a huge balloon payment for the mortgage on the Heart." Maple was having trouble following the conversation. He was worried about her.

Birdie jumped in. "We don't have enough to pay the taxes due in September, and we've promised to give loans to the three witches who are moving in and don't have the money to build yet. If we piss off the town, they could decide not to donate or come after us for more building permits or something and make life really hard for us."

"And you know how hard it is to get contractors. When the new people start to build, they might be unable to find anyone to work for them. The local guys could decide they don't want to come out here." Maple said. "Everyone's home could be in jeopardy."

The group was silent for thirty seconds, an eternity to Maple.

"How about some spell work?" he said.

"I think I suggested a binding spell quite a while ago," Victoria said sweetly.

"That's right," Dandelion said. "Anyone else on stack?" Maple was glad to see that she was still trying to maintain control.

"I have to take a bio break," Boreus said. "Go on without me." He moved slowly toward the door, and Amethyst followed. Maple was afraid that the meeting would dissolve rapidly.

"Wait, we're not finished," Maple said. "We need to do something! And we haven't opened the circle yet."

"May I say something?" A quiet voice from the back.

"Go ahead, Lois. Sorry – I didn't see you there." Maple had a soft spot for Lois, the eldest of the witches at The Old Witches Home, 95 years young. No one had seen her, council member emeritus, come in; she was so small and frail, but there she was, with her walker.

"I'm just thinking that they probably are underestimating us. The lawyer probably thinks we're not quite with it because we're old, and he wants to take advantage of us. They think we're strange. They may laugh at us, but we're smarter than them.

"We need to be strategic about what we do next, or they will take away our homes and independence. We may be old, but we still have magical power. We can be confident about that.

"We need to consider the Wiccan Rede – 'an it harms none, do what thou wilt' – and the rule of three. You know that whatever we do will come back to us threefold."

"What about that stupid Rede? We're not going to curse him; we're simply going to stop him from taking our land!" Bjorn bellowed.

"We don't want any harm to come back to us, right?" continued Lois calmly. "We need to be careful. Our intent is everything."

"I agree," said Maple. "How about if we ask the gods to prevent the transfer from going through? That's not harming him; it's just saving us."

"I think we should ask the gods to give him exactly what he deserves!" shouted Dandelion.

"Nothing" yelled several people in unison.

"And by the way, you weren't on stack, Maple," Dandelion said.

Just then, Diego, who generally remained aloof from the rest of the witches, said, "I believe you are planning to do some mischief! It is important to make sure your work is done correctly."

For once, the rest of the witches were silent. Maple had always admired Diego, impressed by his dignity and strength. He was surprised when Diego applied to become a resident since he had never met a curandero who considered themselves a witch or a pagan. Many still had ties to the Catholic church and their pantheon of saints. There were reports that they liked to conduct blood sacrifices with animals, which scared Maple.

"Sure. Tell us what you think," he managed to squeak. Diego, tall, with black hair streaked with gray, dark eyes, warm brown skin, and a bullfighter's body, strode into the center of the room as everyone watched him. Maya patted the cushion next to her and smiled seductively at him. Maple grunted.

"Great magic requires great sacrifice. What are you willing to commit to the spell to stop this man from harming us?" asked Diego.

Good question, thought Maple. "I'm committing my time, my energy, and the first zucchini that's ripe," he said. He assumed the gods knew just how much he loved his zucchini bread.

Each of the participants pondered.

"I'll shave off my beard and commit it to the cause," boomed Boreus. "If that's what it takes to save our land, I'll do it." Maple wondered if he really had a chin under there.

Everyone else came up with something precious to them, and that represented their connection to the Old Witches Home, from the dream catcher that hung in Dandelion's kitchen window to Victoria's black lace shawl to a rock Charlie dug out from the ground to make room for the community garden. They promised to bring their offerings to be placed on the altar.

Victoria made a proposal to conduct a binding ritual to stop Huffstickler from taking their land. After asking for blocks, stand asides, and support for the proposal, Maple said, "We have consensus. We use magic to stop Huffstickler."

They decided to complete the ritual that night, three nights before the full moon. The Luncheons & Dragons club would have to postpone the second game of their tournament.

The meeting wasn't finished yet. They still needed to write the intention and craft the spell. Maya offered to lead the group in a dropped and open trance, and Birdie said she was willing to work with Amethyst, Lois, and Charlie to do the final wordsmithing. Then, for this group, the rest of the process was relatively quick – only 48 minutes from start to finish. Maya provided hibiscus iced tea, more muffins and trail mix, and a plate of cheese and crackers with dark chocolate. No one complained, at least not about the snacks.

We claim our rights to the land of The Old Witches Home. We bind anyone who attempts to take that land from The Old Witches Home Collective.

Seemed pretty obvious to Maple, but the debate about using "our rights" was fierce. Some just thought it should read "claim the land." Others thought they should name the tribes from whom the land was originally stolen. That led to a discussion of whether they really 'owned' the land at all.

"Ownership of land is a fiction created by European colonialists to rob indigenous people of their homelands," Dirty Swan said.

"That's the world we live in, sweetie," Charlie said.

"What did you just call me?" Dirty Swan towered over Charlie, and Maple could see him cringing just a bit.

"Let's focus, shall we?" Birdie said. "We don't have much time. The Festival is in three days, and we must do this now."

Dirty Swan walked to her Barcalounger and sat, still staring at Charlie. Charlie said, "Sorry," and retreated to the other side of the room.

"Great, let's move on, shall we?" Maple said.

Then came the inevitable wrangling over which deities to invite to the ritual. Bjorn demanded that Thor, Odin, and Loki be allowed to lead the charge. Boreus said the Druids were adamant that it must be a Celtic god, preferably Lugh, or at least Hecate or Cerridwen, but Mnemosyne, with Dianic roots, thought it would be better to fight toxic masculinity with Athena and Diana. Amethyst cautioned that they needed to invoke positive energy if they were going to heal their community. Victoria insisted that there be a balance between male and female energies. Dirty Swan said, fuck the deities, we need human bodies!

Witches began moving around the room and setting it up for a basic binding spell. Birdie put a black cloth on the largest table she could find, a card table that she moved to the center of the room to be used as the altar. Dandelion found an old scale for measuring pot and thought it would be perfect to represent the scales of justice.

Dirty Swan discovered a foot-and-a-half-high statue of a garden gnome, which she put on the altar to represent Huffstickler. The bearded gnome had a pointy hat, holding a crudely lettered "Go Away" sign with one hand and showing his middle finger with the other. Seemed appropriate, they all agreed.

Victoria suggested they all bring ribbons, string, or rope to knot around the statue to create a net to capture his energy and prevent him from winning his court case. She moved Lightning's chair to the side of the table to hold the binding supplies and votive candles.

Birdie and Boreus wrote a chant rhyming "Old Witches House" with "Bad Rich Louse" and set it to three-quarter time. Maple saw it wasn't going well and wished Lightning could help them. His ritual music was legendary. They were still working on the melody when the rest of the group finally opened the circle, leaving them time to go back to their homes to get something to eat, dress, purify themselves, and gather their tokens for the altar.

Maple saw Bjorn approach Maya from behind as she bent down and looked through the crystals on the shelf. He had a lecherous look on his face, and he reached out to give her butt an appreciative pat. Maya turned and moved quickly away, glowering at him. He chuckled and walked in the other direction.

Maya found a place on the altar for the tall glass bodega candle decorated by all the residents with healing sigils, hearts, flowers, and pentacles. They had given it to him that last week before Lightning passed. Then she gazed at the framed pencil drawing, their initial design for The Old Witches Home layout, and placed it in the center of the altar, touching the drawing in a kind of benediction.

She turned to look at Maple and said, "Maybe we could honor Lightning tonight, too. We wouldn't be here without him, right?"

Maple nodded. The room felt empty without larger-than-life Lightning. Birdie joined them and looked wistfully at the drawing. Mnemosyne still stood on the other side of the room, muttering at her computer.

The four left to go home to prepare for the evening.

Hermes hesitated. He sniffed the garden gnome. The comical creature stared back at the cat with a sinister smile.

5

BINDING RITUAL

The garden gnome sat innocently on the altar when the residents gathered in the ritual room to try to stop Huffstickler's seizure of the land belonging to The Old Witches Home. Each of the major traditions was there, some in full regalia, others looking as if they had left their dinner cooking on the stove and were ready to rush back any minute.

The night was warm. When Birdie arrived, there was still light in the sky, but the dusk was deepening. Maple had retracted the translucent roof, inviting the soft shushing of the gentle breeze and the calls of the evening songbirds into the space. The room's energy was rich with the history of the community, Lightning's bright presence still lingering in the corners.

Birdie was pleased with the turnout. It meant that the residents were taking this threat seriously. She wore her long flowing purple dress, always a good standby costume for any ritual, with her largest pentacle necklace, figuring that she needed protection and power to repel this invader to her Home.

Bjorn and Charlie were conferring in the corner, both clad in black t-shirts with Viking wolves on the front. Bjorn had added a formal Viking tie to his t-shirt that landed on his protruding belly. Ever since they had been on the Council, she had felt a certain disquiet. She attributed it to the strong overtones of toxic masculinity in their practices and her ignorance of their beliefs and traditions. It was important to be inclusive and open, she reminded herself. All pagans are welcome at The Old Witches Home.

Birdie took a seat in the west on a low Adirondack chair. As she waited for the ritual to begin, she watched Maple pace around the room. As usual, he was quite nervous, and she didn't understand. He was so strong and smart, but he didn't know it for some reason. She wondered, not for the first time, what had happened in his life to make him doubt himself so much. She had known his wife, Juniper, and Birdie didn't think she had undermined Maple's confidence. Maybe it was from his childhood. Birdie didn't know – she just knew she wished he felt more comfortable with his power.

Maple didn't feel especially confident as he watched people arriving. He would start the ritual when everyone got there, but he couldn't remember who was planning to attend. There were 13 members on the Council, and they all made it to the earlier meeting. But hadn't they agreed that partners could participate in the ritual too? He couldn't remember; so many people had been talking, and he couldn't always hear what people were saying – they seemed to mumble all the time. He had forgotten his hearing aid that afternoon. He suspected that all the talk wouldn't have made sense to him even if he had brought it. Besides, the dang thing made his ears itch. He had it in now, though.

"Okay, everyone, settle down," he said, but no one seemed to hear him. They still kept milling about and talking with each other.

"We're going to get started now."

Still no response. Lois was hobbling across the room on her walker, and Boreus was following her to the wide plush couch on the north side of the space. Amethyst, dressed in a pastel-colored, flowing gown, was already there, gesturing to the seat beside her and smiling at them both.

Dirty Swan and Dandelion were standing in the east, laughing about something, and Victoria was approaching them with a royal presence.

Charlie and Bjorn sat in the south, looking nasty and suspicious. What was up with them? Were they just mad at Huffstickler?

"Ahem," Maple tried again. A little louder. "Could we get started, please?"

From the other side of the room, Birdie spoke up like an umpire at a minor league baseball game.

"Yo, could you all please sit? We want to get home sometime before midnight!"

Maple winced. Once again, he thought, she had to take over for me.

But it worked.

Everyone sat, and Maple walked to the center of the space. He stood next to the altar with the garden gnome in the center, the scales of justice behind it, and the various tokens people had brought surrounding the gnome. He had put a roll of duct tape and scissors on Lightning's chair next to the altar for the witches to attach their binding cords to the gnome.

He reminded the group of why they were there and the intention of the ritual –

We claim our rights to the land of The Old Witches Home. We bind anyone who attempts to take that land from The Old Witches Home Collective.

The witches spoke the intention three times, and Maple started the ritual. He held a branch from one of the sugar maples in the meadow above the village and walked around the circle, inscribing a pentacle in each direction to cast sacred space.

The rest of the opening went smoothly enough, especially for a bunch of witches who all do things differently in their own traditions. Maple felt a sense of unity and strength as they called on the energies of the various directions and settled into the rhythm of the ritual.

After the deities were called, Victoria stepped forth and described how they would take their binding cords, whatever they had brought, and attach them to the gnome. Then, some would walk widdershins (counterclockwise), and others would walk deosil (clockwise) to tie up the gnome and keep Huffstickler from enacting his plan.

Maple stood back as people moved forward with their strings, their ribbons, their chains, and their yarn. Charlie and Bjorn were the first and appeared to be quite eager.

Charlie attached a length of bicycle chain, and Bjorn attached a chain from a chainsaw on top of the gnome's head with duct tape and draped them in front and in the back of the statue. As the other binding cords were attached and wound around, they fell on top of the chains, not actually touching the statue.

Maple thought it was a good idea to have a base for the other binding cords to attach to, but something about the arrangement of chains and ribbons bothered him, and he couldn't figure out what it was.

"This is for Lightning," Maya announced as she affixed a multicolored braided Guatemalan friendship bracelet.

She noticed Diego approaching the altar with a bundle of herbs tied together with a string. She had brought herbs from her own garden. Together, they spread angelica, basil, burdock, and thistle on and around the drawing of the layout. They sprinkled salt on the altar and placed dried acorns and birch strips in vacant spots until the altar was swathed in a woodsy scent of protection.

She heard him quietly repeating something as he circled his right-hand palm downward over the items on the altar. Maya closed her eyes and imagined the village enveloped in a pink bubble, translucent and impenetrable.

Someone – Maya wasn't sure who – started the chant Victoria and Boreus wrote earlier. Every time they got to the words "bad, rich, louse," they stomped their feet and yelled the words. The room filled with strong scents of chain oil, incense and sweat. Some people danced around the gnome; others were seated on the edge, Maya among them.

As the chant peaked and dipped, Maya could feel another presence twirling on the room's edges. Light lavender and rose replaced the musky incense. A vibrant swish of nylon and silk brocade announced Lightning's presence. An image of a purple, blue, and red bodice neatly covered with gold-trimmed embroidered roses and held up by two thin pieces of elastic shimmered as it spun at the periphery of her vision. He laughed as he performed flawless pique turns encircling the group, his arms whipping around, his gaze pulling his body forward, sealing the spell that secured his legacy.

With Lightning's appearance, Maya relaxed and no longer felt the anxiety that had been gripping her all day. She found Birdie's eyes across the circle and smiled a giddy smile. Birdie's eyes were wide, and she was grinning. She, too, had felt the whirlwind of energy Lightning had generated.

The garden gnome was almost completely encircled when Maya heard the unsettling sounds of clacking computer keys and the click of a mouse. She looked to Birdie and Maple to see if they had heard anything, but they were chanting and swaying and seemed caught up in the ritual, beaming with ritual intoxication.

Silly old lady, Maya thought. You're always hearing things. I just have tinnitus from all those rock concerts. Forget it.

The chant climbed into the air, and an energetic cone of power flew off into the ether. Lightning raised his arms to the sky and faded, the tulle edges of his tutu the last to disappear.

Maya heard Maple as from a distance, "We bind this man from harming anyone on this land. Whatever he does, let it return to him threefold."

"For the good of all and the harm of none. In perfect love and perfect trust. So mote it be." The group chanted as one.

"So mote it be." Maya joined the rest of the group, echoing Maple. The hairs on her arms were raised. She was sure the magic would make a difference.

"Don't forget to take your altar offerings," she heard Birdie say after they devoked and released the elements. "And add them to your altars at Home. We're not out of the woods yet."

"Also, you can come back any time and light a votive. Let's keep this spell going," Victoria added.

When the circle was open and she was helping to put chairs away, Maya was settled again. For once, she felt like they were a strong, unified community instead of a bunch of difficult misfits, each with their own way of doing things.

The bound and chained gnome stood upright on the altar, surrounded by votive candles that residents could light whenever they wanted to. Until the threat was gone for good, they wouldn't let Huffistickler's and the brother's energy spread into the world.

Their work was done for the moment. Now, the only thing they could do was wait for the magic to take effect. And hope it doesn't come back on them.

6

MNEMOSYNE IS AFFLICTED

During their post-ritual gathering, she realized that Mnemosyne hadn't been there. Birdie's feelings of unity and accomplishment dissolved.

"Did you see Mnemosyne at the ritual?" Birdie asked Maya and Maple.

"Nope," Maple said. "But she was really tired at the Council meeting. Maybe she went to bed early."

"You think so? She seemed pretty committed to stopping Huffstickler. I don't think she would have wanted to miss the binding spell," Birdie said.

"I'm surprised she wasn't there. Maybe we should check on her," Maya said. "I hope she doesn't have the same thing that Angie has. It's like a sleeping sickness. I stopped by before the ritual, and she was still out of it. I tried to wake her to drink some water, and she sat up and started singing with her eyes closed – *Moon River*, I think. She drank the water, but then she went right back to sleep. She seemed in a good mood, like she was having really sexy dreams and didn't want to leave them. She didn't appear to be sick or anything. I'll go over again after I leave here. I'm starting to get worried."

"Oscar was still out of it when I stopped by on my way here, too," Birdie added. "Rabbit said he's been sleeping all day, making strange noises and pawing at the sheets. He didn't have a fever, and the cut was healing. I don't get it. There's probably no connection between the two of them, right?"

"Oscar often stays up all night playing on his farm game," Maple said. "Lack of sleep probably just caught up with him. He's as strong as a bull. I wouldn't worry about him."

"I don't know what we can do anyway at this point. Angie's safe, and you'll stop by on your way home, right, Maya? And Rabbit is with Oscar. She'll let someone know if Oscar gets worse." Maya nodded, and Maple shrugged. Birdie's sense of unease kicked up a notch.

"Let's see if we can find Mnemosyne. Maybe she's still in her office." They put their mugs in the sink, and Birdie led the two of them down the hall to the DWI office. This wouldn't have been the first time Mnemosyne fell asleep at her desk.

Birdie saw Mnemosyne lying on the floor by her desk as soon as she walked in.

It looked like she fell from her swivel chair and got wedged between it and her desk. One ankle was hooked around a leg of the desk and stuck out at a strange angle. The fingers on her outstretched arms were tapping on the carpet, like on a keyboard.

Goddess, damn it!! What the hell is happening here? Birdie feared something like this when Mnemosyne acted strangely at the Council meeting. First Oscar, then Angie, and now Mnemosyne!! Sleeping sickness, that's what Maya called it. Nonsense, that's what it was. Birdie wouldn't let something as silly as sleeping take them out.

"Maple, you need to get Lois now. Take one of the golf carts and wake her up if necessary. This doesn't look good," Birdie said. Maple obeyed immediately.

It was only 9:25 – hopefully, Lois would still be awake. Birdie regretted not hiring a professional nurse to be on-site, preferring instead to be self-reliant. A perfectly good physician lived in the nearby town – Birdie was well aware of him – but when someone needed help at odd times, like now, they had to rely on Lois, who used to be an emergency room nurse, and she wasn't getting any younger.

Maya squatted, her full skirt expanding as she sat on the floor beside her and put her ear to Mnemosyne's chest. "She's still breathing."

"I know that, Maya. I would have called an ambulance otherwise, not just Lois. Let's put something under her head."

Birdie looked around the tidy office. She grabbed a stack of file folders from the shelves against the wall, and Maya gently raised Mnemosyne's head and placed it on the manila pile. Birdie straightened the edges and made sure no random pieces of paper were sticking out, just as she knew Mnemosyne would have wanted her to.

Then she found some stick incense in the desk drawer, lit it, and began waving it around the room, first widdershins, attempting to remove any stray negative energy and then deosil to invite the positive forces to join them. When she was done, she sat at the desk and began rifling through the papers and envelopes.

Maya remained on the floor with Mnemosyne's head on her lap. Mnemosyne's eyes darted rapidly left and right, but her breathing was steady. Maya softly called her name, but Mnemosyne didn't seem to hear.

While Maya was tending to Mnemosyne, Birdie found the large envelope with Huffstickler's name in the corner and resisted the urge to rip it up. Instead, she took a deep breath and read carefully. The legalese felt like a swampy marsh. She wasn't sure she understood it all, but the gist was clear. His brother, William Gordon O'Neill, was claiming that Lightning had been mentally incapable of writing a will from his hospice bed. He stated that The Old Witches Home residents that had been at his deathbed had forced him to sign it. He could not legally bequeath the land to The Old Witches Home Collective. That's why probate was stalled.

Birdie felt a spike of fear in her gut. She suspected Huffstickler behind it all. She had never heard of this William Gordon person, and she knew that Huffstickler wanted to tear down their homes and develop a weekend resort. He had been making inquiries all around town. She would have to move to some random old age home if he succeeded. She didn't have children to care for her like the others did. This place was her Home. These people were her family. They had invested so much time, energy, and savings in this collection of cabins, houses, and huts. They didn't have time to go somewhere else.

She realized she was holding her breath and exhaled slowly as she heard footsteps in the hall.

When she entered the office, diminutive Lois projected the air of an experienced professional. Even with her walker, she was brisk and efficient. A stethoscope hung around her neck, and a watch brooch was pinned to her blouse.

Maple arrived right behind her, holding a black satchel and breathing heavily.

"What happened?" Lois asked. Maple was leaning against the desk, in a tee shirt with a red dragon that seemed to be spitting sparks of fire as Maple struggled to recover from keeping stride with Lois.

"I have no idea," Birdie said. "But this is getting out of hand. We need to get to the bottom of this."

"Help me sit down." Birdie got off the swivel chair and helped Lois onto it, standing behind it to keep it steady. Lois adjusted the chair to its lowest position. Maple and Maya lifted Mnemosyne's torso to meet Lois halfway.

Lois leaned over, took Mnemosyne's wrist in her hand, and focused on the watch on her shirt. She opened Mnemosyne's eyes and felt her forehead. She pulled a blood pressure cuff out of her bag, wrapped it around Mnemosyne's upper arm, inflated it, deflated it, and listened to her pulse in her elbow.

"Maple told me about Oscar and Angie on the way here. Do you know what's going on? Did she and Oscar and Angie all eat something? Or go somewhere? Were they contaminated, maybe? With someone's nasty energy? Or an actual toxin?" Lois asked as she rolled up the blood pressure cuff and put it back in her bag.

"I know Mnemosyne went to the post office yesterday. Did she pick up something there? Remember anthrax?" Maya said. "Is this a sleeping sickness?"

They all looked at the manila envelope still on the desk; no one wanted to touch it. Birdie looked down at her hands – no white powder. Phew.

"She picked up that claim against us," Maple said. "Maybe there was a hex in that envelope."

"It came from insomniac lawyers," Birdie said. "I don't think they know how to do hexes."

"Maybe they all took some kind of drug. Didn't Mnemosyne say she was having trouble sleeping? She mentioned taking CBD. Maybe she just had a weird reaction to it. You know, like those people who take Ambien, then wander around in their nightgowns and do stuff?" Maya said as she leaned over and pressed her hand to Mnemosyne's forehead. "She doesn't have a fever."

"And look at her eyes. They're moving back and forth; she must be dreaming, but she doesn't look very happy. I hope it's not a nightmare," Maple said.

Birdie steadied the desk chair, which was too big for Lois and not nearly as comfortable as it looked.

Lois was staring at Mnemosyne and hadn't said a word.

"What do you think?" Birdie asked her.

"I think we should call Dr. Payne," she said.

"No," Birdie said. "I don't want any of the townspeople to know what's happening here. What if they think we're infected with something? Then no one will come to the Festival. We need their money." Besides, she thought, I can't be around that guy. He makes me nervous. "Can't we call an ambulance instead?"

"We might need to, but you know it takes them at least 45 minutes to get here from Warren. We should talk with the doctor first. I don't think she's in imminent danger, but I don't know what it is, Birdie," Lois said. "And I can't do anything if I don't know what it is. It could be serious.

You say Angie and Oscar are also infected? How do you know it's not contagious?"

"Well, yeah, but it might not be the same thing," Birdie said hopefully.

"Oh, I hope it's nothing I cooked. I've been adding almond milk to the cookies. It couldn't have gone bad, could it?" Maya said.

"No, Maya, I don't think so," Birdie said and sighed. "Besides, Oscar hasn't been eating your cookies. He's on a diet."

"Except for the late-night ice cream," Maple said.

Lois pulled out her cell phone with the abnormally large numbers and quickly punched the doctor's phone number.

"I have an ethical obligation to do what I need to do to take care of my patient," she said. "There are times when magic just isn't enough. We need medical help."

"And you know his number by heart," Birdie observed, imagining a concerned look on the ruggedly good-looking doctor as he answered the phone in his pajamas. She sighed.

The number 62 hung in Mnemosyne's vision, dripping with rainwater from the trees above. She sensed her friends hovering around her as she drifted in and out of old and present realities. The scene in her mind awakened the memory of the ritual on her 62nd birthday, the night she came out of the broom closet, rejected her Baptist background (except for the hats and the singing), and proclaimed her power.

That year, her birthday, a full moon, and Samhain – the day nackers call Halloween – all fell on the same day! It was epic.

Mnemosyne had heard the call of Sekhmet, the Egyptian warrior goddess of fire and medicine, that night and looked for her now. Many witches focus on one god or goddess from a tradition they feel called to, devoting time to learning about that deity and spending time in trance exploring their qualities and strengths and discovering the challenges they ask of their disciples. You could never predict exactly where the lessons of a powerful deity might take you. Did Sekhmet have a special connection to the dollar signs that were flying in the air around Mnemosyne's head now?

The equations, symbols, and numbers flickered on and off like the sparks from the fire she and her Dianic coven, the Queen Bees, had built in Mnemosyne's backyard, larger than any they had ever had before. The neighbors may have been a bit worried, but the circle her covenmate, Cruella, cast that night blocked the neighborhood energy and dampened the sounds that drifted into their hearing range.

There were thirteen that night, and Mnemosyne took her place in the circle's center, standing next to the fire. When the time came to rid herself of the toxic persona she had become, she shed her clothes and howled to the moon. Her corporate ID badge, her most powerful dark blue suit, and the glasses she wore at work were all thrown into the blaze and sparked purple, orange, and pink as the plastic burned.

Sekhmet was in rare form that night – the bonfire lit up the sky. The process of healing and transformation from Mnemosyne's old life to her new had begun. But that was a long time ago. What was she doing now?

That long-ago night, Mnemosyne crouched into a fetal position on the ground next to the fire while the coven covered Mnemosyne with a rose-colored blanket. They piled on top of her and made shushing, soothing sounds as Cruella walked deosil around the circle and called to Sekhmet, to Gaia, the earth mother of the gods, and to Cerridwen, the Celtic goddess of rebirth, transformation, and inspiration.

"Come to this circle! Birth your daughter! Let her be made anew." Mnemosyne heard the voices in her head now as screeches, fingernails on a blackboard, set against the murmur of worried voices of her friends in her office.

She remembered the sky broke open with torrential rainfall – she and the blanket were soaked. The fire sputtered but continued its march into the sky. The coven was cooled by the downpour but not deterred. They danced around the flames, stirring energy and cleansing the figure on the ground with their song. Now x's, +'s, and division signs fell around her amidst the raindrops.

> *Oh, Mother, hear us calling. We, your daughters, seek healing.*
> *Oh, Mother, hear us calling. We, your daughters, seek healing.*
> *Power, power, your love is our power.*
> *Power, power, our love is our power.*

Her coven sang the chant over and over, some with the Mother lines, others with the Power lines. The sounds dipped and soared and enveloped the huddled supplicant. The verses played leapfrog with each other and sometimes landed on each other's backs. The air hummed with drops of moisture, scatterings of ashes, and molten love. Time was transcendent, and the earth stopped revolving for the thirteen witches. It may have only been a few minutes, but it may have been eons – there was no way to measure such earthly and mundane trivia.

In her memory, she began to stir. A toe, a sole, an ankle slipped out from under the soft, sodden blanket. A hand emerged and then a whole arm. The midwives around her provided protection as they helped Mnemosyne birth herself. She felt their affection and wonder as she shook the blanket from her back, rested on all fours, and then carefully rose to stand on newly formed feet. The arms that reached up to the stars reflected moonlight, smooth and fierce. She was her own perfect child.

On the floor in her office, her limbs resisted and she remained inert, glued to the floor.

"I am strong. I have grace. I share my gifts with all I meet and make this earth a better place," Mnemosyne shouted, over and over and over as she rose from the mud that night.

The women danced and sang around her until the sound liquefied into a clear, bright tone. From pitches above, below, and in all harmonic variations, the sound coalesced into one. It may have been loud, or it may have been just a whisper, but who could tell? The sound was intense, and at the perfect moment, it shot up into the sky, searching for the moon and landing in its brilliance.

The women fell to the ground, breathing hard, some laughing, some crying, some moaning. Only Mnemosyne continued standing, arms upstretched, face turned toward the moon, smiling a smile that held the wisdom of the ages and the laughter of the cosmos.

Mnemosyne was not surprised when Birdie called her the next day and said that she and Lightning, Maple, and Maya wanted to build The Old Witches Home. Of course, she would help and tendered her resignation to the insurance company immediately.

As the fire sputtered, defeated by the rain, Mnemosyne succumbed to dreams of numbers, formulas, and dollar signs. She could feel her friends holding vigil, but she could do nothing. Sekhmet had abandoned her.

Looking down at Mnemosyne, Birdie knew this wasn't a mere case of fatigue from working too late – they were being cursed. She felt her anger growing. Lois sat by the desk, making notes in a little spiral notebook, and Maya cradled Mnemosyne and made soothing noises as Mnemosyne chattered softly, moved her head back and forth, and tapped on the floor with her fingers.

When the doctor called to say he had arrived, Maple took a golf cart to the village entrance to pick him up. Birdie told Lois everything she knew about Angie and Oscar as they waited.

"I don't think this is something that a nacker doctor can do anything about," Birdie said.

"Maybe not," Lois said. "But we have to give him a chance."

"You have more faith in the medical establishment than I do," Birdie said.

"Of course I do. I've devoted my life to healing people," Lois said. "Sometimes it takes more than medicine – it takes magic – but medicine and medical care can give us information we can't get otherwise. We can decide what to do once we know what he knows."

Birdie was still skeptical. But the door opened before she could say anything more, and Maple and Dr. Tom Payne hurried in.

Tom Payne was not tall but not short, either. He was one of those men that seemed to fit everywhere. His brownish-gray hair was too short to pull back into a ponytail at the nape of his neck, but he had tried. Strands of hair fell into his eyes, and he kept pushing them back absent-mindedly with strong, tanned hands.

He and Lois immediately started babbling medicalese. Birdie perched on the edge of the desk and looked down at Maya and Mnemosyne. She didn't want to get too close to Tom Payne. The static she felt near him was distracting, and she needed to focus. She just had to ignore the tingle she had when she looked at him. She thought instead about how important Mnemosyne was to her and The Old Witches Home.

Birdie relied on Mnemosyne to keep her grounded and remind her that insomniacs aren't out to get the witches. Mnemosyne's intelligence and organizational skills kept The Old Witches Home running smoothly. What would they do if they lost her?

Dr. Payne shone a light into Mnemosyne's eyes. After feeling her neck and her forehead and taking her pulse, he turned to Lois.

"Did you take her blood pressure?"

"Yes, 110 over 80."

"Hmmm... let's wake her up and see what's going on," he suggested.

Birdie, Maple, and Maya sat Mnemosyne up, Maple behind her shoulders and Maya and Birdie on either side of her. Her eyes flew open as soon as she was upright, and she started mumbling again. Mostly numbers, but also nonsense words.

"Wow," Maple said. "Do you know what she's talking about?"

"I have no idea," Birdie said. The five of them just stared while Mnemosyne kept talking, her eyes darting left and right but not appearing to land on anything.

"Well, doc?" Maple said. "What do you think?"

"I'm not sure, but maybe she'll be better after a good night's rest. Her vitals are strong. She doesn't have any broken bones or even bruising. Maybe it's just a form of narcolepsy or sleepwalking."

"Yeah, sure," Birdie said. Why did they call this guy?

"You said there are two others?" he asked. "With this sleeping sickness?"

Maya told him about Angie, her voice cracking. Birdie described what had happened with Oscar that morning.

"Are you sure he didn't need stitches?" Lois asked.

"The cut wasn't very deep. There was a lot of blood initially, but after I cleaned the wound, it completely stopped. Rabbit put him to bed without a problem."

"And Angie is still sleeping, too?" Lois said.

"Yes, I checked on her on my way to the Heart this evening, and she seemed perfectly fine. I fed Kumquat and left. I'm sorry. Should I have done something else?" Maya said.

"Not necessarily. But I'd like to check on her tomorrow. And Oscar too," Dr. Payne said. "Let me do some research, check the CDC's Morbidity and Mortality Weekly Report, and see if anyone else has seen something like this. For now, just keep a close eye on them all and let me know if anything changes."

"I'll go with you, Dr.," Lois said. "I can drive you back to your car. But what about Mnemosyne?"

"I think we can manage her," Birdie said. "Let's see if she'll be able to walk if we can get her standing."

"I'd be happy to help you get her home," Dr. Payne said, smiling at Birdie.

"Why don't you let Lois take you back to your car, and we can get Mnemosyne home," Birdie said, avoiding his gaze. "We'll call you if we need you."

Dr. Payne helped Lois out of the chair, and they started packing their bags and conferring. It was hard to tell if Lois was worried; she was always so even-keeled, but Birdie felt a tension in her that wasn't usually there.

Once they got her up, Mnemosyne began walking very quickly out the door and in the direction of the Wisdom lane of the village pentacle. The three witches scurried behind her, trying to catch up.

Maya gave up first and yelled to the others. "I can't do it. I'm going to Angie's. I'll see you tomorrow." She turned around and headed south to Joy Lane. The light summer breeze rippled her skirt as she walked.

Maple and Birdie caught up to Mnemosyne and looked at each other.

"She seems fine," Maple said. "I don't get it."

"Try talking to her."

"Mnemosyne," he said softly. "Mnemosyne, how ya doing?"

"45, 89, 323, 4666, minus liability, lies, lies, lies, assets, assets, assets, ass-licking, assassins, asses..."

She trailed off as they reached her door. Mnemosyne had built a sturdy, traditional Cape Cod house with character. The purple hardwood door had panels curved in a dragon shape around a stained-glass pentacle window at the top. She had installed a camera above the door and a newfangled doorbell hooked into a system that could turn on the heat before she got home. Mnemosyne's home was the most modern of the dwellings at The Old Witches Home and the one they usually showed to visitors to the property.

Birdie watched Mnemosyne type a code on the box next to the door. They heard a click, and the door swung gently open. A lamp on the table near the door turned on at the same time. Mnemosyne walked in, the door closed behind her, and they heard nothing else.

The porch light faded. The only sounds were the frogs in the pond and the crickets. The mountains to the north loomed on the horizon, only their silhouettes visible in the dark. At the end of the lane, there were few lights. Most people had gone to bed for the night, and only a few solar-powered walkway lights guided them back toward the Heart.

"I feel like we should be doing something else," Maple said, looking at Birdie.

She shrugged. "I don't know what to do. Maya's checking on Angie, and Rabbit is with Oscar. I could stay here, I suppose."

"The doc did say she was fine for now."

"Yeah, I'll come back in the morning. I'm exhausted. I need my own bed. Let's give her some protection. How about a dragon?"

"Good idea," Maple agreed. The two of them took deep breaths and called forth dragons to surround the house. They invited the dragons to notify them if danger developed. They started off again once they were satisfied that Mnemosyne wasn't completely alone.

The warm summer air felt peaceful as the two friends made their way down the lane paved with cobbles, easy for golf carts to drive on but permeable, allowing rainwater to sink into the earth to minimize flooding and replenish the water table. Birdie wanted to relax, but she had to admit that she was starting to get scared. This unexplained illness that was incapacitating her friends made the dark seem like a sinister cavern rather than a comforting blanket like it usually did.

"I wish I knew what to do. Why are they so out of it?"

"You can't control everything, Birdie. We have to wait and see."

She thought I may not be able to control everything, but I have to get a handle on this. I have a really bad feeling. What if I were to come down with this thing? What would happen to the Old Witches Home? I had better make a will and leave instructions on what to do with my stuff and me.

"Lightning only wrote his will when he was dying," she said to Maple. "I think we need to get everyone to write one as soon as possible if they haven't already."

"Yeah, that's probably a good idea."

The sky was clear, and the stars above were plentiful. The moon was almost full. Birdie felt small – almost, but not quite, powerless.

There were only two more days to the Festival.

7

THURSDAY MORNING

The next morning, Birdie woke from disturbing dreams of a larger-than-life tuxedo cat jumping in and out of her computer monitor, hissing and scratching. Still half-asleep, she grumbled and rolled over on top of her real-life cat, Hermes. He squealed and scooted out from under Birdie. She struggled to sit upright, and cursed her aches and pains. The cat with a mind of his own jumped down, cursed and stretched and they both got out of bed to go to the bathroom. Definitely not the peace and tranquility she usually felt in the mornings.

She decided to go to the pond for her usual early morning meditation. She thought twenty minutes or so lapping back and forth across the pond might put her in the right frame of mind to face the day. She knew the fish by name and could tell from the birds' calls when they were excited and happy. She could smell whether they would be in for a rain shower later. For the last five minutes, she floated, caressed by the soft, cool water, looking up into the clouds, watching the leaves swaying overhead, then closing her eyes and simply being connected to all around her on a cellular level, inside and outside of the edges of her body.

She had to find out what was going on with her friends, who were delirious. Reluctantly, she had agreed to escort the doctor to examine Angie, Oscar, and Mnemosyne again while Lois had her weekly video conference with her grandchildren in Minnesota. Maybe by the time she was out of the pond, she would be inspired. She would know what to do.

Birdie was waiting on the circular road, sitting in a golf cart, when Tom Payne returned to the village. She heard his cranky old Jeep coming up the hill and felt her breath quicken. She watched him get out and lean into the back seat to grab a bag. She felt a little fluttery, watching him from the back. She had an urge to reach out and touch him.

"So where are my patients with this sleeping sickness?" he asked, almost too softly for her to hear.

"Follow me, Dr. Payne," she said, turning away so he wouldn't see her blush.

"Dr. Payne? Come on, Birdie. I thought we were on a first-name basis."

Birdie didn't mean to be offensive. It's just that she had been hesitant to get too close to him since his wife died. She thought acting professionally would help her keep her distance.

"This is serious. My friends are really out of it. I don't have time to chat with you. I can call you Tom if that makes you feel more comfortable instead of Dr. Payne. But we're not here to be friends."

"Okay, okay," he chuckled. "I won't try to be friends. I have enjoyed our conversations in the past, but I'll keep it strictly medical today." The twinkle around his eyes was almost too much for Birdie. She wanted to slap him and kiss him at the same time.

He was right, though. At one time, they had great conversations, like when they found themselves in the dentist's office waiting room. She was there with a hole in her tooth where a crown used to be, and he was in for a routine cleaning. Or when their paths would cross at the farmers' market and they would fondle vegetables together. Their talks ranged from where they grew up – him a military brat all over the country and her in New Jersey – to politics, gardening, sports, and old music. She had felt comfortable with him and had difficulty shutting down their chats when she had to leave.

But that had been before Ruth died. When Tom was still only her doctor, there was no chance anything could happen between him and Birdie. She had felt a freedom with him then. But not now. In the three years since Tom became a widower, Birdie had avoided him and watched as every single woman in Winkton threw themselves at him. She wouldn't be desperate like that, she vowed to herself. She was just fine without him.

Tom left his car in the visitors' parking lot and climbed into the battered electric golf cart that Birdie was disconnecting from the power stand. He held his mottled brown leather doctor's bag on his lap with both hands. With a lurch, they left the main entrance, a metal gate domed by a wooden arch covered with clematis and started off down the circular drive that ringed the village to go to Angie's house on Fulfillment East. Birdie concentrated on the task ahead.

They turned right. It only took a couple of minutes to arrive at Angie's bungalow where Maya had left the door open. The kitchen had been cleaned and the clothes in the bedroom were neatly folded on top of the dresser.

Angie was curled on her bed with a beatific smile on her face. She seemed to be sleeping comfortably. Birdie recognized the tune she was humming from *Camelot* and wondered who Angie was vowing never to leave in summer.

"Hmmm....." Tom gently turned her so he could open her eyes, which gazed contentedly up at him, not seeing him. He shone a light in her eye and hmm'ed again. When he put his stethoscope on her chest, he looked very serious as he listened. The blood pressure cuff whistled as it inflated and sighed when it went down. He tickled the bottoms of her feet, and she giggled.

Finally, he felt her forehead and neck, and she cuddled up to him without opening her eyes.

"This woman is as healthy as an ox," he stated flatly. "You say she's been like this since yesterday?"

"Yep. And she's not the only one who's out of it. What should we do?"

"Keep watch. If she develops a fever, call me immediately. But for now, perhaps all she needs to do is sleep. There doesn't appear to be anything wrong with her."

Birdie was not reassured. "I'll take you to Oscar," she said. They got back in the cart and went back the way they had come, past the parking lot to Joy East.

Rabbit was in the garden when they arrived at the house next to Birdie's.

"How has he been?" Birdie asked.

"He's slept since yesterday morning," Rabbit said. "Normally I would assume he just wants to get out of weeding, but this is too much, even for him." She took off her garden gloves, wiped the sweat off her brow and offered them a glass of water.

She took them into the bedroom. Oscar seemed to be milking something; he kept squeezing something that looked like an imaginary teat with both his hands reaching forward and pulling down. He was humming and smiling.

Tom chuckled and also pronounced him healthy and strong. But his brow was furrowed. He asked Rabbit if he had been eating, and Rabbit said she had tried to get him to eat, but all he wanted to do was sleep. Oscar mooed.

"But Dr., this isn't like him. He usually has so much energy I can't get him to sleep. He stays up all night playing on his computer," Rabbit protested.

"I understand," Tom said. "Something is happening. I'm not sure exactly what it is yet, so I don't want to propose a treatment without some idea of what I'm treating. As long as his vitals are strong, we shouldn't worry. I've contacted colleagues at the CDC to see if anyone else has had to deal with something like this. We'll get to the bottom of it, I'm sure."

Rabbit let out a breath. "Okay." Birdie hugged her for an extra few seconds before they left.

They continued around the circle to Wisdom West to Mnemosyne's fancy home by the hillside. Her door was locked but she opened it when they rang the bell, dressed in a cotton nightgown and muttering to herself. She was in a daze and unable to focus on what they were saying. She didn't resist when Tom examined her, and her reflexes were still strong. As Tom was packing his bag, she got up, went into the bedroom, laid down and went back to sleep. They let themselves out.

Tom was quiet as they drove back to the Heart, and Birdie softened. She was inclined to open up to this soft-spoken, kind man who exuded an air of contentment and peace. She reluctantly admitted to herself that sitting next to him felt comfortable and easy. When he spoke, he looked at her with soft blue eyes behind wire-rimmed glasses, and she had to fight the urge to sink into those eyes.

We're here to do a job, she thought, stay focused. She turned back to watch the road. As she passed Whale Tooth's tent, Hermes sat in his lawn chair, gazing out as they drove past. Slow down, she reminded herself. You never know when someone's cat will dart out of the hedges.

They arrived at the Healing Center in the Heart where Lois waited for them, eager to hear the doctor's appraisal. Birdie sat on the swivel chair they used when treating people, and Tom made himself comfortable in one of the big lounge chairs.

"What's going on? What should we do?" Birdie didn't want to sound desperate, but she hoped that Tom would have some answers for them.

"I think we need to give it more time," he confessed. "I saw something like this before when the owner of Rite-Aid had a beef with the kid at the computer store."

"Hal? The guy who lives up on Rte. 30?" Lois asked.

"Yes, his wife said he was angry with the kid about a marketing ad he posted online, but no one could click on the link. After they argued, he acted weird for a couple of days, wandering around the store aimlessly and refilling the same prescriptions over and over. Luckily, it didn't last long. His wife was worried, but I couldn't find anything wrong with him. Maybe there's some kind of latent virus that can get activated somehow. At that time, I attributed it to Hal's intake of marijuana and Guinness. But maybe there's more to it."

"That's weird," Birdie said, thinking the doctor was losing it himself.

"What do you think, medically speaking? It's not really sleeping sickness, is it?" asked Lois.

"It's unlikely unless there are tsetse flies here," Tom said. "All their vitals are normal. It seems more cognitive – like a delirium or something."

"Are we sure it's not contagious?" Birdie asked.

"I really don't know – we don't know how they got it. So we can't prevent others from getting it too." The three were silent, trying to think of some common factor that would have affected Oscar, Angie, and Mnemosyne.

"But that's not the only problem right now," Tom said. "When was the last time your friends had water?"

Birdie thought back. Oscar first fell ill yesterday, on Wednesday, her Healing Center day. Angie got sick that day, too, and they found Mnemosyne in her office that night.

"Only since yesterday," she said. "Why?"

"Oh, no," Lois said, a stricken look on her face.

"They haven't had any water for over 24 hours?" he said. "If they don't drink, they'll become dehydrated, which could lead to all sorts of problems – serious complications, such as urinary and kidney problems, maybe urinary tract infections, kidney stones, or in the worst case, kidney failure. Also, there could be dementia, confusion, disorientation, and seizures due to low levels of potassium and sodium. Or maybe heat exhaustion or heatstroke."

"Remember when Crystal Dove was dying?" Lois said. "Her dementia was mostly due to dehydration."

"Jesus," Birdie said. With most of the people at The Old Witches Home, she wasn't sure she could distinguish delirium due to dehydration from just plain being old and odd. Hopefully, Lois could tell.

Dr. Tom went on. "Dehydration is more serious in seniors because you have less water in your bodies naturally. It usually takes about three days for dehydration to set in, but the time could be much shorter for older adults. Humans can go without food for a few weeks but not without water."

Birdie thought about Angie, who had an autoimmune disease. She needed a special diet to keep her Guillain-Barre disease at bay. If she didn't get it, she could get very ill and maybe even die. How long could she go without food and water?

"What can we do? Are they dying?" Birdie wanted the facts.

"You need to get some fluids into them sooner rather than later," he said.

"I'll work out a plan," Lois said. "Maybe Diego can help." She brought out her large phone and began scrolling through her contacts.

8

BUILDING THE BONFIRE

Meanwhile, on the hill, Maple could use all the help he could get. Preparations for the Summer Solstice Festival were well underway. Maple and his crew of helpers were clearing the upper meadow area for the bonfire on Saturday. It needed to be open and welcoming for the witches and townspeople to drum, dance, sing, and celebrate the sun on the longest day and shortest night of the year. Maple wanted the land to be perfect.

He hated being the one that was responsible for creating the magical setting – he had no idea how to create magic. He just knew how to let it happen.

Maple was grateful the three workers had shown up that morning. Oscar usually organizes this kind of work. Maple had to call these guys and set them up to work by himself this time. After Mnemosyne convinced him to buy a new-fangled smartphone, he started having trouble answering calls, often hanging up on the caller instead of talking to them. When he tried to call people, he was never quite sure which buttons to push.

To make matters worse, Eddie, the burly White man who used to be a firefighter and now had PTSD, used an old flip phone, had very little reception, no internet, and his only power source was his solar-powered generator. He lived alone in a cabin he rented from Elmer, the dairy farmer on the next ridge over. Eddie didn't talk much, but he was reliable and a hard worker when you could get him.

At least he reached Taylor, the 42-year-old eco-anarchist staying in the Heart for the summer who might forget to charge his phone for days at a time. A calm man who looked as comfortable in the suit he wore to Lightning's funeral as in the jeans he wore when he was working, Taylor had been in and out of prisons. Dirty Swan claimed he had been incarcerated just because he was a Black man in America, which left Maple feeling vaguely guilty. Taylor filled the silences that Eddie left open, carried a small notebook in his back pocket, and was frequently seen jotting in it. Maple had no idea what he was writing. Poetry, maybe?

Twig, the youngest, only 22 years old, was the only helper who could be reached consistently – they always had their earbuds in and often sang swatches of songs that no one else could hear.

Maple walked stiffly up the rise to the top of the meadow, where they had already started creating the bonfire pile. He loved this part of the property. The trees and mountains to the west and north sheltered the high meadow, making it a perfect place for rituals and bonfires. The stars filled the sky on clear nights, and you could see the Milky Way and all the constellations.

Maple remembered lying on his back in this meadow during a trance in which he had 'died.' The ritual intention was to honor the cycles of birth, life, and death. They had reached the death phase and were slowly being composted into the earth, waiting to be born again as mushrooms and mycelium. The magnificence of the starry sky that night made the chilliness of the earth bearable, underscoring his insignificance as a mere speck of sand in the immenseness of the universe. He almost didn't rise when called – there was something quite comforting about melting into the earth as rotten carbon and water.

He was too old to stay awake all night; still, Maple would bring his sleeping bag and a soft pad to lie on and let the drums lull him to dreams. He still feels that tug in his groin when he remembers holding Maya close to him through the night. There were even a couple of years when Birdie would join them, and the three of them would open the sleeping bag and spread it over them, a light touch of heat for those spots where there was no friendly, warm flesh. He missed those days, but now his old friends claimed they couldn't sleep on the ground anymore and retired to their beds long before sunrise.

He looked down at the dining pavilion next to the ritual circle from the meadow. He was proud of the work he and the others had done building the wooden structure with open sides, a plank floor, and a sloped roof. In the pavilion, they were protected from the rain but still in the fresh air. They had even wired the structure to power lights, fans, and outlets for a small refrigerator and coffee maker. Solar panels on the roof provided all the juice they needed, even in winter, when a few hardy souls used the pavilion for outdoor ceremonies.

Now, looking down the hill, he noticed someone parking a golf cart and a large, stocky gentleman in denim overalls beginning to walk up the path to the meadow.

"Elmer, what are you doing here?" he called.

"Just wanting to see if you need any help. I had a couple of free hours, and it's a beautiful day, so I thought I'd check out the preparations."

Elmer grabbed Maple's arm and shook his hand. The men's calluses seemed glad to see each other.

"Thanks, but I think we're okay here. I got the youngun's doing all the hard stuff. I'm just supervising."

"I see that. But what's he doing? Or is that a she?" Elmer pointed toward Twig, who was off to the side, swaying back and forth to a beat only they could hear.

"Twig's a they," Maple said. Elmer looked at him.

"I know – don't ask. Kids these days got different rules. They're just listening to music, I guess."

Maple couldn't get used to using the singular pronoun 'they' for non-binary folks. He understood the rationale and could clearly see that some of these 'kids' were many genders, not just two. But Mrs. Norcross, his fifth-grade English teacher, just kept squawking about the agreement of nouns and verbs in his barely conscious mind, and his younger self cringed from the sound of the wooden pointer she kept tapping on the blackboard in the back of his brain. Still, he wanted to support Twig, so he kept trying.

"How's the farm doing?" he asked Elmer.

"Not bad. The cows are happy. That's all that matters. Ginny's cousin is here, and they're excited about the Festival. She's been making cakes for two days already."

"Great. Can't wait to try them. Heard from anyone else?"

"The word is that a bunch of people in town are scared to come to the Festival because they think you'll put a hex on them or something. That old lawyer, Huffstickler, has been spreading some nasty rumors. Stuff about Satan and animal sacrifices – weird shit. He's even saying you put a curse on Lightning so that he would leave you all the land. But some of us knew Lightning; he would never have let you take advantage of him. It's clear you all loved each other. So we don't believe it. We'll be here. It's the event of the year!"

"Thanks for the support. And are you going to dance the spiral this year?"

"Not a chance. I'll let Ginny, Sally and the young people do it. I'll sit in the middle and just smile like I usually do."

"You're going to miss out on a good time!"

"I don't think so. I'll get to watch you all dancing and singing together. You have such a strong community. It's so rare in this day and age to see people who really help each other. You did a good job building this place."

"It wasn't me. Lightning was the one with the vision. He, Maya, and Birdie really thought this place up. I just went along for the ride."

"You should take more credit. Don't get me wrong – I like Birdie – but you're the backbone of the place."

"Thanks, Elmer. I find it much safer to stay in the background."

"Well, don't hesitate to ask for help. Everyone needs a hand sometimes, especially old farts like us."

Maple's thoughts turned to his best friend, Oscar. What was wrong with him? What would happen if the community, the old farmers, and the townspeople discovered his strange state of mind? Townspeople generally stuck together. Would they turn against the witches? Maple felt he had become a part of the rural community, but that could change if they thought the witches were cursed.

"Oh, before I forget, I picked this up in town for you. Yesterday, Rosie forgot to give it to the tall lady who runs things. It looks official." Elmer reached into the inside pocket of his overalls and handed Maple a folded dirt-stained envelope with the County Clerk's office in the return address. It was addressed to Lauren Sanders, The Old Witches Home Administrator.

"Thanks, Elmer. I'll make sure she gets it." When she comes out of it, Maple thought, his heart beating faster.

After Elmer left, Maple noticed that the beat Twig was dancing to had become much wilder. Instead of stacking wood, they swung back and forth, reaching for the sky and dropping to the earth. They were caught up in a song no one else could hear, erratically singing words of a verse, then a partial chorus, missing the connecting notes. Maple thought he couldn't hear the flow of the music because Twig was the only one with the earbuds in, but then he noticed Twig's ears were empty.

Between the scattered lyrics, Eddie and Taylor yelled for Twig to help them, but Twig was oblivious.

Maple walked forward slowly, trying to appear unconcerned. Even as the fear that Twig might be like Oscar and Mnemosyne was beginning to blossom, he couldn't help but admire Twig's style and their striking appearance. An adoptee from Vietnam, Twig was of medium height and build with short, brown hair, curly in the front and clipped and shaven in the back, a style that gave no hint as to their gender. A nose ring balanced a pentacle in one earlobe. Twig's face was stunning, perfectly proportioned with dark brown eyes and a light beige complexion. They wore tight jeans over small buttocks and a loose red and gray flannel shirt. Maple felt protective and paternal when he gazed at Twig.

Now Maple was perplexed. He looked at Eddie and Taylor, but they looked just as confused. They all approached Twig and yelled their name, but Twig didn't appear to hear them. They kept smiling, laughing, and dancing even when Maple touched their shoulders and asked Twig to stop.

"What should we do?" Eddie asked Maple as though Maple had a secret dance-stopping solution.

"How long has Twig been doing this?" Maple asked. But he didn't really think it mattered. Just something to say to buy time and sound like he knew how to handle a situation like this. It's always good to let the youngsters know the value of old age, he thought.

"About a half hour," Eddie said.

"Hmmm..." Maple pondered. Another one? He hadn't told Eddie and Taylor about Oscar, Mnemosyne, and Angie, hoping that whatever was wrong with them was just a fluke, but now Twig was out of it, too? Maple could feel his heartbeat getting louder. He didn't need his hearing aid for that.

"Maybe we should take them to the Healing Center?" Eddie suggested, but just then, Twig plopped on the ground, laid on their side, curled up in a fetal position and went to sleep. Oh no, he had the sleeping sickness, too.

Maple called Twig's name, but the only response was soft breathing and light snoring. Twig seemed so peaceful that Maple's anxiety turned to envy momentarily. But not for long.

"Let's move them out of the way and keep building the bonfire," Maple said in what he hoped was a strong, commanding voice and watched as Eddie and Taylor scooped Twig's shoulders and legs and gently placed them in the grass off to the side.

Maple left Eddie and Taylor to finish the work and rushed to the

Healing Center to talk to Birdie about this situation. Now he was really scared. Birdie better know what to do.

"What's going on?" she said. "Did someone get hurt?"

Maple didn't realize how bad he looked, but when Birdie saw him come into the kitchen, she became agitated. He usually tried to be cheerful, but now he couldn't even manage a smile.

"No, it's Twig. I think he – they – have the sleeping sickness, too. Just like Mnemosyne."

"Crap," Birdie said. "Angie is completely gone, too. Oscar is still laid up. What the fuck is going on? The doctor was absolutely no help this morning."

Maya went to the huge refrigerator against the wall, pulled out a big pitcher of hibiscus iced tea, and set it on the counter in front of Birdie. She walked over and hugged Maple. He held on. Her touch made it seem like everything was going to be all right. Not for the first time, Maple realized how much he loved Maya.

"We'll figure it out," Birdie said.

"That's four now. That we know of. Should we try to find out if there are any others?" Maya added, letting go of Maple.

"I'm not sure. I don't want to get people all riled up if it's nothing. You saw how excited they got when we told them about Huffstickler. One of these days, Bjorn and Swan will come to blows. I'd rather wait until after Solstice." Birdie got glasses down from the shelf and poured two glasses of tea.

"Want some iced tea?" she asked Maple.

"Shouldn't we do something about Bjorn? Isn't he violating the Principles of Community acting that way?" Maple asked, frustrated that they let people act so badly. If anyone was sexist and racist, it was definitely him. Even if they couldn't fix their delirious friends, they could confront Bjorn.

He looked at Maya to see what she thought, but Maya turned away and took the jug back to the refrigerator. Maple had seen how Bjorn treated Maya and couldn't understand why she let him get away with his sleazy behavior.

"He's an asshole, for sure," Birdie said. "But I don't think he violated any of the principles. He just talks big."

Sure, Maple thought, disappointed.

"What should I do about Twig?" Maple thought he sounded kind of whiny.

"Is anyone with him?" Birdie asked.

"Yeah. Eddie and Taylor are watching him. I told them to stay with him until I got back."

"Good. Why don't we meet after lunch and see if we can do something with Twig? An energy healing or something."

Thank the Goddess Birdie could always be counted on to devise a plan.

"How can I help?" Maple asked. "You know I don't have any magic abilities like you two."

"Maple, just do what you always do. You've got just as much magic as we do. You just don't trust it. " He wasn't sure what he always did, but he felt better.

"Twig's still young. Maybe we can get into their brain and figure out what the heck is happening," Birdie said. "Then we can do the same thing to the others if it works. It's probably better than waiting for that doctor to figure it out."

"Good idea," Maya agreed.

"By the way, Elmer gave me this letter he got from the post office this morning. It's addressed to Mnemosyne, and it looks official. It's from the court. Should we open it? Since she's out of it?" Maple said, pulling the letter from his pocket.

"No, we should wait for her," Maya said, just as Birdie took the envelope out of Maple's hands and ripped it open.

"Oh, great, just what we need," she said. "There's a hearing on Monday to determine whether the will is valid. Mnemosyne is required to be there. Otherwise, they will invalidate the will and give the land to Lightning's brother."

"Shit." Both Maple and Maya said at the same time.

"Maybe we could talk with him. Reason with him," Maya suggested. "He can't be that bad. Maybe he just doesn't know us or understand why the land is so important to us."

"Yeah," Maple said. "Maybe he's just a regular guy who gets nervous around witches." Maple was trying to give him the benefit of the doubt, but he could tell Birdie wasn't buying it.

"You think?" Birdie said. "My guess is that he's a ruthless businessman who wants to make money with our land."

"But it could be worth a try to talk with him. Let's invite him for lunch and see what he's like. I can make something really special for a land-grubbing evil capitalist." Maya said, smiling.

They chuckled. Birdie folded up the letter and put it back in the envelope.

"I'll call Huffstickler and see if he can come here today. It's still early. Is one o'clock too soon for you, Maya?" Birdie asked.

"No, that gives me almost three hours. I can make lunch in that amount of time, for sure."

"Okay, I'll call him, and we'll meet in the dining room at 12:30." They left Maya standing in front of the open refrigerator. Maple followed Birdie to the office to find Huffstickler's number.

9

MAYA MAKES LUNCH

How about a salad with some of the veggies from our garden? Maya thought as she rooted through the bins in the refrigerator. We have to use them before the feast on Saturday anyway. They won't last that long.

Perhaps some bread and cheese, too? And don't forget the iced tea.

Maya pulled out what she needed from the fridge – her arms were full of tomatoes, cucumber, lettuce, radishes, and green onions when she turned and almost ran into Bjorn.

"Why, hello," he said. There was something suspicious about his smile under his long, scraggly gray beard. He had one hand tucked into his red, white, and blue suspenders, and the other held an aluminum water bottle with a fading black rune. His gray hair matched his full beard; the t-shirt that once was white but now had stains under the arms and across his belly was tucked into his baggy jeans.

"What are you doing here?"

"I was just in the Fire Room meeting with the rest of the Heathens, and I thought I would get some water. I didn't know you would be here."

"I'm always here," Maya said. "We're having lunch with Huffstickler, and I'm getting ready for the Solstice feast. The water's over there."

Maya pointed to the faucet on the other side of the room as if Bjorn hadn't been in the kitchen a hundred times and didn't know where the water was.

Bjorn smiled again, this time a bit broader, making the hair on Maya's neck stand up. What was it about him that bothered her so much? At least he wasn't drinking this early in the day.

"You're meeting with Huffstickler, huh? You know, maybe that guy's onto something. I bet we could make a lot more money selling lots and building up the land than we make at the Festival."

"Yeah, probably, but then we'd lose control, and we wouldn't be able to live the way we want to. We'd just become profit-driven instead of sticking to our ideals." Maya turned away from Bjorn and placed the veggies on the counter next to the food prep sink.

"Yeah, I guess you're right. We might have to wear bathing suits at the pond!" He laughed, and suddenly, the Old Witches Home clothing optional policy felt sordid rather than liberating.

"Don't get me wrong – I like seeing you naked," he said. "But I think I'd like to make some money, too."

Maya thought about the many times she had swam nude in the pond with the rest of the witches. They all enjoyed their bodies, no matter how many wrinkles and rolls of flab they had acquired over the years. She wondered if she would think twice next time if Bjorn was there.

"I like things the way they are," she said. "And I've got work to do." She found a cutting board at the end of the counter and grabbed a long knife from the block next to it. When she turned back toward the sink, he stood in front of the basin, very close to her.

Maya smiled politely. "Have a nice day."

He slid his arm around her waist and pulled her closer to him. "Thank you. I will," he said. She pushed him away with her left hand. A jolt of fear pulsed in her stomach.

"Get out of here. Please." She raised the knife in her right hand, not quite threatening, but it felt good to show it to him.

He hunched up his jeans, turned on the faucet, and filled his aluminum water bottle. Before he left, he turned back to her and leered.

Maya shook herself as if shedding cobwebs and slimy goo. She tried to push away the thoughts always at the edge of her consciousness. No matter how good life was, she knew that something could visit you in the nighttime and take it all away.

Maya hated hot nights like the nights had been lately. They always reminded her of her childhood as Maria Consuela Garcia del Rodriguez in El Paso, Texas, a second-generation immigrant from Guatemala. She was sure her ancestors had lived in the cool mountain rainforests; she loved rainy days.

Maya's family strongly believed in spirits and unseen forces, even though they worshiped the Catholic saints and lived a life bounded by tradition and obligation. When she was a toddler, she was given a bracelet made of red beads to ward off evil spirits, but it didn't work.

When Consuela – the name her mother called her – was six, her maternal grandmother, her abuela, visited from Guatemala. Maya was fascinated by the old woman who seemed so powerful and imposing. She was sure she would never be that old herself.

Her abuela taught her to encourage unwanted visitors to leave the house by propping up a broom next to the front door. It worked every time, to Maya's amazement. Maya always kept a broom handy in the kitchen and should have brought it out as soon as she saw Bjorn.

When she was a kid, she thought everyone did that. She thought the visitors saw the broom coming out and knew it was their time to go. Nothing too magical about that. Later, she learned that other people didn't treat their guests that way and just put up with them until they decided to leave on their own.

Maya grabbed a large bowl from the cupboard filled with serving bowls of all sizes in several rows, some lost in the back that never got used and those in the front that were on the table for every communal meal. Maya remembered how often she felt lost in the family, between her two older sisters, older brother, and younger brother. There was always so much commotion in the house, and it was easier to take a book and disappear than to find a safe place with so many others in the house. She never feels the need to retreat now as she did then – to the banks of the Rio Grande – now she enjoys the company of her fellow kindred spirits when she sits at the pond.

Maya started with the lettuce. Grabbing one after another from the box of heads picked that morning, she ripped the leaves into shreds and dumped them into the basin of cool water.

Damn, she thought, here we go. She knew where her mind was going to take her. She had healed much of the trauma over the years, but the memories had lives of her own. Long ago, she had decided to simply let them play out when they showed up. The images were so much stronger and more painful when she resisted them. Better to try to simply distract herself. She focused on the lettuce.

A picture of her parents in their split-level home floated up from the water. Her family lived the American Dream; her mom was a bookkeeper for the local car dealership, and her father was a property assessor for the city. They worked long hours, and it was time to let go when they got home. They celebrated their middle-class success every night with neighbors, barbecues, loud music, and plenty of booze.

No matter how often she was told to enjoy the parties, she couldn't. She watched her siblings sneak beers from the fridge and finish drinks forgotten by guests long gone. She could have joined them, she supposed, but she wasn't interested. That wasn't the way she wanted to be, out of control.

She knew what would happen after everyone went home. If her mom had already passed out, her dad would want to find someone else to spend time with. Her two older sisters shared a room; her brothers also shared a room, and Maya slept in a small bedroom over the garage. She loved the privacy and the solitude except on the nights her father visited her.

The knot of fear tightened. Okay, come on, let's get it over with, she thought as she grabbed one head of lettuce after another. I don't understand why he won't go away. He's dead, and I don't ever have to go back to El Paso. Why do I have to remember? She had moved far away and was only occasionally in touch with her siblings since her parents died. Still, she hadn't forgotten.

Shredding the romaine lettuce felt good: Tearing each tender leaf into pieces. She felt the tug as she pulled and heard the soft ripping sound, the cool, slick texture. Reducing a big long head to small green rafts, floating in the water, ready to be dried and eaten. She swirled the leaves in the water, watching as the specks of dirt sank to the bottom of the basin.

Maya grabbed a cucumber from the pile on the counter. Prickly, dark and hefty. Its weight in her hand made her feel strong. She picked up the peeler. She denuded it from one end of the cucumber to the other, removing strip after strip and leaving the cucumber exposed, vulnerable, raw. Just the way it should be.

She was only 14 when her father first visited her on a hot night. At that time, she had developed breasts almost as large as her mother's – before most girls in her grade. That must have been it. He would have left her alone if she hadn't developed so early. No, she shouldn't think that way. It wasn't her fault.

Dang! Do I have to think about this shit? That slob, Bjorn, triggered me. I shouldn't let him get under my skin.

She started slicing. Quickly. Skillfully. Thud, thud, thwack, thwack thwack. The knife reduced that cucumber to small green rounds – in no time at all, the cylinder beneath her hands lost itself.

But the memories had taken hold and flooded her mind as she worked.

The first time he came to her room, she was surprised. Waking, she saw him standing in the doorway. At first, she was glad to see the father, who had always been gentle and warm with her. Maybe he came to talk with her about the book he had given her for her birthday. He liked science fiction and fantasy too; they had often talked about what it would be like to live in another world.

She dumped the cucumber into the bowl. What a laugh, she thought. Gentle and warm. Yep. She should have known better. No one goes to their daughter's room in the middle of the night, reeking of tequila and beer, just to have a quick chat about the latest young adult fantasy novel.

Then she became afraid. "Dad, what are you doing here? Has something happened?" She sat up, letting the sheet fall, revealing the light nightgown she wore. Even though she was hot in that small room above the garage, she liked the feel of the cotton on her skin.

"I just want to lie with you for a while, baby. Your mom is asleep, and I just want some company." His voice was gruff, and his words slurred. He was a big man, dressed in boxer shorts and a t-shirt, sweaty from the summer heat. When he laid down next to her, she could feel his stubby cheek on her shoulder and his hairy legs next to hers.

The room felt stuffy and small. He took up so much room in her small bed that there was barely room for her. She felt confused and scared. Why was he here? His rough hand was on her leg. She tried to breathe. But all she could think of was the river, the tree she usually sat beside, the bumpy banks of the Rio Grande.

At the time, she didn't think of his visits as abuse because he wasn't rough with her. She had loved him. He always told her how beautiful she was. His hands were tender and strong, except when he accidentally hit her or pushed her because he lost his balance. Otherwise, he caressed her and kissed her skin lovingly. How could he not notice that she lay there unmoving, tense, and silent, just waiting for it to end?

Maya placed another cucumber on the cutting board, peeled it forcefully, and hoisted the knife to slice it thin.

He never went inside her. He just rubbed his hands all over her body, but one time, he grabbed her underwear and pushed the flimsy cotton down to her ankles. He got on top of her in that tiny twin bed, groaning with the box spring. He laid that slimy, hot piece of flesh and skin between her legs and moved up and down until it grew and became firm.

In the kitchen, she saw bread dough rising and burning in the oven.

In bed, Maya kept her eyes closed. She just kept imagining the water flowing, the wind swaying in the trees, the sounds of the birds and the fish. When he rubbed his penis on her stomach or between her breasts until it burst with sticky liquid smearing all over her torso, she lay there quietly, just waiting, frozen, somewhere else in her mind.

She knew what he was doing – her older sister, Elena, had given her all the relevant info about boys. So Maya was patient; she let the disgust and nausea spread through her body and leave with her breath. He didn't take long. And she was learning that she could escape.

Maya now knows that what he was doing was criminal, but at the time, all she knew was that it was just not worth fighting about, not in her family. She always lost. No one ever listened, and it was easier to just go her own way.

Maya finished slicing the cucumber, wiped down the knife, and brought out her next victim – a tomato. It was going to succumb – it had no choice.

She remembered telling her older sister about her father. Elena didn't believe her. She was convinced Maya was lying. She said you live in another world. Daddy wouldn't do something like that. Most of the time, Maya had lived in another world, a fantastical place populated by dragons, fairies, and magic. But this time, she hadn't made it up.

She remembers the night her imagination became real. She had been thinking about the river and the bench she usually sat on, and then suddenly, she was there. Actually there. She could see the dark water. She could feel the moist air. She could hear the birds in the trees nearby. When she looked down at herself, she saw only an outline, translucent, filmy. She realized she was not in her body – only her mind had traveled to the river.

Maya was amazed. She knew her father was still on top of her, but she wasn't under him. Somehow, she had left. She had liberated herself. She was safe.

The first night was only for a few minutes, but the trips became longer and longer over time. She sent her consciousness to the ceiling, watched from above for a moment or two, and then left the little room altogether to soar over the river and the mountains in search of a safer place. She left the nausea, the shame, and the fear in her bed.

She tried going to other places to soar around the city but liked the river best. It was peaceful, and there was no one there at night. She found she couldn't stay out long and didn't need to. He didn't usually linger in her room after he finished what he came to do. She wanted to be back in her body by the time he left.

She was afraid he might want to talk with her before he left, although that had changed, too. They used to have conversations. She had loved telling her father about characters in her imagination and what she was reading. Now, she avoided him as much as possible, shrinking from his touch, moving away when he was near. Trying to make sure no one could hear the rapid beat of her heart.

He didn't interact with her anymore, except for the nights. When he saw her during the day, he looked down, lowered his voice, and spoke little.

Over time, she became so skilled at the art of astral traveling that she could do it even when her father wasn't there. Maya called it relocating her mind. She practiced her newfound ability whenever she felt safe enough to leave her body behind. She learned how far she could travel and what she could do when out of her body. She discovered that no one could see her and she couldn't talk to them, but she could observe. And she could fly. When she was airborne, she was powerful and strong; she could do anything.

She never told anyone in her family about this new power. She was sure they would think she was crazy. Knowing she could escape kept her sane. Sometimes, she didn't want to return, but Maya was practical. She knew what was real in this world and made sure she had a foot planted firmly, if only metaphorically, on the ground.

The salad was almost finished. Just a few slices of radish, cool dark pink and white to complement the green and red. Her knife was sharp and steady. But the memories weren't finished. She knew this tape – she had heard it many times before. Just let it go until it's over. One more scene.

"Shh, shh," her father said as he stumbled off the bed. "You're so beautiful. I love you the best, you know. You're my sweet, sweet baby., My sweet, sweet Consuela."

Maya said nothing and waited. He lurched toward the door. He missed and smashed his head on the door frame and fell down. She lay in bed, hoping he wouldn't get up and wishing he would disappear.

"Fuck. Fuck!" He got on his knees and pushed himself up, holding on to the doorknob for support.

"Oh, I'm sorry, honey. I shouldn't use that word. I'm sorry, I'm sorry." He mumbled as he finally made it through the door and down the stairs. She heard the door to the kitchen close.

After giving him a few minutes to make it to his bedroom, Maya stood up, wiped off her stomach and breasts with the towel she had learned to keep beside the bed, and went to the bathroom to pee and take a shower before trying to sleep.

Once back in her room, she lit the small candle on her dresser and prayed to the Virgin Mary to keep her father away from her. She didn't know what else to do; perhaps the saints would help her.

Mary must have heard her pleas because she finally came through for Maya. That was the last time her father frightened and abused her.

The next week, her abuela came to live with them, and there was nowhere to put her but in the room over the garage with Maya. Maya thought she would resent the intrusion, but she loved listening to her abuela's stories of Guatemala and the ways of the curanderas. Maya learned healing and the use of herbs. She also learned to cook from her abuela and always 'cooked with love' just as she taught her.

So that's what I do now. I cook with love and use my healing powers for my friends.

She wiped her wet hands on her apron. Cucumber seeds and pieces of tomato dotted the fabric. She never seemed to be able to keep her clothes clean when she was in the kitchen. But the salad was done.

Maya was back in The Old Witches Home. She din't have to relocate her mind anymore, at least not for the moment. Hopefully, she wouldn't need to relocate her body, either.

10

LUNCH WITH HUFFSTICKLER

Birdie was grateful for Maya's seating choice, near a window with a view of the mountains in the north, a divine example of the Goddess' work. Off to the left, past the Knowledge North and Wisdom West dwellings, trees obscured the ritual circle's hiding place. They could see the outdoor dining pavilion just past the access road to the valley east.

Surely, the beauty of this land had to soften even the hardest capitalist's Heart.

"Branches up, roots down," Maya said when Maple joined them. In just a few seconds, the familiar exercise centered and readied them.

"Huffstickler didn't seem too excited about coming to lunch today," Birdie told her friends. She shushed Hermes out of the room before she moved to the sideboard to get the dishes and silverware.

"Do you remember that Samhain weekend when Lightning told us about this place?" Birdie asked her friends as they began to set the table.

"Yeah, you were complaining about being too old to dance," Maya chuckled. "I think that was the first time I heard you admit that the years were creeping up on you. We were sitting around the fire at the drum circle. You had just retired, and it was one of the rare times we could all get together other than at Witch Camp."

"I guess it was inevitable that I would have to acknowledge my aches and pains. But Lightning got so excited, remember?" Birdie stood up straighter, tilted her head, and tried to imitate her friend. "I know what you mean, sisters! No matter how much I flirt and swivel my hips, none of these young faeries give me a second glance. And when I go home alone after camp, I feel so lonely. I enjoy my own company, no mistake, but wouldn't it be nice to have someone to come home to?"

She batted her eyelashes and delicately lifted a strand of her short gray hair out of her eyes as though it were Lightning's long blond hair. She seductively turned her head away and pointed to the top of her head, where Lightning had tucked the tin foil silver lightning bolt in a tight hair knot. She remembered how it twinkled in the moonlight. A gay witch for over 30 years, Lightning had been known for his incredible dancing – he had been a member of Les Ballets Trockadero in his youth and could still rise on pointe and tower above everyone else in the circle.

Maya and Maple smiled and chuckled.

"Dang, but Lightning was something," Maple said. "He seemed to mellow the longer I knew him, but I was scared of that sharp tongue of his. Then that night, out of nowhere, he hugged me and said, 'What the hell did you do that for?' while kissing me on both cheeks."

"Remember how he flew into the dining hall the next morning? That was the beginning, wasn't it?" Maya added. "I can't forget what he said – 'The goddess and the gods, just everyone, wants me to do this!! It's going to be fabulous. It will make such a difference in the world. Nothing will be the same again.'" Maya looked at Birdie and Maple with tears in her eyes.

"I want to build a retirement home for witches!! I inherited land from my great aunt Estella that is just sitting in the mountains. It's near this tiny town called Winkton. I know there's a small hunting cabin on the site, but I couldn't stand looking at a wall filled with antlers and heads without bodies, so I haven't gone to look at it yet. There's a pond, good water, lots of sunshine, a hill, a beautiful meadow, and incredible fairy energy. We could build something there!" Birdie rose, opened her arms wide, and stood on tiptoe, pretending again to be the tall gay dancer.

They laughed and got back to the task at hand.

The clothes Birdie had changed into in preparation for this lunch felt odd and uncomfortable. She hadn't used the professional persona in years, but today, she thought it would help to dress the part. She wore the remnants of the old life when she worked a demanding job at a toxic non-profit – sensible black slacks, a flowered print blouse, and a gray cardigan in case it was too cool in the dining hall. She had combed her hair, patting it down from the spikes it usually ended up in, and put on makeup for the first time in years. When she looked in the mirror, she felt like she was looking at a photo of herself that someone had added wrinkles to. It was all she could do to not smear the mascara and remember to dab, not rub the eyeshadow.

Yet here she was, being her most cheerful imitation of a nacker, just like before that fateful weekend.

"Perhaps Huffistickler didn't want to come because he thinks we will curse him," Maple said. She would have liked to, but that wasn't how she did things. They would just have to convince him. Maybe the spell they did last night would already be working on him.

"Elmer said that the mayor and the town council are supporting Huffstickler," Maple continued. "They want to get their hands on this land as well."

"They've been complaining for years that this place is an eyesore," Birdie said.

"They don't think we're paying our fair share for the town utilities," Maple said.

"We have our own well, and all our electricity is supplied by the solar collectors," Maya said. "We even have a state-of-the-art environmentally friendly septic system. Maybe they don't like the candle bits and cast-off altar cloths we bring to the town dump. They're scared we'll bring down demons on them with that little bit of non-biodegradable stuff we toss."

Maple laughed. "You never know. We'll see who comes to the Festival."

Maya had outdone herself this morning. The heirloom tomatoes were the most vibrant shade of crimson. Just that morning, she had picked the ripe cucumber and fresh lettuce from the community garden, a testament to abundant plant magic. She carefully took the sourdough bread out of the oven and placed it on the table next to the soft goat cheese from Elmer's dairy farm. Maya had even brewed an enticing iced tea from fresh hibiscus and mint. Finally, the almond flour brownies with coconut crème icing were among Birdie's favorites and were sure to please the sour old lawyer.

Maple sat on the bench in front of the window, back erect, wearing a Grateful Dead t-shirt. He was clean-shaven and was tapping his foot.

Suddenly, an unfamiliar shadow darkened the doorway.

"Please come in, Mr. Huffstickler. We're so happy you could make it." Birdie put on her most welcoming and diplomatic smile as she strode toward him, hand outstretched. He returned the gesture with a weak shake, barely touching her fingers.

Huffstickler strode into the room as though he owned the place. His wrinkled gray pinstriped suit reminded Birdie of a 1940s zoot suit without the two-toned shoes. There was something of the gangster about him, albeit one who had seen better days. He had declined Maple's offer of a ride from the parking lot on the golf cart. Said he preferred to walk and enjoy the sights.

Hmmph, he's pretty sure of himself, Birdie thought. Okay, we'll play.

"Mr. Huffstickler, may I offer you some iced tea?" Maya was the picture of hospitality with her colorful Mexican blouse, full yellow skirt, and gingham apron.

"Thank you," he said as he brushed away non-existent crumbs from the bench facing the window before he sat.

Maple looked at Birdie, who shrugged. Maya sat on the chair closest to the kitchen.

"I hope you had a pleasant drive up here. How was the walk from the parking area?" Birdie asked.

"Fine, just fine. Although I have to admit you have some – uh, interesting – houses on the property. That tent looks like the wind will blow it away in the next storm."

"Construction on that property is still underway," Birdie said. Birdie thought it would go a lot more quickly if Whale Tooth could get his funding.

Maya placed a salad bowl in front of each of them. The white of the creamy poppyseed dressing delicately complemented the colors of the hand-painted apples, currants, and cherries on the four matching ceramic bowls and plates. Biride was surprised; usually, the table settings were a mishmash of whatever was clean and whatever people brought to the dining room to share. Residents of the Old Witches Home rarely bought anything new, preferring to repurpose perfectly good items. It seemed that everyone had varying versions of landfill nightmares.

"Enjoy," Maya said. "Please let me know if you need anything else."

Huffstickler sniffed as he picked up his fork. He speared a shred of lettuce and cucumber and brought it to his mouth.

"Thank you so much. It's a delight to see fresh vegetables," he said without much conviction. He began crunching.

"We asked you to come to lunch because we received notice that you're representing Lightning's brother. I'm so sorry we haven't had a chance to meet him yet. Have you heard from him? I hope he's feeling well," Birdie said.

"Oh yes, he's doing much better. He's currently indisposed and unable to travel, but no worries. I have his complete confidence and can speak on his behalf."

I bet you will, thought Birdie. "I understand he feels we pressured his brother to leave the land to us. I assure you that nothing is further from the truth. We thought we could discuss the situation and reach a mutually satisfactory resolution." Birdie was amazed at herself that she could still talk like that.

"That is my hope as well," Huffstickler's smile was slimy. "By the way, where is your Administrator, Lauren Sanders?"

"Unfortunately, she's currently indisposed as well. But I'm sure she will be better soon. And who knows? Maybe the hearing on Monday will be unnecessary." Birdie could put it out there, couldn't she? Or maybe the binding spell was already doing its work.

"I'm sure you understand that there is nothing personal in William's claim. He is simply concerned that Edward was responding to an unhealthy influence from his caretakers. He used the words 'they put a spell on him,' but I assured him that was unlikely."

"Do you have a personal interest in the outcome of the probate?" Maple asked.

"Oh, no," Huffstickler replied quickly. "I would just like to fulfill my dear great-grandmother's wishes. She was so devoted to her granddaughter, my mother, Isabel, and I wouldn't want her legacy to go astray."

"Of course," Birdie said. "Lightning – I mean, Edward – besides being a generous benefactor, was a beloved member of our collective. We're like a family, you know. I'm sure he would not want to see his dear Great-Aunt Estella's wishes to be ignored." As she spoke, she felt a light breeze like someone were twirling their skirts around the room. There was a faint scent of lavender and roses. She gazed directly at Huffstickler with a slight smile on her face. "I feel confident we can work this all out."

As she began to eat, Birdie noticed movement in Huffstickler's salad. He was speaking about the summers he spent as a child with his great-grandmother in her home in the city. He remarked that he rarely saw Edward there.

Birdie tried not to stare at the bowl in front of him. She explained how they were committed to taking care of lower-income elderly in the region. She didn't think that would be a strong selling point to Huffstickler, but she wanted to deflect his attention away from his salad.

Birdie looked over at Maya, who was busy slicing the bread. She nodded in Huffstickler's direction, but Maya couldn't see her. Maple creased his brow and looked at Birdie quizzically. She raised her eyebrows and nodded again, but Maple shook his head and creased his brow – what?

The movement was moving again, little and green. Birdie stood up, "Would you like more tea?"

"No thanks, I have plenty." Huffstickler lifted his glass in a mock toast to the other three.

"Let me get you more salad," Birdie thought she might be able to take his plate away from him before disaster struck. She stood up, ready to grab his dish, but he blocked her approach with a protective arm across his food, while his other hand snagged a piece of bread from the other side of the table.

"No, thank you," he said firmly, raising his fork in the air as if to illustrate a point. As soon as he moved away, Maya added more salad to his dish and assertively tossed it with the dressing. Birdie was transfixed by the jumbled pieces flying around the plate, trying not to stare too intently as she kept an eye out for the little green thing.

When Maya sat back down, Birdie breathed a tiny bit more easily. Maybe it had been her imagination, or the little green thing had surreptitiously moved somewhere else. She took a bite of her own salad. Delicious. That poppyseed dressing was dreamy.

Huffstickler was saying something about the weather in the region and the potential for flooding this summer. Property values were most likely to go down, he was sure. He stabbed a spear of lettuce, and there it was again! Slithering away from his fork and burying itself under the radishes and cucumber slices.

Shit. Doesn't Maya see it? But Maya was slicing the goat cheese with that special ceramic cheese knife she loved. How about Maple? He was also focused on his own food and oblivious to Birdie's attempts to contact him telepathically.

Huffstickler seemed to be enjoying himself.

"If the courts rule in William's favor, perhaps we could reach an agreement to buy the land from him over time," Birdie said. "After all, if property values are decreasing, he won't want this land to weigh him down. Perhaps you could broker that for us?" Maybe there was a slim chance they could work this out amicably?

Huffstickler didn't respond; he seemed to be thinking it over. He jabbed the fork into the salad, speared tomato, cucumber, and radish, along with a bite of lettuce, and deftly inserted it into his greedy mouth.

"My great grandmother was a – aackk!! Yeech!" He spat out the lettuce, cucumber, and .... A plump green caterpillar. Maple attempted to spear the bug with his fork but only succeeded in upending Huffstickler's salad bowl. He kept at it, attacking over and over, but the caterpillar wouldn't be caught.

Creamy poppyseed dressing, bits of tomato, cucumber, lettuce, and radish rained down on Huffstickler's gray suit.

Those stains won't be easy to get out.

"What are you doing?" Huffstickler sputtered. Maya ran over to him, pouring tea on her napkin as she approached. She started patting the front of his jacket, moving perilously close to his private parts.

The caterpillar squirmed under his plate, and Birdie saw it slither down the tablecloth and plop onto the floor.

"Are you trying to poison me? What is wrong with you people?" Huffstickler jumped up. His napkin and the phone he had been holding in his lap, taping the conversation, flew to the floor. Birdie heard a nasty glass-breaking sound as the phone fell under his chair. The napkin landed on the caterpillar, scurrying away as fast as possible which wasn't very fast at all. Birdie was sure he would step on it, and then he would have squashed caterpillar goo all over the sole of his shoe. That would serve him right, she thought.

"I'm so sorry," all three of them said. Birdie jumped up and wasn't sure what to do as he held his glass up, inspected it, and then gulped down the whole glass of iced tea. She held out the pitcher to refill it, but he slammed the glass on the table.

"Yeech," he said. "You'll hear from my colleagues."

"I washed the lettuce, I promise!" Maya said. "But I just picked it this morning. That little bugger must have been hiding." She was rooting through the salad with her hands, picking out lettuce leaves and examining them in the light, poppy seeds clinging to her fingers.

"You just weren't careful, were you?" he spluttered. "That's how you people are, with your 'organic' food and your 'organic' houses, all helter-skelter all over the place. There are still people living in tents on this property! What are you, barbarians?"

"Now, just a minute," Maple said and stood to face Huffstickler. "That's not fair." He tried to approach Huffstickler menacingly, still holding the fork in his hand, but he was sitting in the middle of the bench and had to climb over it, which wasn't easy with his achy back and sluggish hips. This slowed his assault somewhat and allowed Huffstickler to reach the door unimpeded.

"You haven't heard the last from me," Huffstickler said. "I can't wait until this place is mine. I'll clean it up and make it a respectable place. Not some aging hippie commune. Passion of Fire Room? Really? Water Purification Space? I'll show you what cleansing and purification mean when I tear down those hovels you call houses."

"I'm so sorry," Maya said. "That happens with fresh veggies sometimes." She was still pawing through the salad, looking for anything else that might still be alive.

Birdie sighed. No matter how she tried, it seemed she couldn't communicate with insomniacs. Once again, she had failed; this time, her friends' homes were at risk. All she could do now was save face and minimize the damage.

"Thank you for coming," Birdie said as she walked Huffstickler to the entrance, trying to smile and remain friendly. "Don't forget to join us for the Summer Solstice Festival this Saturday! We look forward to your donation."

"Harrumph," he said. He stumbled as Hermes zigzagged in front of him. "Damn cat!"

Hermes ran down the hall. Birdie sat down. Maya gave up on the salad and sighed as she also sat down. Maple climbed back over the bench.

"Well, that went well," Birdie said. "I just hope our spell is working." She pushed her lettuce around. The knot in her stomach was tight. Her only comfort was the thought of coconut crème brownies. She felt a swish of air and heard a bit of soft laughter.

Maple grabbed a piece of bread and smushed some goat cheese on it. Maya looked like she was going to cry.

11
HUFFSTICKLER'S PLAN

Huffstickler smiled as he felt his resolve harden. He was driving away from that accursed place and was reveling in his plan to enact revenge. He wouldn't allow them to make a fool of him. He would get that land, tear down all those ramshackle huts and build an upscale resort for city folks. He would make millions, and their silly village in the shape of a pentacle would be wiped away forever. He would pave the place with asphalt and concrete! No more bumpy, scraggly, permeable pavers that strained his BMW's suspension and forced him to drive so slowly it made his teeth ache.

He chuckled at his own ingenuity. They will never know what he did, and they will be so disarmed that they won't even be able to curse him to spoil his plans. Those old hippies don't have the brains or the stamina to fight him. They're going senile and don't even remember what they did the day before, much less how to outsmart a man like him. He would be much more in control when he got to that age. He tried not to think of himself as aging, even though he was already 69. He refused to contemplate needing someone to take care of him.

Huffstickler was devastated when his parents were killed in an auto accident during his first year of college. He never quite got over the loss – he just never talked about it. When he learned that the accident was caused by a drunk gay man dressed as a wood nymph returning home from a Halloween party, it confirmed his opinion about 'silly fairies' and those 'unnatural degenerates.'

He had started spending more time with his great-grandmother after that, perhaps longing for a parental influence of some sort. When Estella fought to stay alive for so long, even after her companion Alice died, he took care of her, managing her affairs, making sure the aides, and eventually the hospice volunteers, did what they were supposed to. But in the end, the cancer was just too much for her. Where was Lightning when she needed someone to help her to the bathroom? Huffstickler still grieved for the only woman who had ever accepted him just as he was, single, a bit overweight and not very attractive.

He was her only great-grandchild, and when he convinced her to allow him to be the executor of her estate, he assumed that he would inherit everything. He loved the batty old woman, even if she and Alice were probably more than just friends. If he didn't give their relationship much thought, it wasn't too difficult to pretend she was like everyone else's dear old grandma.

When he thought about her life, he did have some sympathy for his great-grandmother, even if she was somewhat deviant. After one New Year's Eve, when she had too much sherry, and Alice had gone to bed right after the ball fell, Estella Amato told her great-grandson where his mother came from. She was determined that he wouldn't be a man like those she had known, and she slurringly accused him of being insensitive with his last girlfriend. There was probably some truth to her accusation, and Huffstickler knew it. He just had no idea how to act differently. Women were alien to him.

Huffstickler's mother, Isabel, was Estella's grandchild. He already knew that. But the rest of the story was new information. He knew Estella had raised Isabel since her daughter, Harriet, died. He didn't know that it had been due to a drug overdose shortly after Isabel was born. He also learned for the first time that Harriet had been born when Estella was only 15, the product of an assault by Estella's father's best friend, a neighbor and pillar of the tight-knit Italian community. After the rape, Estella was sent away to a New York City unwed mother's home. There, she tasted independence and never returned to the small town in New Jersey where she grew up.

She said she met Alice in Greenwich Village shortly after Harriet was born when Estella was trying to find a job and a place to stay. There was no support for unwed mothers then, but Estella had made friends with one of the orderlies at home, and he had broken the rules by letting her stay at his apartment until she could find a place of her own.

Huffstickler didn't want to hear the rest, but Estella told him he'd be cut out of her will if he didn't sit there and listen. She said Alice worked at the coffee shop in the neighborhood. She was the only friend the young mother had; she gave her free coffee while Estella pored over the want ads and rocked the stroller back and forth. Alice told her that she was smitten when she saw the curly black hair and full breasts ready to feed her daughter. Estella knew that Alice had girlfriends before, which made her curious. They succumbed to their growing infatuation and fell deeply in love. They raised Harriet together, and then Isabel after Harriet's death.

Oh my god, he thought at the time. Shut up. I don't want to know this.

Benjamin Huffstickler, the only child of Isabel Amato and Adam Huffstickler, simply wanted to think of Estella as a loving grandmother who ignored his social ineptness and awkward conversations. Her bohemian apartment in the Village was full of relics from a long life in the hub of creativity and progressive politics. When she died, Huffstickler was pleased with the proceeds from the estate sale and felt relieved he didn't have to pay any more attention to her aberrant lifestyle.

He was furious that she left the upstate land to Lightning. It was just a ramshackle hunting cabin in the middle of nowhere, but Estella had decreed that she wanted Lightning to have a special place in the woods that he could do with as he chose. At the time, he resigned himself to letting Lightning have it. Huffstickler told himself he didn't care. No one ever went there; why would they? He got everything else, including the apartment and the art. He had profited, but still – it wasn't fair, and it wasn't right. He was the one who was on Estella's deathbed. He had loved her as best he could. Wasn't it enough?

Huffstickler began plotting immediately after Estella's will was read. He convinced other elderly women to rely on him, and he began to amass a sizable portfolio of land, houses, and other securities after their deaths. He would get the Winkton land, too, he vowed. He would avenge Estella – she must have been bamboozled by that effeminate dancer who got all her attention while Huffstickler was ignored and taken for granted.

Huffstickler thought he had plenty of time. No one cared about this property. It was just a bunch of trees. No one knew this area would become so popular, and weekenders would start coming to the region to get away from the city to breathe fresh air and pretend they were doing something useful for the environment.

It only took ten years. Lightning's death from AIDS six months ago was a welcome gift for Huffstickler. He knew he could find a way to delay probate and bankrupt the witches. He was in a perfect position. They needed money to make it through the year. That silly bank manager, Louella Cartwright, had been flirting with him for years. It had been so easy for him to convince her to call in the balloon payment on the mortgage. Then, he just had to contest the will.

He was going to turn the town against them. And he was going to seize that land. He had already started a Twitter thread with the hashtag "BadWitches." It had 203 followers!

He found Billy, Lightning's brother, in a trailer in rural Missouri. It didn't take much to convince the aging alcoholic to contest the will. Billy regretted the pain he had inflicted on the brother he called a nogood fairy. Maybe he could move onto the land and develop it how his little brother Eddie would have liked. Maybe somehow, he could redeem himself.

Huffstickler humored Billy, offering to take care of the details himself. All Billy asked him to do was pay for rehab and ensure that he would get a sizable chunk of money whenever the land was sold or developed. Billy promised to get sober, change his ways and make amends. While

Billy was locked away in rehab, he couldn't get in the way. As long as he had his signature, Huffstickler would act on his behalf and do whatever he wanted.

Then, two weeks ago, he had had another brainstorm. He needed a backup plan just in case the contest didn't work. What if it looked like Lightning had never transferred the deed to himself from Estella after she died? Then, it would seem that he didn't own the land, and Huffstickler could claim he was Estella's only rightful heir. He had heard of cases like that. Even if Lightning had squirreled away a paper copy, if there was no record at the County Clerk's office, he could delay the proceedings long enough for the bank to foreclose on the property. But he would need help.

Two weeks before the lunch that was so devastating for the caterpillar, Huffstickler had driven to the only computer store in town. He told the soft-spoken 20-something man with dark-rimmed glasses at the Olde Magick Tech Store – a ridiculous name for a store – he wanted state-of-the-art security. He heard the young man was a wizard at hacking and security.

Henry turned around from the computer he had been working on and placed his hands on the counter in front of him. Huffstickler noticed the spider web trailing up Henry's dark-skinned arms, and a red-eyed spider peeking out from under the sleeve of a dark grey t-shirt.

"Yeah, I'm good at security. No one gets through my firewalls," Henry confidently assured Huffstickler. A poster of *Anansi, Spider God of Knowledge, Stories, Trickery, and Wisdom*, on the wall behind the counter appraised Huffstickler.

After negotiating the security project, Huffstickler decided to take a chance on the next step.

"One more thing," Huffstickler said in a low voice. "Can you hack into the County Records and remove a file?"

Henry looked around to ensure no one had entered the shop while they were talking. The shop was a crypt, as usual. Henry didn't take long to think about it. "Okay, I can probably do it," he said. "What do you need?"

"Just a quick hack to hide the deed transfer to Edward O'Neill from his aunt ten years ago. I want it to look like he forgot to register the transfer, so the land wasn't really his when he died."

"I can remove the record of the file from the registers and indexes. But I can't get to a paper copy if there is one."

"No worries. Since Mac took over the office, it's been a royal mess. I can get in and take the hard copy."

"Okay, just give me the deets. It will cost you, you know."

"No worries. It's worth it," Huffstickler conceded.

"Cool. I don't like that place anyway. But what if I get caught?" Henry looked directly at Huffstickler. Huffstickler looked right back, admiring the arrogance of the kid. He felt the kid's anger and wondered about it.

"Don't worry. I'm a lawyer. I'll take care of you. You won't get caught. And I have friends in the sheriff's office if you do."

Henry had given him a price that actually seemed very low to Huffstickler. But he didn't tell Henry that. He simply said he needed the work done as soon as possible.

"I'm sure you know how that place is stealing all of our water and is contaminating our creeks with runoff from their 'eco-friendly' septic system." Huffstickler used air quotes around 'eco-friendly.' "And they don't hire any locals – they only use people from the city or some other strange place. They're not like us, you know."

"Yeah, they wouldn't hire me when I applied. They had already hired someone else, they said. They're snobs, and they think they're better than everyone." Huffstickler sensed that Henry had been nursing this grudge for quite a while. Being one of only a few Black kids in town, he wondered what it had been like for Henry growing up here.

"Besides, this is only Plan B," he reassured him. "I'm sure we can get the will thrown out. The hacking is just our insurance if that doesn't work."

Both Henry and Anansi studied Huffstickler. "I may have a better idea. I think I can create chaos and ruin the Solstice Festival. If they can't hold the Festival, they won't get any donations and'll have to shut down anyway."

"Tell me," Huffstickler said. "I'm all ears."

Henry told Huffstickler about a computer virus he had been experimenting with that would incapacitate the witches. Huffstickler was skeptical.

"If they want their world to be 'natural,'" Henry explained, "what is more natural than using their own games and fantasies against them? Whatever programs they use or play with would get into their heads and take over. Their thoughts would be slowly wiped away, replaced with images and sounds from the places they visit on the internet." Henry's wariness seemed to be fading as his excitement grew.

"Really?" Huffstickler said. Magic wasn't real, was it? But he had to admit, this idea would be rather ingenious if it worked. The Old Witches Home would be crippled. They couldn't pull off the Festival if everyone was out of it. Most people today can't live without computers, and they're just regular people, right? Let's see what happens when they're stuck inside their own programs!

"Meanwhile, I can still hack into the county system and hide the deed transfer," Henry added. "I can make it look like it was never there in the first place."

"Great idea. That will confuse them and make them wonder if they know what they're doing."

Huffstickler chuckled and marveled at his own magnificence. He offered Henry a position in his organization when he turned the place into a weekend resort.

But he could see that money wasn't Henry's motivator; he felt wronged and wanted vindication. Good. I can use that against him if I need to. He's mine now, he thought.

That was the plot they set in motion two weeks ago. Today, he needed to repair his phone. The cover had cracked when he jumped up after spitting out that foul caterpillar. He also wanted a progress report.

He told Henry the story of his lunch. Henry listened. He was meticulous as he gently removed the broken glass from the phone.

"Just a minute," Henry said. "This repair is going to need some extra care. We must be super careful to remove all the impurity and toxins it picked up from the floor of that place."

While Henry was working on the phone, he told Huffstickler what he had done. He had called on the powerful West African god Anansi to create a spell that would spread a virus throughout The Old Witches Home computer system. Anansi was known for his ability to outsmart oppressors and turn weaknesses into strengths, perfect for a scheme against a bunch of crazy witches who had underestimated him and thought they were better than him. When he worked on the server, he installed the virus and set it to contaminate individual computers as soon as someone logged on to the Wi-Fi. Finally, when he installed it on someone's laptop directly, it created a positive feedback loop that increased the power of the spell every time that person was on the internet.

Huffstickler didn't think trickster gods were real and certainly didn't think this young techie could manifest them if they did exist. He listened to humor the kid; honestly, he didn't care what he had done as long as it worked.

Henry carefully cleaned the phone, not just with solvent but by sprinkling a bit of salt water on it and passing it through the smoke from some incense he already had burning on his desk. Huffstickler was impressed – it couldn't hurt to fight fire with fire. Maybe this was going to work.

"Your phone is clean," Henry said. "And the virus is in place. I've been to The Old Witches Home office, and no one knows what I did to the server. Also, one of the old guys picked up an infected loaner a couple of days ago when he dropped off his laptop for repair. Shouldn't be long before they're all infected."

"Excellent," Huffstickler said. "I'll be in touch," he added as he left the smoky shop. He squinted in the sunlight and smiled.

Now he just had to deal with that old witch, Birdie. She was going to be a problem, he knew. He had encountered women like her before, those who didn't know their places, who thought they were smarter than everyone. He had once been attracted to someone like her. The sting from that rejection lingered, but it wouldn't for long. Just wait until Birdie opens her laptop!

12

TWIG

"Now what do we do?" Maple asked as he finished the last brownie, a bit of crumb on his lip.

"I guess we better see if we can help Twig. The doctor couldn't figure out what was going on. Maybe it's magical," Birdie said. "And if it is, we're the best people to deal with it, right?"

"Maybe you guys are, but not me," Maple said. "I just like the singing and dancing and the circle's energy. I don't have a clue what to do."

"Oh, shush," Birdie said. "Magic happens all the time with you. I've seen how you can bring people together to do stuff – just look at the work on the dining pavilion and the ritual meadow. If 'magic is the art of changing consciousness at will,' like Doreen Valiente said, then you are quite magical. We all are. We created this place from our imaginations, remember? That's magic!"

She didn't like the way Maple still looked worried. She turned to Maya. "Let's see what we can do with Twig, okay? Do you have any healing herbs that you can use?"

"Sure. I'll find some. Be back in a few."

Maya left to go to her house to get some feverfew and rosemary. Maple went off to find Twig – was he still lying on the grass in the meadow? Birdie cleaned up the dishes from lunch and pondered their situation.

There were only two days until the festival, and the stress affected everyone. That morning, she had seen Maya muttering, "Was it two gallons of cider or two quarts of cream?" with a crumpled piece of paper that looked like it was trying to escape from the very small jail cell of her fingers. Maya opened and closed it continuously, looking at it over and over, but it made no sense to her. Birdie suspected that all Maya could focus on was Angie's voice singing *The Music of the Night* and not her shopping list for the festival.

Birdie's thoughts were consumed with Mnemosyne's fingers tip-tapping on the ground and her wrinkled brow saying, "It doesn't add up, it doesn't add up. 99, 42, one thousand six hundred twenty-six, three." She remembered Oscar curled up in bed and Rabbit's concerned face.

Then she thought about Huffstickler, and her blood began to boil. They had to fight him. She'd light a votive before they worked with Twig. The bindings on the gnome could use strengthening. Huffstickler definitely didn't seem very restrained when he was at lunch.

When Maya returned, Birdie joined her in the ritual room, lighting candles to reinforce the binding spell.

Birdie was surprised that she felt nothing as they studied the gnome with ribbons, chains, and ropes around it. She expected some kind of energy, resistance, or churning. It made her uncomfortable, but she wasn't sure why.

Soon, Maple joined them with Twig in tow and Hermes not far behind. Twig was smiling, giggling, bouncing up and down, singing to themselves in a reggae beat. It wasn't odd for Twig to be upbeat and happy, but this was a bit much for them.

The old witches had decided to work on Twig first because Twig was young. Their brain was still being formed, and the neural pathways might be more amenable to taking detours than older brains. They thought that if they could get inside and find the bugs causing the misfiring, they could rewire the circuits and then do the same thing, whatever it was, to the others.

The three witches guided Twig to the center of the room, seating them on a cushion. Maple, Birdie, and Maya marched around the circle, drawing pentacles at each of the four directions. Birdie invoked the element of air in the East and asked for inspiration, a cleansing breath, and a new beginning for Twig. Maya invoked fire in the South, requesting transformation, a burning away of that which Twig no longer needed, and the innocence and joy of a child. Birdie called to water in the West, asking that they be allowed to see beneath the surface and that the water purify Twig's brain. Maple stood in the North, drawing earth energy and requesting healing, strength, and perseverance. Finally, they all gathered in the center, calling on the energies of spirit and community. They inscribed a pentacle above Twig and on top of them, then pushed it down through the floor below them. Twig was fast asleep.

"All right, now what?" said Maya, looking at Birdie. Birdie looked at Maple, who cleared his throat and looked back at her. Birdie was frustrated. He was just as old (maybe older?) and had faced as many demons as Birdie had, hadn't he? Why didn't anyone see him as the wise old elder? Why did they always come to Birdie?

"I don't know," Birdie said. "You two have been around as long as I have. Why do you always expect me to have the answers?"

"Ahem," said Maple, and they both turned on him. "What?"

"Maybe we should ask the Goddess?" he ventured.

"And what does she know?" Birdie grumbled. "Okay. Grab some chairs and let's meditate."

There was a time when they would simply sit where they were standing but all three of them were afraid that they wouldn't have been able to get up again, so they searched the room for comfortable chairs. Maya pushed a swivel Barcalounger toward the center, wincing at the squealing as the legs scraped the floor. The chair had a lovely floral pattern and big soft cushions, just right for Maya's ample butt. Birdie wheeled the black desk chair to the middle. "For my back," she stated as she grabbed a cardboard box to put under her feet. Maple went out to the atrium and brought a chaise lounge with cushions and a cup holder. Hermes snuggled up to Twig on the pillow on the floor.

Maya grabbed a frame drum from the pile in the corner and began a simple heartbeat rhythm. Ta dum dum. Ta dum dum. They were all experienced at trance work and were able to quickly submerge their consciousness in an open green meadow where the Goddess stood.

"She is welcoming us and eager to help with our problems," said Maya, as always the peacemaker. Everyone appears to Maya as generous and loving.

"Why haven't you asked Twig what they need?" the Goddess said in Birdie's thoughts, in that chastising tone Birdie used with Hermes.

"More will be revealed. All will be well in its own time," intoned Maple in the smooth bass tones of a guru, soothing everyone in the circle.

Hmmph, thought Birdie, as she sent tendrils of thoughts out to Twig on the floor. She felt Maple and Maya do the same, and the three of them twisted and braided their thought streams around Twig, protecting and wrapping them.

"Gently now," Maya cautioned softly as their thought streams began to penetrate Twig's aura and find their way into their neural networks. Bursts of light buzzed around them, occasionally blasting into sounds of indie vibe music, which made them all want to tap their feet.

"Twig? How can we help?" Birdie stepped around the music bulbs blooming up from the floor of the network.

I've found him – Maple's thought appeared in her mind. She saw him gesturing to a figure laying in a fetal position among x's and o's, beeps and chirps, on a flat green bed. Green walls, floor, and ceiling enveloped the young person with an innocent smile on their face in a translucent bubble. Twig looked about six years old.

Okay, let's go in, thought Birdie. She felt Maya and Maple by her side as she looked for a way into Twig's consciousness. They walked around the figure and reached out with their thoughts.

"Stay positive," she said. "Twig won't let us in if we feel like a threat." Rosy, warm pictures of butterflies and flowers grew up around Maple; Maya conjured the image of pancakes with blueberries and sweet syrup. Along with Birdie's thoughts of floating in a cool mountain lake, their approach was gentle, soft-footed, and welcoming. But the shield around

Twig was solid. The x's and o's flashed brightly as they approached and grew larger when they reached out. The green screen enveloped Twig so completely that they were only a two-dimensional image in a bubble, smiling and cooing as they slept.

Birdie heard the sound of Maya's drum becoming softer and slower. She felt herself leaning further and further back in her chair until the chair swiveled a bit to the right, startling her. She opened her eyes and saw Maya and Maple in their comfortable chairs, eyes closed, lips partly open. Maple was breathing deeply, with a little ripple of sound as he exhaled. Maya's hands gently rubbed her stomach, and she had a small, childish smile.

This won't do, Birdie thought. We need to get in and help this poor kid. She closed her eyes again and focused on the energy sphere. She tapped on the green walls in her mind, looking for an opening, any weakness. Tiny bursts of light shot out from the wall, and the wall quickly restored itself to being a solid barrier.

Okay, that won't work. Is there another way in?

I'm sorry, Twig. I just want to heal you. But I need help.

She formed an image of Chiron, the wounded healer god in Centaur form. He reared up on his hind legs and shot an enchanted arrow into the wall in front of Twig. This time, the multicolored bursts of light filled the air around them, clearly outlining the sphere where Twig was captured. Light static sparked around Twig and seemed to push Chiron, Birdie, and the others farther away from the figure on the floor. Twig writhed and twitched but didn't appear to be hurt.

Birdie felt a kinship with Chiron, the most famous Centaur in the Greek pantheon. He had been mortally injured while trying to protect a friend. When he surrendered his immortality in exchange for relief from the pain, he became a resident of Mt. Olympus and a mentor to many. He had the torso and legs of a human and was known for his wisdom and knowledge of medicine.

The founders of the Old Witches Home felt that Chiron's healing abilities would be crucial as they cared for each other in their waning years. They had invoked him during their inaugural ritual ten years ago and called on him many times. This might be his greatest challenge yet.

Chiron galloped widdershins around the circle, engraving a path around Twig, flecks of shiny gold swirling up from the ground, dusting the walls of Twig's enclosure, blending with the translucent green and seeming to solidify the barrier rather than weakening it. The sound of his hoof beats overlaid the softening sound of the drum.

Maya roused. Birdie could hear her shift position in her chair, slowly beginning to match the drum beat to the hooves. As he galloped, he continued to shoot his arrows against the enclosure. A storm of multicolored sparks lit the air around them every time they connected with the wall, highlighting the figure inside the bubble.

Maple, too, was wakening to the galloping noise and the presence of Chiron. The three witches reached out to each other in their minds, holding the space, protecting the sleeping form, and lending their strength and energy to the majestic horseman, determinedly attempting to break down the walls and free Twig from within.

In a trance, there is no sense of time. Chiron could have galloped and shot for hours or seconds, but it made no difference. The walls stood firm, and Twig was captive. Birdie felt no pain or suffering from Twig; quite the opposite – there was a sense of peace and joy and an echo of a reggae tune, the offbeat coinciding with Maya's drum and the stomp of Chiron's hoof. Birdie was at a loss. What could they do?

She sensed the energy connecting her to Maya and Maple, marking the limits of the circle. Chiron's galloping slowed. Birdie was afraid he was defeated. She looked at the proud and tall Chiron as he stopped before them, his bow low. He nodded solemnly to each of the three witches and moved around the circle once more. As he completed the circle and faced Birdie again, Chiron slowly disappeared.

In his place, a tall figure in a brocade tutu with a lightning bolt in his blond knot stood on toe, long arms upraised, face upturned, a ferocious straight spine. The muscles in his legs appeared to be worn, solid stone – impenetrable.

The wooden toe shoes beat a rhythm on the green floor, tapping out a miniature light show. An aroma of lavender and rose filled the room.

"We will free Twig," Lightning said. "I'll take care of this special young person. They have my heart. Go back now and prepare the festival."

Birdie was reluctant to give up so soon. There must be more she could do. She felt Maple and Maya release the bond of energy holding them together. They trusted Lightning. If he said he would protect Twig, he would ensure Twig's safety. She had to let go.

Still, she was perplexed. What could possibly be holding Twig captive? What was that green glow? Why couldn't they reach them?

Maya was the first to open her eyes and begin patting herself down. Birdie walked around Twig one last time and still saw no opening in their defenses. Lightning was on his knees near the captive figure inside the enclosure. How had he penetrated it?

Maple was motionless in his chair, softly snoring and sputtering.

"Now what are we going to do?" asked Maya when Birdie finally sat up and rejoined her in the room.

"Let them sleep, I guess," said Birdie as she grabbed an afghan and placed it over Twig. "Let's wake Maple up and figure out your shopping list." She didn't want to attempt working on anyone else until they could figure this out.

Maple grumbled a bit as they roused him but offered to watch over Twig and get them back to their room when they awoke. He promptly closed his eyes and went back to sleep himself.

As Maya and Birdie moved toward the kitchen, Birdie silently thanked Lightning. Still, she was afraid. She had always known what to do. *What the heck is going on here? How can I fix this?*

Twig didn't notice the witches' exit. Their sleep was peaceful. They heard enchanting reggae music, enclosed in a purple, yellow, dark blue, and white iris. Twig wanted to descend into the iris like a Georgia O'Keeffe painting. The labia felt damp and soft and sweet. Like their first lover, Spring, a nonbinary friend from high school.

Images of high school and Spring forced their way into Twig's consciousness. A memory of Twig's parents, usually so understanding and supportive, challenging them that afternoon when the guidance counselor called Twig's mom. The counselor used Twig's chosen name and their chosen pronouns to talk about the senior prom.

Twig was in their bedroom when they heard their mother hang up the phone. Then, there were only muffled voices as they assumed their mother was calling their father at work. Lots of silence, and then a plaintive voice, louder than before.

"I don't know what it means. Could you just come home? I think we need to talk to him together. For once, could you please be part of this family?"

Then silence again, and Twig heard, "Dammit, Greg. Just come home."

Twig put on their headphones to listen to the non-binary playlist on Spotify. They lay back on the bed with the railroad print bedspread Twig had had since early childhood. They had always enjoyed traveling across the country in a sleeper car, watching hills and mountains, streams, and farm fields drift by to the beat of a rhythmic clacking. Someday, maybe.

The tinkling keyboard sounds of *It's Okay to Cry* by Sophie soothed Twig as they waited for the inevitable confrontation with their parents. Twig breathed deeply and idly scanned the internet for non-gendered haircuts.

The front door slammed and brought Twig out of their reverie. More muffled talking, some raised voices, and then, "Danny, could you get down here, please? Your father and I would like to talk to you."

Twig knew there was no way to avoid it, and soon, they were all sitting in the living room on the salmon-colored couch. There were two drinks on the glass-topped oval coffee table, clear martinis with one olive each on square coasters with images of Parisian dancers. A print of an oil painting depicting a Vietnamese village hung over the couch, a token nod to the culture of Twig's birth.

Twig's mother told Twig about the phone call she had just received that afternoon.

"We just don't understand. Can't you explain it to us? I thought you were gay. I don't know what the word – nonbinary – means. Did I say it right?" Their mother, tall, thin, in a neat blouse and slacks, had a pained look. They knew she wanted to help, but this was too much for her.

Twig remembered the way their father scowled as Twig tried to say something, anything, that would make sense to them.

"I'm – I'm sorry. It's just that – I don't know – 'they' feels right somehow. I'm not a 'he' or a 'she.' I'm different."

"That doesn't make any sense at all," Twig's father's voice was getting close to yelling, but Twig could tell he was trying to control himself. He was still in his dark suit and white shirt from work, tie loosened at his neck.

"You have balls and a prick. You're a boy. You may be gay, but you're something." He pulled off the sky-blue tie and sighed deeply.

"Language, sweetheart," Twig's mom said. "We're still Christian."

"I know, I know... I'm sorry." He sighed again and took a long sip from his martini. Twig's eyes filled with tears, and the room's edges blurred. They felt dizzy.

"Oh, honey, it's just that you didn't tell us. I didn't know who Mr. Hofstra was talking about when he said, 'your child, Twig.' Can you imagine how embarrassing that was?"

"You're not being fair to your mother. You know she tries to support you, but you must meet her halfway. It's unacceptable for the school counselor to know more about you than we do. You owe us an explanation," their father said.

Twig looked down and tried, really tried, to think of a way to explain it to them. Mr. Hofstra and the teachers at school seemed to understand and accept them. That is, of course, except for the gym teacher, Mr. Brandon. He didn't know what to do with Twig when assigning them to a sports team. Mr. Hofstra solved the problem by letting Twig use the time for independent study instead. It didn't help Twig's popularity, but at least they had a refuge for a few hours when everyone else was swaggering, flirting, and competing with each other.

"I'm sorry, mom. Maybe I could change... I don't know." But Twig did know. Even the thought of declaring girlness or boyness gave them sharp pains in their stomach, their groin and their head. They felt out of place, a stranger in their own home.

"I give up. I have work I need to do." Twig's father walked out of the living room, entered his office, and closed the door. Twig could hear his father start a phone conversation with what sounded like a coworker. "Sorry, Jim. Just a little family stuff. Teenagers, you know. He'll get over it."

Twig's mom moved over to the couch next to Twig, patted Twig's hands, and gazed at them with a sad look on her face. "I don't know what to say, hon. What should I tell your grandparents? You know how much they love you. We've all tried hard to make you a part of this family."

Twig couldn't say anything. They didn't know how to explain it in a way anyone would understand. They just weren't like the rest of the world.

Twig's mom looked at Twig as though she were about to say something but gave up. "I have to start dinner," she said, picked up her glass, and walked out the door.

Twig sat there alone until dinner was ready, feeling hopeless. Their younger sister looked in and saw Twig crying. She started to say something, maybe ask a question, they thought. Twig tried to smile at her – they felt protective of the ten-year-old, the biological child his parents had so desperately wanted when they settled for Twig.

"You shouldn't get them so upset, you know," she said softly. "They're not very smart." She looked away and started for the kitchen. "You never know what they're going to do."

A half hour later, they all sat down for dinner, and it was as if nothing had happened. Twig's mother talked about the garden sale the church was having. Their father said he couldn't wait to get back to the golf course and reviewed the weather forecast for the weekend. The younger sister babbled on about the softball team she had succeeded in joining. No one looked at Twig or asked about their day. No one chastised them for not eating all their dinner, either. Twig's stomach just couldn't handle it.

The rest of senior year went by quickly. Whatever Twig's sister thought their parents would do never materialized. They ignored Twig's fashion choices, said nothing about their friends, and didn't object when Twig decided not to attend college in the fall. Twig was relieved to be left alone and felt more disconnected from the family than ever.

Twig spent most of their free time with their best friend, Spring, but Spring was leaving for college at the end of the summer, and Twig still hadn't decided what to do yet. Organic farming appealed to Twig; it meant getting away from the suburbs on Long Island and being in nature, with dirt under their nails.

Spring said she heard from a friend who lived upstate that a farm called The Old Witches Home was looking for workers. She said it was a retirement village for witches.

Witches? Did they do spells and curses? Twig had never met a witch; at least, they didn't think so. But it was worth checking out. Maybe they were weird enough that they would accept them. Twig took a day-long bus ride upstate and fell in love with the view from the greasy window.

The first question Mnemosyne asked during the interview was what Twig's pronouns were. What a breath of fresh air, in more ways than one. Eddie gave Twig a ride back home to get their stuff. It wasn't long before Twig was fully acclimated to the old people, forgetting almost completely about the awkward family they had left behind.

That was five years ago. Twig fell back into sleep; butterflies tickled their face and clung to their legs. The fresh, light smell of the iris and the soft embrace of the labia enveloped Twig, and they knew they were safe and at home. Twig heard the sounds of *Mellow Mood* and gently hummed along.

Lightning gazed down at Twig, then looked around to see if there were malevolent spirits nearby. Satisfied that Twig was safe, he twirled and danced away.

"I'll be back soon, precious," he said. "Rest."

13

GATHERING THE HEALERS

"Okay, the mind meld didn't work," Birdie said to Maya after they left Twig in the ritual room. "What do you think about a regular old healing circle?"

Maya mumbled something about apple pie and baked beans. Maple was still asleep in the ritual room with Twig.

"I guess I'll just have to get it together myself," Birdie grumbled. She said a loud goodbye and left without waiting for a reply.

Walking home, Birdie tried to remember the last time she had been on the computer. She had looked up Nixon's running mate when no one could recall that night Mnemosyne, Maple, and Maya had come for dinner. Was that the last time? That was at least a month ago. I hope the damn thing still works.

Birdie turned on her computer. She was frustrated and scared. She needed help, and she didn't want to admit it. As she waited for the home screen to show the photo of the architect's drawing of The Old Witches Home village to load, Hermes jumped in her lap. She was so lost in her thoughts about Angie and Twig and Oscar and Mnemosyne that she couldn't tell if it was her impatience or if it really was taking longer than usual to flash this and that and give her the chance to shut it down.

Finally, the familiar pentacle-shaped layout appeared.

Now let's see, how do I send an email? That's right, click on the O with the open envelope icon.

Microsoft Outlook started up, and Birdie examined the screen. There it was, the little envelope that said, 'new email.' She tried to click on it, but her mouse cursor missed, and she deleted an old email message instead.

She tried to click again. This time, nothing happened at all. She didn't even hear or feel that 'clicking' sound. It was like pressing Jell-O.

Maybe I should press the other side of the mouse. Whoa – what is all that? A long list of suggestions showed up. Do I want any of these? I don't think so.

How about 'collapse the ribbon'? That sounds ominous. Better stay away from that one.

Let me try again. Maybe the contraption will work this time. She hovered over the 'new email' envelope and clicked. Nothing. No new letter. Nothing.

Aren't you supposed to click twice? Or was it once? She clicked again, just for good measure.

Okay, there it is. A blank email template. And isn't it nice the way her signature is at the bottom? Birdie had humored Mnemosyne when she suggested the signature, and there it was. She thought Birdie should have an official signature since she was one of the founders. It felt a bit too much like work for Birdie.

She moved her cursor to the 'To' box and started to type "OWH Residents," the list that included everyone's email addresses automatically. Mnemosyne made sure everyone got one when they moved in. This way, she could notify the whole village at once if there was something they needed to know, like when the Girl Scouts were coming to sell cookies or if a storm was on its way. Birdie thought that this is a perfect time to notify the whole village. Maybe someone can do something.

But when she tried to spell out OWH, the letters on the screen kept changing to other letters. She typed OWH, and it came out as NPX. She tried again, and QGB showed up. Then HSRT. Then they kept changing independently without her doing anything, flashing and disappearing and reappearing and changing colors and sizes and fonts and beeping and buzzing and ringing.

Birdie could feel tingling in the fingers still on the mouse. A subtle burning sensation was starting to move up toward her wrist. Her pointer finger was hot and getting hotter. This was not carpal tunnel syndrome. The other fingers were turning red, and thin, snaky lines appeared on her hand, crawling up toward her wrist.

"Ack" she screamed and tried to pull her hand away. But it felt like her hand was super glued to the mouse.

Crap, this is magic, she thought. Okay, I can fight this. She knew better than to let a few doubts get in her way.

She stood up, scrunched over with her hand still stuck to the mouse, closed her eyes, and concentrated.

May the white light of love and truth surround me and protect me!

Over and over, she repeated the mantra, all the while visualizing a crystal knife cutting the energy under her fingers.

Every time she chipped away and started to pry loose a finger, another one was pulled back down.

I can do this. I can do this. I am woman, hear me roar!

Damn, this is tough. Maybe brute force is not the answer. Instead of the crystal knife, she envisioned hand lotion. Silky, smooth, luxurious globs of pine-scented hand lotion under her fingers, between her hand and the mouse, slipping all around and allowing her hand to slide, slide, slide easily off!

Phew. That did it, and now her hand was softened. She wiggled her fingers, still feeling a tingle here and there. The red lines looked like a subway map on the back of her hand.

Once she was released, the screen on her computer went blank. She could still hear clicks, beeps, and whirring, but she had no idea what the dang thing was doing. She knew she was supposed to tell it to shut down nicely but screw that. She crawled under the desk and unplugged it from the wall. The thing was a monster.

She shook her hand, watching the thin red lines dwindle into dots and then disappear. There was still a faint shimmer around her hand that was slowly fading, and the tips of her fingers still tingled and itched.

Whatever had happened, Birdie suspected it had something to do with the nasty illness that was wiping out her friends. She wasn't sure how, but she would find out. Meanwhile, she had to heal them and bring them back. The Old Witches Home residents had to combine their energies and do some healing. People needed to know about the threat and unite to fight it!

But obviously, a blast email was not going to work. I guess we do this the old-fashioned way. I need to talk to people face to face. Birdie grabbed a felt-tip pen and a pack of Post-it notes.

She started on Joy West and headed north. The village's lanes formed a pentacle with the Heart at the center. Lanes were designed for five lots on each side, for a maximum of fifty dwellings. Only thirty-seven were occupied so far. The backyards abutted an alley between the lanes, allowing people to visit with friends on the next lane or with their neighbors to either side. Lots of opportunities for hanging out and getting to know each other.

Birdie planned to inscribe a banishing pentacle as she walked. By the time she returned to the end of Joy East, she wanted to call in as many protective energies and healing deities as she could think of.

She wished she could have asked Maya to join her, but Maya was up to her elbows in feast planning. Maple had enough to do with getting the property ready, the bonfire built, and the tables set up. Without Twig, Angie, Oscar, and Mnemosyne, their resources were depleted. She would have to handle this on her own.

Still, she missed Maya's tranquil, nourishing, healing energy. Maya had softened Birdie's rough edges for many years – for Birdie, Maya was the childhood blanket that kept her safe and warm no matter what was going on around them. She was glad their houses were close to each other.

House was a generous term for the structures within the village. People built whatever they wanted on their little plots. The witches were nothing if not creative. They felt it was a divine calling to live in whatever kind of dwelling spoke to them.

Most people started with a tent as soon as they secured their plot. Each plot was approximately a quarter acre and was already equipped with a connector to the eco-friendly septic system and the spring-fed water reserve. New homes could also connect to the electric grid powered by a combination solar grid, windmill, and hydraulic generator on the mountain behind the village.

Owners had to deal with their own heating and cooling needs. Most folks chose to install air-source heat pumps, but that only happened once they had actual walls. In the beginning, it was a tent, a campfire, a water pump, and one electrical outlet. New residents had to choose whether to hook up their electric shaver, toothbrush, or computer.

Most important, of course, was the long-range Wi-Fi that extended throughout the village. Except for up on the mountain, the signal was excellent, and, since the recent upgrades, the system accommodated all residents with no problems. The Wi-Fi was included in the monthly HOA fee, and everyone enjoyed streaming TV, Pandora (with reason, of course, given what one might release!), and games. Each resident was also given their email account connected to the Old Witches Home server.

Birdie knew that sending a blast email to everyone about the healing circle would have been easier, but she also knew many folks never checked their inboxes. No, this task was too urgent, she rationalized. Best to speak to people directly. And to see if other people were afflicted with this sleeping sickness.

Birdie spent the rest of the afternoon going up and down the village lanes, knocking on doors, inviting people to the ritual room that evening for a healing circle.

Each lane was named for one of the points of the Old Witch Pentacle, representing the fruits of aging: Wisdom, Reflection, Fulfillment, Joy, and Knowledge.

An altar with the symbols of that energy anchored the lane at the access road end. Wooden circular signs with shelves beneath them hung proudly on poles set deep into the ground behind each altar, thanks to Lightning's graphics designer friend.

Birdie's favorite altar was Reflection. A birdbath on the shelf with mirrors of all sizes beneath the sign could be used to fix your hair before leaving the village. A journal in a zippered oilcloth bag hung from the shelf, where people could write their reflections for others to read.

She didn't have time to read today, though, and sighed. She took a quick look at herself in one of the mirrors and moved on. Only one more lane to get back to her home on Joy East. She contemplated taking a cart back up to the Heart that evening instead of walking. She had enough exercise for one day.

The heat from the strong summer sun had given Birdie's arthritis a rest, but she was tired. The light breeze from the mountains to the North cooled her just enough, with a hint of birdsong and fragrance from the garden flowers along her way. She felt proud of her community as she strode down the lanes of this magical place they had built from their dreams.

Then she thought about Huffstickler and her friends who needed help. The Goddess used the beautiful sunshine and perfect day to trick Birdie into complacency. She shuddered, breathed deeply, and kept walking.

She answered many questions, drank enough iced tea that she needed to pee at every fifth house, and marveled at the various configurations of hanging toilet paper near the seat. By the time Birdie had finished knocking on all 37 doors and chatting with the 22 witches who were awake and coherent, she was famished and needed to pee again. She listed everyone who seemed to be overcome with the illness, another 11 witches. Okay. Now, she was really starting to freak out.

Hermes met her at the door to her cabin. After running to the bathroom with only a few drips, she fed him and collapsed on the couch. She would figure out food in a minute. Hermes jumped up beside her. Birdie's eyes closed, but just for a minute.

14

OSCAR AT THE FARM

Maple was disoriented when he woke up. He could faintly hear Maya in the kitchen. Twig was sleeping peacefully on the floor of the ritual room. Maple didn't want to wake them, but he thought he should get Twig to their room upstairs.

Maple's sciatica twinged when he stood, but after stretching a little this way and that, he felt limber enough to bend down and touch Twig on their shoulder. Twig swayed a little as they rose to a seated position and then uncoiled to their full height. They were rocking to each side, swinging their arms in and out, clearly hearing a beat lost to Maple. Twig was looking up with a soft smile and followed Maple with no resistance when he pointed him to the stairs in the hall.

After settling Twig in their room, Maple's thoughts turned to his friend, Oscar. He was worried about him. He usually powered through minor cuts and scrapes. But this time was different, and Maple had to see what was wrong.

He might have recovered by now. Maybe he didn't have the same thing Twig, Angie, and Mnemosyne had. Maybe it was just a reaction to the cut in his hand. Whatever it was, he wanted to fix it as soon as possible. They needed all hands on deck to host the festival and stop Huffstickler.

Walking down the lane from the Heart to Rabbit and Oscar's bungalow took only ten minutes. Their homey place reminded Maple of his and Juniper's home and the care she had taken to create the perfect home for their kids. He always felt like a stranger there, like the apple in the vegetable bin that looks perfect, but when you pick it up, you see where the worm ate a huge hole.

Rabbit and Oscar had moved in just a month or two after the founders. They built a bungalow on Joy East with large south-facing views and a vegetable garden with a hothouse on one end with irises, lilies, lavender, and daisies around the seven-foot-high chicken wire fence that enclosed the large rectangular plot. On the north side of the house was a lovely stone patio with a tarpaulin roof for shade, bird feeders, and wind chimes. Maple learned the hard way to avoid the whirly twirly lawn ornament that could put you in a trance if you looked at it too long.

When she arrived, Rabbit sat in her chaise lounge reading *A Discovery of Witches* on the patio.

"Hi," Maple said, and Rabbit started as though someone had pinched her. "Didn't mean to scare you."

"I was just getting to the good part," Rabbit said. "But no worries. I won't lose my place – they're not going anywhere. I'll get us some tea."

She put down the book and stood up. Rabbit was over six feet tall and towered over Maple. He tried not to be intimidated by Rabbit, who smiled and laughed easily and had the greenest thumb on the planet. He wondered if Rabbit had named herself after Harvey, the pink pooka in the old film with James Stewart.

"How's Oscar doing?" he asked when Rabbit came out of the house with a metal tray painted with big yellow sunflowers and two glasses of purple iced passion tea.

"He's sleeping. I don't know what's going on with him. He's been muttering in his sleep, and it's worsening. The cut in his hand seems to be healing nicely, but he doesn't want to wake up."

"Was he sick before he cut himself?" Maple asked.

"He started acting strangely when he got back from town on Tuesday. I wasn't worried, though. He's got the immune system of a bull."

"What did he go to town for? Maybe he picked up something there." Maple was hoping they could identify a virus or bug of some kind that they could fix.

"He was having computer trouble, so he took it to that store – what's it called? Magick Tech Store or something? But he wasn't there long. He picked up a loaner that he's still having trouble with. Personally, I think it's a user error. He's a luddite like the rest of us, you know. What do you think it is?" Rabbit's brow was furrowed.

"You know, there are a couple of others who are out of it, too," Maple told Rabbit everything about Angie, Mnemosyne, and now Twig. Maybe there was a connection.

"What the hell is going on?" Rabbit asked. Spikes of tension crackled in the air.

"Even the doctor doesn't know what to do," Maple said resignedly. Maple had been relying on Oscar since the beginning, for the last ten years. Maple's old job as manager of an upscale hardware store made him and Oscar, who had been a general contractor, natural partners. Maple had always been the Operations Manager, and Oscar approved all new construction. Whenever Maple needed help, Oscar was always there, except for now.

They fell into a tense silence.

"You sure there's nothing we can do?" Rabbit asked. "I hate this."

"Just wait and watch?" Maple suggested. He felt so inadequate.

"Okay, I'll let you know if anything changes. I'm not leaving here." Rabbit picked up her book. She looked at Maple.

"You okay?" she said to him.

"Yeah, I'm just not sure how I can get everything done before Saturday. We still have to finish the bonfire, set up all the vendor's tents, bring out all the chairs from the shed, set up the stone altar, and rewire part of the dining pavilion because the last storm took out the area where the coffeemaker and small fridge live. I don't know if I can do it all by myself. I'm so used to relying on Oscar."

It wasn't like Maple to share so much.

"Isn't there anyone else?" Rabbit didn't seem ready to let Oscar out of her sight.

He sighed. "Nah, but I'll figure it out. It's not rocket science. And Eddie and Taylor are really helpful. I miss Twig's help, though."

"You mind if I just check on him?" Maple said.

"Sure. I'll stay here. I was in there just before you came," Rabbit said without looking up, an edge in her voice. She appeared to be focused on her book, but Maple realized her eyes weren't moving, and she hadn't turned a page in quite a while.

He walked into the bedroom and found Oscar in a fetal position on top of the floral bedspread. He was clucking and muttering in a low tone that sounded like mooing. Maple was mesmerized and wondered what the heck was going on in his mind. Maple laid a hand on his friend's shoulder, but Oscar didn't move. Rabbit stood behind them in the doorway, barely breathing.

As Oscar lay sleeping peacefully, images of farm animals were scampering in his brain. They kept popping up out of nowhere and then, poof, disappearing just as quickly. The visions ran randomly from the back of his head to the sides to the front to the sides to the back, like a billiard ball on a very bad but powerful hit, bouncing excitedly around the edges of the pool table without actually contacting another ball. His eyes weren't connected to their muscles and simply danced about in his head like they were on hot coals that kept getting hotter. As the farm animals mooed and oinked and snorted and bleated, Oscar's brain lost control over his thoughts and simply lay down in the mud.

If Oscar could speak, which he clearly couldn't because anything that came out of his mouth might only communicate with the goats in his visions, he might tell Maple that his brain started its rural pilgrimage two days ago when he figured out how to load his favorite farming simulation game on the loaner computer he got from the nacker kid at the tech store. He was playing the game, just about to ascend to another level, when the chickens started clucking in his head. At first, he clucked right back, telling them they would be nuggets soon if they didn't start laying for him.

His clucking, however, soon didn't need a translator. He could feel feathers on his chest and around his head, bobbing forward and backward uncontrollably. He understood perfectly that Annie wouldn't lay anything until she got a coop with more sunlight, and Denise didn't want to be stuck next to Gertrude, that old hen, any longer! Oscar apologized and commiserated and promised to move them wherever they wanted just as soon as he could meld into the screen.

Oscar was a little confused then and decided to join Rabbit in bed to do what the birds and the bees do. They had quite a bit of fun. In his mind, it sounded like Rabbit was honking and purring. Oscar roared like a bull. Not bad for some old dude, he thought.

After Rabbit fell asleep, he returned to the computer to play on his farm. He fell asleep clucking and snoring with his head on the keyboard.

When Rabbit came in at 3:22 in the morning, he woke just enough to remember where he was – in his house with Rabbit. He was grinning like a neon KFC sign, happy to be among his animals, not far from his farm.

When he sat up, the animals on the screen were hopping and scratching. They glared at Rabbit when she pried his hand off the squeaky mouse. She gingerly grabbed the device – he was sure that she was going to suffer a bite and need a rabies shot. Oscar watched her move to the little window at the bottom of the screen and click on the "shut down" option just as he had shown her. Screaming violet, purple, hot pink, and lime green ribbons blazed while the screen said, "Closing all apps – are you sure, sucker??" – and shut down.

When she touched his shoulder, he leaped out of his seat, braying loudly, his arms and hands pawing the air in front of him. She stroked his head and the back of his neck instinctively. He settled down, and she led him away from the computer.

Oscar was still oinking and mooing as she coaxed him into bed,

"Shh, shh, it's all right. You're all right." He felt an urge to ask if he would get eaten before Yule but couldn't find the words.

The next morning, Oscar seemed okay, although he waddled a bit when he walked and would occasionally bleat like a sheep. He assured Rabbit that he was fine and ready to work in the garden with her, occasionally letting out a "waa" as though he had Tourette's syndrome but was otherwise fit for duty. He even seemed to crave the weeds in a way he hadn't previously. As he dug them out of the ground, he sniffed them and licked the leaves as though they were popsicles. He was sure all these plants were incredibly precious, even the ones that got in the way.

The pain in his paw from the trowel was excruciating. He clucked and then barked and then brayed like a mule. He felt like his body was growing and shrinking and rapidly changing shapes, one minute with feathers, the next with a leather hide, the next with wool.

The next thing he knew, two humans were leaning over him and wrapping his hoof with something soft. An insistent part of his brain was telling him to run away and hide, that these humans around him were dangerous and they didn't smell right.

The short one examined him in a way that made him very uncomfortable. When he looked into her eyes as she leaned over him, he saw his own reflection – noting the chuck, the loin, the flank, and the shank in dashed lines across his body. The human voice in his brain struggled to make itself heard over the cacophony of squeals and roars and ruffling feathers.

He managed to communicate and even stand up for a minute, on only two legs, even! He could smell the garden just down the road and all the trees and ditches where some creature had marked their turf with their pee. His nose worked overtime, twitching and burning and savoring. Finally, the familiar smells of lavender and laundry soap from the sheets on the clothesline soothed him. He laid down on a soft spot amid the vegetables and settled in.

He saw Rabbit sitting next to him. He raised his head and rubbed his snout on her. She helped him up, and he was able to walk, slowly but deliberately, back to his bungalow. She led him with an invisible tether into the house and onto his bed. Then, Rabbit gave him a blanket, tucked him in, and left him to snuffle in his pen, sleeping and dreaming of grass, weeds, garbage, and corn. English words succumbed to more expressive and demanding sounds, and he slept on his own little virtual farm.

He was still at the farm and might never leave. He had no idea that Maple was watching him.

15

Healing Ritual

While Birdie and Oscar napped, Maya readied the ritual room. Healing rituals were Maya's favorite type of ritual. She hummed to herself as she sprinkled salt water around the ritual room, cleansing and purifying. Make sure you get in the corners, she reminded herself. You never know what kind of energy is left over from the last ritual.

She laid big multicolored pillows in the center and draped blankets and scarves over them. She placed several folding chairs around the room's edges, not knowing who or how many people would be there. But she knew not everyone would be ambulatory.

At each corner of the room, she pulled out the small foldable table leaning against the wall. She pulled a piece of cloth from the fabric bin that felt right for that direction and element. In the East, she draped a pale-yellow scarf with fringe. In the South, it was a dark red piece of velvet. In the West, a blue moiré fabric that looked like ocean waves, and in the North, a dark green cotton cloth covered the table.

Then, she found a pillar candle from the candle box to add to each altar. Maya added just one token on each table, feeling the need to keep it all simple to allow the energy to flow freely both into the circle and out of it. She found an owl feather for the East, a piece of fire agate for the South, a small abalone shell that she filled with water for the West, and an oak branch for the North.

Just as she was finishing, witches started to arrive. Bjorn came in, leaning on his staff with a scowl. "What is this all about? Why has Birdie called us here?"

"I'll let her tell you when she gets here," Maya said. Bjorn walked over to her, looked at her face menacingly, and smiled. She moved away quickly.

Charlie arrived next with his swagger, taking up more space in the room than anyone else. His t-shirt was taut over his belly.

Lois came in accompanied by Boreus and found chairs between West and North. She wore a white blouse and slacks, reminiscent of her nurse's uniform. She folded her walker, placing it behind her. Boreus' face, now divested of its long beard, sagged with wrinkles, his eyebrows almost obscuring his eyes.

Amethyst, in a sheer pastel long sleeveless dress, and Victoria, in her usual black tunic and skirt, staked out their places in the southwest quadrant. Whale Tooth sat in a lounger near the drums. Soon, all the chairs were filled.

Rabbit held Oscar's arm as he ambled into the room, and she carefully led him to the cushions in the center. She plopped down next to him and gently coaxed him to lie with his head in her lap. He was smiling and cooing to himself as she stroked his hair absentmindedly.

Maple and Taylor were on either side of Mnemosyne as she came in. Maple still had on his Grateful Dead t-shirt but Taylor had changed into a soft yellow print caftan that complemented his warm brown skin and looked cool and comfortable.

Mnemosyne was agitated, counting on her fingers and mumbling. Her eyes were half-closed, and her pupils were moving back and forth rapidly. They brought her into the center, sat her on a cushion, and Taylor sat down cross-legged beside her. Maple went to stand next to Maya, who was still waiting in front of the North altar.

Eddie was carrying Twig over his shoulders in a fireman's carry as though Twig were no more than a bag of groceries. He set Twig down gently and held his arm as Twig began to bounce up and down. They were dancing and giggling so much that Eddie could barely keep hold of Twig to lead them into the center. But once Twig sat down, they immediately laid on their side and began snoring lightly. Eddie stood over them and looked down protectively.

Angie also took up quite a bit of space as she entered. Birdie and Dandelion were behind her, barely keeping up with Angie's long strides as she lifted her arms above her shoulders and belted out the chorus from *Don't Rain on My Parade.*

Birdie pushed Angie down, not so gently, and she fell onto a cushion, her outstretched jazz hands flailing above her and her mouth open for the next line. Dandelion nudged her, and Angie fell on her side, closed her eyes, and the rest of the song was lost. Dandelion kneeled beside her and swung her legs to one side, settling in for the duration.

Dandelion wore a sleeveless pink lace tank top which matched her toenails. The delicacy of the outfit seemed at odds with Dandelion's girth and muscled arms, but that was Dandelion. A picture of contrasts.

"Okay, we're here," Maya said. "Now what?" She looked around the room and counted – exactly 13 witches had gathered this evening. A good sign, she thought. We should be powerful enough to do some healing.

Birdie explained what had happened in the past couple of days. She told everyone about Oscar's injury and passing out, as well as Angie's incurable musical optimism. She described how they found Mnemosyne on the floor of her office and how Twig had danced and slept instead of building the bonfire. She mentioned that she counted another 11 from her walk around the village that could also be afflicted. They would check on them as soon as they could after the healing ritual.

Birdie looked tired, Maya thought. She had changed from the casual business attire she had worn for their lunch with Huffstickler to a cotton blue sundress and sandals, but she didn't look cool.

Dandelion spoke up. "I've heard that others are acting strange. Nighthawk told me that Sky was out of it, and she was concerned about Arden and Anastasia too."

Maya didn't know the people that Dandelion mentioned very well. They were fairly new residents and lived on Knowledge North. They weren't on the Council and hadn't attended many community gatherings. She took a deep breath and prayed to the Goddess for patience and clarity.

Birdie shushed the murmurs around the room as the group talked about afflicted others.

"Okay. Maybe this is a bigger problem than we realized," Birdie admitted. "But maybe healing these four here now will heal everyone else simultaneously."

"Maybe," grumbled Bjorn. "And maybe not. Do we have any idea what is causing their craziness? What does the doctor say?" Charlie looked at Birdie and sneered. It felt to Maya like they knew something.

"Lois?" asked Birdie.

"The doctor was here this morning," Lois said. "He's very concerned but couldn't find anything obviously wrong with anyone. He's contacted colleagues and the CDC for more information to see if this is happening anywhere else. He'll be here again tomorrow. At this point, we just don't know what's causing their behavior. I won't speculate without more information. I've checked their vitals, and no one is in imminent danger. They're all seemingly quite healthy. We just need to make sure they stay hydrated. That's the most important thing."

Murmurs started again, and Maya could feel the tension gathering.

"Sounds like magic to me," Victoria said. "We need to do something."

"That's why we're here," Birdie said. Maya appreciated her calm resolve. The others seemed to settle down, looking to Birdie for their next steps.

Maya suggested a simple intention: *We gather together to heal our fellow witches and community*. No one had any objections.

"Short and simple, that's what I like," Bjorn said.
"Eloquent," said Victoria. "I like it."

A consensus was reached, and they moved on to design the rest of the ritual. Let's hope we can do this quickly, Maya thought. We don't have lots of time. We have to finish prepping for the Festival. Who will do the decorations now?

The group developed the specifics, calling on their years of experience in co-creating rituals spontaneously. The most difficult decision was which chant to sing. Maya tuned it out, figuring she would simply join whatever they decided to do and that it would all work out.

Instead, she quietly walked around the edge of the room, widdershins, using an imaginary broom to sweep out whatever negative energy had entered with the witches. She gently gathered energy and pushed it out the windows and doors. The air felt prickly and sharp – she felt like she was sweeping shards of glass as she moved. Eventually, the air was clear, and she noticed the voices had softened from eager, jagged, separate tones to a harmonic hum, with voices blending with each other in a smooth rhythm.

"Let's all stand and get started," Birdie said finally.

Maya stood in the East. Boreus began the grounding as everyone else fell silent. Maya could feel their roots below the ground and their branches above, reaching out to touch each other. A grove was growing in the room, connected and strong. Maya took a deep, hopeful breath.

Victoria cast the circle, and Maya felt the air around her thicken and solidify. When she inscribed the pentacle above and below, the orb of energy encompassed them all, safe and secure. The outside world was gone, she thought. At least it was for her.

Maya didn't pay much attention as the directions were called and elements honored. She moved 90 degrees to her right, lifted her arms, and repeated, "Air is sacred. Welcome, Air, " changing the element as she went. It all felt so familiar and comfortable.

Finally, they were ready to begin their magical work.

The witches moved forward, clasped hands, and circled the bodies in the middle. Rabbit, Dandelion, Eddie, and Taylor stood and joined them.

Every step I take is a sacred step;
Every step I take is a healing step.
Healing, healing, healing our bodies.
Healing, healing, healing the land.

The song started slow and ragged while voices warmed up and remembered the words. The witches in this circle had sung and danced this spell many times over the past ten years. Sometimes, the healing helped someone recover from an illness or grief; sometimes, it helped them pass into the Summerland. Those who sang and danced always felt better afterward.

Her right foot automatically crossed over her left, then her left foot stepped out to the left. Then the right went behind, and the left reached out again. Over and over, Maya moved with the rest of the witches as they stirred the cauldron of energy, building warmth and a potion to rid the ones in the center of the awful poison sickening them.

The dance was slow and relentless. Lois, Bjorn, and a couple of the other witches who had difficulty dancing, released themselves and sat on the outside with arms outstretched, singing and holding the energy, reflecting it back to the center. Now, there were too few to hold hands, and Maya moved into the center to hold Angie, sense what was afflicting her, and transform and release it.

But when she held her, Maya felt only a slight twinge of static. She was alarmed. She had a strong connection to Angie; they had been working together for years, and Maya depended on Angie's steady, solid presence. But now she felt she was holding a blank piece of paper with fading invisible ink and a shimmer of green on the edges.

Angie had joined the Old Witches Home Collective after a long illness had rendered her unable to work at a regular job. Her irritable bowel and Guillain-Barre syndromes made her sensitive to certain types of foods and environmental irritants. The Council had approved her membership application to give her a place to recover even though she didn't meet the age requirements. Maya rocked her back and forth, humming the healing chant, hoping to rouse her. But Angie's breathing was shallow and quiet. She had a small smile, and her eyes slowly moved back and forth in what appeared to be some kind of dream.

The dancers continued moving, and the chant dug a trench into Maya's unconscious. She didn't know what else she could do. Where was Lightning? He had made that spectacular appearance at the binding spell ritual and again when they tried to reach Twig. Where was he now? They could really use him.

When she silently pleaded to him to join them, she heard a rustle of skirts, but that was all. It was as though he didn't want to be there. She recalled Lightning and his disdain for new things after he was given an email address when the Wi-Fi was installed. "It's my Midwestern upbringing," he said in an exaggerated accent. "I just don't cotton to those newfangled gadgets. Give me a piece of paper and a good sturdy pencil, and I'm fine."

But what did that memory snippet have to do with this illness? She was so confused.

She moved to Twig and brought Twig's head onto her lap. Again, just the shimmer of green but nothing else. The same with Oscar and Mnemosyne. What else could they do? They all seemed to be fading into the ether. Maya was scared.

The dance was sluggish, with only a few people still moving around but not in sync with each other. Holes in the circle will make it difficult to accumulate enough energy to make a difference, Maya thought.

Suddenly, Diego entered the room with Dirty Swan carrying a chicken in a cat carrier. He was dressed all in white, with a red scarf on his head and a large bowl in his hands. Dirty Swan wore her ragged work jeans and a t-shirt with Che Guevara over her chest.

Diego took out a dagger and mimed opening a door into the area where the ritual occurred. All eyes turned to him and Dirty Swan as they walked to the center of the room, to the middle of the cushions.

"We need to gather great energy for this healing," Diego said. "After Birdie summoned us this afternoon, I prayed to Oggun, and he instructed me to sacrifice for our friends. We need more energy than we can gather by ourselves; we need the energy of the gods."

Birdie looked skeptical, and Dirty Swan made shushing noises at the chicken. Maya could see Bjorn and Charlie become visibly excited and Dandelion visibly anxious.

Dirty Swan glowered at anyone who came near to her chicken to get a look at it but respectfully stepped aside when Diego approached. He had what appeared to be a very sharp, thin knife in his belt. He pulled the chicken out of the carrier and examined it closely, scraping away some of the feathers on its neck.

"I have asked our sister, Dirty Swan, to make this sacred offering," Diego said, holding up the bird by its neck. "This chicken will sacrifice its life so that our friends may live. Let us all gather around this sacred bird and give thanks."

The few dancers who were left melded with the people sitting outside to form a circle with Diego in the center with the chicken. He waited patiently for people to gingerly rise from their chairs and shuffle forward.

Lois shuffled to the center, holding on to Boreus' arm, looking intently at the chicken. Maya imagined Lois in an operating room, with a nurse's hat on, solemnly assisting the surgeon. Amethyst appeared floating toward the center, her face a little green and her mouth opening and closing as though she wanted to say something but couldn't find the words, a rare occurrence for her.

While waiting, Diego's eyes were closed, and he appeared to be praying.

She also noted that Diego's large hand-painted ceramic bowl came from her kitchen. She wasn't sure she liked the idea of her good bowls filling with blood. But they routinely ate the chickens that lived at the Old Witches Home anyway, and this time it was for a good cause.

Everyone shifted their gaze to Diego as he opened his eyes and slowly walked around the circle, staring intently into each person's face as he passed. When he came back to the center, he held the chicken high in the air. He nodded to Whale Tooth, who grabbed a djembe from the drums in the corner of the room.

Diego gestured to him to begin drumming. He began an intricate rhythm that made everyone sway and transported them to a different plane of consciousness.

"Oggun, we call you! Take this sacrifice! Use this blood to heal our sisters and brothers. Take from them the poison that is afflicting them. We offer this creature to you. Your wisdom and strength guide us. Strengthen, heal, and protect your children."

He held the knife high in one hand, the chicken in the other. He slashed its neck with one quick swipe. The witches gasped, transfixed.

Holding the chicken over the bowl, Diego let the blood drip, drip, drip. The drumbeat was rapid, insistent, and powerful.

"Oggun is here," Diego proclaimed. "Our friends are safe. They will heal." He strode to the sleeping bodies and dipped his thumb into the bowl of blood. He dabbed a red mark on each of their foreheads and then held the bowl high as he marched around the circle widdershins.

Maya saw Charlie surreptitiously stick his foot out just before Diego reached him. Diego stumbled. There was a gasp from the group as the blood swished into the bowl, and it threatened to tip onto Lois and Boreus. Eddie, standing next to Lois, stepped forward and grabbed the bowl. Diego straightened himself, nodded to Eddie, took the bowl back, glared at Charlie, and continued his circuit.

Charlie chuckled. Dirty Swan was still holding the dead chicken and motioned it toward Charlie as if she could cut his throat, too.

Finally, Diego finished walking, and the tension began to ease. Dirty Swan wrapped the chicken in a kitchen towel; Whale Tooth slowed the pace of the drums.

"Farewell, Oggun. Thank you for being here and for caring for our friends. We honor you and are in your service." His stentorian voice sealed the intention.

The witches who had called directions now released them, their voices shaky and tentative. By the time they opened the circle, the energy in the room was heavy but peaceful. Maya helped Maple lift Angie, who burst into a chorus of *June is Busting Out All Over,* and everyone laughed.

Lois reminded everyone that if they knew of someone afflicted with this sleeping sickness, they should call her so she could put them on a list for the doctor to visit the next day.

The ritual was over, and hopefully, recovery had begun.

Maya had hope. Then she saw Bjorn striding across the room, his eyes boring into Birdie.

He confronted her from ten feet away. "You mean, I just spent my whole evening chanting a silly song, doing a stupid dance, and watching a chicken get slaughtered? You ReDreaming witches don't know what you're doing. The only good thing out of tonight is that we'll get to eat the chicken."

"You didn't have to come," Birdie said. Maya moved closer to support her.

"You mean, no Heathens have been affected? You all are perfectly fine?" Maple asked as he joined Maya and Birdie.

"Of course, we're fine; we're powerful and pure."

"What about Andy?" Charlie asked. "He's been out of it for two days." To Maya, Charlie looked like he was actually worried. Then he shook his head as if he were remembering something.

"He just has a flu. It's seasonal," said Bjorn, as he gave Charlie a look that said, 'shut up.' "These ReDreaming witches are manufacturing lies. This is a hoax."

"No, it's not," Birdie protested. "You can see them." She pointed to the four witches who still slept in the center of the circle. "You can see they're not well."

"They're taking naps; that's all I see. Don't call me again unless you really need something." He snapped his red, white, and blue suspenders, nodded to Charlie, and they left the room. Maya watched them leave, just the two of them, ignored by everyone else, as usual.

Rabbit approached Maya and Birdie. "I'm going to get Oscar home now. I'm still worried."

"I know," said Birdie. "We'll keep working on it. You know how magic works. Sometimes it takes a while."

"Damn it!" Birdie shouted as she stubbed her toe on one of the folding tables. "What the fuck is this thing doing here?"

"I'm taking it down. It was our west altar." Maya tried to sound soothing but not condescending. She knew how Birdie reacted when she thought someone was patronizing her. She also knew that Birdie only got angry like this when she was scared. She hated being scared.

Maya looked again at Angie, so sweetly tucked into herself, and reminded herself that it would all be okay. You just have to have faith.

Taylor picked up Twig and carried them out of the ritual room. Eddie tapped Mnemosyne on the shoulder, and she bolted upright, stood, and began walking quickly toward the door. Eddie scampered to catch up.

Maple guided Angie to the doorway as best he could while Angie danced lazy jazz squares and switched to *Get Me to the Church on Time*. Birdie was gathering the altar cloths, blowing out the candles, and putting everything away.

Maya thought that she seemed so small and fragile. I hope she's okay. She'll figure it out, I'm sure. Just like I'll figure out this darn festival feast. At least we'll have fresh roast chicken.

Maya caught up with Maple and took Angie's other arm.

16

FRIDAY MORNING

The next morning, Maple walked over to the dining hall to refill his water bottle from the water jug in the corner before continuing to work on the setup for the Festival. He saw Bjorn and Charlie sitting at one of the tables by the window. As usual, they looked like they were conspiring, but Maple figured that was their normal appearance.

"Hey, Maple, what does Birdie have you doing now?" Charlie yelled.

"What are you talking about?"

"You're her boy, aren't you? You do everything she asks."

"No, I don't." Then he thought about it. He hated to admit it, but he usually did. "Well, yes, I do, I guess. But that's because she has good ideas and common sense. I trust her."

They snickered.

Maple wished he could think of a better comeback. He knew it would come to him as he fell asleep, but for now, all he could think of was, 'And your mother, too.' But that didn't make sense, so he was grateful he hadn't said it.

He filled his Gryffindor lion stainless-steel water bottle and started to walk out. Bjorn and Charlie were huddling again, and he thought he could make it out without talking with them if he were quiet. He turned away from the water jug and tripped over the trash can by the side of the table.

Damn.

Bjorn called, "Hey, Maple, do you know how much this land would go for?"

Crap. Does he have to answer? Maybe he could pretend he didn't hear. They all knew he was hard of hearing.

"Maple, I know you heard me."

He stopped, but he didn't turn around. Bjorn and Charlie stood up and began moving toward him. Neither one was actually bigger than Maple, but something about the two of them together made him feel small, and he could feel his flesh crawl as they neared him from behind.

"What do you think? How much is this land worth? What would we get if we sold to Huffstickler?" Bjorn's voice was cool.

"He doesn't want to buy it. He wants to steal it from us." Maple turned to face them and quickly regretted it. They were standing on either side of him, and he felt like he was in a cage.

"How do you know?" Charlie said. "Maybe if we offered a fair price, he would buy it instead. Save him the legal fees and such. A win-win. If the brother wins, he will buy it from the brother. But if we win, we could sell it to him and make the money."

"Yeah," Bjorn added. "He's a businessman. He's going to do whatever makes the most profit. Smart. A good American. We could make some money off him. God knows we could use it. My social security doesn't really go that far."

Maple sputtered. "But then what? Where would we go? This is our home."

"Maybe it's your home, but to me, it's just land," Bjorn said. "I didn't grow up here. We're not really family, just a bunch of outcasts who happened to end up here. How do we know you all didn't coerce Lightning into leaving the land to you?"

"What are you talking about?"

"I wasn't there when Lightning died, but you were. I don't understand you ReDreaming witches. You are all so tight; it isn't hard to imagine someone saying you put a spell on him or something."

Maple had to think about that. They were tight. Did Bjorn feel left out? Is that why he was so nasty?

"Just saying – what if someone testified in court that the four of you, or maybe just Birdie – you know, the ones who were with him at the end – what if someone told the court they knew you had influenced him? Huffstickler might find such testimony quite valuable. But if you wanted to prevent that from happening...." Bjorn let his words trail off and just looked at Maple calmly.

Maple couldn't believe what he was hearing. Was Bjorn really trying to extort him? He could feel the anger and fear starting to rise.

"You're wrong. No way," Maple sputtered. "No one can say we influenced Lightning. We didn't, and we'll prove it. We are family. This place is special."

"Calm down, Maple," Charlie stepped between him and Bjorn. "We're just saying that we might be able to turn this situation to our advantage. None of us are rich here. If Huffstickler is willing to pay a good price, maybe we could make out okay. Just think about it."

"Oh, I'll think about it all right. But we didn't put a spell on him. We don't do that kind of thing!"

"I know that, but Huffstickler doesn't," Charlie conceded. "If I weren't so strapped for cash, you know, with the heart meds going up and all, I wouldn't even consider selling to him."

Maple forgot that Charlie had been in the hospital last month for a mild heart attack.

"Let's go, Charlie. Maple's no help. C'mon." Bjorn tapped Charlie's arm. "Let him go back to Birdie."

"Think about it," Charlie said as he turned to go.

Maple felt helpless as he watched them head out the door that would take them to their cabins on Knowledge Lane. He was pretty sure they would sit on Charlie's porch and drink beer all afternoon. He fantasized about throwing the beer in their faces or, like on Survivor, voting them off the island.

Maple chided himself for being so weak. Damn. Why can't I stand up to them? They're wrong – I know they are. This place deserves to stay the way it is. We need this community. At least I do. And Birdie doesn't tell me what to do. I just follow her suggestions. If I were as powerful and had as much magic in me as she does, I would be able to do more on my own. But I'm just not wired that way.

Maple left the Heart to check on the preparations in the meadow, just like Birdie had asked him to. The anger began to subside. He was needed. It felt good to be on the mountain. For a few minutes, he forgot about their troubles.

He forgot about Oscar and the others. He forgot that the land was not yet theirs. He felt the sun and smelled the fresh air. Life was good. Everyone would recover and have the money they needed to keep the land. The Festival would be magnificent, and the Goddess would provide. He was sure of it, wasn't he?

When Birdie entered the Healing Center, she got annoyed. Lois had all the medical supplies, the bandages, the instruments, the medications, the herbs, the vials of tinctures and decoctions, on the counter. She was carefully placing each item in the cabinet.

I had them the way I like them, Birdie thought. Alphabetically.

"What are you doing?"

"I want to be ready when the doctor gets here. I'm a little tense, I think. People have been calling me with the names of more people who are out of it, and I'm worried about what's going on. So I thought I'd do something useful until he gets here. These supplies should be placed together with others that serve similar purposes, like pain medications or wound care, all in the same area. That's the way it's done in hospitals and clinics. It makes so much more sense than the higgeldy piggeldy way they were before."

Birdie took offense at that, but Lois was so sincere that she chose to keep her mouth shut. I'm learning, she thought. Restraint of tongue and pen.

"Can I help you? You're holding your hand," Lois observed.

"Yes. I woke up with pain in my fingers and shooting up my arm. It hurts to move my ring finger and my middle finger, and they keep popping when I try to straighten them. I just need pain meds, I think."

"Oh, dear. Come over here, sit down, and let me look at it."

Birdie sat in the chair and laid her right arm on the desk. Lois held Birdie's hand in hers. As she probed Birdie's muscles and tendons, her fingers were soft, moist, and cool.

Birdie could almost see right through her hand, like a rice paper vegetable roll. Her skin had a shimmery angelic translucence as though the walls of the cells had been worn away over time, leaving just a papery thin barrier between her and the world.

Lois turned Birdie's hand over, pressed her wrist, manipulated her fingers, and pulled her ring finger until it popped.

"Feel better?"

"A little. What is it?"

"Just trigger finger. It's common in the elderly."

"I'm not elderly. Just a little old."

"Yes, dear." How can a 90-something be so condescending? "We have a couple of options. You could go into town, and Dr. Payne could give you a cortisone shot, or he could give you a referral for surgery. Or we can do a moxa moxa treatment. You know, Chinese herbal medicine. Several treatments will take a bit longer, but you'll feel better. There's also Reiki, but I'm not sure it will give you immediate relief either."

"I need to feel better now. The Festival is tomorrow, and I have way too much to do. Maya's overwhelmed and I need to fill in for Mnemosyne. How about just some pain meds?"

"You could do that, but it will only mask the symptoms for a little while. And you still won't be able to fully use your hand. Here, let's see how you're doing. Open this."

Lois handed Birdie a jar of ointment, and Birdie wrapped her hand around it to turn the lid.

"Ow! Shit." She dropped the jar on the desk and shook her hand. "Dang, that hurt. Okay, what's the fastest thing I can do?"

"Well, a cortisone shot usually takes a couple of days to fully take effect. Moxa moxa requires more than one treatment, and I have no idea how soon you would be able to schedule surgery. I have some ibuprofen if you'd like."

"I guess I'll take the ibuprofen. I don't have time for anything else," Birdie argued. "I need to be able to use my hand now. I have to be able to write down the donations that come in and keep track of the vendor donations, and I'm sure there's other stuff. And I can't touch my computer. The damn thing's possessed."

"Let me take your blood pressure. You're getting all riled up." Lois made soothing sounds as she wrapped the cuff around Birdie's forearm. "How's your wrist these days?"

"Damn thing still hurts like crazy, especially when I wake up in the morning. Even if I wear my wrist brace."

"You probably have arthritis along with your carpal tunnel. That sprain last year just exacerbated everything. Your body is wearing down, you know."

"No, it's not! I can still dance." *Not for very long, but I can dance.*

Birdie took the ibuprofen and promised to call Dr. Payne. She hated the thought of having to ask him for help. Again. She didn't want him to think of her as needy. But he was always so warm and generous – old fool. Why did he pop into her mind when she was falling asleep or sometimes when she was meditating? What was it about him?

Forget it. There's too much to do. Let me go to the office and see if I can figure out the finances for this damn Festival. Lois went back to rearranging.

Maya was rushing around in the kitchen, preparing everything for the Festival. Thank the Goddess she didn't have to make desserts. The townspeople would bring those. But The Old Witches Home was responsible for the appetizers, salads, main dishes, and sides. That's how they got the generous donations – by providing food and entertainment. The ritual was the entertainment, and the food was her job.

She studied the crumpled sheet of notebook paper that listed the dishes they had planned to provide – a Celtic Cheese and Cracker Spread, Blessed Baked Beans, Cosmic Corn On The Cob, Summer Solstice Potato Salad, Dragon Barbeque Chicken, Haunted Hamburgers, Wicked Wieners, vegetable burgers, green salad, macaroni and cheese, vegetable spread, Out of This World Onion Dip, tortilla chips and Ghostly Guacamole (her specialty), and an assortment of breads and buns. She also needed to concoct five gallons of hibiscus raspberry iced tea for the guests.

She pulled the worn pink vinyl notebook from the shelf. She leafed through her favorite recipes from fifty years of catering and cooking for friends and loved ones. Twelve other notebooks sat on the shelf with many more recipes, but these were her go-to recipes for large groups with the gigantic amounts needed to feed 100 people.

Just as she started perusing the baked beans recipe, trying to decipher the instructions still legible between the brown and greasy stains of previous batches, Gwion arrived. The diminutive White man of Irish descent with curly red-gray hair was wearing his green Kitchen Witch apron and smiling broadly.

"Thank you for calling me," he yelled. "I am at your service, milady." And with that, he bowed forward with one arm outstretched and the other sweeping in front of him as though he had a large hat in his hand. Maya almost lurched forward to catch him before he fell, but he straightened without a problem and stood smartly at attention in the doorway.

Gwion's hearing wasn't what it used to be. He spoke very loudly and kept repeating whatever Maya said. But Maya loved Gwion – he had been such a gifted cook in his day – so she left him alone and let him do what he wanted. She was grateful he had come.

"Why don't you get started on the potato salad?" she said and gestured to the sack of potatoes at the end of the counter near the sink.

"The tomato salad? Why, certainly." And he moved toward the crates of tomatoes and lettuces that had been picked the day before.

Sure, why not. We'll do the potato salad later. Her blood pressure increased slightly, and she could feel her heart pumping. I'm fine. I can handle this.

Phoenix bounced in the door a few minutes later. A tall, thin, White woman, she was a spry 82-year-old with purple hair tied up in a bun, wearing a lavender sundress, and eager to help.

"You called me?" she said. "I was doing chair yoga, but that can wait. What can I do?"

"Can you get started on the Out of This World Onion Dip? The sour cream is in the fridge."

Maya turned back to the baked beans recipe. Phoenix opened the huge walk-in refrigerator door and went in to get the sour cream.

Gwion was whistling loudly as he was chopping tomatoes. No one heard the solid metal door shut.

Nighthawk, a gray-haired woman of Indian descent, medium height with thick dark glasses, trudged in with a dour look on her face and a frumpy cotton apron that looked as if it could use strong detergent.

"I was polishing my altar stones when you called," she said. "Where are all of your usual helpers?" Nighthawk stood in the doorway with legs akimbo and hands on her hips.

"I called everyone, but so far, it's only you three," Maya said, and her blood pressure inched up another notch. "Could you start chopping the potatoes for the potato salad?"

"Where is a knife? And a cutting board?"

Maya gave Nighthawk the smallest utility knife she could find and a wooden cutting board. She pointed to the sack of potatoes on the counter.

"Help. Help." A soft, muffled sound wafted into the kitchen.

Maya thought she heard something but wasn't sure. Maybe she was imagining things.

Gwion started with Danny Boy, whistling with his whole Irish soul. Maya turned back to the baked beans recipe, and the blood in her heart pumped even stronger. A throbbing in her temple near her right eye momentarily distracted her.

Now Gwion had moved to the singing part of the song and was regaling the kitchen with his finest baritone, loud enough to reach the back of the auditorium. It was a lovely song, but – Maya was having trouble concentrating.

Maple syrup or brown sugar? What did she put in the baked beans last time when they turned out so well?

When she turned to move to the pantry, Nighthawk was standing right behind her with the knife in her hand.

"Oh," Maya felt a jolt of fear, and her blood pressure slid further.

"I've finished chopping the potatoes." Maya looked at the pile of potatoes on the cutting board and saw bits of dirt and grass amidst the small white pieces with their brown skins still on.

That's right. I told her to chop the potatoes, not wash or peel them, just chop them. And she did what I told her to.

"Help!" And banging. Something was definitely happening.

She began to look around the kitchen for the sound when Eddie burst through the swinging doors. He had on his heavy fire-fighting boots and a wild look in his eyes.

"Where's Birdie?"

"I don't know. What's wrong?"

"We were setting up the vendor's tent, and Maple smashed his foot with the iron mallet. I took him to the Healing Center, but no one was there. I don't know what to do."

"Help. Please. Help!"

Birdie sauntered into the kitchen, her right wrist wrapped with an Ace bandage. She was pulling her right ring finger and massaging her hand.

"What's going on?"

"Maple's hurt. He's in the Healing Center. Where's Lois?" Maya wished she could return to her recipe; her head was starting to throb.

"She just went to the bathroom; she should be back there by now."

"Please. I'm cold." Where was that sound?

"Shhh, Gwion." But he didn't hear her and moved on to verse two.

"Gwion, shush!" she said more forcefully. She turned around to try to make the sound.

Lois hobbled in with her walker. "We have to call the doctor."

"No," Birdie said.

"Yes," Lois said. "Maple may have broken his toe, and you need a cortisone shot. We need a medical professional. I can only do so much."

"Help, please! I'm cold." Gwion's whistling trills were other-worldly.

"Gwion, shut up!" Maya blurted.

"What did you say?" Gwion turned toward her, smiling affably.

"I said, shut up. Please."

Gwion closed his mouth and hung his head.

"Whatever you say, milady." Maya immediately felt guilty and walked over to hug him.

"I'm sorry, Gwion. I didn't mean to…"

Lois opened her mouth to respond to Birdie but was cut short by Taylor rushing in with a worried look on his face. His calm demeanor seemed to have deserted him. He was clutching his notebook.

"Help! Please! Help!"

The fridge. Maya swung around. Where was Phoenix? Oh, no. She locked herself in the refrigerator. Blood pressure must be up to 160 by now.

Taylor went over to Birdie. He consulted his notebook. "I just went by Acorn and Rose's place to get more help for setup, and they're both out of it. Just like Twig. So I swung by Dandelion's to see if she might be available, but she's sitting on the floor humming and swaying back and forth. Then I ran into Victoria on my way here, and she said that Amethyst and the little old lady she lives with, Topaz, are also goners. What's going on? Who's doing the decorations? Where are the banners?"

Maya tried to get to the refrigerator, but she had to elbow her way past Birdie, sidestep Lois' walker, and move Eddie and Taylor aside, which is difficult for a short woman to accomplish with such big men. She finally reached the large, heavy steel door. When she opened it, Phoenix had her arms full with two gallons of sour cream and a frozen smile.

"Oh, thank you. I don't know what happened. I closed the door because you don't want to let the air conditioning out. But then I couldn't get out."

Lois pushed her walker into the kitchen. She was uncharacteristically agitated. "We need to do something about this now. There are way too many people 'out of it'. I thought we had healed them with the chicken. "

"Crap, I don't know what's going on," Birdie said. "But we're going to find out."

"Meanwhile, Maple needs medical attention. Now. And it's obvious that maybe others do, too," Lois said. "We have to call the doctor again."

"I don't trust him," Birdie said. "He's not one of us. He's an insomniac."

"He may not be a witch, but he's always been good to us, Birdie. You know that. I know you think nackers have nothing to offer us, but at this point, we should be open-minded, don't you think? Don't be so uptight about it."

"All right, all right. Just keep that man away from me," Birdie said. Maya was surprised Birdie was so adamant. She thought Birdie liked the doctor.

She felt a pounding in her head. Her blood pressure was spiking. Dizziness forced her to sit down quickly. No one noticed her defeat.

Lois moved to the kitchen phone to call Dr. Payne.

Gwion was whistling again, softly this time. Maya took a deep breath and started looking for a colander so Nighthawk could wash the potatoes. Phoenix was still shivering as she sliced onions for the onion dip.

Eddie was looking over Taylor's list. "Who does that leave?" he said. "Is there anyone who can help us?"

Lois put down the phone and turned to Maya and Birdie. "He's still busy with patients in his office, but he was already planning to come by later this afternoon. I'll do what I can for Maple, and he'll probably be fine for a while. If not, we'll go to urgent care."

Birdie left with Lois to go to the Healing Center to see Maple. Phew, a little bit of quiet.

The phone rang again.

"Hello?"

"Hello, this is Louella from the Central Mountain Bank. Is Lauren Sanders available?"

"No, I'm sorry. She's ill. May I help you?"

"I'm sorry to hear that. But I have urgent business. Are you on the executive board?"

"Hold on. I'll get our president." Maya called down the hall for Birdie. She returned with a puzzled look on her face. Maya handed her the phone and turned back to the kitchen. A few minutes later, Birdie approached her.

"That was the bank," Birdie told her after she hung up. "That awful woman bank manager said that Lightning must have forgotten to transfer the deed from Estella ten years ago because, apparently, the county has no record of the transfer in their system. She said the bank would need to foreclose on the Heart immediately if we can't prove Lightning owned the land. The sheriff's office will be here Monday to seize the property."

Birdie looked frantic. "I have to find the deed," she said. "This was what Mnemosyne was scared would happen. Got any ideas where to look?"

"I've got no clue. But if I know Mnemosyne, it's clearly labeled in a file that says, 'Deed Transfer.' Somewhere."

"Of course. But where is Mnemosyne? What the hell are we going to do?" Birdie sounded shrill.

Maya really wanted to comfort Birdie, but she felt panicky. She could hear her heart beating in her head. "I don't know, Birdie. We have to have faith."

"Sure," Birdie said without much conviction. "I'll find it. And I'll take care of the people who are out of it. And I'll figure out the decorations. And the ritual. And the finances. And oh yes, I'll see you tonight at my house. Pre-Solstice dinner, remember?" Maya stared after her as she hurried down the hall to the DWI office.

All Maya needed was a few minutes of peace and quiet. She recited her usual prayer – Goddess, please help me.

17

HARDWARE AND NAPS

After lunch, Maple leaned against the door frame of the shed. *Goddess, help me get this Festival together,* he prayed. Lois had taped his toes together and securely bandaged them. He held his injured foot up and put his weight on the healthy foot. The crutches they had found in the Healing Center closet were nearby, waiting for him. The pain had subsided to a dull roar.

The setup for the Festival was only half-finished, and now there was another problem besides the fact that the banners had not been finished. The damn raccoons had eaten through the squeaky-clean plastic waste bins looking for food, not believing there was nothing left from the last Festival at Beltane, not even a tortilla chip. Still, those sneaky critters ate huge holes in the sides and lids. Much as Maple appreciated nature and felt a kinship with ignored, displaced, and unfairly maligned creatures in the modern world, this was too much for him.

Metal bins – that would fix them! Even though the Festival was tomorrow, Maple decided he had enough time to get to the hardware store, buy a couple of aluminum trash cans, and finish the setup. He wished he had a helper to run into town for him, but most young people were like

Twig, not on this planet now. Even Oscar, his old buddy, was visiting the moon. He would just have to do it himself. Besides, going into town meant he could take a break from the heavy lifting of setting up tables and tents. His aching back thanked him for the respite, and his throbbing toe reminded him to sink into a recliner sooner rather than later.

The morning had taken its toll on Maya. She wasn't used to running a kitchen like this anymore. Even though Phoenix, Gwion, and Nighthawk had their hearts in the right place, they were exhausting.

She left them to have lunch on their own and searched for a place to rest. In between the larger communal areas, the kitchen, dining hall, administrative offices, and Healing Center, they had built small rooms with elemental themes, perfect for small groups to meet or just for meditating on that element. Residents had decorated and accessorized the rooms as the element spoke to them. Green and brown plants grounded the north Mother Earth room; flutes, recorders, and feathers sang in the east Clean Air room; drums and kazoos, toys, candles, and bright primary colors played in the south Passion of Fire room; and blue fountains and flowing scarves and wall-hangings streamed in the west Water Purification room.

Maya went across the hall into her favorite, the Passion of Fire Room, and found the pile of pillows stacked against the wall, next to the easels with oil and watercolor paints lined up on them. She laid the cushions on the floor and gratefully sank down on the paisley prints. I'll never get up, she thought, but at least my feet and legs will have a break.

The breeze from the half-open windows was warm and heavy, perfect for a summertime snooze. As soon as she laid her head down and closed her eyes, Maya felt herself detach from her body, just like she did when her father was on top of her. It was a light feeling but one that also felt a little nauseating. Even though she knew her body was safe and that no harm would come to her while in this trance, she felt an uneasy sense of danger.

She had wanted to sleep, but ... maybe a little flight in the country would be just as restful.

She looked down and saw The Old Witches Home village from above in its familiar pentacle shape. She loved the haphazard nature of the structures on the five lanes that surrounded the pentagon community building in the center. After ten years, some trees were starting to provide good shade, and the paths with permeable paving stones had become slightly erratic.

She gazed toward Winkton at the end of Route 29, that sleepy town growing and gentrifying, and saw cars with out-of-state license plates parked on the street. A woman with a wide sun hat emerged from the hardware store on Main St. Behind her, a man was pulling two carts, one with bright, colorful flowers and the other laden with a spade, a hoe, a rake, and other assorted gardening tools.

Her attention was suddenly drawn to the dark and dingy store on the corner, and she was sucked inside. At first, she was confused. Where was she? Then she saw the sign on the glass door that read "Olde Magickal Tech Store" backward next to a picture of an old-fashioned computer.

There he was, bent over his keyboard, his face contorted and scowling. She couldn't see exactly what he was doing, but she could hear him muttering, "With air and fire, with stone and light, Anansi, god of spiders, god of stories, infect and blight, infect and blight."

Then, she recognized the laptop he was working on. That was Oscar's laptop! She had given him some of those sheep and pig stickers for his birthday. What was that kid doing with it?

Incense hung in the air around him. Cobwebs in the corners of the room waved in the breeze and seemed to sparkle with malevolence. On the wall behind the young Black man was a tin poster from the French film Anansi. Maya remembered what she had learned about the spider god from Africa, that he was a trickster and a storyteller and had helped the enslaved people in America resist their captivity. He was known for his wisdom and knowledge and his ability to outsmart powerful opponents. She hoped Anansi hadn't been responsible for the cobwebs.

Maya didn't know Henry. She had heard that there was an IT whiz in town, and Angie swore that he could fix anything with a computer. Maya knew he had been in the Heart – was it last week? – to do something with the Wi-Fi, fix the – what was it called – the servant? Angie liked him, but Maya felt something was off. Henry looked like a lost young man who had no sense of style to her. His black jeans and white t-shirt were wrinkled, and he had orange peels and pistachio shells all over his desk.

Maya could see into the room, but the protective aura seemed to repel her every time she started to descend. She felt the presence of a protective pentacle above and below, around the office, enveloping the room in a silvery glow. It flickered as she tried to get closer, and she quickly rose higher.

She saw Henry moving his hands as though he were shaping a dumpling. They were cupped together over Oscar's laptop, and he was rolling something between them, up and down, left and right, patting and shaping. She could see flashes of green and brown goo, as though it were a ball of nasty lime Jell-o that was burned at the edges. An orb of evil intent.

Dang. I wish I could get closer. If he'd only move out of the way.

The drone of his chant was getting louder. It sounded like radio static, like a station just out of range. The incense smoke and the dim light from the greasy windows looked like a scene on an old black and white television set, like an Outer Limits episode. She heard a voice from her past.

There is nothing wrong with your television set. ...We can change the focus to a soft blur or sharpen it to crystal clarity. Sit quietly, and we will control all that you see and hear. .... You are about to experience the awe and mystery that reaches from the inner mind to... The Outer Limits.

Maya felt woozy. She tried to focus on the man below. She tried to hear above the static.

Henry looked up, and Maya shrank back. Did he see her? He caressed the orb in his hands, pressed them together, and flung the orb toward her.

Without thinking, Maya ducked. She watched the orb fly past her, gaining speed as it flew. Flecks of silver, lime green, and brown streamed from it, and she reached out her hand as if she could grab its tail and bring it back.

But it was too fast. She looked down once again, and Henry had passed out on the desk. The image was mottled and losing color. Maya felt herself being pulled back to The Old Witches Home.

She gasped, and her eyes opened. Her body felt heavy and stuck to the pillows beneath her.

What had she seen? She tried to make sense of it, but there was an awful pounding of footsteps approaching her.

Nighthawk was running down the hall, poking her head into all the rooms and calling to her. "Maya! There's a fire in the kitchen! Fire!"

Maple was scuttling as quickly as he could on his crutches. He needed to buy the trash bins and then get back to The Old Witches Home and finish the setup.

"Hey, Sammy," Maple said as he entered the familiar store with its scent of metal and sawdust. He was tempted to browse the aisle of hammers, screwdrivers, and other tools just because he liked picking them up and feeling their weight in his hands. But he had a mission and didn't want to waste time.

Sammy, the 30-something short White woman perched on a bar stool behind the cash register, wore no makeup, and her otherwise clean white polo shirt had what appeared to be a few drops of spittle on the shoulder. She spoke so intently and patiently to a woman with a cart full of pansies, impatiens, and marigolds that she didn't notice Maple's crutches when he came in. The woman's husband – he had that hangdog whatever-you-say-dear look about him – followed her with another cart full of brightly colored garden tools. Maple could hear Sammy explaining that the flowers were annuals, meaning they wouldn't stay alive through the winter and needed full sun. And no, they couldn't get a refund when the plants died in the fall. The line behind the couple was already three people deep, a crowd for this store, and grumbling was getting louder.

Maple remembered how people had treated him when they first moved up here. Plenty of grumbling then, too. But now they recognized him, and he was on a first-name basis with most of the guys who hung around the store, which functioned as an all-purpose town hall for the old farmers in the area.

As he limped down the hardware aisle to the back of the store where the garbage bins lived, he heard low voices from the electrical cords.

"I told you, I fixed it," a youngish, squeaky voice said.

"Then why is the Festival still happening?" an older voice with a slight rasp asked.

Maple turned up his hearing aid. For once, the dang thing would come in handy.

"I don't know. It's active. The loaner transferred the virus to the system. I monitor it from my shop, knowing it's infected at least five units. Probably more. It's hard to tell unless I knew all the IP addresses."

"You said they would be blubbering idiots once this virus got ahold of them. But they're still planning to have this Festival tomorrow. If they get enough donations to keep going, they might be able to pay lawyers too."

"Don't worry. All they have to do is log on and go to their favorite program. It'll mess with their heads, I promise you."

"You better be right. I don't know why I thought a spell would fix them. There's no such thing as magic. If they get the money to fight me, it'll be you who has to pay."

Uh oh. What the heck were these two talking about? He tried to move quietly to the back of the store to sneak a glance up the electronics aisle. But he wasn't used to these damn crutches, and he knocked one of them into a freestanding rack of wind chimes. The tinkling chorus was lovely and loud as though a strong breeze had flown through the store. He pressed himself against the shelves and looked the other way. He waited for them to come around to see what had happened, but he was lucky. They just kept talking.

He recognized the old guy's voice. That lawyer, Huffstickler, came to lunch the other day! The guy who wants to take their land. What a snake!

Maple stumbled to the end of the aisle and peered around the corner. They were at the other end, almost on top of the display of surge protectors, heads nearly touching as they conspired. Huffstickler was in his frumpy gray suit, tie and all, still looking like an imitation of a gangster from the 40's. The other guy in the white t-shirt and black jeans had to be that computer kid who fixed their Wi-Fi.

Or did he fix it? Maybe he did something to mess it up instead. Maybe whatever he did started the illness. Computers have viruses, right? Maybe one got out. What was he saying about the programs messing with their heads?

Maple turned to go back toward the front of the store but banged his injured toe with the crutch and barely missed knocking down the display of macrame pot hangers. Owwww.... He bit his lip to keep his scream to himself.

"Get back to the store and make sure that virus is good and strong and doing what it's supposed to," the growly voice said. "We've got the hearing on Monday. I've got two witnesses who will say that O'Neill was under a spell, but I'm not sure how reliable they are. They're witches, too. They keep saying they need to consult some god with a hammer to which they owe allegiance. Weird. Thank goodness you got rid of the deed transfer. You did do that, didn't you? I want the court to think Lightning never really owned the land in the first place."

"Yes, yes. There's no record of the transfer. They would have to find the actual hard copy of the deed, which you've already taken care of. Those damn witches are going to get it."

"Good. Louella is calling in the loan. They can't have enough money to pay lawyers and the bank too. She'll have to foreclose, that's for sure. One way or another, I'll get the place."

That was all Maple needed to hear. He watched the entrance from behind a display of brooms and mops, breathing slowly and letting the pain in his foot subside. Finally, a frumpy suit and a pair of black jeans headed for the exit.

"Watch where you're going, lady," the suit said to the woman with the flowers after she stopped to admire a swan lawn ornament near the entrance.

"You watch yourself," she replied. Her husband, pulling the two carts, collided with black jeans guy. Behind him, a heavyset woman with a soda can in one hand and an armful of cushions in the other fell forward, spilling the soda. Her cushions landed on purple, yellow, and red flowers in the husband's cart.

"Oh, damn," she said, dabbing at the stains on her oversized American flag t-shirt.

"I'm so sorry," the harried husband said.

"Well, let's just all move it, don't you think?" She grabbed her cushions from the deflated flowers and pushed everyone aside. The automatic doors whooshed open just in time to let her out. The others followed.

Maple waited another minute to ensure the coast was clear and to catch his breath. All was quiet. Finally. He covered the side of his face with his hand and began his move.

"Did you find everything you need, Maple?" Sammy asked as he hobbled past. "What's up with your foot?"

"Nothing. All good," he grunted, feeling bad that he was being rude, but it was urgent.

Forget the aluminum bins, he thought. We'll just use garbage bags. Sorry, planet, I know you don't like plastic. I have to get back to the village. I have to talk with Birdie and Maya.

18

THE SLEEPING SICKNESS

Birdie was busy. She had agreed to be the doctor's driver. But when she came to pick up Lois to go with them, she saw Lois wrapping Gwion's hand. Phoenix was standing off to the side, agitated and teary. She could hear Maya in the kitchen banging pots and cursing.

"What happened?" Birdie asked.

Lois described the situation as if she were reporting symptoms during clinical rounds. "Some dishcloths were left on the stove. They caught fire when Phoenix went to boil some water for tea. Gwion grabbed them, got burned, and dropped them into the skillet on the range. The bacon grease in the skillet lit up. Gwion poured water on it, which made the flames jump to the potholders on the counter. Nothing else burned. Maya put the whole thing out with a fire blanket. She's cleaning it all up now."

"Wow," said Birdie. "Just what we need. Was anyone else hurt?"

"Just Gwion here. He'll be okay."

"I am so sorry," Gwion said, looking quite chagrined. "I thought I was doing the right thing. I forgot you're not supposed to throw water on a grease fire."

"I'm so sorry, too," Phoenix said. "I should have known better. We had a fire when I was a girl. We had to run out of the house in the middle of the night, and I lost my doll, Suzette. She was so pretty, with blond hair and blue eyes. Not like me at all, but I didn't care." Phoenix continued recalling the Disney doll, her childhood, her sister who tried to steal Suzette from her, her dog, Cassidy, her cat, Ginger, all the other pets in the neighborhood, her friends from school, and all the streets in the town in New Hampshire where she lived.

She'll go on for another hour, Birdie thought.

"What time is the doctor getting here?" she interrupted.

Ever patient and calm, Lois looked at Birdie as though she were a troublesome toddler.

"Soon, dear. You're going to have to take him. I can't leave here right now. Could you hand me those scissors?" Birdie grabbed the scissors off the counter and gave them to Lois. As she did, she noticed lime green goo and brown-speckled ash on the counter, no doubt blown in from the kitchen.

Birdie tried to brush the ash off the counter but only smeared it and created a sooty green and brown blob. Her vision became blurry, and her fingers tingled and burned. She realized that it wasn't just ash, but her mind was too foggy to complete the thought and figure out what it really was.

"Don't worry; I'll clean it up," she heard Lois say, realizing she had forgotten other people were there. I'm losing it. I better get out of here.

"I'll go wait for the doctor," she said.

Birdie pulled Lois's list from her pocket of the others stricken. Twenty-two. People had been calling Lois for two days, reporting friends or housemates who couldn't wake up. She had posted a notice outside the Healing Center asking people to notify her when they knew of someone who had been taken ill by the Sleeping Sickness, as they were calling it, even though it really wasn't a sleeping sickness. A Silly Sickness, Maya called it, and Birdie thought that name was more apt.

It would take them all afternoon to visit everyone on the list, meaning she would spend more time with Tom than Birdie was prepared for. She tried to think of safe topics to discuss but decided that the only really safe topic was the patients. He sat beside her in the golf cart, his bag on his lap, exuding calmness as her anxiety mounted.

Each new patient only added to the puzzle. They were as healthy as they had been, most of them being on the youngish side of the Old Witches Home demographic, meaning they were under 60. But they were all "out of it," muttering strange things, moving their bodies in strange ways, tapping their fingers, flexing their thumbs, and appearing to be in another world. They would rouse when Tom tried to wake them up, but they couldn't focus, and nothing they said made sense. He could get most of them to drink water, but some were unresponsive. Body temperatures were low, heart rates were sluggish, and some people had been incontinent, forcing Birdie and Tom to clean them up and find fresh underwear.

Tom was gentle but non-committal when Birdie pressed him for a diagnosis and treatment options.

"I just don't know, Birdie," he said. "I've never seen anything like this. They're fine in most ways, but they're fading. We need to keep an eye on them and keep them hydrated. I've searched the internet and talked to several colleagues, but no one has seen anything like this. Even the CDC has no clue. Their symptoms are like delirium, but there's no obvious cause. I'm afraid we just need to keep searching for more information."

His assessment didn't ease Birdie's worries at all. They didn't have enough caregivers to support everyone, and she couldn't do this daily. And how would they hold the Festival? They needed money to pay the bank and save their land. She knew she was glowering and tried to avoid looking at him.

"How's your hand?" Tom asked, distracting her. They were sitting in the cart, not moving, while Birdie reviewed the list and tried to decide which witch to visit next. "Lois mentioned you were having some issues when she called me."

"Oh, it's fine," Birdie said.

"May I?" He reached toward her, and Birdie felt compelled to extend her right hand to his. He pulled at her finger, and she winced. He turned it over in his hand, probing the wrist and the fleshy mounds of the palm. She knew it was purely medical, but his fingers were warm, and the pressure was right. Her heart sped up a little, and her tongue involuntarily caressed her lower lip.

"If your finger bothers you, I can give you a cortisone shot that might help. I think the sprain in your wrist from last year has healed. Any pain there now is probably arthritis." He smiled reassuringly at Birdie and held her hand for a moment longer.

Birdie pulled her hand back slowly. It had felt so natural, letting him hold her hand. She remembered what it was like to feel the excitement of falling in love. There was no high in the world that could beat it. Then, she remembered the anguish of rejection, misunderstandings, and hurt words. Like alcohol, love could turn on you and change from comfort to conflict, which could cause trouble instead of solving problems. No, she thought, not now. I'm fine. I don't need this.

"Tell me about Ruth," she said to get back to guarded territory until they could get to the next patient. "Where did you meet?"

Tom was open and candid about his marriage and the ups and downs. He said there had been difficulties long before she got sick, but he didn't want to leave her when she needed him.

The more he shared, the more Birdie found herself telling him about her history. She kept telling herself to hold back and then realized she had exposed one more layer of experiences after another.

"Only one more," she said, finally. "On Wisdom West." She turned the cart in that direction and gazed ahead. She could feel Tom's eyes on her.

Back at the Healing Center, they checked in with Lois. Both Tom and Lois were worried that the number of the afflicted was climbing. But Birdie was concerned about their homes.

"I know this is bad for the people who are out of it, but this is also going to put a major damper on the Festival," Birdie said. "A third of the village is afflicted with this silly sleeping sickness, and we don't even know what it is? What if the town finds out about it? No one will want to come here tomorrow. We need their money. If we want to keep the land."

"It's strange – this illness is affecting more young than old people," Lois said, ignoring Birdie and speaking to Tom directly.

"Everyone is basically fine right now, but their vitals are deteriorating. Amethyst's heart rate and blood pressure are dangerously low. And her partner, Topaz, is also unresponsive. I'm concerned that they will only get worse if they don't get water and nutrients," Tom said.

"Oh, dear. We'll have to work on that. I can make sure they get fluids, but there are so many of them. I don't think we have enough caregivers. And we definitely don't have enough beds here in the clinic. Can you help us?" Lois asked.

"Whatever you need," Tom agreed. "I'll bring IV equipment in the morning. Can you monitor them overnight?"

"I'll ask Eddie to go round their houses after dinner. He used to be an EMT, you know. He'll notify me if someone needs anything. Most people have roommates or neighbors who have been staying with them. And then we can do another sweep in the morning with electrolytes or saline solutions." Birdie was impressed with Lois' cool. She wished she felt that way.

"Maya and Maple are meeting at my house for supper," Birdie said. "Would you like to join us? We could talk about it then." She looked at Lois and Tom.

"I'm exhausted," Lois said. "I'd like to head home and work on the hydration plan tonight. Maybe Diego can help me. Thanks anyway."

"I'd love to join you," Tom said. His eager smile made Birdie wonder whether letting him into her house was such a good idea. Lois picked up the phone with the extra-large numbers to call Diego.

19

DINNER AT BIRDIE'S HOUSE

Birdie took Tom back to her house, where she set about making pasta and salad.

"Thanks so much for inviting me to dinner," he said, sitting at the kitchen table. "I get pretty tired of eating alone."

"Doesn't Louella make dinner for you?" Birdie had seen Tom with the 50-something bank manager going to the diner in town for lunch one day.

"Louella and I are just friends," Tom said. "She's too busy with her teenagers to have time for me. And that's quite okay with me. Besides, I think she's been seeing Mr. Huffstickler, the lawyer in town."

Birdie grunted, both pleased and disquieted by Tom's candor and worried about the liaison between Louella and Huffstickler. She put the pot of water on the stove to boil and took the vegetables out of the refrigerator for the salad.

While she worked, she could feel Tom watching her. They were both quiet. When she dropped the chopping knife, Tom jumped up to grab it, but she had already picked it up.

She broke the awkward silence by mentioning that the vegetables in the salad were ones that Oscar and Rabbit had given her. Tom then talked about his successes with his own garden. The tension between them lessened somewhat but was still filled with more than her concern about Mnemosyne and the others. Birdie's head throbbed like someone was lightly rapping on a door, and her right hand still felt overcharged and tingly. She was glad when Maya and Maple arrived to distract her.

Maya walked in without knocking like she usually did.

"Did you hear about the fire?" she said. "I've never had a fire in my kitchen before. You would think they're trying to burn us out."

"Who?" asked Tom.

"That awful lawyer and his capitalist cronies." Maya had her I'm-your-mother-don't-you-dare-cross-me look on her face. "I wouldn't put it past that man."

"That doesn't make sense," Birdie said. "There's no way he could have gotten into the kitchen without you or someone else knowing. You were in there all day."

They heard a stomping sound out on the walkway, followed by a swishing as though someone was banging on a drum and then feathering it. The sounds repeated, getting louder as whoever made them got closer.

Finally, there was a knock. Maya opened it, and Maple was in the doorway, leaning against the frame and huffing.

"I just came back from the hardware store," he said. "They were there, and they're in on it together."

"Who's in on what?" Birdie asked.

"Huffstickler. And the kid from the computer store." Maple shared everything he overheard in the electronics aisle.

"Crap," Birdie said.

"Yeah," Maya agreed. "I haven't told you what I saw when I napped this afternoon. With all the craziness in the kitchen today, I almost forgot," she said, then glanced at Tom sitting at the table. She gave Birdie a questioning look, but Birdie just shrugged.

"You might as well spill it. Hopefully, this nacker is on our side," Birdie said with a wary look at Tom.

"I did my astral traveling thing," Maya said, trying not to notice what Tom might think of her for saying such a thing.

"Yeah? Where did you go?" Birdie wasn't sure she believed Maya could travel anywhere but saw no harm in humoring her. Maple had sat down, and his good leg was jiggling rapidly.

"I went into town. Have you noticed how many weekenders are in town? There wasn't even one parking spot on Main Street. There was this lady coming out of the hardware store – all dressed up, with makeup and a hat and a bunch of flowers and gardening tools."

"I saw her!" Maple said. "Her poor husband." He chuckled.

"I know, right?" Maya said and chuckled too.

"Okay. And?" Birdie said.

"Oh, yeah, I got pulled into the Tech Store for some reason. The kid in there was working on Oscar's laptop. I recognized it from all the stickers he had on it. He's got cows, horses, sheep, goats, and even baby chicks. It's so cute, like a little farm on the laptop.

"And – there was something else, like a neon cloud over the kid's head. But it wasn't really a cloud. It was a circle of energy, with spikes all over it, like this." Maya pointed her fingers and jabbed the air to the left and right in front of her.

"It was very creepy – it seemed like there were cobwebs everywhere. And he was muttering something. I didn't like it."

Birdie glanced at Tom. He had a scowl on his face.

"That's weird," Birdie said.

"It is. I told you the kid is in on it," Maple said excitedly. "He said everyone should be infected by now." He jumped up on his bad foot, grimaced, and quickly sat back down.

"Yeah, the store is called The Olde Magick Tech Store," Maya added.

"The name doesn't mean anything," Birdie said. "I'm sure that's not it. I can't believe that nacker kid would know how to put a spell on us like that. I bet our problems are closer to home." She was thinking of Bjorn and his antagonism toward the ReDreaming witches. He always seemed to be objecting, no matter what they did. Maybe he was trying to take over and slipped some kind of weird poison into people's food.

"No, he's definitely in on it," Maple said. "He and Huffstickler were conspiring, and Huffstickler told him that if the Festival went well, the kid would pay. He also said he has two people who will testify in court that we coerced Lightning to leave us the land."

"Who?" Maya asked.

"He said they worshipped a god with a hammer, so it must be Bjorn and Charlie," Maple said.

"Huffstickler has also been spreading rumors," Birdie said. "When she showed me the letter, Mnemosyne told me what the lady at the post office said. Then she said something about hash and eggs named 'bad witches.' I'm not sure what she was talking about."

Birdie dropped the salad tongs, bringing the salad to the table, and that time, Tom got to them before she did. He rinsed them off in the sink and touched Birdie's arm before giving them to her. His touch was soft, a gentle caress that Birdie felt throughout her torso, an unfamiliar but quite welcome sensation.

"Can't we do something about Bjorn and Charlie now?" Maple said.

"Let's just wait until after the Festival," Birdie said, feeling overwhelmed. She just wanted to sit and do nothing for a while.

"I really thought that the chicken we sacrificed would bring us strength and protection, but I guess it didn't," Maya said. "Magic doesn't always work, does it?"

"You never know," Birdie said. "There may be other things that aren't apparent to us. You know how magic works, sometimes behind the scenes or under the radar. Don't lose hope. We'll get Huffstickler yet."

"Well, I also have to figure out a way to collect garbage that the raccoons won't get at," Maple said. "I tried putting a banishing spell on the garbage bins to keep those critters out, but it doesn't seem to have worked. And where are the banners and the other decorations? Twig and Angie were supposed to do them."

No one said anything. Birdie looked at Tom, but he was looking down with a faraway look on his face. What was he thinking? She chastised herself for hoping that he would rescue them.

Birdie told Maya and Maple about the discussion with Lois about dehydration and food deprivation.

"We gave everyone water this afternoon, and left instructions with whoever was taking care of them to give them water regularly, but not everyone had someone staying with them. Some just had neighbors checking in. And if they don't get enough water, they could get really sick, like crazy sick! Delirious more than they already are."

"I checked everyone's vitals and no one is in imminent danger," Tom reassured the group. "But I know some of them have underlying conditions that could get worse. Soon."

"Or bladder or kidney infections or seizures!" Birdie added.

Maya offered to make soup for everyone, but Birdie said she had enough to do with the feast and that they had to let Lois handle it. She would get Diego and Eddie to help her.

"Dang, that's scary," Maple said, and everyone nodded. The anxiety in the air was palpable.

"Don't worry," Tom said. "I'll work with Lois and we can hydrate people with IVs if necessary."

Supper was a glum affair. Everyone appeared to be lost in their own thoughts. No one had any good suggestions for what to do about the illness. Or anything else, for that matter.

Birdie was thinking about magic, how you could have what you thought were the best intentions in the world, how you could know exactly what you wanted, how you could do the most perfect spell and the most powerful ritual, and then how the Goddess would make something happen that you weren't expecting and could never have imagined, and how it was exactly what you needed. She usually had faith in the Goddess, she usually knew how it worked. But today, she wasn't so sure. All she wanted was to keep her home with her friends. Did the Goddess really have their backs?

She tried to lighten the mood with Almond Joy ice cream for dessert, of which Tom had a large bowl with chocolate sprinkles, but nothing helped.

Finally, Maple blurted out what he was thinking.

"The Summer Solstice Festival is tomorrow! We need people to run the damn thing, and a whole bunch of them are sick. Isn't there anything you can do?"

He looked at Tom and then quickly looked down at his bowl of ice cream. Birdie knew he thought a man with an MD ought to do more than simply suggest waiting and giving people water.

Maya burst out. "I can't do this," she said. "This Festival is going to be the death of me. I have no idea what people are bringing, who's making what, or what we need. And now this stupid illness. I can't believe I let Angie talk me into using that cursed computer. Now everyone will think this old lady can't even handle a potluck. And my friends are going to die because I can't even feed them."

"No, they won't. We'll figure it out. You've been a caterer longer than anyone in this town. Your feasts are famous! You'll get it. We'll help you. And we'll figure out how to help everyone else, too." Birdie was starting to feel a bit panicky herself.

"We don't have time," Maple said. "I need the help now. I can't set everything up without Oscar, and all the young guys are out of it." His uncharacteristic whine scared Birdie more than Maya's tears. If these two were falling apart, and she didn't have Mnemosyne, what hope did she have of keeping it together? Why did Lightning have to die?

To Birdie's annoyance, Tom remained calm. He sipped his chamomile tea silently. He had caused enough trouble already, what with scaring them about the water and food thing. It was only a couple of days. Everyone would be all right. Wouldn't they?

"Anything I can do to help?" Tom offered.

"Can you lead a Spiral Dance?" Birdie retorted. She began clearing dishes. Maya began to help her, but Birdie shooed her away. She had a system; Maya only messed things up.

Maple stood up and walked over to Maya, enveloping her warmly. She sank into his shoulder.

Birdie soaped up a sponge and began washing the plates. Her hands were slippery; the glass she held fell and smashed into bits. The noise startled everyone. She tried to pick up the pieces, but the glass had splintered, and there were tiny shards all over the bottom of the sink. Her hands were covered with foam and shiny bits of sharp glass. Drops of red were swirling in the water.

"Damn," she yelled. "Damn, damn, damn."

"Let me help you," Tom said. He walked to her side, and she was tempted to lean into him, but she had to get it together. She just had to.

"Thanks, but no," Birdie said, pushing him away. Suddenly, she turned around to face Maple and Maya, leaving the water running and shards of glass in the sink.

"What are we going to do about the hearing on Monday?"

Maya and Maple looked at her, their blank faces revealing they had forgotten about the hearing.

"Someone has to go. Mnemosyne can't do it. Not the way she is now. Huffstickler will win if we can't prove we didn't coerce Lightning. And where is the deed transfer? And where will we get the money to pay the balloon payment? What are we going to do?"

Tom turned off the water.

Birdie looked at Maya. Then she looked at Maple. Finally, she turned and looked at Tom.

"Well?"

No one said anything. They all just stood still and stared at Birdie.

"Oh, forget it," she said, her voice rising as she returned to the sink. "I'll take care of it."

She threw the towel on the counter and turned the water on full force. Her back was an impenetrable wall.

"Why don't you all just go home?" she shouted. "Don't worry. Birdie will handle it. Birdie will figure it out. Birdie will come to the rescue. She always does. I don't need any help. Just go away." She turned, stomped into the bathroom, and shut the door.

The tears just wouldn't be held back any longer.

"Crap," she heard Maple say. She imagined they were still hugging.

She didn't want to listen to them. She didn't want to have anything to do with them. She wanted Mnemosyne. Or Lightning. Someone smarter than her. Someone stronger than her.

"There's nothing anyone can do tonight," she could hear Tom's muffled voice. "Maybe you all should go home. I'll talk with her."

Tom? What the hell does he think he's going to do?

She sat on the toilet, breathing slowly. She heard the front door open and close and the water in the kitchen turn off and on, then off again. She just kept sitting and breathing, sitting and breathing.

The tears subsided. She splashed cold water on her face and relieved her bladder.

All right, she thought. I'm ready. Might as well face him. Let's get this over with.

Finally, Birdie came out of the bathroom. She was never able to stay mad for long. Tom was drying the pasta pot and setting it back on the stove.

"Did they leave? Were they mad at me? I hate it when I blow up like that."

"I don't think they were mad. Everyone is a little upset." His calm voice soothed Birdie.

"I stayed because I was worried about you. But I can leave if you want me to," Tom said. "You must be tired."

"I am, but I'm more confused than anything. You can stay for a while if you'd like."

Birdie sat on the couch and was surprised when Tom sat beside her. There was a perfectly good chair on the other side of the room.

"I just don't understand. What is wrong with everyone? What the heck did those asshole insomniacs do?" Birdie thought keeping the conversation to her afflicted friends might be the wisest course of action. "How can we help them?"

"Tomorrow, we'll figure out how to get some fluids into them. If we have to, we can set up IVs. I'm sure Lois will have a good plan."

He sounded sure of himself and that nothing bad would happen. Birdie wasn't so sure but allowed herself to sink into the couch next to him.

"You know, Birdie, I've watched you for ten years now, and if anyone can figure out what to do, it will be you."

She groaned. "I really wish you hadn't said that."

"Why not?"

"I'm not that strong, and I'm getting old," she said. "Everyone has said, oh, don't worry, Birdie will handle it. And I have. But I don't want to anymore. I'm old. I'm not strong – or smart – anymore. Don't you know what happens to people when they get old? They start to lose it."

"You're not losing it, Birdie. I think you're in great shape."

"For an old broad, I guess."

"No, for any age. I really like you, Birdie. You're amazing."

She was close to tears again; my god, she didn't realize she was this tired. And it certainly wasn't Tom's fault. No need to take it out on him. He's being really nice.

"I'm sorry. Maybe you ought to leave. I'll be fine."

"I could leave, but I don't want to. Is it okay if I stay a while?"

"I guess."

Tom reached over and pulled Birdie into a hug. It felt awkward, but it also felt nice.

"I wish I knew what was wrong with everyone. Then maybe we could fix it," Birdie said.

Tom pulled her closer, and she put her head on his shoulder.

"Should I put on some music?" she said. She had to get up from the couch and straighten out her back.

Tom followed her to the wall shelves where the phonograph and records lived. The arrangement of vinyl, stereo equipment, CDs, and cassettes on the shelves made her feel at home; it was exactly the same as all the other houses and apartments she had lived in for the last forty years.

"Wow, you have some wonderful oldies," Tom said. "You actually have the *White Album*. I haven't listened to that album for years. Music was really music back then, wasn't it?"

"Yeah. That album has the scratches to show for it, too. I'm afraid we won't be listening to that one tonight. I'm not sure why I still have it; it's unplayable. Sentimental value, I guess."

"There are numbered copies of this album on E-Bay that go for a lot of money. Is yours numbered?"

"Since you can't play it, I don't think it matters."

"Well, I could bring the songs up on Pandora if you want to listen." Tom pulled out his phone. "What's the Wi-Fi password here? The network is OldWitchHouseFun, right?"

"Yes. The password is 'OpenSesame60+'."

"Hmmm. It's trying to connect, but it's certainly taking time. Usually, the connection takes only a few seconds."

"Huh. That kid from the computer store worked on the Wi-Fi just a few days ago. He promised that it would run better. It would facilitate a 'free flow of information,' he said. He probably put a bug in it."

"How many people are on it? Sometimes there's a lag if too many people are using the system at the same time."

"But that's what he was supposed to fix. He was supposed to make it so everyone in the village could get on at the same time. I don't get it. What the hell was he doing here? He said he was upgrading our servant." Servant? Butler? Waitress? None of them sounded right.

"Well, I'm on it, but I can't get my Pandora to load. It's taking forever." Birdie heard *"Blackbird singing in the dead of night"*, then nothing for two seconds, then *"Take these broken ..."* and then nothing again.

"That's worse than my scratchy record," she said. "Dang. That must be what that kid messed with. He must have infected the Wi-Fi. Usually, this time of night, no one is using it except Oscar with his farming game. The only other person I know who used the Wi-Fi late at night was Mnemosyne. She used to say that she liked working late at night because it was quiet and the signal was strong."

"Well, neither one of them is on the system now," Tom turned the power off on his phone, waited a few seconds, and then turned it back on.

"You're right. That's it. I wonder who else used the system late at night. Angie? Twig?"

"What are you thinking?" Tom said.

"What did Maple say that the kid in the hardware store said? That everyone should be infected by now? What if what's wrong with Angie and everyone is not a regular virus, but a computer virus?"

"A computer virus?"

"Yeah! What if the kid concocted some kind of spell or hex? He must have. What if it was their computer or the Wi-Fi or the internet or something that infected them? Made them crazy?" Birdie started feeling hopeful again. If they knew what was causing the illness, maybe there was a way out of it.

"That's damn unlikely, Birdie. Those kinds of things don't happen in real life, just fantasy novels."

"Sure, it is unlikely, but maybe...."

"Who are the people who aren't affected? Do they use computers a lot?"

"Well, I don't, and when I tried to send an email, I got this very strange feeling up my arm, and my computer got all wonky. Maple never uses the computer – he says they're for younguns – and Maya prides herself on perfect handwriting. A lot of the people here haven't even figured out how to read their emails."

"A computer virus? Are you sure?" Tom chuckled. "Maybe you really are losing it, Birdie."

"Magic is real," she said. "If that kid put a spell on our computers ..." Birdie felt stung – was he laughing at her? Then, the realization that something awful had infected their system and she didn't know what to do about it intruded and began to blossom. "I just didn't think that kid had it in him. Shit. What do we do now?"

"There's nothing to do tonight. Let's listen to some music, have some tea, and deal with it in the morning."

"That's easy for you to say. You seem pretty nonchalant about it. Shouldn't we come up with a plan?" Birdie's voice was becoming shrill again.

"Use the Serenity Prayer," he said. "Accept the things you cannot change."

"That's just like a nacker. Let someone else handle it. Thanks a lot."

"Birdie, it's okay. We'll fix it. I don't know how, but we will. Everyone I saw this afternoon is as healthy as can be. Let them rest. And you should get some rest, too. We'll figure out a way to get them hydrated tomorrow. They'll be okay."

"I don't need rest. I need to figure out what to do. And no, they won't. You don't know anything about them. Or about us. You think everything will be okay because it's always been okay for you. You're a middle-class white man. You don't even know what kind of privilege you have. But it's not okay, and it has never been for us. We used to be burned at the stake, you know?"

"Birdie, relax. Come here. Sit down."

"No, I won't sit down. You're like every other man I've ever known, thinking you know everything. Mansplaining. You don't know anything. Magic is real; magic works and these people have used magic against us."

"Okay, okay, I get it. You don't need to yell at me."

She spoke louder this time. "No, you don't get it. You don't get anything. You don't know what it's like to feel like you're different, that you don't belong anywhere, that no one trusts or likes you. That people are laughing at you behind your back. Nackers like you have really screwed up our world, our planet. We're trying to do something different here, and Huffstickler's trying to stop us. We have a home here. And that man wants to take it away from us."

She was close to tears again, but she was damned if she was going to let him see her cry.

"Birdie, you're getting emotional. Maybe we ought to talk about this another time." His voice was calm and low.

"Don't put me off! Of course, I'm emotional. If you're not enraged, you're not paying attention. My home is under attack!"

"I'm sorry, Birdie, I didn't mean to imply…" He put his phone in his pocket and moved toward the couch.

"No, no one ever does. They don't mean to… but they do it anyway.

It's not their problem. And then they leave – letting other people clean up their mess. So why don't you get it over with? Just leave. Leave now. You know you want to." She got up to go into the kitchen.

"No, I don't. Birdie..."

"Well, I want you to. Go. Leave. Let me be. We'll figure this out without you." She turned back to him.

Birdie scowled, daring him to look at her and be nice. She refused to believe a word he said.

He stood still, looking at her. She could see that he was trying to find a chink in her armor. But she was practiced at defending herself. It wasn't there. He gave up.

"Okay." He grabbed his medical bag by the door. "I'll see you tomorrow at the Festival. I'll talk to Lois in the morning. But call me if you need anything. Anything." Again, he searched her eyes.

"I won't." She turned her back to him and started putting the dishes away. She should thank him for washing them, but she wouldn't. He got a free meal out of her.

"Well, I guess, bye then." He hesitated and looked back at her. Birdie didn't look up. She heard the door latch, then went over and flipped the deadbolt.

She heard a soft meow. She opened the door and let Hermes in. She looked into the night, a bright, almost full moon casting shadows through the trees. A dark figure walked down the familiar path away from her.

After Tom left, Birdie sat on the couch. She thought some meditation would calm her enough so that she could sleep. But the basketball of anxiety in her stomach was dribbling down the court.

She lit her mustard-colored creativity candle and began the deep breathing that usually took her into a tranquil frame of mind and opened her heart. Still nothing, just a jump shot into her head.

Danger was creeping around the edges of her mind and taking root in her solar plexus. It wasn't just the fact that she was in pain due to being old, or that there was a computer virus infecting her friends, and people may be dying due to lack of food and water, or that they were in danger of losing their home to a nasty lawyer. There was something else tightening that knot and filling her with dread.

She had to get rid of the knot in order to function. It was up to her to figure out what to do about the hearing, the computer virus, the balloon payment, and everything else. She was having trouble thinking. Meditating was the only way she knew to relax her mind and clear the fuzz away.

She hadn't felt quite this way for years, but there it was, that feeling of knife-edged butterflies. It was always there when she was about to expose herself in one way or another, about to let the world see her warts and her failings. So many people saw her as strong, confident, in control, but she knew the real story. She was puny and scared and absolutely incompetent. She had no idea what she was doing and was too afraid to ask for help. She never had, and now she's too old to learn. That was the real Birdie.

That was why Birdie had to become a witch. That was the Birdie that made up spells at night to protect herself because she didn't know what else to do, and she couldn't admit to anyone that she felt threatened. She worked with the pictures inside her head and used them to empower her and keep her safe. She reached out to spirit guides, angels, gods and goddesses, and anyone she could think of to come to her aid, as long as she didn't have to tell another human being what she needed. She was fine as long as she didn't have to voice her fears or admit her insecurities out loud in front of others. She had the unseen world at her back, and that was enough.

Or so she thought. But she knew that reliance on her ethereal support system had its drawbacks. It meant she was always holding secrets, sometimes even from herself. And it meant that no one could ever come close because they could never get through the cosmic security checkpoint Birdie had set up. No one could get inside her dreams and her conscious mind to touch her heart.

Birdie had been safe, stable, and satisfied for so many years. She had her friends, good, close, loving, supportive friends whom she trusted and would do anything for. Maya, Maple, Mnemosyne, Lightning, and all the others at the Old Witches Home – she loved them fiercely and loyally – even Bjorn, that right-wing reactionary whose beliefs were diametrically opposed to hers. She would fight to the death for her community, for their right to thrive in this world, and she would enlist all her demons, angels, and goblins to fight by her side if she needed to.

Now, it was all threatened. She was getting old, and maybe she really was losing it. Maybe Tom was right, and she was really a joke. Maybe she was just a caricature, an old witch with a cat. Where was her pointy hat? Oh, that's right, it was in the closet, right next to the brooms.

But no, the perils were real. Huffstickler would take the land and build condos and a golf course. All their work to build a sustainable community that would honor the land, improve the soil, and sequester carbon was about to be destroyed. Instead of being part of the solution, their homes would be part of the problem, just like the world they had all chosen to leave.

She thought about how hard they worked to govern themselves differently, to create a community that respected all voices and empowered those who had been on the fringes of mainstream society. They built systems to take care of each other and provide for those who needed more help than others. Now, the community was falling apart. Bjorn had angered over half the witches, and this virus incapacitated the others. How could they ever unite to fight for their homes?

And what would she do if she lost Mnemosyne, that stable voice of reason, the connection to the established world they could trust? Mnemosyne was always able to explain how white supremacy, capitalism, and overculture worked in a way that made some kind of sense and gave them some way of maintaining their own way of living and coexisting peacefully in the world. She needed Mnemosyne more than she wanted to admit.

She needed the young people like Twig too. They gave her hope for the future and a sense that everything the Old Witches Home stood for, everything they had fought for, everything they had risked their sanity for, would result in a better world. A world where everyone was welcome and loved. A world where it didn't matter if you were different and didn't fit into the predetermined box that was checked when the midwife first gazed at you as you slipped out of your mother's sanctuary. Twig was special, bright, and brilliant as a gem polished by the gods. She needed Twig to come back to her.

Birdie checked in with her gut again. Has she clearly articulated to herself what she's scared of? Is it the whole truth?

No, her gut said. No, it's something else. You're scared of something else, something more.

Okay. She breathed, slowly and deliberately. She sat quietly on the couch and gazed into the candle flame. Okay, I'm ready. What am I so scared of?

Him.

The word seemed to come from somewhere else, somewhere outside of her.

Him? That's ridiculous. Who? Tom? What's so scary about him? I've been in lots of relationships over the years. He's just an insomniac, a nacker who doesn't understand anything.

Even as she chastised herself, she knew it was true. He wasn't a witch. He didn't understand myths, gods and goddesses, chants and rituals. He lived in this world and this world only. He couldn't imagine another world where people lived with each other and nature in harmony, open and trusting, respectful and grateful. Where social justice wasn't just a convenient phrase but a way of life.

Tom didn't feel the energy emanating from a tree or the power generated by a Spiral Dance. He wasn't like them. He was an insomniac. He hadn't dreamed of another world where everyone's voice was heard, and resources were shared – he couldn't redream his visions.

But she liked him anyway. He was a nacker, yes, but he was a good man. There was something about him, an innocence, a willingness. She liked his gray hair and long, dark eyelashes. His hug was close and genuine, and his arms made her feel safe. He cared, really cared about everyone.

And he seemed to get her. Whenever she wanted to attack, he stepped to the side and deflected her arrows. Then he said something that showed that he understood. He was smarter than she was – she hadn't been around anyone smarter in a long time, well, maybe not ever. Smarter in the "I can see what you're doing, and I know how you're feeling" kind of way. Not just book smart. Heart smart.

And he liked her. That was new, too. Men had recoiled from her since she wasn't a pretty young thing but a strong older woman. She found sex partners over the years, sure, but no one who stuck around. She was used to them running when it got too hot.

She had a choice to make. She could dismiss him and pretend she hadn't felt the pull toward him. She could ignore him. Or she could let him in, however dangerous that might be.

Well, he told her how he felt. Now, she needed to do the same. He deserved honesty and straight talk. If she liked him, she needed to tell him.

He would laugh at her, she was sure. He wouldn't understand why the Old Witches Home was so important to her. He hadn't been experimenting with the powers of his mind since he was a kid. He thought there was reality, and you could tell if something was real just by looking at it. She knew there were many shades of reality, and they didn't look the same to everyone. He wouldn't understand how her belief in magic had saved her life. More than once. He would laugh, she was sure. And then he would leave.

God, this is crazy. I haven't felt this way since I was a teenager.

But even as a teenager, her feelings weren't this solid, this mundane. She had always bought the tragic fantasy that she was 'meant to be' with whatever love interest was current, that the Goddess had brought them to each other, and that their attraction was cosmic and foretold. That they weren't responsible for whatever they did. That it was magic and there was nothing she could do about it.

But it was different with Tom. With him, she felt an earthly affection. This was loving someone who had seen you with your warts and your wrinkles and who wanted to be with you anyway. She had been going to Tom as Dr. Payne for years. He had diagnosed her arthritis and her sciatica. He had prescribed statins for her cholesterol and had checked her ears when she thought she couldn't hear because of excessive earwax. She knew he had tried not to chuckle about that one, as he told her patiently that her ears looked clear and that frequently older people had hearing loss. He had watched her gain weight as she aged and prescribed melatonin when she complained of difficulty getting to sleep. He knew her in a way no one else did.

So why was she afraid of showing herself to him now?

She took a deep breath and quieted herself. She listened.

It's all on the line now, she heard her inner voice saying.

If they lost The Old Witches Home, she'd be all alone. Maya and Maple could go live with their kids, but where could Birdie go? What could she do? She was afraid to be so completely, so irrevocably, alone.

She was tired. She couldn't keep fighting.

I'm old, and I have to admit it, she thought. Maybe I belong in one of those senior living apartments where they play card games and go to matinees because they can't stay up late enough for an evening performance. I could get the senior discount at the diner if I showed up at 5 pm instead of a reasonable adult dinner time.

She didn't want Tom to know how vulnerable she felt. She was afraid that he would abandon her and find someone else, someone younger, someone easier than her, someone more together than her. She was afraid he wouldn't like her if he knew how miserably pathetic she was. Just how much she had been relying on The Old Witches Home to stave off the fear of losing her faculties, with no one to care for her.

Birdie took a deep breath and blew it out slowly. She opened her eyes, looked around the room, and turned her face to the moonshine pouring in the east window. The knot in her gut began to unravel.

Phew, at least she figured it out. Now it made sense why her stomach was in a knot. Now, she could get on with figuring out the other stuff. She blew out the candle with a short puff and uncrossed her legs.

That was enough of that. She had to get to sleep. The Solstice Festival is tomorrow, and they need to get ready. And they need to figure out what to do about Huffstickler. She'd worry about Tom later.

Birdie took a breath and realized she still wasn't sleepy at all. Maybe a walk will help. She could stop at the kitchen in the Heart and get some of the chamomile blend that Maya concocts. Some tea will be good.

20

A RESTLESS MIDNIGHT

Maya was exhausted. After all that commotion in the kitchen, Birdie flying off the handle at dinner, and Dr. Payne warning them about the sick people – well, it was all too much. Maya had always been good at compartmentalizing her worries, and she had every intention of doing that tonight. Her job was the Festival feast, that's all. Let everyone else handle the other stuff.

Maya rebraided her long gray hair and twisted it into a pile on top of her head. She took off the greasy dress that smelled of smoke and had bits of brown ash on it. After wrapping herself in her pink cotton bathrobe, she put on her eco-friendly satin shower cap and turned on the water.

Maya had started showering at night after her father began his visits to her. She found that the warm water soothed her whenever she was troubled or felt tense and allowed her to let go of the day.

She hung the robe on a hook by the door and stepped in. Even though the night was still warm, the water had to be hot enough to steam the mirror. Maya stood under the stream for a few minutes, letting the droplets grab the negative energy and flush it down the drain. She lifted her face, opened her hands, and reached out her arms as though she were receiving a gift from the shower goddess.

Let it go, let it all go. Goddess, wash me clean of the anger, the fear, and the doubt. Maya looked down, and she thought she saw green and brown specks whirling and eddying as they were sucked into the drain.

Once rinsed, Maya began soaping her whole body. She rejoiced as she lifted each breast, held them lovingly, and washed all around, tweaking each nipple playfully. Those breasts had nourished her children and had brought her hours of pleasure by herself, with her husband, and with her other lovers throughout the years.

Maya remembered when her breasts had begun to grow. At first, she was embarrassed – her development was earlier than her classmates. The boys would snicker and stare, and when she began wearing bras, they started grabbing the strap in the back, pulling it back, and letting it go so that it smacked her back, smarting and making her whirl around to confront them.

"Are you a turtle?" they said.

"No," she responded angrily.

"Then why do you snap?" They laughed and ran down the hall.

Maya sputtered, wishing she could say something or get them back, but by then, the other kids were laughing too, and all she could do was rush into class.

Then her father noticed her breasts, and everything got much worse. It was years before she finally made friends with her breasts. A weeklong exploration of her Body Temple at Witch Camp made all the difference, giving her a chance to talk with them and caress them and repair her relationship with the body that she thought had betrayed her so many years before.

Ben helped a lot, too. She had met him at a political protest when she was 25. Their marriage had been raucous and difficult – Ben drank way too much and took too many drugs – but also passionate and loving. Despite the drama and craziness, they managed to stay together, raise three kids, and have lots of wild, sexy, and frequent sex. He never quite understood witchcraft, but he was sympathetic and cared for the kids when she went to camp. His death from liver disease twelve years after he got sober was hard on Maya. But the kids loved their mom, tried to care for her, and ultimately let her run her own life, just as Maya asked them to. She resumed her catering business, put on hold while she nursed Ben, returned to Witch Camp, and ended up with her best friends at the Old Witches Home.

Maya loved her body now. The extra pounds she gained at menopause gave her gravitas, she thought. And now that she didn't have to stand on her feet as much as she did when she was working, her legs didn't hurt as much. She could feel the strong thigh muscles and the tight abs under the rolls.

Maya got out of the shower and slathered lotion all over. It felt so good. She didn't want to don a nightgown. So she didn't. She laid down, eyes closing as soon as she arranged herself under the sheet and was drifting away.

The night air twinkled with the few stars that could peek through the darkness despite the almost full moon. Maya felt light, airy, and deliciously free. She could float above the village, above the town, forever.

Suddenly, Maya was pulled downward into the Heart kitchen. Instantly, she knew why when she saw who was there.

Damn, who let those bastards in my kitchen? I'm going to have to get better locks on the door.

Bjorn and Charlie were laughing. They both had spoons in their hands and arrayed before them on the worktable were three bowls.

"This potato salad is really good," Charlie said, plopping a big scoop into his mouth.

"I'm partial to the bean salad," Bjorn countered as he dug into the metal bowl, spilling oil and bits of onion on the counter.

"Let's try the macaroni salad. It goes really well with beer."

Maya saw four St. Pauli Girl bottles on the counter, two more lying on their sides.

Damn those guys. They're nothing more than big kids, but I'll get them out of there.

All the peace and serenity she had been feeling disappeared. She was angry. Instantly, she was back in her body, sitting up and shaking her head. How dare they!

She got out of bed and threw on a sundress.

Maple's big toe was throbbing. He could feel every heartbeat, every pump of blood that went from his chest to his foot as if a five-year-old drummer was exploring his new toy.

This is ridiculous. I'm a grown man. So I banged my foot? Big deal. Yeah. Owwww.....

The more he chided himself, the more it hurt, the pain traveling from his toe to the rest of his foot, to his ankle, to his calf...

Maybe if he laid on the other side? Shit! That's not it. His toe screamed at him as he brushed it against the sheet in the turnover dance.

The house was too quiet. Everything was too quiet. He missed his wife. He hadn't thought about Juniper for the past few days; everything had been so busy, but she was never far from him. He had always felt strong with Juniper, like the sweet tree for which he had been named.

Maple had been told that maple trees symbolized practical magic, balance, longevity, generosity, and intelligence and that they could adapt to different soil types and climates.

Yeah, I guess that's what I've done. Adapted to different climates. When Juniper needed me to be stable, I worked at the hardware store. When Maya and Birdie needed me to help with The Old Witches Home, I was generous with my retirement fund and helped with all the logistics and the buildings. I've always done what needed to be done and never really complained about it.

A mosquito buzzed near Maple's ear. He swatted at it, but it came back. The sheets were tangled in his legs, and the moonlight was too bright.

Usually, he talked with Juniper when he felt restless like this, even now, after she'd been gone for over twelve years. Or Oscar would tire of his farming game and coax Maple outside to sit on the porch and share a beer with him. Someone always had a good idea of how to urge the body toward sleep; someone always knew what he should do next.

The mosquito buzzed again, and Maple jumped up to hit it.

Aargh! The pain in his foot woke him completely.

Maple limped out of bed, relieved himself in the bathroom, and put on his pants and a t-shirt. No sense in just lying there. You might as well go to the shed and dig out the tables that the vendors will use. Might need tarps, too, if it rains.

People are depending on me, Maple thought. So what if I'm in pain? They need me. I can take care of it. His ever-present feeling that he wasn't quite enough and that he was somehow responsible for the injustice in the world was an ache in his brain. He pushed it aside as he always did.

As Maple headed toward the shed by the dining pavilion, he noticed lights in the communal kitchen. Two men burst out of the kitchen onto the grass, laughing as they walked away.

Maple recognized those laughs. The Heathens were drunk again. The moonlight reflected off their suspender clips, zigzagging across the lawn as they stumbled toward their homes. Maple tried to run after them, but the aching in his foot stopped him. He stood in the dark.

I can't even run anymore, he thought. And what would I have done if I had caught up to them? They would have laughed at me, and I would have taken it just to keep the peace.

Maybe they're right. Maybe we should give in and let Huffstickler take the place. We can take our shares and go to a retirement home where everything is handled. I wouldn't be the odd one then, and nobody would need me. I wouldn't be letting my friends down. Without Juniper, without Oscar, I'm just not strong enough. I'm not a maple. I'm a sapling.

They left the light on. Of course. I guess the least I can do is go in and turn off the light.

Birdie was sitting at the counter with Maya, each with a cup of tea, when Maple arrived.

"All right. I'm not proud of myself, but he was mansplaining," Birdie said.

"Tolerance, Birdie. Patience. No wonder you've never been married," Maya said.

"What happened?" Maple asked as he limped into the kitchen. He groaned as he leaned up against the door frame. "Any chance we can sit somewhere more comfortable?"

"Birdie was just telling me that it's a computer virus infecting everyone. She and Dr. Payne figured it out, but then she kicked him out," Maya said. "We're trying to come up with what to do. Want some tea, Maple?"

"Shit, I'm sorry," Birdie said. "I'm just not doing well tonight. Let's go in the Water Purification Room."

"No, just some water. And to get off my feet. I'm too old for this shit. My foot really hurts. Oh, all right, I'll have your Sacred Sleeping brew."

Maya found a bottle of ibuprofen with the first aid kit in the cupboard. She poured him some tea, put the ibuprofen in her pocket, and grabbed her mug. She followed Birdie, who was helping Maple into the Water Purification Room next door, between the kitchen and the Healing Center. A solar battery-powered fountain sat on a driftwood shelf in front of the large west-facing window. Jars of water, seashells, and beach glass on flowing blue, green, and white cloths decorated the shelves against one wall.

Birdie deposited Maple into a beach chair, grabbed another for herself and one for Maya, and brought them close together in a small circle. She found some pillows to put under Maple's hurt foot.

At first, no one said anything. The light from the moon in the window shone a spotlight on their helplessness. Birdie considered turning on a lamp – there were several on the shelves around the room – but rethought it, feeling that darkness was fitting for their current situation.

"Couldn't sleep, either?" Maple said finally.

"No. I saw those guys eating my potato salad, and I had to come to rescue it. By the time I got here, they were gone, and there were just lime green and brown specks, like burned guacamole, on the counters. I cleaned it up."

"Yeah, I saw those guys leaving," Maple said. "Did they burn something?"

"I don't think so. I'm not sure what it was. Birdie showed up just as I was finishing. I used quite a bit of vinegar to get that grease off the counter."

They lapsed into silence again. Tears threatened to leak out of Birdie's eyes again. What was going on with her?

"I'm sorry I was such a bitch," Birdie said. "I'm just scared. What if we lose this place?"

"We're all on edge," Maya said. "I don't know how to fight Huffstickler. I can barely turn on a computer, much less figure out how to fight a tech guy who uses computers against us."

"Yeah, who ever heard of a computer virus that infects humans?" Maple said.

"I know. Crazy." Birdie said. "But Tom couldn't even get on the system to play some music on his phone. That kid infected everything! That's why I couldn't send an email. I almost got infected, too."

"That's so nuts. I didn't think that's the way computer viruses work," Maya said.

"Maybe magical computer viruses work that way. We have to get rid of it," Birdie said.

"We don't have any time. We have to do something about that kid and Huffstickler now." Maple tried to cradle his foot in his arm, but Birdie didn't think his back would lean over that far. He winced.

"We know." Maya and Birdie said the same thing at the same time. Then, they were silent. They could hear an owl hooting up on the ridge. They couldn't lose this magical property. It was perfect for them.

"What should we do?" Maya said without much enthusiasm. Birdie had never heard Maya sound so depressed.

"I don't think we should tell anyone," Birdie said. "We don't want to start a panic, and maybe it would be better not to let Huffy and his sidekick know that we know. We should handle this ourselves."

"Can we put a counter-spell on them?" Maple suggested.

Hmmm... they all thought for a few minutes. Birdie thought that maybe this was beyond their skill level. They had all done political spells to bind a politician from doing nasty stuff. Or protection spells to keep them all safe. And, of course, they set wards and did a land-blessing spell when they first moved to the land. But a counter-spell? Against something as nasty as this? Birdie was skeptical.

"If Huffstickler thinks we're too old, maybe we need to live up to his expectations. We can just unplug all the computers," Maple said.

Well, that's kind of obvious, Birdie thought. Huh.

"That's not a problem," Maya said. "I wouldn't turn on a computer now if you paid me."

"Me neither," Maple said.

"What if we spread the word that the computer system is down and see if anyone argues with us. That way, no one else gets infected, and we'll find out if anyone else knows about the virus." Birdie suggested.

"You think Bjorn and his buddies are in on it?" Maya said.

"I wouldn't put it past them," Maple said. "Remember, Huffstickler said he had two people who would testify that we coerced Lightning to leave the land to us. I think they want Huffstickler to win. They think they'll make money if he does. I'm not sure why we ever let them move here."

Maple told Birdie and Maya about his confrontation with them in the dining hall the day before.

"I don't trust that Bjorn. He harassed me in the kitchen the other day, too," Maya said.

"That's another reason not to tell anyone. We don't want any of the Heathens to find out what we're doing," Birdie said. "Not all of them are like Bjorn and Charlie – I really like Andy and his partner, Raven – but I'm sure they talk."

"I'm not sure we're strong enough to fight Huffstickler, the computer store kid, and the Heathens," Maple said.

"Sure we are," Birdie said, starting to feel her hackles rise. What are hackles anyway? "We've been gathering strength for years. We're powerful witches. We can do this. I know we can."

They looked at her skeptically.

"Sure. We've been doing magic for years, haven't we? What about the time we did the magical protest against the crazy President? He was voted out of office, wasn't he?"

"Yeah, but he caused incredible chaos," Maya said.

"And every year, we get together at camp and heal ourselves and our planet. That's powerful work, isn't it?"

"Of course it is," Maple said. "But that's just personal work."

"It may be personal, but we regularly fight childhood abuse and trauma with magic, and it works." Birdie remembered what Maya had shared about her work to heal her relationship with her body. She was on a roll now.

"I guess so," Maya said.

"So this is the biggest thing we've ever had to do, but we can do it. I know we can." Birdie looked at them. They had to believe her.

"So you know how to make a computer virus antidote?" Maple asked.

"Come on. We're witches. We can figure this out."

"Maybe something with crystals," Maya said hesitantly. "And herbs. They have incredible power that can change all sorts of energy. How about mushrooms? Oyster mushrooms are used to clean up oil spills."

"How about a crystal water fountain? Didn't the kid say he would increase the free flow of information?" Maple suggested.

"Yeah, didn't you make something last year for Samhain? A waterfall thingy?" Birdie asked.

"Yeah, I used a little solar battery to power the fountain, so the water is recycled. Just like that one." He pointed to the fountain in the window. "It was easy."

"And I'll bring the protection herbs from the binding ritual. Let's put them in the water. That will increase the purification power of the water. And maybe I can find some mushrooms to spread around the grounds."

"Now we're cooking," Birdie said. They decided to place the new fountain in the center of the ritual space. It would be hidden by the drummers, and they could fill the bowl with herbs and crystals – blue agate, rose quartz, yellow topaz, and green malachite, with clear crystal quartz around them. If they concentrated on using the crystals to focus the energy from the Spiral Dance, then... Birdie was sure they would be just as powerful as that computer kid.

"What are we going to do about Angie and the others? Don't we need to get them food and water?" Maya asked.

"Yeah, that's scary. But Tom said he would call Lois, and he would handle that. I'll check with him." Birdie said. She figured apologizing for tonight would probably be a good idea anyway. "Lois said she would call Diego too."

Maple took a jar of Waters of the World off the shelf. The small jar held water that witches had brought to The Old Witches Home from far corners of the globe to become a symbol of the unity of the human race. The waters didn't recognize political boundaries and flowed freely from nation to nation. Not fit for drinking, perhaps, but definitely filled with magic from diverse beliefs and perspectives.

He picked out several various-sized crystals and a large ceramic bowl. They decided to go down to the DWI office and unplug the server. At least no one would be able to get on the Wi-Fi.

Maple shivered as they opened the door. He hadn't been in this room since finding Mnemosyne two nights ago.

Maya turned the desk lamp on, and the shadows disappeared. Maple chided himself for being silly. As he went to the shelves in the back of the office where the machinery lived, he noticed Maya and Birdie looking through the papers on the desk. The big manila envelope and the crumpled letter summoning Mnemosyne to court on Monday were still there. They were murmuring at each other, and Maple couldn't hear what they were saying.

He turned his attention to the tall black rectangle that sat on the middle shelf. Rows of lights, some blinking lime green, some not lit, and some blinking red, stared back at him. This rigid, impenetrable, and incomprehensible monster was contaminating his friends. He had to find the switch. He began searching, starting with the top row, planning to work his way down.

Birdie appeared next to him.

"Aren't you going to turn it off?"

"Yeah, I'm just looking for the switch."

"It's right here." She reached out and pressed a small black bar. Nothing happened. "Hmm. Maybe that's not it."

"What are you two doing?" Maya said as she approached them. "Come on. I'm tired and want to get back to bed."

"Maple can't find the off button," Birdie said. Neither could she, Maple thought.

He watched Maya and Birdie study the unit like apes examining an obelisk.

"I got it," Birdie said, reaching behind the shelf and pulling the plug out of the wall. "That should take care of it."

Dang, Maple thought. I should have thought of that. He turned to go, but Birdie stopped him.

"We can do this," she said, looking directly at him. He glanced at Maya and then came back to Birdie.

Maple said, "We can do this. I know we can." He felt a strength that he had never known before.

The three of them moved in for a group hug.

As they all got ready to leave, Birdie said, "I'll check with Tom and Lois first thing in the morning. Maya, let us know if we can help with the feast."

"Sure, if I ever figure it out. At least we still have some potato salad."

"And a plan," Birdie said.

I can do this, Maple thought.

21

BIRDIE AND TOM

After Maya and Maple turned left outside the Heart, and Birdie turned right, her near-panic returned. She could still hear the owl hooting in the hills; now, it felt like a warning. The large dark trees loomed around her and cast moon shadows as she walked down the lane. Even the sound of Whale Tooth's cot squeaking didn't make her smile as usual, but instead made her think of Pandora's box of evil. The nacker computer kid had unleashed evil at the Old Witches Home, her home. She was angry. And scared.

As she approached her cabin, she saw a figure sitting on the steps to her front door.

Shit. He came back, she thought. Now, what do I do? She was too tired to run and knew she would have to face him soon anyway. She took a deep breath and kept walking.

"You're here," she said.

"Yes. I'm sorry – I know it's late. But I just couldn't leave it like that."

"Come on in. It's not that late. And I can make us some tea." Birdie didn't want another cup of tea – she would be up all night peeing – but she felt obligated to be gracious. And she had to admit, she was glad to see him. She was still too keyed up to sleep anyway.

Hermes tried to scoot out the door when she opened it, but she blocked his exit with her foot.

"You know better," she said to the cat. "There are nasty critters out there. You'll get eaten."

Hermes appeared to shrug and trotted off to his pillows on the floor near the wood stove. Once settled, he looked up at them expectantly.

"Have a seat," Birdie said. "I'll get the tea started." She turned toward the kitchen, stopped, and returned to Tom.

"I'm sorry," she said quietly.

"I'm sorry," Tom said, a half beat later.

"What was that?" she said, turning toward him.

"What did you say?" he said.

"You first," she said.

"No, you."

"Oh, all right," Birdie conceded. "I'm sorry. I shouldn't have yelled at you tonight. Okay? I'm sorry. Now let's just forget it." She turned back to tea preparation.

He grabbed her arm, and she turned to face him, but she still didn't look him in the eye.

"I'm sorry, too. It's okay. I know you're stressed with everything that's going on."

"Yeah, I suppose."

"Birdie, I admire you. You're handling a lot. I'm just glad you're letting me help."

"Thanks."

"Maybe we can spend more time together when this is over?"

She wouldn't tell him how much she would like that. His kind confidence was a security blanket holding her tight.

"Okay, I guess. Let's sit down and drink tea. It's late." She could tell he still wanted to hug her, and it was tempting, but she hesitated.

She crossed to the kitchen and poured the tea into rainbow mugs.

Tom chose a record and placed it on the turntable. The sounds of Joni Mitchell filled the room.

When she turned away from the stove, Tom was across the room from her. He looked at her, and she returned his gaze. They took their cups and moved to the couch. It was too warm to build a fire in the fireplace, but the moonlight from the window over the sofa lit the pile of winter ashes with a soft glow.

Birdie closed her eyes and leaned back into the couch, willing herself to relax and just enjoy the moment. The familiar music soothed her. Somehow, this would turn out all right; she just had to have faith.

"Birdie, my wife died three years ago – you know that, right?" Tom's voice was a gentle opening into the quiet energy that enveloped them.

"Yeah…."

"She was strong like you and had a sense of magic. I couldn't save her. The cancer was stronger than both of us. I miss her. But I think it's time to move forward with my life."

"Of course you miss her." Birdie was sure she knew where this was going – she realized she wanted it to go there. Still, little alarm bells were tinkling, her shoulders were stiff, and the knot in her stomach was maintaining its determination.

"Would it be okay if I kissed you?"

"You want to kiss – me?"

"Is that crazy? I'm sorry. I'm not sure I remember how to do it, but I think it's like riding a bike, right?"

"Well, okay," she said. She turned to him and couldn't decide whether to tilt her head left or right. She looked into his eyes, searching for a clue, but he looked just as befuddled.

He tilted right just as she tilted left, and they bumped noses.

"Sorry, sorry…" they both mumbled.

"Let's try again," Tom said. He cupped Birdie's face in both his hands and brought her closer to him. She closed her eyes in anticipation.

Then he stopped. *Shit, my breath must be bad or something*, she thought.

She opened her eyes. He was smiling and looking at her.

"You're just so beautiful."
"Bullshit. I'm old."
"Yep. And beautiful."

Birdie's neck and shoulder were really starting to hurt. "Do you mind if we switch sides?"

"Oh, of course, I'm sorry."

They both stood up and started to move forward, but they had the same problem with the kiss.

"You stay there, I'll go around," Birdie said. She scooted past him and sat back on the couch. When Tom joined her, this time, he put an arm around her and leaned over.

He kissed her. This time, it worked.

Tom's mouth was scratchy and moist. His tongue reached into her mouth and sought out hers. They played with each other, exploring, dipping into sensation, and allowing the feelings to spread throughout her body.

It felt like the first good kiss she had when she was young – Tony Colangelo in the skate park when she was fourteen. He was sixteen and knew what he was doing. She trusted him completely. Until he made fun of her in front of his friends. Relationships had gone downhill since then. Men were clearly not trustworthy. Right? Shhh......

They lingered on the couch, kissing, talking, and holding hands.

"I haven't done anything like this in a really long time," Birdie said. "I used to be good at it."

"I'm sure you were. You still are."

They lapsed into silence again as Birdie leaned on his shoulder, and he stroked her arm gently. The night was still. All the problems Birdie was dealing with were still there, but they were muted. She had been given a reprieve, a respite from the pressure. If she had allowed herself to think about it, she would have still been afraid for her friends' lives and their homes, but those thoughts were far away for the moment.

They listened to the music and sipped tea. Soon, their hands were exploring thighs and breasts and other parts that hadn't been caressed in years. Their lips became friends.

Tom told Birdie he hadn't had sex since his wife was diagnosed with cancer, over five years now, and wasn't sure if he could do it.

"I'm not sure I can either. Are we ready for that?" Birdie asked.

He didn't answer; he leaned over and started kissing Birdie again. His soft lips lingered on her neck and nibbled her earlobe. Her body remembered what it felt like when those sensitive spots were awakened. She sank backward and allowed the sensations to spread throughout her body.

Oh my Goddess, she thought, this is fun. And she turned her face to his, playfully pulling on his lower lip.

"You know," Birdie said softly into his ear as she kissed his neck. "There are lots of things we can do besides intercourse." His hands were roaming on her thighs, bunching the sundress up near her waist.

He had brought pills, he said.

"I don't think you'll need them," she whispered. She stroked his thigh and felt the bulge in his crotch begin to grow and throb.

Her resistance to him was fading. She just wanted to be loved. Why not let him? She wasn't getting any younger. What was there to be afraid of?

"I guess we're doing this," she purred.

"Do you want to?"

"Yes, I do," she replied. The knot in her stomach had almost dissolved, just a tiny tickle of apprehension remaining.

Finally, when the next record change was due, they rose, still kissing and caressing each other, and moved to the bedroom.

They reached the bed and stopped. She turned toward him. He looked at her.

She knew that this time, she was deeper than she had ever been before. She wanted this man to know her, really know her, and right now, in this moment, she was open and naked. Taking her clothes off was only a gesture; the first kiss was crucial, and she survived it.

"Please don't laugh," Tom said. "This old man hasn't had his clothes off in front of anyone for quite a while."

Birdie chuckled, reflecting on her morning nude swims in the pond. At those times, it never occurred to her to worry about what someone thought of her body. When she got out, she would don a sundress because it was comfortable. She had no qualms about using the co-ed sauna either, but this was different. No one ever noticed her when she was in the pond – now all those wrinkles and sagging skin were on full display.

Oh, heck, just jump in. The water's warm.

"It's okay. We don't need to do anything. Let's just cuddle and see what happens."

Getting undressed was a cooperative endeavor, with Tom bringing her dress over her head and Birdie unbuckling his pants and letting them fall to the floor. They stood and looked at each other as each garment fell away.

Birdie felt proud of her flab and her wrinkles. Each one represented a year in her life, a hard-won moment, a promise that had been fulfilled. Together, they showed him who she was and who she could be.

As he dropped his pants on the floor, she admired how the hair on his chest was white and wiry, and his breasts were sagging just a little. Several layers of flesh above a semi-erect penis were asking to be fondled. He lay down on the bed. She climbed in and stretched out next to him.

Birdie's fingers traveled the folds and crevices of Tom's body. On his back, she found scars and ravines, memories and moments, reminding her of the joy of connection and consummation. The feel of his hands on her thighs and her butt fluttered throughout her body, especially deep within her, where the juices that had long been dammed were beginning to flow again.

Birdie reached down between Tom's legs and gently rubbed him, feeling the blood gather and grow his pleasure. He definitely did not need to take his blue pill; his erection was strong and solid, maybe not as rock hard as it once was, but it felt good to Birdie.

She reached into the drawer of her nightstand and pulled out a condom. She couldn't believe she still had one. The expiration date was probably long past, but... it was probably better than nothing.

"Is it okay?" she asked, holding the package so he could see.

"I promise I don't have any STDs," he said. "But you're right. I suppose we should be responsible adults. I don't know where you've been," he said, giggling.

She ripped the package open. The condom slid on easily – they did it together. She heard him moan as she rubbed lubricant up and down his penis. The feeling of satisfaction in giving someone pleasure warmed her in a way she hadn't felt in a long time.

It was early in the morning by the time he entered her. They had explored in delight, remarking on what they found and sharing stories. Birdie was wet enough to feel only pleasure. The pain she expected from disuse wasn't there. The vagina that hadn't been enjoyed for so long opened eagerly, and there was only a twinge as he started to move.

Their lovemaking was slow but steady. Birdie felt the familiar rise of sensation from her vulva to her nipples, from her lips to her toes. They fit together so easily, kissing and caressing and rocking, first him on top of her and then her sitting astride him, knees bent.

The crescendo took her by surprise. She had been so lost in the feel of her legs against his, his hands on her back, his penis in her vagina, that she hadn't noticed her own steadily increasing arousal. She was usually so conscious of its rise when she masturbated – she could stop and prolong the climax and often achieve multiple orgasms. But this time, she was unaware, adrift in pleasure, so many more sensations flooding her that the peak happened without her permission.

There it was – the shudder, the wave, the letting go. A cone of power shooting to the stars. A burst of magic releasing her intention to love and be loved in return. To not be alone anymore.

"Oh, Goddess." She fell forward onto him and buried her face in his shoulder.

He turned her head to his and kissed her deeply and passionately.

She slid onto her back, allowing him to be on top again. It felt so good to let him be in charge and to surrender.

She could still feel tingling as he began to thrust again, and her excitement mounted.

His orgasm was gentle. He pushed hard and then squeaked a moan; his back arched, and the muscles of his buttocks clutched as he drove into her one last time. When he let go and relaxed onto her, his weight was light, his skin soft and slightly moist.

He rolled off her, and they turned to face each other, their knees touching and their arms at each other's waists.

"Well, that worked, I think," Birdie said.

"Yes, I think it did."

They continued to look at each other, and the knot in Birdie's stomach knocked feebly on the door of her consciousness, but she waved it away. A prickle of fear started to grow, a reminder that something was seriously wrong. She kissed him, and he kissed her back.

I am fine. We are fine. Just leave it at that.

She curled into a fetal position on the bed with him spooning behind her. She reached out and caressed his butt. The skin was soft and thin without much muscle tone, and she loved how she could grab the cheek. She could feel him stroking her stomach and breasts slowly. His breath was becoming deep and regular. She could feel his nose nuzzling her ear.

How could this be so comfortable? She was always so happy that she didn't have to share a bed with anyone; she couldn't remember being so at ease in bed with a lover before. She complained she was never able to sleep with someone else there. This is good magic, she thought. The kind we make together.

She ran her tongue around her mouth and felt something was missing. She hadn't put in her night guard – that was it. Well, she wasn't going to do it now. What if he wanted to kiss her again? Something she never worried about when she was alone. She was grateful she had brushed her teeth.

She found herself sinking deeper and deeper into the mattress. Her eyes were closed, and she had no desire to move or adjust her body; it all felt like it was exactly where it was supposed to be. Images of computers, ceramic Tree of Life mugs, and official-looking papers started appearing before her. Mnemosyne curled on the floor, muttering. The images scattered and danced as darkness soothed her.

A light pressure near her feet let her know that Hermes had jumped on the bed and circled near her feet. He didn't want to be left out; she was glad he had joined them. The bed was a bit crowded but in a good way.

22

SATURDAY MORNING

The next morning, they had run out of time. Maple had to create the anti-computer-virus weapon, and he had to do it now. His friends' lives depended on him.

He was in the shed, picking up and putting down lawn mower parts, weed whacker string, zip ties, tools, nozzles, random screws, nuts and bolts. Dang. I know there's some tubing somewhere here, he said to himself.

He had to finish it quickly. And get the device into the center of the circle before anyone arrives. He looked at the half-finished fountain in the ceramic basin. The solar-powered battery was attached to the pump and ready to go. He had gathered crystals from the ritual room and surreptitiously plucked the herbs off the altar. Now all he had to do was add the tubing and the water and place the damn thing.

Wait, he thought. I haven't blessed or consecrated it. No wonder it's not ready to go. I should know better. Well, I guess I do now.

Maple planted his feet on the shed floor and took three deep breaths, letting each out with a sigh. He held the fountain up to each of the directions, starting in the east, and asked the spirits of the elements to bless and consecrate this magical tool. He asked for their assistance dispelling the virus curse, healing his friends, and saving their home. Instead of the awkwardness he usually felt when doing things like this, it all felt right this time. Maybe he really did know what he was doing.

When he set the fountain back on the table, he saw from the corner of his eye a length of tubing hanging from a hook on the wall.

See, you just need to ask for help sometimes.

Maple quickly added the tubing to the device, threw a shop rag over it, and peered out the door. He looked from side to side, didn't see anyone, and started up the hill to the meadow. He had left his crutches in his cabin; they only slowed him down. He was doing just fine, limping along. It was only his toe, after all.

Lost in his thoughts, he didn't see the exposed root on the path. His bum foot, which he had been dragging behind him, dug a crevice in the soil and connected with the root. He lurched forward. The solar collector flew out of his hands and landed with a thud.

Owww! He had no free hand to muffle his scream, so he bit his lip. He placed the fountain on the ground and grabbed the collector. It was still intact. Phew.

He decided to take a moment to rest. Uphill was the worst. His heart was pounding, and his breath wasn't quite filling his lungs. The throbbing in his toe was chanting, "You're old, you're old." He held the fountain against his stomach and sighed. Then he heard the voices.

"There must be something we can do," Charlie said. They were in the clearing where people usually gathered before beginning a ritual in the meadow. Maple couldn't see them around the bend of the path.

He turned up his hearing aid. He was getting some good use out of this thing.

"Just act normal. We don't want anyone to know we're involved with Huffstickler. No one knows that we're testifying on Monday. But watch out. If anyone tries anything, we may need to fight back. For now, let's just let the virus do its work. It's taking them out one by one. Pretty soon, they'll be happy to let Huffstickler take over."

"Yeah, I can't wait to really start developing this place. We'll make boatloads off the tourists and weekenders. And I won't need to worry about getting my meds."

"Just stay off the computer," Bjorn said, and they started approaching him. Maple got himself to his feet and began walking up the path. He rounded the bend and feigned surprise when he saw them.

"Look who's here," Charlie said with a sneer.

"Good morning. Hope it doesn't rain," Maple said and kept walking, trying to act nonchalant, past them.

"What you got there?" Bjorn asked, moving in front of Maple and stopping him.

"Just a little fountain for the altar. Hopefully, it will convince the rain gods we don't need more water." The clouds were already gathering in the west in a mostly blue sky.

Bjorn lifted the cloth and peered intently at the fountain. Maple held his breath. After a minute, Bjorn dropped the cloth.

"Looks kind of tacky to me," he said. "Thor may need an offering that is a bit sturdier to stay away today."

"He's not the only god we'll be working with today," Maple replied, convincing his bum foot to move around Bjorn and keep heading up the hill.

"Happy Solstice!" Charlie shouted.

"You too!" Maple turned down his hearing aid. He had no desire to listen to them anymore.

Once he reached the meadow, Maple noticed someone had brought the garden gnome up the hill. It was still wrapped with all the ribbons and cords they had attached during the binding spell ritual. He looked at it for a few seconds, perplexed. Something was wrong. It didn't seem that Huffstickler had slowed down since the binding ritual. Why hadn't it worked?

The chain draped over the small statue glinted in the sun. That was it, he realized! The chain kept all of the other bindings from touching the gnome. It protected Huffstickler like a coat of armor. It was strong and durable, a symbol of the industrial age. No wonder their flimsy ribbons and yarn hadn't done anything. How could ribbons stand up to a chain?

Maple quickly removed the ribbons, strings, and cords from the gnome and set them to the side. Then, he dismantled the chain configuration and dumped the chains on the ground. Since he didn't have the duct tape to attach the ribbons to the gnome, he tried to tie them together in a kind of net to drop over the gnome.

Macrame is really not my thing, he thought, as the collection of yarn, string, ribbons, and leather cords quickly became a tangled mess. Okay, breathe.

Start again. He grounded himself and asked for help from Frigg, the Norse Goddess of weaving and wife of Odin. She'll know how to handle Odin's son, Thor, he thought. He took a deep breath.

He pulled them all apart and took one piece of leather cord from the pile. He wrapped it around the gnome's neck, made a slip knot at one end, and pulled the other end through. Then he grabbed a ribbon and tied it to the end of the cord. He wrapped it around the torso, looping it up over the shoulders and down around the legs. He continued with each string and piece of yarn or ribbon until the whole thing was fully covered. And fully contained.

There. That ought to do it. He threw the chains into the trees beyond the meadow.

He placed the gnome on the stone pedestal in the center and the fountain underneath it. He walked up the hill to the bonfire, grabbed one of the gallon jugs of water, and returned to the fountain to fill it. He pulled out the jar of waters of the world from his pocket and added some to the basin, feeling a connection to the global community of witches. Then he finished filling it with the jug of water.

The south-facing solar collector was glowing, and he could feel energy beginning to build. A cloud darkened the sky, then moved quickly past, allowing the sun to shine on the fountain again. Maple brought his hands together at his heart and looked up.

Lugh, Sun God, please charge this fountain and be with us today.

He looked around the meadow. The chairs were off to the side, ready to be placed in a circle amidst the drums. In past years, they had as many as ten drummers, but this year, he thought there would be only three. Maple knew what had happened to the others – they were 'dancing to the beat of a different drum' that only they could hear.

The bonfire further up the hill was built and ready to go. It was not as tall as usual, and many of the logs were more helter-skelter than he liked, but it was up asking to be lit.

He started down the hill. The rest of the village was beginning to stir.

Birdie woke that morning from the most restful sleep she had in years. Before she even opened her eyes, she felt herself smiling, a little tingly all over. The memory of the previous night rolled in comfortable waves across her consciousness.

Tom wasn't in bed with her, which was just fine. She wasn't ready to face him directly. She stretched and slowly started moving her body, aware of Hermes pacing on the floor in front of her. Her heart began racing as she thought of her friends, and the Festival they weren't ready for.

After her trip to the bathroom and filling Hermes' food dish, she noticed the note on the kitchen counter.

"Had to get supplies. See you later. Tom." A little heart next to his name. How cute. Just like junior high school.

Birdie dressed quickly, let Hermes out, and hurried to the Healing Center to talk with Lois.

"Have you heard from Dr. Payne?" Birdie asked.

"Not yet. I don't want to call him too early. It's only 8:30. I imagine he'll be here soon," Lois replied.

"You look rested," Lois remarked. "I didn't sleep a wink worrying about all the people who haven't eaten or drank for three days. What's your secret?"

"Just some chamomile tea," Birdie said, chuckling. "And a little exercise."

"Whatever you did, it worked."

"Do you know how many have been affected?"

"I believe we're up to 43. Almost all of the young people, and so many people who live alone. I'm not even sure we've found them all. I'm planning to go door to door."

"That's almost half the witches who live here," Birdie said. "Do you have enough help? You said you were calling Diego, but maybe Eddie and Taylor can help, too. The setup outside is pretty much done."

"I've got some supplies ready. I think Dr. Payne is bringing IV hookups if we need them. We have to get them hydrated as soon as possible. Oh, dear. Do you know what can happen if they become dehydrated?" Lois had a significant wrinkle on her brow, even more pronounced than all the other ones she already had.

"Yes, you and Dr. Payne were very clear about that. Will you be able to get to them all?"

"Oh, I hope so. We'll do the best we can. Don't you worry, dear? You have other things to do."

She certainly did.

Lois was concerned there were not enough supplies and immediately consulted with Dr. Payne when they returned to the drive outside the Heart.

As usual, Taylor appeared unaffected by what was going on around him. He sat calmly at the steering wheel, writing in his little notebook.

Diego held up the ring of keys. Eddie and Charlie followed him. They split the keys with Taylor, and all three golf carts took off again.

While they were traveling to their next stop, Lois thought about what they were doing.

She looked down at her list and counted the names without checkmarks beside them. She was frowning; so many people they couldn't see because their doors were locked and they lived alone. What happened to a welcoming environment where everyone felt safe?

Lois sighed. She thought that no matter how far we travel, we can never really leave the society we grew up in. She wondered how many of her friends had firearms they hadn't told anyone about.

Lois' training as a surgical nurse had prepared her for crises like this. Her faith in the Goddess gave her an optimism that had differentiated her from many of her colleagues. She knew there were more forces at work than the science of medicine could explain. She had learned how to tap into those forces after her own bout of ovarian cancer.

Lois remembered how she had found solace in sharing her experiences with others who had similar struggles when she attended a support group of women who were all battling some form of cancer. There, she had made friends with Beatrice, who told her about an eclectic form of nature worship that brought Beatrice peace.

That month, she invited Lois for a full moon healing circle. It changed her life. When Lois sat in the middle of the circle of women in Beatrice's candle-lit living room, she had no expectations. She simply hoped she wouldn't be so depressed when she left. The doctors had not been very optimistic about her prognosis but were unwilling to speculate on the likely progression of the cancer.

The women chanted and danced around her, enveloping Lois in a bubble of warmth and love. Lois felt like she was being lifted out of the chair, that her atoms and molecules had split apart, and that she was floating in a gaseous cloud. The waves of the chant rocked her as though she were a baby in a cradle. With her eyes closed, the mist around her was twinkling with starlight.

Suddenly, a figure appeared, not just in front of her but above, below, and around her. Embracing and enveloping her, it felt feminine, maternal, and ephemeral. Without distinct edges, just shades of white, feathery, and light.

"You are healed," Lois heard the Goddess say in her mind. "Now go forth and heal others."

While sitting in the golf cart moving toward the next bungalow, Lois reached out to that Goddess. "Please let us heal our friends," she implored.

Maya was bustling back and forth between the dining hall and the kitchen. The feast that was supposed to be held in the outdoor dining pavilion before the bonfire had been downsized. Normally, they would have set up extra tables outside, but the clouds had been growing all morning, and Maya was in no mood to take chances. The dining hall was big enough; at least there, she could keep an eye on things.

The three elderly witches who became her assistants yesterday, now that her regular helpers were out for the count, moved very slowly, and she wasn't sure any of them really understood her directions. Phoenix could never remember if Maya had said teaspoon or tablespoon, salt or sugar. She just tried everything and tasted it afterward, proclaiming, "Delicious!" as though her sense of smell and taste hadn't been destroyed when she had the coronavirus years ago.

Gwion loudly hummed *When Irish Eyes are Smiling,* placing cheese slices on a platter. When Maya asked him to place the platter on the sideboard in the dining hall, Gwion happily assured her that he did not splatter anything. It was all good, and he returned to what he was doing. Maya sighed. I'll try again later, she thought.

Maya turned to Nighthawk for help. She was Maya's rock. She did everything Maya asked – literally. Then she waited for more instructions – right behind Maya. Every time Maya turned, there she was. She was like a cat who always gets under your feet. Maya was sure she would seriously injure Nighthawk or herself if she moved too quickly.

She asked Nighthawk to put the forks and knives on the table. Nighthawk obeyed. She dumped the forks and knives on the table with no order, no placement whatsoever. Nighthawk was exhausting.

But somehow, it was all coming together. The checked yellow tablecloths were laid; the Cosmic Cheese and Crackers were set out; and the Royal Potato Salad had been put in four dishes in every direction. Luckily, she had made more than enough, and Bjorn and Charlie's midnight feast didn't deplete the supply.

Maya found some kids from the town to set up the chairs, and she was as ready as she was going to be.

By the time Maple reached the Festival grounds near the dining pavilion, the clouds were dripping slightly, adding to the haphazard, half-baked nature of the day. Vendors from town were setting up their tables, and the place was beginning to look like a flea market. Eddie and Taylor were supposed to be helping them, but Maple didn't see them.

Were there fewer vendors this year? Maple wondered if he was just being paranoid. He could see the ladies with the knitted scarfs, hats, and mittens, the quilters with their wall hangings and table linen, the potters with their ceramic dishware, and the artists with their paintings. Elmer's wife sat at her table with the flower arrangements in the milk cans. Even the woman who made art out of leaves was there. He loved how she created squirrels, dragonflies, and birds using the droppings from the trees in her garden.

Maple had to stop at the table the hardware store workers set up. They had brought flowers, small garden tools, and saws with landscapes painted on them. Sally was arguing with the vendors set up next to them.

"You're in our space," she said loudly. "We're always here, every year. And we always have two tables." She stood solidly, looking up at a young brown-skinned man in a light yellow polo. The boxes beside him were filled with framed aerial photographs of the area.

"I'm sorry," he said. "This is our first year, and there wasn't anyone here to tell us where to set up. Do you know where we should go, sir?" he asked Maple.

Damn, Maple thought. No, I don't know where you should go. Oscar would.

"How about that table over there?" He pointed to an empty table down the line of vendors and hoped it hadn't been promised to someone else.

Sally harrumphed. "Damn weekenders," she muttered under her breath. Maple hoped the new vendor would sell many photos and donate a sizable amount to The Old Witches Home.

The woman from the community-supported-agriculture farm called him, but he just waved back to her. He still had too much to do to get caught up in gossiping.

So many people were out of commission, it was a miracle that anything was getting set up. The banner tied between two poles at the entrance to the meadow read "Welcome" without the final "e," and there was only a sun and flowers at one end of the banner; the other was bare, waiting for someone to finish it. However, it didn't matter much as the ink began dissolving into misshapen blots from the mist anyway.

Some of the brave townspeople were arriving with raincoats and umbrellas. He called out to Rosie from the post office.

"So good to see you," he yelled across the lawn.

"Wouldn't miss this for the world," she yelled back. "What's a little rain?" Two boys about ten years old ran ahead of her, kicking up moist dirt from their rubber galoshes.

Soon, the kids would be eating fairy cakes, playing games, and dancing to the music from the Celtic folk band.

He watched as the bass and guitar players started to set up at the end of the pavilion. They were missing two of their four members. The tune they started playing sounded like a sad dirge with no melody. Perhaps the fiddle player and the lead vocal were lying on their beds somewhere singing rap songs and clicking their right thumbs on the sheets.

Maple turned his hearing aid down a bit.

Maple wondered what else he could do to prepare for the ritual that celebrated the year's longest day. He mouthed a prayer of gratitude to Lugh, the Celtic sun god, for this place and these witches who were his family. He knew that the Old Witches Home could be foreclosed on in a minute if they couldn't raise the money they needed for the balloon payment. Now, they needed money for lawyers, too. He believed with all his heart that their magic would protect them and that the gods would provide.

He looked up at the sun, high in the sky. It seemed to be having a quiet disagreement with the clouds. The sun would win for a few minutes and proclaim its summer sovereignty, and then the clouds would wrap it in grey and sap its strength, misting the sky and moistening the earth.

There was nothing he could do but watch. He certainly didn't have power over the weather. The circle was set, the bonfire was built, the garden gnome was properly bound, and the fountain was in place. Townspeople were starting to arrive. Now, all that was needed were the witches.

Birdie was late to the meeting in the Fire Room with the only witches left in the ritual planning cell.

She felt more energetic than she had yesterday. Even though she was trying to help Maya with the feast, figure out how to get everyone fed and watered, and keep everyone moving in the same direction, she wasn't straining. A glow deep within her fueled her.

Still, it was a lot. Without Mnemosyne, she had to figure out how to handle the vendors' donations and tithes. She didn't have those kinds of skills. She was impatient with numbers. And most of the people who were still functional had more than one screw loose at this point in their lives.

She looked around at the witches who had created this ritual.

"Okay, I know everyone's tired. It's been a difficult couple of days, and we're missing a few people," Birdie said. "But let's try to be quick, okay? We don't have much time. Now, who is doing what?"

Birdie always tried to incorporate everyone's tradition into the ceremony. She knew this public gathering was crucial to squash the notion that the witches were Satanists with evil intent. It was true that a couple of demon-lovers lived in the village, but they weren't very well organized and didn't seem to get much done. Mostly, everyone else just wanted to make sure their favorite ritual practice was included and that the town knew who the real witches were.

Solstice Rituals from previous years came to mind. She remembered the exhilaration she felt afterward, knowing she was in a tight community of people who loved each other and had each other's backs. She always felt transported to an ethereal realm where the boundaries between bodies were only suggestions, and hearts melded with each other without hesitation.

It was that euphoria that brought the townspeople back year after year. Some of them had begun attending the classes held occasionally by residents. Not just young people, either. Farming fostered a connection to the land and Mother Earth, compatible with most pagan traditions. Winkton was becoming a magical town.

But today, they had to make several changes in the ritual as the witches slated to take important roles were found asleep or mumbling something incoherent and scary. Instead of each direction being invoked by a group of witches from different traditions, now they were lucky if they had one person from each tradition to call forth the energies of the elemental spirits. The average age of the celebrants was getting older and older as the days went on, with basically no people under 50 still being functional.

Boreus, the Archdruid, was gesticulating with his staff to anyone who would listen. He had agreed to represent the masculine God energy in the ritual. But they had lost the Dianic priestess who was to be his feminine counterpart to re-enactments of Buffy the Vampire Slayer stabbing the Master, screaming, "You won't open Hellmouth while I'm alive!" Victoria volunteered to step in to fill her place.

Boreus stood, harrumphed, and stated, "The Druids use flaming wands to represent the sun's return." He remained standing, looking straight ahead.

"That's just reenacting the patriarchy and has nothing to do with the Solstice and the goddess," Dirty Swan said.

Macha, the high priestess of the Celtic Reconstructionists, spoke. She was no longer a member of the council since she had been diagnosed with dementia, but she wanted to make sure that everyone had a chance to jump over the bonfire. She also wanted to reenact the fight between the Holly King and the Oak King.

"We need to have the initiates jump together," she said. "Where is my high priest?"

"The bonfire will be after the ritual," Birdie explained patiently. "And Aiden, your high priest, passed five years ago. He won't be with us. You're at The Old Witches Home. We're a mixture of a bunch of traditions. This is not an initiation. It's a Solstice ritual."

"Well, what about Emerald, my daughter?"

This is going to take forever, thought Birdie. Can't we just move on? But no, every voice has a right to be heard. Don't be so impatient.

"She's not with us, either. Would you like to do the opening declaration, my lady?" It always helped to address her with the kind of deference and respect she had demanded from her initiates.

"Of course I will. I always do it." Good, she's got something to focus on now.

"Wait, wait," said Birdie. "We need to be inclusive. Is there a way we can honor the Holly King, the Oak King, and the Goddess?"

"The Goddess and the God both are part of nature." Victoria sounded like she was teaching a bunch of first-graders, probably just like when she had been a teacher for 35 years. She was a third-degree Gardnerian and just couldn't understand these witches who didn't understand that. "We have to appeal to them both and adhere to their teachings and forms in ritual. That's how we make the magic."

"Gender is fluid," Birdie said, wishing Dandelion were there. "Remember that it's the perspective that's important, not the deity's sex."

"I don't care who shows up, as long as there's a blot with plenty of mead!" grumbled Charlie.

"No substances," Dirty Swan reminded him. "You know that. Inebriation skews the energies, and we could send fire energy to the Evangelists, for goddess' sake."

"Also, not everyone can jump over the bonfire," she complained. "How are we going to make accommodations for those who cannot jump? And what about the Spiral Dance? Not everyone can dance either."

"Don't worry, Swan. There will be plenty of chairs in the center," Birdie said. How many times has Dirty Swan brought this up? It seems like she says this at every public ritual. Maybe she's just a little forgetful these days.

"Maybe they don't want to be in the center!" And cranky, too.

"Well, then they can sit wherever they would like!" Birdie was rapidly losing her cool. She took a deep breath, sent her roots down into the earth, and silently asked Gaia for patience.

The discussion dissolved into an argument over whether they should include the Spiral Dance. Birdie said it was a tradition – they had always had a Spiral Dance at the solstice rituals!

But Dirty Swan said, "Times change, and since when do we have to do things the way they've always been done? Isn't change good? Aren't we trying to manifest social justice and take down the capitalist system?"

"Thor doesn't dance!" thundered Bjorn, one of the two Heathens in the room. Don't those two ever use computers? Why weren't they affected by the virus? She wouldn't have such a headache if they weren't around. "This should be a solemn occasion! The death of Baldur, the beautiful, the son of Odin!"

"We have to do a Spiral Dance," said Birdie when Victoria suggested that perhaps there weren't enough drummers and musicians to make it work. "The townspeople expect it. Gives them a chance to check out our horns. They enjoy it, and we need to stay on their good side. I'll lead it if I have to."

And we have to build enough energy to counteract the computer virus spell.

"Okay. I'll take the tail," Victoria agreed. "But make sure you go slow – not everyone can skip and dance like they used to."

Birdie wondered, not for the first time, why she had ever thought it would be a good idea to get all kinds of pagans together in one place. Maybe she thought they'd get less cranky as they got old.

She looked around the room. Boreus' brown, green, and gold-ribboned robe had been quite resplendent at one time but now had frayed edges around the bottom and a coffee stain just above his navel. Victoria was wearing her flower crown, but several flowers had lost petals, which seemed more like suggestions than the real thing. Macha's delegation, three witches from Wisdom West, whom Birdie hadn't seen all summer, had a walker, a cane, and a knee brace, respectively.

Dang, she thought. This lot is a sorry bunch. We need to get Silver Sneakers going again.

"Okay, let's practice the chant. I'm not sure how many drummers we're going to have, so we may need to carry the energy with just the singing."

The chant was one they had sung many times before, and everyone knew the words. But people's memories being what they were, it was always a good idea to rehearse a bit. Birdie started strong but floundering as other voices joined, some slower than others, many who didn't remember the words, and others just plain off-key. She started stomping her foot to make the old fools keep the beat, and soon her ankle started complaining.

Good enough, she thought. "Okay. Let's do it," she said aloud. "We'll meet in the meadow at 1:00."

Birdie watched them move to the dining hall to get something to eat. They still had two hours before the ritual would actually start, which was good because it appeared that several of them needed to rest. She was sure Macha's contingent would fall asleep in their chairs.

23

THE HYDRATION PROJECT

After the planning was as complete as it could be, Lois and Diego strode into the Fire room, taking up more space than all of the witches who had been there that morning combined. They found Birdie sitting in an Adirondack chair with closed eyes. Lois hated to disturb her, knowing she felt responsible for everything. But this was important, and Birdie needed to handle this.

"Three of the souls we went to tend to did not answer their doors," Diego told Birdie. "Does anyone have keys to their homes? Their doors were locked."

Eddie came in right after Diego.

"Yeah, we had the same problem," he said. "What should we do?"

"What did you and the doctor do when you visited people yesterday, Birdie?" Lois asked.

"We just knocked and went in if the door was open, which most of them were. If it was locked and no one answered, we looked in all the windows. If we didn't see anyone, we talked to their neighbors," Birdie replied. "Some people are out of town."

That was like Birdie, relying on the shortcut rather than fully completing the task.

"So you don't know if people inside had the sickness who just couldn't answer the door?" Lois said.

"It only happened once that we didn't know where the person was – at Garnet's house. Tom checked with her next-door neighbor, Willow Wand. Garnet wasn't on the list, and it had only been two days." She sighed, realizing how stupid she had been. "I left a note!"

"Hell, I'm sorry," Birdie said. "We never had to get into anyone's house before. Should we have broken down their doors? What do we do now? Don't we have security for this? Damn, Mnemosyne would know."

Charlie poked his head in. "I was getting some water, and I overheard you. Don't you remember? We set up a security detail last year after you had your concussion. We wanted to be able to get to people who live alone if something happened to them."

"Damn," Birdie said, "I forgot."

Lois knew that Birdie didn't want to remember. She hated the idea of someone having to break into her house because she couldn't answer the door. She tended to ignore such things. Lois recalled the argument that Maple used to convince Birdie to give Mnemosyne a copy of her key just in case. He asked what would happen to Hermes if something happened to her.

They got keys from everyone else at the same time.

"Right," she said. "Let's go to Mnemosyne's office. We should be able to find them."

Lois started down the hall, her walker clip-clopping ahead of her. Eddie, Diego, and Charlie waited for Birdie to lead the way.

"Uh, Charlie, I think we can handle this," she heard Birdie say behind her. Lois stopped and waited for the rest of the group.

"You don't need any help?" Charlie said.

"No, we're okay," Birdie replied, but Lois wasn't sure.

"But I thought people were in danger. Don't you need everyone?" Charlie insisted.

"How did you hear that?" Lois was alarmed. Is their situation common knowledge?

"I saw Dr. Payne arriving and asked him what was going on," he said. "You really shouldn't keep news like that from the residents. We need to know if there's a threat to our health. I thought you all were all about transparency."

"We're taking care of it, okay? We don't want people to panic," Birdie explained. "Please keep your alarmist ideas to yourself."

"Maybe we should call off the Festival," Charlie said.

"No," Birdie said. "People are already setting up. We need to go ahead. We can do this."

Charlie shrugged and smiled. "Whatever I can do to help, I'm here," he said.

Lois looked at Charlie and tried to read him. She decided to give him the benefit of the doubt. She didn't think he wanted people to die.

"Well, okay, why don't you go with Diego?" Birdie said. Seemed like a good idea to Lois. They really could use the help.

Everyone caught up with Lois and went into the DWI office together. Luckily, Mnemosyne's penchant for organization manifested itself in a desk drawer labeled 'keys' with a huge ring with keys labeled with names. Diego took it from Birdie, and they left.

Lois led the crew back to the carts.

Lois was concerned there were not enough supplies, and immediately consulted with Dr. Payne when they returned to the drive outside the Heart.

As usual Taylor appeared unaffected by what was going on around him. He was sitting calmly at the steering wheel writing in his little notebook.

Lois looked down at her list, and counted the names without checkmarks beside them. She was frowning; so many people who they hadn't been able to see because their doors were locked and they lived alone. What happened to a welcoming environment where everyone felt safe?

Lois sighed. No matter how far we travel, we can never really leave the society we grew up in, she thought. She wondered how many of her friends had firearms they hadn't told anyone about.

Lois' training as a surgical nurse had prepared her for crises like this. Her faith in the Goddess gave her an optimism that had differentiated her from many of her colleagues. She knew there were more forces at work in the world than the science of medicine could explain. She had learned how to tap into those forces after her own bout of ovarian cancer.

Lois remembered how she had found solace sharing her experiences with others who had similar struggles when she attended a support group of women that were all battling some form of cancer. There, she had made friends with Beatrice, who told her about an eclectic form of nature worship that brought Beatrice peace.

That month, she invited Lois to join her for a full moon healing circle. It changed her life. When Lois sat down in the middle of the circle of women in Beatrice's candle-lit living room, she had no expectations. She simply hoped that she wouldn't be quite so depressed when she left. The doctors had not been very optimistic about her prognosis, but were unwilling to speculate on the likely progression of the cancer.

The women chanted and danced around her, enveloping Lois in a bubble of warmth and love. Lois felt like she was being lifted out of the chair, that her atoms and molecules had split apart and she was floating in a gaseous cloud. The waves of the chant rocked her as though she were a baby in a cradle. With her eyes closed, the mist around her was twinkling with starlight.

Suddenly, a figure appeared, not just in front of her, but above, below and around her as well. Embracing and enveloping her, it felt feminine, maternal, ephemeral. Without distinct edges, just shades of white, feathery and light.

"You are healed," Lois heard the Goddess say in her mind. "Now go forth and heal others."

While she was waiting in the golf cart, Lois reached out to that Goddess. "Please let us heal our friends," she implored.

Diego held up the ring of keys. Eddie and Charlie followed him. They split up the keys with Taylor, and all three golf carts took off again.

The keys worked for everyone's house except Mnemosyne's. Her fancy door didn't just use a key; it had a security code, and no one knew what it was.

"What are we going to do?" Taylor asked Lois. "Do you want me to try to break in?"

"No, that would set off the alarm, and the police would come. She must have the code written down somewhere in her office."

Taylor walked around the neat yard, peering in windows.

"She's on the floor in the bathroom," Taylor yelled. "She's breathing. Her lips are moving, and her fingers are tapping the tiles."

Lois hobbled over to the window Taylor was looking in and strained to reach the sill to see for herself.

"Would you like me to help?" Taylor said.

"Oh, sure," Lois said, admonishing herself that there was no need to feel embarrassed just because she had to be lifted in order to see through the window.

Mnemosyne was dressed in a summer nightgown that had gathered at her waist, revealing sexy flowered cotton panties. Taylor was right – she was breathing and didn't appear to be in any immediate danger. But how long had she been like that?

The hem of Mnemosyne's nightgown lifted off the floor and gently floated. That's when Lois realized that the bathtub was overflowing. Mnemosyne must have been preparing to take a bath when she lost consciousness. The water was rising quickly.

Let's hope that bathroom isn't watertight, Lois thought, although, knowing Mnemosyne, it probably was.

Diego and Charlie drove up to the house. They had finished their list and had stopped to see if Lois and Taylor needed help.

"Go to the DWI office and see if you can find the code for Mnemosyne's house," Lois said to Diego.

"It's right here," Diego said, showing Lois the tag on the large ring from which they'd split up the keys.

"Oh, thank the Goddess," Lois said. "Let's get in, turn off the water, and get Mnemosyne to bed."

She was sure she didn't need so many men to help her take care of Mnemosyne, but she was grateful for their company. Mnemosyne's heart was racing and her skin had a bluish tint. She was having trouble breathing and kept coughing. Taylor propped her up in her bed while Lois tried to pour some Gatorade down her throat.

"Honey, can you drink this?" Lois asked her.

"78, 49, equals sum A7 to X58," Mnemosyne responded in a murmur. Her eyes opened, but she didn't focus. She looked straight through Lois and appeared to be in a different room altogether. Lois put the bottle to her lips, but the liquid flowed down her chin. Then she laid back down, closed her eyes, and continued murmuring. Diego stood over her and chanted something as he gently waved his hands back and forth.

"I'll need to get an IV in her," Lois said. "She's not doing well. Eddie, can you help me? Everyone else should leave. The ritual will be starting soon."

Lois had been planning to invoke the energy of Center/Spirit at the ritual. She hadn't had a role in ritual since 1973 when her stage fright had caused the young witch to hide beneath the altar for over a half hour, seriously disrupting the circle's energy. But she knew it might be her last chance this year, and she was determined to redeem herself.

She told herself one step at a time, just do the next right thing. She wouldn't let Mnemosyne die. Maybe next year.

She took a deep breath and began prepping Mnemosyne's arm as the others left. Goddess, don't leave me now, she prayed.

24

THE SUMMER SOLSTICE RITUAL

Birdie saw Rosie, the lady from the post office, making her way up the meadow path with several people behind her. She realized that no one had put out the signs they usually posted to guide people from the community building up the hill, but luckily, there were enough townsfolk who had been to previous rituals that they knew where they were going. The meadow was filling with dozens of people of all ages in colorful t-shirts and shorts, looking like they were ready for a 4th of July barbecue.

Birdie's mouth watered when she saw the dishes in the hands of several townspeople. She was pleased to see that Sally, the town librarian, had directed the food back to the dining pavilion, where tables were set up to receive the cookies, brownies, cakes, and pies.

Normally, Angie or one of the young helpers would have organized the food, but they were in another world now, weren't they? Thank the Goddess for the friendly folks who didn't even seem to notice that people were missing. Their excitement was contagious.

"Time for ritual," Birdie announced to the witches, nodding in the dining hall.

Slowly, the group coalesced into a moving blob, and haltingly, with cane, walker, and wheelchair, the planning cell made their way to the ritual meadow just south of the bonfire. As Birdie looked around, she gave thanks to the Goddess again, relieved that they had mustered enough witches to have something that resembled a proper Solstice celebration. So many had the silly sleeping sickness, lying in their beds or wandering around their rooms, chanting or singing or muttering as their fingers twitched and their eyes darted back and forth a quarter inch to each side. She couldn't reach them. They were in their own worlds, and Birdie felt helpless and confused.

Well, no matter now. She took a deep breath. She closed her eyes and asked Gaia for strength to get through the day and to bring forth abundance for her very special home. The sky was still clear, with just a few clouds gathering in the West. The air was electric and jubilant.

The energy in the meadow swirled around Birdie with an insistent hum, rising and falling with laughter and little kids shrieking. Small bodies ran across the circle, chasing each other. The very little ones hid behind their mothers' skirts, eyes wide and smiling. Even the Old Witches Home residents seemed to be more alive than usual.

They formed a ragged circle around the meadow. Townspeople and residents placed lawn chairs, camp chairs, folding chairs, and Lazy Boys to create an amoeba-shaped assembly. Some townspeople tried to corral the children scampering about in front of the people in the seats, but the witches didn't notice. Perhaps they couldn't see them, their vision not being what it used to be.

Goddess, please give them enough strength to dance the spiral, Birdie silently pleaded. Thank the stars there are enough townsfolk to balance out the energy. There were fewer townspeople than in previous years, though, and she was worried.

The drummers moved into the center with their benches, their stools, their djembes, their dunduns, their batas, and bougarabous. One old witch had even brought a snare drum and her hi-hat cymbal. They moved slowly, forming a living sculpture of wild gray hair, tie-dyed t-shirts, and flowing skirts. Whale Tooth's tight leather pants that had been to countless rock concerts had ridges at the knees and the groin and appeared so brittle Birdie was afraid they would split down the middle and clatter to the ground when the drummer sat.

When the flow of incoming visitors slowed to a straggler or two and Sally had joined the group in the meadow, Birdie nodded to Maple.

She watched Maple settle into his high priestess stance in the circle's center, looking strong and confident. His booming voice rang out.

"Gather round, fair townsfolk. Gather round, witches, and pagans of the land. Today is the longest day of the year. The sun is high and strong. The fields are fertile and thriving. Today, we celebrate the friendship between the town and the witches of The Old Witches Home. Join us to feast, play games, revel in each other, and dance our most sacred dance, the Spiral Dance. After the ritual and the feast, the bonfire will be lit as we honor the Old Gods and Goddesses, the Oak King, the Holly King, and Lugh, the Sun God. Join us in the circle as we set our sacred space and invoke the elemental deities, our ancestors, and the spirits of the land."

As he retreated to the circle's edge, Maya stepped into the center to lead the grounding exercise. Her warm and genuine manner soothed Birdie and brought everyone together. Maya planted her feet firmly, stretched out her arms, and entreated the gathered to become trees, to send taproots deep into the earth, to send branches up into the sky, and to intertwine their roots and branches with all the others in the circle. By the time she was finished, a forest of souls was enjoying the sunlight that had broken through the clouds.

Birdie felt the presence of Huffstickler before she saw him. As she was basking in the forest sunlight, a dark shadow entered the glade from slightly behind and to her left. Instead of his usual frumpy suit, he wore smartly creased blue jeans and a white t-shirt with fold lines as if it had just come out of a box. Birdie wondered if there was still a tag on the back of the neck.

Great, he's here, she thought. We'll show him that we are the rightful stewards of this land!!

A vaguely familiar person walked just behind Huffstickler. The 20-something ebony-skinned man in black jeans seemed to have a cloud of brown and lime green swirling around his head. His gaze was about a foot behind Huffstickler, grazing the grass as he moved. Birdie felt a screechy chattering as though there were banshees vying for his attention.

She looked around to see if anyone else had noticed, but no one else was reacting. Just two more townspeople in the crowd, as far as everyone else was concerned.

Oscar was scheduled to cast the circle, but since he was incapacitated, Maple limped deosil around the circle and created sacred space. He brandished his hoe in the air above him to inscribe a pentacle in each direction, requesting all to envision a verdant field of flowers and grain around, above and below them, protecting and embracing them in the light of the Goddess. Then, he used the hoe as a cane to get to the next point.

Dirty Swan spoke the land acknowledgment, honoring the Haudenosaunee Confederacy, the Mohawk, the Lenape, and the Oneida who had lived on this land before the Europeans, who had suffered from colonization, and who had taught the settlers so much. She asked for their ancestors and their descendants to permit them to celebrate that day and to join them in their expressions of gratitude to the land, the animals, and the plants.

The elemental deities were invited into the circle next, each invocation echoed by the group. Townspeople and a couple of the witches with impaired hearing were just a couple of beats behind, which gave the invocations Alpine echoes.

As usual, the Gardnerians invoked the East in the traditional way:

"Ye Lords of the Watchtowers of the East, ye Lords of Air; I do summon, stir, and call you up to witness our rites and to guard the Circle."

The group murmured, "Air is sacred. Welcome, Air." Air is sacred..... Air is sacred..... Air is sacred.....welcome....welcome....welcome.

The Radical Faeries invoked the South and Fire, dancing and whistling and waving sparklers in the Air.

The group giggled, "Fire is sacred. Welcome, Fire." Fire.... fire.... fire.... fire.....

So far, so good. But this is taking forever. Birdie's stomach was in knots, and her spidey sense that notified her when the energy was off was squealing.

The three elderly women of the Dianic Grove waved blue scarves around, undulating and cooing as they called to the powers of the West, the womb of the Mother, and the spirits of Water. Birdie watched the ancient witches and was sure that at least one would sink beneath the sea as she rolled her hips in imitation of the ocean's surf. The group hummed, "Water is sacred. Water is life. Welcome, Water." Water....water.....water..... The echoes sounded right for this invocation, as though the whole group was submerged and gasping for Air.

In the north, the senior Druids planted their feet and bellowed to the meadow's oaks, maples, and birch trees. The voices proclaimed, "Earth is sacred. Welcome, Earth." Welcome....welcome....welcome.... and the echoes dribbled off, turning the sound of the earth into a muddy chorus.

Phoenix strode to the center and read from a 3X5 index card that Birdie had given her just before the ritual when she learned that Lois wouldn't join them.

"We call upon the energies of Spirit, energies of the Center. Cauldron of Cerridwen. The magic melting pot. Join us. Spirit is sacred," she whispered as loudly as she could, giggling a little as she read.

Luckily, the group was trained by now since no one had heard a word. "Spirit is sacred. Welcome, Spirit." And the echoes reached the heavens, knitting them together in community.

After Lugh, the Sun God, the Holly King, the Oak King, and all the Gods and Goddesses that have anything to do with fertility were invoked (32, to be exact), most participants were restless or nodding in their chairs. The kids had disappeared into the woods and could be heard playing tag. The sun had disappeared behind a light gray cloud and was rapidly obscured by ominous slate clouds moving across the sky.

Finally, we better do this quickly, though, Birdie. That sky looks scary. But one more person needed to speak.

Macha, the old Celtic Reconstructionist, slowly stepped into the center of the circle.

"We come together to celebrate the Summer Solstice: the highest arc of the sun and the rich abundance of the year. Flowers, fruit, and vegetables are plentiful. We delight in long, warm days and balmy, scent-filled nights. Under the warming touch of the sun, we open to the beauty of all around us. We cherish our family and our friends. We surrender ourselves to this moment of joy." Macha smiled broadly around the circle, then gingerly stepped back to her chair.

Birdie thought it wouldn't be a good idea to be too open or to surrender too quickly. As far as the warming touch went, she remembered the feeling when her hand was on the mouse, and the jolt went up her arm. She glanced at Maple and then Maya, spaced at strategic points equidistant from her. They both looked a bit scared.

Birdie nodded at them and tried to look confident. She had no idea whether their counter-spell would work, but they had no choice. She prayed to her patron goddess, Athena, Goddess of war, and mentally touched each of the crystals in the fountain they had placed in the center of the circle. She raised her voice so everyone could hear.

"As is our custom on the longest day of the year, we dance the Spiral Dance. This is our chance to greet each other and come together in friendship. We will be walking slowly in a circle, singing the chant many of us learned before ritual. If you don't know the words, don't worry. We will sing it over many times. After you've heard it a few times, join in whenever you want.

"Think of what you've been growing this year. Ponder on the projects, the crops, and the efforts you've put time and energy into, which are at fruition. The summer solstice is the height of the sun's powers. We will channel that power to manifest what we've been working on all year since the winter solstice. This is the time to make it real."

Birdie saw Bjorn and Charlie nod to each other, and Huffstickler looked at Henry, who was still looking at his feet.

Then Birdie instructed the people who weren't going to dance to bring their chairs to the center and to encircle the drummers, facing outward. A couple of the younger townspeople moved in to help some of the elderly witches with their chairs, but the process still took over five minutes for everyone to get situated. The clouds had begun morphing and darkening, and the gentle wind occasionally was a strong breeze. This ritual was taking forever.

"Gather round and grab hands," she said. The amoeba bulged into an oval, and Whale Tooth, the head drummer, nodded to the others who started a beat. It took twenty seconds or so before all the drummers were on the same beat, but eventually, they all found it, with only an occasional wayward boom or cymbal crash. Good enough, she thought.

"Remember to look into the eyes of each person you pass. We want to acknowledge and greet each other and open our hearts to our community."

Weave and spin, weave and spin.
This is how the work begins.
Mend and heal, mend and heal
Take the dream and make it real
Strand by strand, hand by hand,
Thread by thread, we weave a web

Birdie dropped her left hand and began moving slowly to her left, the rest of the circle starting to move behind her. She stepped out with her left foot, crossed her right foot over, and gently pulled the woman next to her in line to follow her. The young woman from town, with spiky red hair, heavy-duty hiking boots, jean shorts, and a bright orange tank top, was belting out the chant, energizing Birdie.

The townsfolk sang as though they were skipping rope, compensating for the unsure elderly voices in the circle. Gradually, everyone became more confident. Nothing wrong with this community, Birdie thought, and not for the first time, her anger at Huffstickler began to rise. Why did he have to attack a bunch of old witches? What did they ever do to him? She knew she needed to be focused, though. She couldn't let the anger flare too soon. She willed the red-hot ball of rage in her stomach to remain there until she was ready.

Thank you, Goddess, for placing this young lady next to me right now. She'll keep me grounded.

As they moved around the circle to the left, Birdie led the dancers following her into a spiral just inside the outer edge of the circle. Their backs faced the people still standing, waiting for the person next to them to begin. Birdie could sense the line of people starting to flow. It was like a slow wave that wasn't sure it wanted to crest but knew it was inevitable. One by one, they began moving, a couple of people tripping over themselves as they sidled, hand in hand with an old friend to the left and a new friend to the right.

It was tradition that the witches spaced themselves out around the circle so that townsfolk were flanked by them, and everyone was thoroughly enmeshed in the same circle, with no distinctions whatsoever between townie and witch.

It seemed to take a very long time to make one full spiral into the center. Birdie felt the looming clouds. Finally, she reached the center and turned to shape the spiral for the rest of the dance. As she turned right, back in on herself, she smiled at the red-headed hiking boots woman beside her. Then, the bearded witch next to the hiking boots woman. The bouncy ten-year-old next to the bearded witch.

Down the line she went, twisting the spiral in on itself and winding it outwards. She gazed into each person's eyes, finding the twinkle and awe in some and the confusion and forgetfulness in others. Each person added a bit of life to the ocean of energy in the circle. Each person was crucial, and yet each was only a small ripple, insignificant alone but vital together.

The drummers had really found their rhythm and were buoying the dancers with some extra special licks. The chant was getting louder and louder and everyone seemed to be infusing the sound with their own joy, their own sunshine, and their own hopes for the rest of the year.

Birdie almost forgot her rage and the darkening sky as she reveled in the faces she passed, even the ones with suspicion and anxiety. She beamed at them as if to say, for now, it's all good, and we're together.

Just before she got to the end of the line to make her inward turn, she saw him – Huffstickler. He, too, was part of the dance, and when he looked at her, he sneered. That computer kid in black jeans was also there, one dancer away, looking anywhere but at the person in front of him.

A cold shiver ran down her spine. She knew, finally and with certainty that the illness at The Old Witches Home was their doing. She knew. She was damn well going to do something about it.

She made the turn. Faced toward the center of the circle. Snaking through the lines of people still on their outward journey. Gazing into the eyes in front of her. People smiling and singing. The edges of Birdie's vision began to blur. Her voice was still part of the chorus, but the music sounded far away. All she could feel was the beat of the drums – reverberating up her legs into her body. Compelling her to move and sing.

She reached the center again and again made a turn. Now she wasn't sure anymore whether the people she was seeing in front of her were witches or townspeople. Her mouth was stuck in a smile. Her voice was a record with a deep scratch in it. The same phrase over and over again. That's the way chants work – everyone singing the same thing with their own favorite phrases.

Birdie felt the energy building as they danced in and danced out, in and out, three times in and out, smiling and singing. By the third time she led them back into the center, the group was one entity, one tight, squirming blob of sound and movement, one heartbeat and one breath. They dropped hands as their bodies surged toward the drummers, writhing and slithering, toning and chanting. Some were still singing the chant as written. Others had created their own verses or had dropped words altogether in favor of pure sounds, joyous, loud, insistent.

The drums shifted and all the complex rhythms stepped back into a single file of one beat, relentless and strong. The voices, too, coalesced into one, a morphing and blossoming tone, a deep, rich note with overtones of high-pitched angelic chords and undertones of dark, loamy, rocky earth, ever-shifting, becoming softer and louder, first in the center, then from the outer edges of the circle and then back again.

Suddenly, the sky ruptured. Lightning split the Air. Less than a second later, thunder bellowed. A few dancers screamed. But most people didn't hear. They just kept singing. The sky swallowed the screams.

As the energy built and swelled, as the sound spread and shot up to the sky, another bolt of lightning sprouted from the cloud, followed by the rumble of thunder as though a train were barreling down on the dance from above.

Faces turned toward the sky – anticipating – but there was no rain. The lightning and thunder crashed again, high in the clouds. The sky was dry. More and more eyes were drawn to the spectacle played out by the gods, Thor and Lightning battling above.

The beat continued; dancers still moved. Even townspeople were caught up in the trance. Consciousness took a rest. Thoughts no longer linear and sharp, just round and hazy. Everyone in the same dream, another universe, hurtling through space, timeless, motionless, only here, only now. A blob of awareness, a bottomless lake of existence.

Slowly, they gathered, staring up, intoning that sound, stomping their feet, the drum beat propelling them into the center.

The protective shell Maple had created was strong. Shafts of bright lightning illuminated the edges. A rainbow bubble enveloped them, safe and shimmery.

The wind gathered speed. Darkness encircled them as though it were a starless night. Branches whooshed just outside the circle. Twigs and leaves flew, chaos. Lightning and thunder crashed again and again, the pauses between shorter and shorter each time.

Birdie only barely heard the drums that were keeping time with the thunder, the cymbal clanging with the lightning and swishing with the leaves.

Maple's toe no longer throbbed. Maya felt power radiating from her heart. Elmer, sitting in the center, lost inside the vortex of energy, couldn't feel the chair beneath his butt. Whale Tooth's pants split in two – he just kept drumming.

Oooommmmmm..... Louder and louder, they toned until their voices were a shrill scream into the heavens, and then the energy they were shaping became a cone. Round and tight at the bottom, widening, gathering speed as it rose, pure energy, open to the sky, filled with hope, with love and ...

With Huffstickler's evil spell! Birdie could see it now, a neon green and brown spiky orb in the middle of the cone of power.

She shouted, "Focus! Manifest! Bring forth your love. Welcome the Sun God! Welcome Gaia! Together!! Together! Love is all!!"

She concentrated on the crystals in Maple's fountain in the center. She felt Maya and Maple's energy also focused on the crystals. The flow of the water over the faceted gems directed and amplified their combined rage, expanding and sharpening their intentions. Three spears of red, blistering energy aimed at that orb. The sounds around her intensified.

But the orb was emitting its own energy pulse, and it was getting stronger and denser. There were forces in the crowd strengthening and protecting that orb. The Heathens!

Birdie and the others fought back.

All her training, all her years of experience, all those days and nights playing with love spells, house blessings, protection spells, she called on it all to assist them now.

She called on Maya's warmth, Maple's strength, Whale Tooth's rhythm, Nighthawk's loyalty, and the gallantry of Gwion. She intermingled Elmer's compassion, Rosie's openness, the redhead's passion, and the 10-year-old's innocence. Everyone in the circle. Everyone's energy, all focused in a cone of power, united, full of love.

Then she felt him, whooshing tulle and chiffon as Lightning twirled around the circle. The scents of lavender and rose mingled with the musky Air.

Lightning, in his element, sixty feet tall, toes pointed, arms outstretched. Turning, jumping, coiling, leaping. Widdershins. Dispersing. Banishing. Dissipating the Heathen energy. Protecting his – their – land. Opening space for the crystal flow.

Birdie felt the red-headed hiking boots woman, the ten-year-old, Tom somewhere on the other side of the circle, Rosie from the post office, Elmer in the center, Dirty Swan, Boreus, Whale Tooth, and the cashier from the grocery store. All in it together. It didn't matter that they didn't know what they were doing.

Maple, Maya and Birdie – three points of a cosmic triangle – coalescing, directing everyone's energy upward and into the clouds.

Focus. Birdie aimed her mind, her intention, and her will into a laser. She braided her strength with her friends. The rest of the ritual receded. Only a faint background murmur. The column of force created by the chant rose. Gathering strength, concentrating itself, condensing, confronting the danger.

Whistling. Crackling. Whooshing.

Connecting.

BOOM.

The orb exploded.

Blasts of energy scattered in all directions. Echoes reverberated. Tiny shreds of neon green and brown ashes drifted down from the sky, lit with rainbow sparks. Clouds raced overhead. Sprays like fireworks burst above them. Dazzling streaks showered the group with magic.

They did it.

They broke the spell.

A shout from the crowd echoed through the trees. Birds scattered into the heights of the mountain. Squirrels, chipmunks, and all manner of small rodents scampered up the trees or burrowed into the earth.

Rain burst forth.

The witches and townspeople chanted, dripping, and drenched. The din of the droplets drowned their song.

The ribbons, bits of yarn and string, even the leather cords, on the gnome – burst into flame. Its sinister smile dissolved as it lit up like a Christmas tree. The rain quickly dowsed the nasty little figure, leaving it a smoldering, wretched mess.

Birdie looked up, empty and clear. Free of panic, full of magic. Lightning stood over them still, his toes tapping a rapid bourree that vibrated in her bones like a deep earthquake. His fierce countenance a bright shape in the haze.

Owww..... deep within the crowd, Birdie heard Huffstickler moaning. A figure in black jeans writhing on the ground beside him, holding his head, his face contorted in spasms of pain.

Shiiiittttt..... Bjorn bellowed behind her. Nearby, she saw Charlie fall, mud splattering his hands, his face, his shirt.

From somewhere far away in the Heart, she heard a beeping, then a ringtone. From one of the houses nearby, the sound of an old-fashioned phone. Beeps and buzzers and errant snatches of music started popping up all over the village as though everyone's alarm had all gone off at the same time. The noise grew until the air shimmered with the sounds, and the drummers matched the beat. The celebration had begun.

Birdie and the other witches dropped to the ground, placing their palms face down, breathing into the earth. Some of the townspeople did the same. Others were laughing and smiling and turning their sopping-wet heads up to the sky. The rain was soft and steady, with distant sounds of thunder now miles away.

"We bless this earth, we bless this community, and we give thanks to all the Gods and Goddesses of the land on this, the longest day of the year. Blessed be." Maple's voice echoed around them.

Sparkles of rainbow light fell with the raindrops.

Birdie saw Maya grinning and chuckling as the group reformed into the amoeba. She looked at Birdie and beamed. Birdie glanced at Maple, and he, too, had a satisfied smile.

Then, she saw Oscar, Twig, and Angie approaching the circle. They looked confused and stumbled as they walked, but their eyes were clear and comprehending. There was no doubt that they had returned.

Mnemosyne strode down the lane, with Lois and Eddie a step behind her. Others followed and joined the circle.

The crowd cheered. Even townspeople who had no idea what was going on shouted and whooped. People started hugging each other. Some kissed people they had never met and may never see again. The redheaded hiking boots woman took off her tank top and threw it in the air. Children ran around the circle, high-fiving each other as they crossed opposite directions.

Off to the side, Birdie saw Huffstickler holding his head, scowling, and retreating to the parking lot. Good riddance, she thought. The boy in black jeans followed him, groaning, shuffling, and casting backward looks at the group.

As usual, the devocations were much shorter, and the circle was opened quickly. Angie, staggered to the tables in the meadow, and Birdie saw her grabbing the cloth napkins and silverware Nighthawk had set out there. She took them back to the dining hall out of the rain, passing Hermes sitting on the steps waiting for the party.

Magic, Birdie thought. It's magic. We dreamed this.

Magic. Yes, it was exhilarating. And then someone had to clean up afterward.

The lawn was soaked, and all Birdie could hear were squishes and sucking sounds as vendors walked around trying to remove items from their booths to take them inside.

The tables were arrayed against the low walls inside the ritual room and lining the halls. As the sounds of the storm continued outside, striking the windows and occasionally shaking the roof, bedraggled witches and townsfolk mingled and murmured with each other, oohing and aahing over ceramics and jewelry, ritual robes, and scarves. Most items had not been damaged by the rain, as their creators had brought them in quickly, soon after the first thunder had been heard. Only the notecards were truly watercolors.

The next couple of hours were filled with laughter, children running around, loud talking, and lots of eating. Birdie moved from table to table, thanking folks for coming to the celebration and reminding everyone of the various methods to donate to The Old Witches Home Collective – Venmo, PayPal, Zelle, cash, and even the anachronistic check were all acceptable methods.

As Birdie savored the smell of some particularly pungent blue cheese, Mnemosyne approached her.

"What happened?" she whispered as Birdie embraced her with a passion Mnemosyne had never felt from her before.

"I have no idea. All I know is that that evil nacker capitalist was behind it."

"I don't remember anything. One minute, I was working on the spreadsheet for the Festival, trying to calculate what we needed to take in, and the next, I woke up in my bed with numb fingers. All I could see were numbers and equations for the first couple of minutes. I felt like I was inside the spreadsheet.

"But when I opened my eyes and got out of bed, the feeling faded, and I was here again. Shaken but here. I could hear the drums, the thunder, and the chanting. How did I miss the whole ritual?"

"You weren't the only one. I can't tell you how glad I am to have you back. I'm not sure what they did, exactly, but we fixed it."

What did they fix? Mnemosyne decided to go to her office for a moment of reflection. She needed a safe space to collect herself and breathe for a few minutes, but serenity was the last thing she found when she got there.

What had gone on while she was out of it? Someone had clearly been rifling through the file cabinet. It was closed, but the keys were lying on the desk in front of her. The ring of house keys was splayed out next to it.

She next saw a dirt-stained envelope ripped on the short edge. Next to it was a letter with an official-looking letterhead.

Notice to Appear. The document from the Winkton County Clerk said Lauren Sanders, Administrator, The Old Witches Home Collective, LLC, was due to appear in County Court on Mon 6/23, at 9 a.m. to present testimony regarding the Last Will and Testament of Edward Vincent O'Neill. It said to bring their articles of incorporation and documentation of the registration of the deed transfer from Estella Amato to Edward Vincent O'Neill.

Dang! She had no idea where the copy of the deed transfer was. Was that what they had been looking for? She vaguely remembered Lightning celebrating with Almond Joy ice cream after he received official confirmation of his ownership of the land ten years ago. But this document said there was no record. Had he done something wrong? Why didn't they know about this before now? She knew his lawyer had filed it with the county court, but then Lightning fired that lawyer, didn't he? And took all his official records back. But where did he put them?

No problem, she thought. I'll find the email acknowledging the transfer and take it with me on Monday.

She sat down at her desk and turned on her computer. It started okay, but it wasn't connected to the internet. She was confused.

Wasn't it on the Wi-Fi? It was always hooked into their system. Then she noticed that the server on the shelf was dark and quiet. She walked over, examined it, and plugged it in.

She waited. She heard a low hum, like usual. She listened for another few seconds, but there were no other sounds. She walked back to her desk and sat down.

She was still a little light-headed and felt a strong sense of apprehension as she gingerly grabbed the mouse.

Whiz, crackle, grind. She wasn't sure what her computer was doing, but it struggled. The screen lit up, then went to black, then lit up again. Spreadsheets started scrolling right to left as though she were rapidly flipping through a book.

Pop! The image of the last spreadsheet she was working on stabilized on her desktop. The expense sheet for the Festival. Okay. That looks normal.

She closed it, opened the browser, and went to the County Clerk's website. She typed in their address, and there it was. Winkton County Form 9983, Transfer of Ownership of Real Property, stared back at her. She wasn't sure, but there appeared to be a slight green sheen around the page on the screen.

She examined it carefully. Everything appeared to be in order. Estella's name and date of death, Lightning's name, and property details. She went to File Properties and checked the history of the document.

Created 22 Apr, ten years ago. Deleted 5 Jun this year. Restored 21 Jun. Huh?? Why was it deleted? Who did that?

Someone must have been tampering with the files. Damn. But it was back now.

Okay, she thought. We're okay. She sank back into the chair and breathed deeply. She reached out to the protective wards she had carefully placed around the room. A tingling electric static buzzed in her ears, and she could swear the room's energy shimmered and glowed. Her body relaxed. She allowed herself to feel at home and content.

Mnemosyne realized something had shifted inside her. She was always concerned about staying in control, convinced the place would fall apart without her. But it hadn't. She had been out of it for three days, and the others had kept everything going and held a successful Festival. They had ensured she was safe and then brought her back to herself. Maybe she didn't need to keep such a tight hold on things. All she needed to do was clean her desk and straighten her files. And it didn't matter if she did that today, tomorrow, or next month.

Maybe she needed to have faith. In her community. In the magic of The Old Witches Home.

Tom found Birdie sitting off to the side of the dining hall. She was leaning against the wall with her eyes closed, musing on the subtle and magnificent power of magic.

He spoke gently, "How are you doing?"

"Oh. Good. I guess I'm a little stunned. I wasn't expecting the rain." She needed to downplay the incredible power she had felt during the ritual, still unsure of Tom's acceptance of magic.

"Yes, that was a surprise. It was an amazing ritual. I don't think previous years have been quite so intense."

That's an understatement.

"Isn't it fabulous that Angie's back?" they heard as Maya rushed past them, headed toward a clump of townspeople sitting at the back of the room.

"It's good to see she's up and moving," Tom said, nodding his head toward Angie, staring at two crockpots, one filled with black beans and another with baked beans. She went back and forth between the two as if expecting one of them to jump into the other. Birdie could faintly hear Angie humming, "Food, glorious food. Hot sausage and mustard." Birdie was sure she had heard that song somewhere before but couldn't place it.

"*Oliver*," said Tom. "It's from the musical. *Oliver*. I haven't heard it for years. I wouldn't think someone as young as Angie would even know it."

"Hmmm..." Birdie said. How did he know what she was thinking?

Just then, Henry and Mr. Huffstickler peeked their heads through the wide double doors that opened to the lane leading to the circular drive. Birdie could see them creeping along the outer wall, slowly advancing toward the food tables. They were both soaked and dripping and looked sheepish as they tried not to be noticed.

Maple appeared at the end of the table, blocking their way.

"Welcome, gents," he said politely. "I'm wondering if you might like to have a word." He gently and firmly grabbed Huffstickler's elbow. Just as Henry tried to slip away, Birdie came up behind him, grabbed Henry's arm, and said, "May I join you?"

"Unhand me," Huffstickler said loudly, obviously designed to get everyone's attention. "Why are you accosting me? I thought you witches were all about hospitality."

"We are," Birdie said softly, as she and Maple began moving Huffstickler and Henry toward the corridor.

"My car won't start, for some ungodly reason," Huffstickler said, emphasizing the 'ungodly.' "I was just hoping to use your phone.."

"Yeah, our cell phones don't work, either. What did you do? Put a spell on them?" Henry added sarcastically.

He was eyeing the fried chicken hungrily.

"Never you mind, young man," Birdie said. Maya came up behind her and handed Henry a chicken leg. Birdie shot her a look, but Maya just shrugged and smiled at Henry like an old grandmother sneaking sweets to her grandchildren while their mother was away.

"You got any aspirin?" Henry whispered to Maya. "My head is killing me."

"I'll get you some," she said quietly and retreated to the kitchen. She came back in a minute and handed Henry a glass of water and a couple of white pills.

"Will you convince Lightning's brother to drop his contest of the will?" Maple asked, confronting Huffstickler directly.

"Are you crazy?" Huffstickler said, again quite loudly, as if he wanted to make sure everyone in the dining hall heard him. "This land isn't worth anything. He'd be doing you a favor if he took it off your hands. I just want to get out of here."

"Would you like something to eat?" Maya asked Huffstickler.

"No, thank you, I'm not eating your insects again," Huffstickler announced. Maya shrugged.

"There's a phone in the kitchen," Maya said. "Why don't you all go there?" She handed Henry a plate.

"Come on then." Birdie and Maple escorted Huffstickler to the kitchen. As they were leaving, Birdie saw Henry glance around suspiciously and then dive into the macaroni salad, grab another piece of chicken, and spear corn on the cob.

In the kitchen, they kept their eyes on Huffstickler as he called the only tow-service in town. He harrumphed into the phone. The mechanics, he told them after he hung up, were at the Festival.

"Would you like a jump?" Maple asked. Birdie imagined Maple's knee in Huffstickler's backside as he leaped in the Air.

"I'll find my own way, thank you very much," Huffstickler replied. "I'll see you in court on Monday. Come on, Henry."

The young man came into the kitchen with a spear of corn in one hand and a brownie in the other. He looked sheepish as he followed Huffstickler.

Bang. Everyone could hear the door from the kitchen to the road when Huffstickler and Henry left. The sound was quite satisfying.

Birdie and Maple returned to the dining hall and saw Maya standing nearby, wiping her hands on a towel and chuckling. Birdie almost felt sorry for Huffstickler. Almost.

No one noticed the lawyer and the computer tech leaving. They were having too much fun, building community, sharing stories, and making new friends as the evening wore on. Outside, they could hear the wind and the rain as it drenched the land.

Dandelion found a few bottles of dandelion wine in the back of the kitchen pantry. Dirty Swan brought beer from her home, supplemented by Whale Tooth's hard cider. Whale Tooth had found some safety pins in the Healing Center and pinned his pants together. White cotton peeked through near his crack, which gave the impression he was wearing a diaper.

The sober witches slipped off to hold a 12-step meeting. Several of the insomniac townspeople joined them, a tradition on solstice evenings. They often went to each other's meetings, either in town or in the Water Purification Room, on Wednesday evenings or Saturday mornings. In those settings, white t-shirts and overalls coexisted comfortably with purple hair and pentacle tattoos.

Birdie usually joined the meetings but felt tonight that it was more important for her to continue to play hostess in the dining hall.

Later that evening, Birdie relaxed with a piece of lemon meringue pie. She could occasionally hear someone say something like, "Wow, that was the best ritual we've had here!" and she smiled to herself. You don't know the half of it.

Maple approached her, only slightly favoring the foot that hadn't been injured. He seemed to have a new determination, a new strength.

"What do you think about the bonfire?" he asked.

"Not while it's coming down like this," she said. "Should we ask the others?"

They polled Boreus, Victoria, Dirty Swan, Dandelion, and Macha. Enough of a quorum, they thought. Everyone agreed that it would be better to wait until the next day.

Birdie was relieved and went to get another piece of that incredible pie and get off her feet. She sat at a table at the far end of the dining hall and watched Tom move about the room, chatting with the townspeople and The Old Witches Home residents equally.

Then she realized that he and Lois were spending a little extra time with each of the people who had been afflicted. She was on one side of the room, and he was on the other. Each time he sat next to one of them, he took the person's hand and looked deep into their eyes. She was amazed that he could be so discreet while still getting vital information.

Finally, he and Lois met each other near the dessert table. He sat beside her and was very quiet as he listened to her. I'll never have to worry about my health care with those two around, Birdie thought.

When he got up to move away, he leaned over and gave Lois a peck on her cheek.

Birdie was surprised that she thought about Tom with such longing. She had long ago given up on romance and was determined to never fall in love again. She remembered what it was like to be obsessed. And ultimately rejected.

Remember Tony in high school? Shut up – absolutely no point going back there.

She and Tom hadn't really talked since they had been together. And that was only last night! But he hadn't called, or texted, or anything...

Birdie turned away from watching him and started gathering plates and silverware to take into the kitchen.

The evening passed, and all those afflicted were learning about what had gone on during their absence. Birdie listened as they told the townspeople what had happened, and a current of concern grew in the room. Some people made joking comments that maybe it was because of the witches consorting with evil spirits that they had been struck ill. But others thought that was nonsense and stated their views in no uncertain terms.

"You know these folks!" shouted Elmer, the stout dairy farmer. "They could no more consort with evil demons than my cows could spout chocolate milk."

"Then what the heck happened to them?" said Sally, the sane and reasonable town librarian. "Dr., do you know what happened? Are they really okay now? I hope whatever it was isn't contagious."

Tom Payne didn't move from the bench where he was sitting next to Lois. He said, "Maybe it was a virus. I've never seen anything like it, but it appears to be gone now. I don't think anyone is in danger anymore."

"Maybe it was a computer virus," Elmer said and laughed. "Those dang machines are going to be the death of us all. Just the other day, when I turned it on, all I got was this blue screen and nothing else. Nothing! I took it to Henry, that kid in town, and he fixed it. He was here a minute ago, wasn't he? Said it was too old or something. He just wanted me to buy a new one, I bet. But it's only ten years old! It's just getting broken in!"

Birdie remembered the green aura she saw around Twig when they were in the healing circle. Green. And bright, like neon. Like a green screen? What is a green screen, anyway?

The discussion continued, and Mnemosyne told them about the squiggly numbers. Angie performed a powerful rendition of *Defying Gravity*. When Twig began to dance to a reggae beat only they could hear, a sudden bolt of lightning struck the roof, and the lights disappeared. The room was as black as molasses.

There wasn't a sound except for the rain hitting the roof. Dandelion went into the Fire room and brought over a few pillar candles. She struck a match and lit one. Slowly, other candles were lit, and people began to move around.

"Anyone who wants to can stay here tonight," Birdie offered. "We've got plenty of blankets and pillows in the ritual room and more in the element rooms."

Children were already piled high on cushions in the ritual room. Maple and Maya embraced Birdie in a very tired embrace. Tom approached them, and Birdie stretched out her hand. He eagerly joined the group hug.

The backup solar generator kicked in, and the lights came back on.

When they let go of each other, Tom said softly to Birdie, "Want to go to your place?"

After Birdie and Tom left, Maple and Maya continued cleaning up. Only a few guests were still hanging out in the Heart. Maya could hear young voices harmonizing and enjoying a bardic circle in the Fire Room. Every once in a while, there was a loud burst of raucous laughter. Without the bonfire, they had to improvise the fiery celebration of the longest day. There was still plenty of energy to work with.

But Maya was tired. She was grateful for the quiet that had settled over the dining hall. It felt comfortable to work alongside Maple. She was clearing the last of the dishes and the condiments from each of the tables, placing them on a cart, while Maple followed behind, wiping them down with a rag soaked in vinegar and water. All that was left was for her to start the dishwasher and for Maple to sweep the floor with the big broom.

The only people still sitting in the hall were Bjorn and Charlie at a table in the back corner.

Bjorn was wearing sunglasses as though the light hurt his eyes. He had a blue and purple bruise on his cheek reaching up to his right temple, outlined by deep scratches punctuated by droplets of coagulated blood. Charlie was sitting next to him with his cap pulled down low, his head in his hands, breathing raggedly. Neither spoke, although occasionally one would moan and the other would say, "I know, man, I know."

Abruptly, Bjorn got up from the table, raised his glass of mead, and looked like he was about to make a toast. He gestured to Maya and Maple.

"Congratulations! You did it. Free enterprise is officially dead at The Old Witches Home. No one can make money off this place now. And I'm screwed."

"What are you talking about?" Maple asked, continuing to wipe down tables and slowly moving closer to their table in the back. Maya tried to ignore them, but they were only one table away.

"Huffstickler was a good American," Bjorn slurred. "He had his priorities straight. He was going to build on this land and actually make money. We would have all been rich! Instead of living like hippies."

"How do you know what he was going to do?" Maple said.

"Wouldn't you like to know? I have sources," Bjorn said, grabbing the bottle to refill his glass. "Some people talk to me. Some people include me in their plans. Some people have respect."

Maya saw the bottle and paused. Maple stood before them with a rag, ready to wipe the table if Bjorn ever moved.

"We're trying to finish up here," she said, moving toward their table. "Maybe you could take your bottle back to your cabin?"

"What, you don't like an old-fashioned celebration? Our ancestors drank mead, and their women had no problem with it."

Maya held her breath. She really didn't want to confront Bjorn when he was like this.

"But maybe you don't know about that. Maybe it was different where you came from. I mean, your people don't know how to make mead, do they? They only know how to make liquor with worms, right?" Bjorn laughed; a little spittle dribbled from his mouth.

"Come on, Bjorn," Charlie said, rising from the bench, and standing shakily. "It's time to put you to bed." Maya hoped Charlie, usually a voice of reason, would get through to him.

"Maybe this little lady would like to join me? I've got plenty of room, and it looks like you've got plenty to share," Bjorn said and laughed again. Charlie chuckled as he swayed and moved around the table toward Bjorn on the bench on the other side. He glanced at Maya apologetically while Bjorn looked at her greedily.

Maple moved closer. Bjorn turned toward him, got a serious look on his face, and put out his hand, palm up. Maple stopped short of confronting him.

Maya stiffened.

"Aren't you hippie witches all about free love, darling?" he crooned. "I've seen you all hugging and kissing each other – don't you want to hug and kiss me, too?"

Maya froze – she was thirteen years old. Again.

Bjorn started to move toward her. Maple went around the table to block Bjorn. Charlie got up and stepped between Maple and Bjorn, like three big dominoes in a row. She was having trouble breathing.

"Stop it," Maple said over Charlie's shoulder. "Leave her alone."

"Oh, I'll leave her alone soon enough," Bjorn said. "And then maybe she'll go back to where she came from and let the real Americans have the country. If only you all had let Huffstickler do what he needed to do, the rest of us would have been rich. You don't know how much we need the money. But no – you have to be inclusive," he said in a singsong voice. "You have to all agree – reach consensus – so everyone makes nice. Well, no one asked me what I need." He was tall enough to see over Charlie and Maple. He didn't take his eyes off Maya and took another step toward her, pushing Charlie into Maple and Maple closer to Maya.

Maya felt herself starting to leave her body. She felt her legs swaying and wanted to close her eyes. She just didn't want to be there anymore.

She heard a whooshing sound behind her. The scents of lavender and rose. Then, it felt like hands were on her back, holding her up and pushing her forward.

"Do it," she heard. "Stand up to him." The voice was soft but clear and resonant. Did anyone else hear it?

"I can't," she thought. "He's too strong."

"Leave her alone," Maple said angrily. Bjorn kept his eyes on Maya.

"He's not going to do anything. He's drunk. He's just fooling around," Charlie said. "It's okay. He's a good guy. Really."

"It's not okay," Maple said. "He needs to leave. Now."

"We will, we will. Don't get your knickers in a twist." Bjorn's bruised face looked forlorn. Then he sneered.

Charlie and Maple were face to face, Charlie swaying a little and Maple leaning on his good foot. Bjorn was still watching Maya as though he were getting ready to pounce.

He reached around Maple and Charlie to touch Maya's face. She could smell his breath. She couldn't move. They were so big. Three men. On top of her.

"So soft and plump. Plenty of woman here, that's for sure. My sweet baby," he cooed.

That was it. Something broke.

The whooshing sound grew louder, and Maya felt the air swirl around them.

"Stop," she yelled. "Leave me alone. Who the hell do you think you are?" She was shaking, still not quite sure she had actually said anything. "Get out of here and go back to the rock you crawled out from, you racist prick."

"Whoa, little lady," Bjorn said. "I wasn't going to hurt you. I wouldn't do anything you didn't want me to do. I just thought we could be friends. You're such a sweet baby."

No. No, no, no. She inhaled, lavender and rose filling her nostrils and masking the beer and mead.

Maya grabbed the industrial broom that was leaning against the wall behind her. She raised it and began to swing at Bjorn. Charlie and Maple scuttled to each side. The wooden broom weighed almost five pounds, too heavy for her to lift higher than his head, but she connected with his torso and knocked him off balance. He fell on his butt.

From the floor, Bjorn reached up and tried to grab the broom. She pulled it away from him. He tried to stand, but he couldn't keep his balance, and she batted him again and again. He tilted back and forth like a bowling pin, trying to decide if it was hit or not. Then he fell again, thudding as his head hit the ground. He sat up and started scooting away from her, groaning in pain.

"Get the hell away from me. Don't you dare come near me again," she screamed as she swung the broom back and forth, pushing him farther and farther away from her.

Maple and Charlie had stopped arguing with each other and were standing with their mouths open.

"What the..." Charlie said.

"Maya," Maple said. "Stop?"

But she wouldn't stop.

"Get away. Leave me alone. Go!!"

"You go, girl," she heard behind her as the whooshing circled the room.

"Maya, Maya, it's okay." Maple was carefully approaching her, trying to reach out and take the broom from her.

"I am strong. I am a witch! You can't touch me!" she yelled and, with one final burst of energy, swung the broom over her head in a wide arc that just missed him as it came down in front of her and split in two.

Bjorn finally was able to get to his feet, breathless and wide-eyed. He retreated quickly to the wall behind the tables. Charlie joined him and stood in front of him just in case she came back.

She threw the broom handle, now light and sharp like a lance, to the floor. Maya plopped on the bench.

The whooshing subsided, and she heard, "Good job. You did it."

Charlie and Bjorn were greedily taking swigs from the bottle Bjorn miraculously still had in his hand.

"I think you guys better leave," Maple said. They were as far from the exit as you could be in that room. They had to sidle along the wall to get to the door. They stumbled once or twice before they made it out into the night. Maya could hear loud talking as they left the building.

"Can you believe that bitch?" one of them said.

"Let's just get out of here," the other answered.

Maple sat down next to Maya. "You okay?"

"Yes, I think I am."

Maya felt lighter than she had in a long time. She was at peace.

"I love you, Maple. I trust you. You are really one of the good guys." she said.

"Thanks. Yeah, I guess I am. I'm really not a sexist, racist, heterosexual white supremacist. I've learned something over the years, and I will never be like those guys."

"No, you won't. You've got more magic and more heart than anyone I know."

She dropped her head on his shoulder.

"And you know what? I love myself, too."

"So do I," Maple said, pulling her close.

They both let out huge breaths. Then Maple stood up. He reached out, and she stood and let herself fall into his embrace.

"Let's finish up and go to bed," he said. "How about I walk you home? Would you like some company tonight?"

"Definitely." She would love to share the magic of the solstice with Maple. Her body was hers, and hers alone. Being with Maple felt like the perfect end to a long day.

She gathered the salt and pepper shakers on the table, and Maple wiped it down. Sweeping could wait.

She hung up her apron and took Maple's hand. She heard Angie's stump fiddle, accompanied by the group singing *The Christians and the Pagans*.

As the clouds moved rapidly across the sky, the rain disappeared. Birdie could hear faint young voices singing one of her favorite songs. Slivers of light occasionally lit the path, then just as quickly ducked back behind the gray clouds.

Tom and Birdie walked in silence. The sounds of their squishing feet and the drips from the trees punctuated their steps. The energy from the ritual remained as a slight buzz in Birdie's body, a substance-free high.

The full moon and the solar path lights should have been more than enough to see, but the lingering mist obscured the world as they walked. Birdie felt like they had stepped into a dream. The fog around them muffled the voices and the music from the dining hall. An occasional laugh pierced the haze.

Birdie felt a slight shudder as she walked. It was not from cold; the air was still warm, and there was only a light breeze now. The mist smelled fresh and alive, pleasant on her skin. The scent of the trees and the potent air around them held them in a strong, safe embrace.

Her mind was in a reverie, for once – no worries, no planning, no memories, no fear. The counter-spell worked, the ritual was powerful, her afflicted friends had all awakened, the feast was a success, and they had banished Huffstickler, at least for now. Tom was beside her.

An owl hooted nearby, waking her.

Ugh, she thought. I should say something. But what? How about – what did you think of the magic we made? Did you notice the evil orb? What do you want for breakfast? My damn sciatica is acting up again. Can you help? How about those crazy witches waking up just in time to not die?

I don't know what to say or how to act, she silently screamed. Gaia, please help me. This is ridiculous.

Gaia must have heard her because, just then, a cool breeze brushed them. Tom reached out and gently took Birdie's hand. She looked at him, and he smiled. They both looked ahead at the path before them and walked.

Then Birdie's brain got involved again. The knot in her stomach tightened.

Why am I feeling this way? I've been with lots of men and some women. I know how to do this.

This felt different. This felt like they were wading through an underground river, through hidden caves near the planet's molten core. Before last night, they had walked on the surface of the earth through forests, meadows, and streams, but now they were somewhere else. They had descended to the world underneath, to the underworld that held up all their dreams, that fed the forests and meadows and streams with the unseen currents, the hidden flows of energy that had been growing for years. The accumulation of experiences, wishes and feelings, disappointments and fears. All was there underneath. And now they were in it. They had stepped through the door in the tree that led to the underworld, the place where shamans take you. The place where spirit animals and transformation live. The crucible from which you return irrevocably changed, forever different, undeniably alive.

Tom seemed to be just as lost in his thoughts.

No turning back now.

Birdie stopped at the front door and put her hand on the knob. "Are you sure?" she said.

"Absolutely."

They went in. Hermes ran inside just as she closed the door.

She crossed to the kitchen and put water in the teapot. Tom chose a record and placed it on the turntable. The sounds of Crosby, Stills, and Nash filled the room.

Hermes jumped up on the sofa and settled in, purring loudly.

25

A WEEK LATER

By Wednesday, June 25, The Old Witches Home was back to normal. Hermes trotted after Tom and Birdie, who were arguing as they left her cabin. The sky was clear, and summer was in full force. They were headed to the pond, so Birdie could get in a quick swim before the weekly meeting, before Tom left for his office.

"I didn't say magic isn't real. I'm just not sure that anyone can do it," Tom said.

"Of course, anyone can do it," Birdie replied. "You've got magic in you. We all do. It's just a matter of tapping into it and directing the energy."

"I don't know. They certainly didn't have a course on magic in med school."

"You saw what happened at the ritual. You don't think that was magic?"

"Something happened, but I can't say what it was."

"But you felt it, didn't you?"

"Yeah. I felt something."

"And we won against Huffstickler and Lightning's brother. That was magic, too."

"Now you're reaching. That's just good lawyering."

"No, it wasn't only lawyering. We set the energy in motion, and it moved the way we intended it to. The lawyers did a great job but they had whatever spirits who chose to join us, and all of our energy, behind them."

A breeze lifted the short strands of Birdie's hair from her neck like a gentle kiss. She heard a small chuckle somewhere off to her left that twirled around them as they walked. The sense that something tall, strong, and lithe was leaping ahead of them was strong. She could swear she smelled lavender.

It's so good to have you with us, Lightning, she thought.

"Can you feel that?" she asked Tom.

"Feel what?"

"The breeze, the laughter, the flying through the air. Lightning is here."

"That's just the wind," Tom said. He laughed and put his arm around Birdie.

She pulled away. "You don't know what you don't know," she said. "Don't patronize me or mansplain to me. If you're going to hang around here, you might as well get used to the idea that magic exists."

"Or what? Are you going to turn me into a toad?"

"I just might." She walked away from him in the direction of the pond.

When he caught up with her, she laid her dress on the bench beside her towel. She was splashing Angie's Sassy Sunscreen on her arms. She spread it on her torso, rubbing it between her breasts, over her nipples, and on her stomach. When she bent over to cover her legs, Tom spoke.

"Would you like me to put some sunscreen on your back?"

She wanted to say, go away, I can do it myself, but she still hadn't mastered the trick of twisting her arms far enough to put lotion on her back. There were just some things a person always needed help with, like reaching the cups in the back of the top shelf of the cupboard.

"Oh, all right." She wasn't ready to be really nice to him yet.

"You know, Birdie, just because I'm not a witch doesn't mean I can't believe in magic."

"You're an insomniac," she said. "You don't know how to make dreams real."

"You're right. I'm probably too old to change now," he continued. "I believe there's a power greater than us, and sometimes we can get on that power's train and go the same way it's going. But I don't think we make the train or lay the tracks."

"Maybe we can throw the switch and make the train go off in another direction," she said. "You just don't know. And neither do I."

"You're right," he said. "I don't know. So, I will choose to believe whatever I need to believe to continue to enjoy being with you. I love the rituals, and if any of the gods or goddesses are listening, I hope they know I respect them."

"Okay." Birdie was softening. She had never imagined herself being content with a non-Witch, with an insomniac. She had always insisted on finding someone like-minded, but there was something endearing about his sincerity, even as he questioned her view of the world.

"And I respect you. I'd like to spend the rest of my life loving you." He was looking at her directly, and she suddenly felt quite naked, which she actually was since she was getting ready to jump in the pond.

"Huh. Okay." She felt a need to protect herself. Maybe she could tell him that the Council didn't approve his residency application. Or maybe she should just jump into the pond and drown. He was leaning forward, moving toward kissing her.

Oh, shit. I have to say something!

Just go for it, something whispered in her ear. Isn't this what you've always wanted?

Birdie took a deep breath. Why not? She certainly wasn't getting any younger. She met him, and they kissed deeply and passionately.

"I love you too. Now take off your clothes and let's swim. We can talk about everything else later."

Tom smiled and leaned over and kissed her on the cheek. It was not a long kiss like the one before, but a light, familiar kiss, as though he had been kissing her his whole life. The kind of kiss that says, yes, we belong with each other. We are one.

Birdie felt tears in her eyes. Shit. She ran to the pond, kicking up sand and dirt as she passed the witches lounging on the beach. She dove headfirst into the cool water and swam as far as she could underwater until she reached the middle, surfacing only when she could no longer hold her breath. She looked back to the shore, and Tom was very small and far away but getting closer by the minute. She exhaled and laid back to allow the sun to warm her body as she floated. She felt weightless, ageless, and free.

Birdie felt at ease at their weekly meeting. She and the others congratulated themselves on another example of successful ReDreaming magic. They had won, and now Huffstickler was under investigation for fraud and embezzlement. The district attorney had discovered that Huffstickler attempted to convince several other elderly women to leave their estates to him and had pressured Lightning's brother to contest the will.

Unfortunately, the brother was nowhere to be found. He had left the alcohol rehab center, and no one had heard from him since. Because he didn't appear or contact the court, Judge Longfellow, the lovely woman who had brought a pecan pie to the Solstice Festival, declared the will as valid and the contest as unsupported.

"I can't imagine Lauren and her friends trying to coerce that lovely man, Edward Vincent O'Neill," she said. "His brother must have just not gotten to know them."

"But I'm the one who took care of Estella. I was there after Alice died. I should have inherited her land, not Edward. He only showed up when he wanted applause." Huffstickler tried to defend himself, but the judge was not moved. "And now I don't have any family at all," he muttered as he closed his briefcase and prepared to leave.

Huffstickler looked so downtrodden that Birdie felt sorry for him and, in her mind, promised to invite him to their next public ritual. At least if he was still out on bail.

"I can't believe I found the deed transfer," Birdie said to Mnemosyne as she took her usual place by the window. "Just like Lightning, to put it with his clippings."

Birdie found it Sunday afternoon in a folder marked *Les Ballets Trockaderos reviews* in one of the boxes she had retrieved from Lightning's shed. Then, Monday morning, the county clerk unexpectedly found the record of the land transfer from Estella to Lightning in the system. However, she was still having trouble locating their official paper copy.

In any case, the legitimacy of the will was no longer in question. Now the land belonged to The Old Witches Home Collective, LLC.

"We still need to pay the balloon payment, though," Mnemosyne remarked.

"Yeah, I think Louella is sweet on Huffstickler," Maple said. "I saw them walking out of the bank together when I went to the hardware store yesterday to get trash bins. He probably convinced her to push the issue. But we do have collateral now. She could have helped us refinance instead of calling the loan."

"We didn't collect quite enough at the Festival," Mnemosyne said. "I think I can finagle something, but I wouldn't mind having more cash."

"I'm sure you'll figure it out," Maya said. She placed a platter of morning-glory muffins on the table in front of the group.

"To Lightning," Birdie said as she held a muffin up.

"To Lightning," the others echoed, also holding their muffins high.

They all looked at each other, sighed, and took big bites.

26

EPILOGUE - LATER

"Uh, excuse me," Henry said from the doorway. Mnemosyne was hunched over her laptop, deep in thought, scowling.

He snuck a glance around the room. It felt familiar to him, even though the only time he had visited previously was when he tampered with the server. The energy didn't seem as tight as it had then. There was a more relaxed quality to the atmosphere. Still, the room had a quiet strength that he knew better than to mess with.

Anansi, please… He reached out to the god who had infused the spell he had created with its powerful trickster energy. But trickster gods sometimes surprise you. He hadn't really thought the whole thing through. Maybe Anansi really is the god that outsmarts oppressors.

"Yes, can I help you?" Mnemosyne looked at him suspiciously, but he knew The Old Witches Home Code of Behavior required being open and non-judgmental. "Come on in. Aren't you the tech who works at The Olde Magick Computer Shoppe?" He saw her try to smile, but her forehead remained creased as if she were having trouble thinking. Maybe she still hadn't quite recovered from her days under the spell of the computer virus.

He couldn't wait. He had to confess. Even though Huffstickler hadn't ratted him out, and the County Clerk still didn't realize their records had been hacked, he felt guilty and wanted to come clean.

"I thought it was the right thing to do," he said. "I don't think I expected that it would actually work." He walked sideways into the room and stood behind the cracked leather easy chair in the corner.

"Okay." When she looked straight at him, he felt himself looking away. He knew he looked a wreck; his white t-shirt was wrinkled, and there were holes in his black jeans. He wore sneakers without socks. He hadn't shaved for a couple of days. He hadn't slept either. He could taste a slight crust of dried saliva caked at the corners of his mouth.

"I was just mad, that's all. I thought everyone here was taking advantage of the town. You seemed to hire only outsiders, not locals. It wasn't fair. And when he told me he'd give me an apartment and a car, it felt like the right thing to do. I didn't know it would work so well!"

"Okay. It wasn't your fault. But what did you do?"

"You know who Anansi is?"

"Sure," she said. "He's a storyteller god from Africa. He was a symbol of freedom for enslaved people. But he was also a bit of a trickster."

"I invoked him. I brought him here."

"You brought him?"

"Yeah, to infect your system. And it worked. And then I hacked into the County system and deleted the land transfer."

Henry told her the whole story.

"Wow." She looked at him. He expected her to say something, but she just stared.

"I'm really sorry. I wasn't sure it would work. I didn't know it would cause so much trouble. I didn't realize that it might endanger people's lives. I was mad, and I thought you all were the oppressors. Then Mr. Huffstickler said he could make my life so much easier. But now he's under investigation and could go to jail. I don't want to go to jail too. I wanted to apologize."

"You came up with that virus? That spell? All by yourself? Are you in a coven or anything?"

"No, it was just me. And Anansi. I didn't think it would work so well. And now I'm sorry. I don't think you're oppressors anymore."

"Well, that's a good thing. We tend to dislike oppressors around here."

He looked down again. He felt stupid that he had misjudged them. And he was pretty proud that he had done what he did. He wasn't sure if he had come to tell her because he wanted credit or to ask forgiveness.

He looked up. Her face had softened.

"Listen, we'll figure this out. I can't believe you could do all that by yourself without support. Do you still feel Anansi or any other trickster gods around you? Did you bring them in with you?" She closed her laptop quickly.

"I haven't felt him since the Summer Solstice ritual. I think you guys banished him or something. I could try to get him back if you want."

"No, no, no... we've had enough of him for a while. What else can you do?"

Henry told Mnemosyne about the store and how they were trying to build a business, but there wasn't enough demand for a full-time computer store in Winkton. Most people got what they needed from the internet. He also told her that two years ago, he had applied for a job as a helper at The Old Witches Home but had been turned down because they had already given the job to Twig. He thought they had lied to him and that they didn't want to hire him because he was Black. Mnemosyne chuckled when he said that.

"Then what am I doing here?" she said. But she understood how he felt and how he could think that way. Even at The Old Witches Home, diversity and fairness couldn't be taken for granted.

She listened intently and then sat quietly, staring at him. He felt naked and checked to see if his fly was open. It wasn't.

After a long few seconds of silence, she spoke. "Want a job doing office work?"

This was not what he had expected. "Sure... I think."

"I need help in this office, and I'm not getting any younger. Most people here don't know how to use a computer or balance a checkbook."

"Do what? I don't think I've ever balanced a checkbook, either."

"Sorry, I forgot. Another lifetime. That's okay. Can you use spreadsheets?"

"Of course." He swallowed. She was still looking at him. "You're really offering me a job?"

"I'd rather have you working for me than against me. When can you start?"

"I suppose I could cut the hours at the shop. How about tomorrow?"

"How about next week? Let me just run it by the Council. We make decisions by consensus here. You'll get used to it."

Henry thought he would start crying from relief, but Mnemosyne embraced him, and he didn't want to get her clothes wet. He left to make arrangements to switch the store to part-time hours.

Twelve weeks later, one day before the Mabon Fall Equinox Festival, Henry gawked at the pile of boards, logs, and branches growing before him. He and the others – Eddie, the old firefighter, in jeans and worn leather work gloves; Taylor, who had started a monthly poetry slam on the new moon and then decided to stick around through the winter; and Twig, an enigmatic creature Henry couldn't take his eyes from – were building the best bonfire Henry had ever seen. Oscar and Maple were sitting on lawn chairs off to the side, supervising, they said, but generally just laughing at their own jokes and occasionally shouting, "Good job, keep it going."

Eddie was the one quietly directing their efforts, ensuring the base was strong and easily lit. Henry was beginning to feel the muscles in his arms and legs, much more developed since he wasn't just sitting in his store all day. He was starting to feel healthy and at home.

He still called on Anansi for wisdom, knowledge, and strength, and Anansi seemed to enjoy being in a multi-cultural pantheon.

Finally, they took a break. Henry saw Twig standing alone, admiring some late-season wildflowers, purple asters, and blue yarrow. Their avocado green crop pants blended in with the grass and leaves and complemented Henry's own bright orange t-shirt. He still wore his black jeans.

Henry approached.

"Hey."

"Hey," Twig replied. "Aren't they beautiful?"

"Yeah, they are." Henry hesitated, afraid that Twig knew how Henry had almost destroyed their home, how he had enchanted Twig and kept them captive in their music. He could never do something like that again now that he knew everyone.

Henry had started attending classes and had been invited to a few private rituals. As a condition of his employment, he had agreed to the new *Principles of Community*, which stipulated that everyone was required to treat everyone else with respect, which they had previously simply assumed people would do. But he knew they had added it to deal with people like Bjorn.

Henry was just starting to get to know the other traditions in the community. He liked the polytheistic worldview of the Heathens, that emphasized free will. He got along with well with Andy and Charlie, although Bjorn was somewhat standoffish since he returned from rehab. Still, Henry enjoyed talking with them about their relationship with Heimdall, the protector god they had transferred their allegiance to from Thor. He imagined Anansi and Heimdall collaborating to keep The Old Witches Home safe.

"I like your voice," Henry said to Twig. "I could hear you singing with your headphones, and it was really nice."

"Thanks," Twig said. "I've been working on it. The hormones only do so much."

"Well, it's working. You sounded beautiful," Henry blushed a little. He was afraid to look around in case the others were watching him.

"Thanks," Twig said. Henry looked up from the dandelions he had been studying and saw a shy smile on Twig's face, their dark eyes warm and glowing.

"Hey, Maple," Twig said and turned away. "You ready for the bonfire? Are you staying up for it, old man?"

Maple laughed. "Of course I am! We're celebrating! The land is ours, and all is in balance."

Henry glanced at Maple and saw Maple studying him. He imagined the old man saying to himself, 'That's right, you little shit. You shouldn't even be here.'

"Cool." Twig tossed another branch on the pile. "You'll be at the bonfire, too, won't you?" they asked Henry.

"Sure, if it's okay."

"Yeah, why not? Right, Maple?"

"I guess." But Maple was still eying him, and Henry felt the hair on his arms.

"I'm going down to the pond for a dip. I'm sweaty. Wanna come?" Twig smiled.

Henry exhaled with gratitude. "Sure!"

As they walked down the hill and through the meadow to the pond, Hermes followed them, occasionally darting off into the trees to chase a chipmunk. Twig laughed easily and reached out for Henry's hand, and Henry felt at peace for the first time in a long, long while.

I think I could grow old here, he thought, smiling.

LIST OF CHANTS

Healing Chant (Oh Mother)
by Alisa Starkweather

Every Step I Take is a Sacred Step
by Donald Engstrom

Weave and Spin
by Starhawk

The Christians and the Pagans
by Dar Williams

Grounds Layout

Heart Building

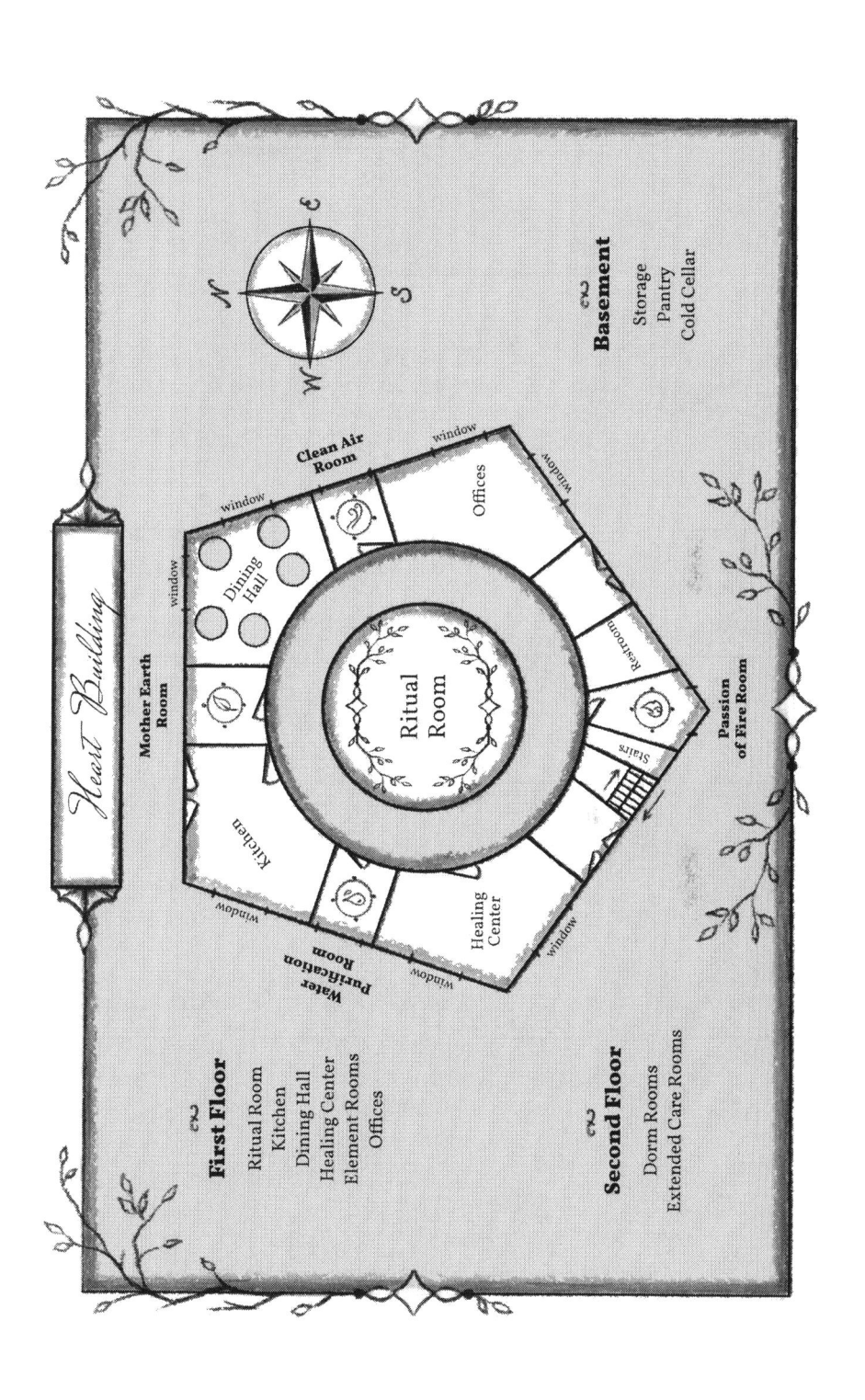

Mother Earth Room

Clean Air Room

Dining Hall

Offices

Ritual Room

Restroom

Kitchen

Stairs

Healing Center

Passion of Fire Room

Water Purification Room

First Floor
Ritual Room
Kitchen
Dining Hall
Healing Center
Element Rooms
Offices

Second Floor
Dorm Rooms
Extended Care Rooms

Basement
Storage
Pantry
Cold Cellar

Lightning's Family Tree

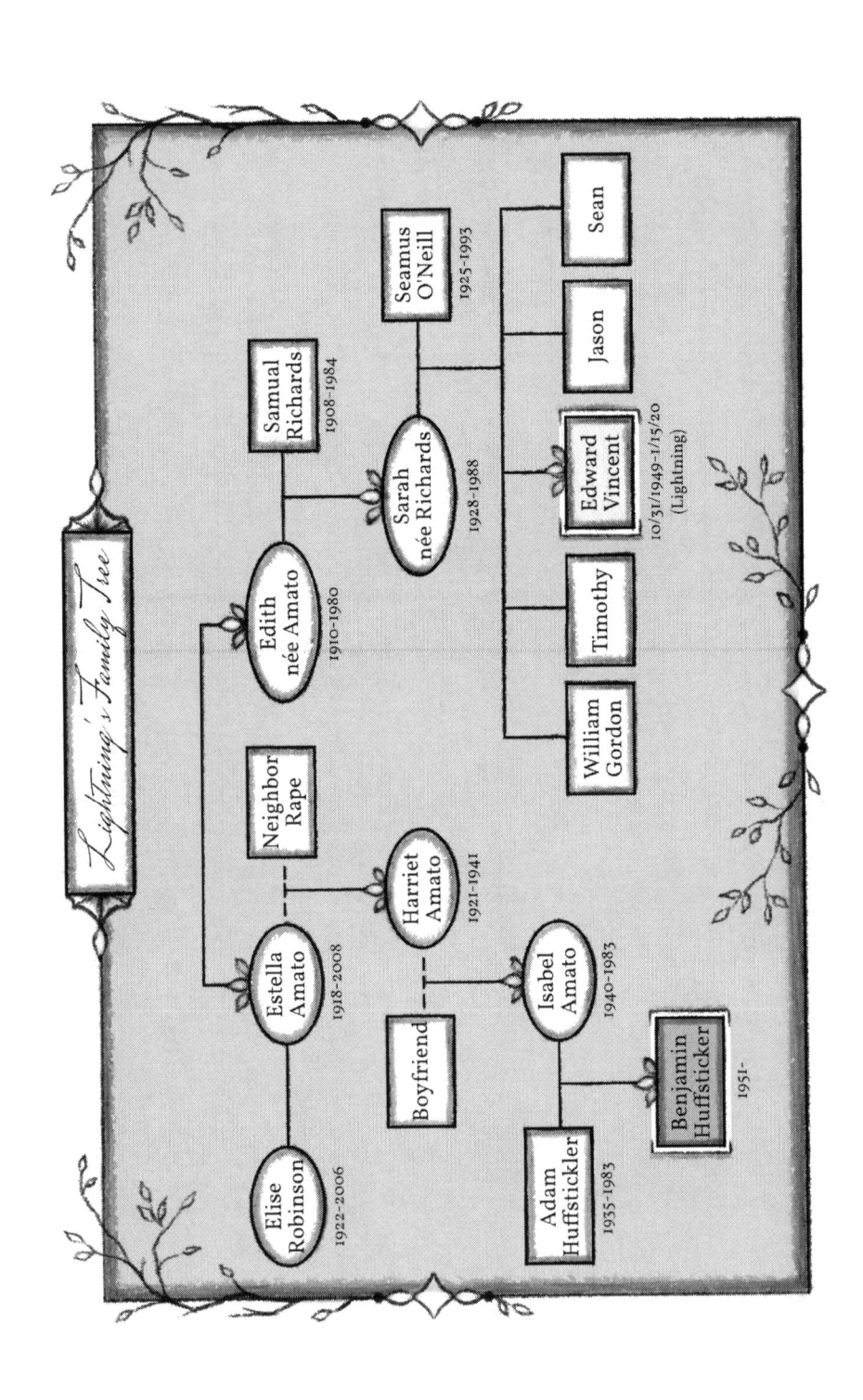

- Samual Richards (1908–1984) — Edith née Amato (1910–1980)
  - Sarah née Richards (1928–1988) — Seamus O'Neill (1925–1993)
    - William Gordon
    - Timothy
    - Edward Vincent — 10/31/1949–1/15/20 (Lightning)
    - Jason
    - Sean
- Estella Amato (1918–2008) — Neighbor Rape
  - Harriet Amato (1921–1941) — Boyfriend
    - Isabel Amato (1940–1983) — Adam Huffstickler (1935–1983)
      - Benjamin Huffsticker (1951–)
- Elise Robinson (1922–2006)

THE OLD WITCHES HOME
PRINCIPLES OF COMMUNITY

The Old Witches Home is founded on the principle that all humans have the right to age gracefully, with dignity and care, among beings that respect and love each other, including non-human and non-living creatures. We believe that divinity is within each and every human, and that our connection to the earth is sacred.

All Pagans, Witches and others who would like to reside at The Old Witches Home must agree to abide by the following principles:

- Inclusivity is of paramount importance at The Old Witches Home. All are welcome, regardless of background, prior experiences, current beliefs or economic status.
- We view diversity as a strength of our community, and actively strive to foster an environment where Witches and Pagans of all genders, sexualities, abilities, races, traditions, and ethnic backgrounds are able to thrive.
- No one is turned away for lack of funds. The Old Witches Home will make every effort to support prospective residents who have financial needs through loans or grants.
- Everyone has a voice at The Old Witches Home. We use consensus-based decision making procedures to ensure that all voices are heard in order to reach mutually acceptable solutions to problems.
- We rotate leadership positions and balance individual responsibility with personal capabilities and health, recognizing that faculties may deteriorate as a person ages.

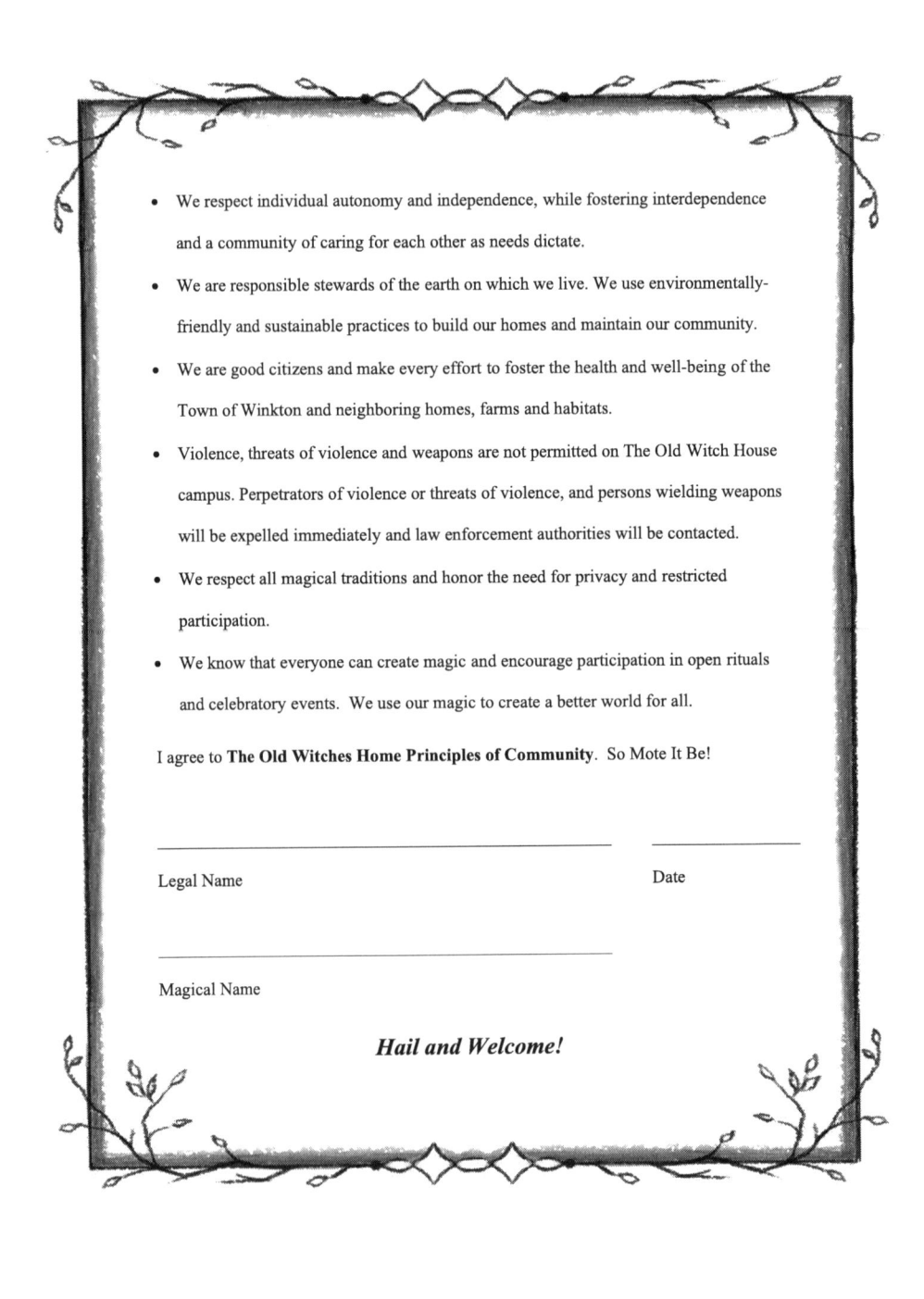

- We respect individual autonomy and independence, while fostering interdependence and a community of caring for each other as needs dictate.
- We are responsible stewards of the earth on which we live. We use environmentally-friendly and sustainable practices to build our homes and maintain our community.
- We are good citizens and make every effort to foster the health and well-being of the Town of Winkton and neighboring homes, farms and habitats.
- Violence, threats of violence and weapons are not permitted on The Old Witch House campus. Perpetrators of violence or threats of violence, and persons wielding weapons will be expelled immediately and law enforcement authorities will be contacted.
- We respect all magical traditions and honor the need for privacy and restricted participation.
- We know that everyone can create magic and encourage participation in open rituals and celebratory events. We use our magic to create a better world for all.

I agree to **The Old Witches Home Principles of Community**. So Mote It Be!

_____   _____
Legal Name   Date

_____
Magical Name

Hail and Welcome!

AVIAN SWANSONG BIO

Avian Swansong is a lifelong witch, guardian of the amazing cat, Opus, and author of The Old Witches Home. She has recently retired from her day job and now spends her time dreaming about a world of justice, community and magic. Her stories have been published in Catskills Literary Journal. Committed to reclaiming a healthy planet, she nourishes her soul each summer at Witch Camp, at home with others who were wild and strange in their youth and still don't want to conform.

Made in the USA
Middletown, DE
03 June 2024

55084062R00170